PRAISE FOR
CATHERINE ANDERSON'S NOVELS

"One of the finest writers of romance."
—#1 *New York Times* bestselling author Debbie Macomber

"Catherine Anderson doesn't shy away from characters who face life's toughest challenges—but she also gifts readers with a romantic tale that celebrates the hope and resilience of the human spirit."
—#1 *New York Times* bestselling author Susan Wiggs

"Catherine Anderson writes with great emotional depth and understanding of complex relationships and family dynamics."
—#1 *New York Times* bestselling author Sherryl Woods

"Catherine Anderson weaves beautiful stories overflowing with emotion and heart. *The Christmas Room* is an absolute keeper, destined to be read again and again."
—*New York Times* bestselling author RaeAnne Thayne

"Master storyteller Anderson has skillfully penned the heart-wrenching story of domestic abuse and its aftermath. . . . Compelling."   —*Booklist* (starred review)

"The minute you open an Anderson novel, you can immediately feel the vision of humanity and warmth that runs through all her books. No one does heartfelt romance better!"   —RT Book Reviews

"Romance veteran Anderson is a pro at making readers weep."   —*Publishers Weekly*

MAPLE LEAF HARVEST

A MYSTIC CREEK NOVEL

Catherine Anderson

JOVE
New York

A JOVE BOOK
Published by Berkley
An imprint of Penguin Random House LLC
penguinrandomhouse.com

A JOVE BOOK, BERKLEY, and the BERKLEY & B colophon
are registered trademarks of Penguin Random House LLC.

ISBN: 9780593198506

First Edition: August 2021

Printed in the United States of America
1   3   5   7   9   10   8   6   4   2

Cover design by Colleen Reinhart
Cover images courtesy of Shutterstock

To my son, John, who has been my rock, my compass, and my guide. Thank you for your understanding and unflagging support. When I needed help, you were there. When everything fell apart, you did everything you could to fix it. When I didn't think I could keep going, you grabbed my hand and encouraged me to take just one more step. And at some point, you had the wisdom to stop holding my hand and pushed me to do things I never dreamed I might, such as driving round-trip across four states. I never would have survived losing your dad if it hadn't been for you. Together we have had so many adventures and have created a wonderful new life in Montana. There are no words strong enough to express how grateful I am or how much I appreciate the sacrifices you've made along the way. Thank you for helping me make so many amazing memories and redefine who I am as an individual.

And to my grandson Jonas Anderson, who lives far away in New Zealand. You were only about seven or eight when I visited your house on the North Shore, and I will never forget sitting with you on the sofa and listening to your outlook on life and the personal challenges we face. You told me that challenges make us better people—kinder and more understanding—and that by dealing with our own difficulties, we learn to appreciate those around us who may be dealing with even worse problems. Such wise words from a little boy. As I created the character of Jonas Sterling, I tried to imagine you as a grown man and how you will relate to others. Only time will tell if I got it right. Regardless, I know you are going to be a person who brightens our world.

Prologue

Lane Driscoll jerked awake and then cried out in pain as she jackknifed to a sitting position. *In my own bed*, she registered as she focused on the floral coverlet lying over her quivering legs. *Safe. It was only a dream, an awful dream.* She dragged in shaky breaths that squeaked going down her windpipe. Sweat pooled beneath her breasts and trickled like rivulets of ice water down her spine and flanks. Even her hair was wet and hung like a fringe of reddish-blond twine over her eyes. *You're fine*, she assured herself, but as she drew up her knees and hugged them to her chest, every part of her body throbbed. She'd dreamed that a tall, scarecrow-thin man was trying to kill her. Beating her with brutal fists, kicking her, and then clamping his hands around her neck to choke her. Now, as she dragged in another breath, her throat felt as if it was actually bruised and swollen. She shook her head. *Impossible*, she thought. *People don't wake up with injuries from what happens in a dream.*

Pale sunlight and leaf patterns cast by the ancient maple tree outside the window danced on the white Priscilla curtains. Relieved to see that it was morning, Lane released a taut breath and tried to stop shaking. Sometimes it was hard for her to root herself in reality again after she had a particularly vivid dream, and this one had been the most vivid of them all. *"Trying to run, are you?"* the man had yelled at her. *"Well, you'll never try it again! I'm gonna teach you a lesson you'll never forget!"*

Attempting to center herself, Lane focused on the dresser that stood against the light blue wall opposite the foot of her bed. The piece was old and battered, but to Lane, the nicks and scratches only made it more beautiful, each mark telling a story about its previous owners. She had personalized it with a white dresser scarf her mom had crocheted. Atop the fluted lace sat a bottle of the vanilla-scented perfume Lane favored, an ancient, ivory hand mirror that had belonged to her great-grandmother, an orchid vase from a long-deceased aunt, and a framed photo of her parents at the beach. Their faces beamed smiles at her through the protective layer of glass, and their dark, wind-tossed hair looked so real that Lane could almost smell the salt-drenched breeze whipping around them.

She took a deep breath and slowly released it. *You're okay*, she assured herself. *It was only a stupid dream. Shrug it off.* A green scrunchie she'd used yesterday to tie back her hair lay on the dresser. Her pink lacy bra dangled over the edge of a partially open drawer. From the apartment next door, she could smell bacon and coffee, ordinary scents that assured her the world was still turning. Mark and Tanya, a couple in their forties, rented the other half of the duplex. Mark was presently unemployed, and they squabbled about money sometimes, but Lane liked both of them. They'd been wary of her at first, believing that someone in her mid-twenties would be a party animal. Now, after a year of living next to her with only a paper-thin wall for privacy, they had switched to worrying about her lack of a social life.

Tossing back the bedding, she struggled to swing her legs over the side of the mattress. When she was finally sitting with her bare feet planted firmly on the floor, she leaned forward and breathed deeply, her lungs burning as if they'd been oxygen deprived. *Crazy, so crazy.* She hadn't actually been choked. With quivering fingertips, she touched her throat, which still ached where she'd imagined her attacker's hands were clenched. As she stood, she felt light-headed, and her bedroom seemed to spin around her, a swirling kaleidoscope of her discarded clothing from yesterday, her flowery bedspread, and the worn, speckled linoleum of the floor.

Palming the walls for support, she made her way into the bathroom, turned to the horizontal mirror over the sink, and gasped when she saw her reflection. Her damp, strawberry blond hair stood out from her head in spikes, resembling carrots julienne. One of her cheeks was bright red. Her lower lip, though not cracked, looked swollen. But what truly alarmed Lane were the scarlet fingerprints on her neck.

"Oh, *God*. It wasn't real. I know it wasn't real. Just a dream." Even her voice rasped as if she'd been relentlessly choked by strong hands. "Get a grip," she ordered herself. "Wake up. Shake it off. It didn't really happen."

She searched for something ordinary to look at again—anything ordinary that might root her firmly in reality. Only she still felt frightened, and that man's voice, vibrant with rage, echoed in her mind. *"I'll kill you the next time you try to run. You got that? I'll slit your throat and toss your body in a dumpster."*

Hands still shaking, Lane grasped the hem of her nightshirt, an old black thing with orange lettering that commemorated her brief college stint at Oregon State. As the worn material slid upward, revealing her hips and belly, she stared fixedly at her reflection, willing the red splotches on her skin to vanish. Seeing them made her feel as if she'd moved back in time to her childhood. Back then, bad dreams had been commonplace for her.

Feeling defeated, she braced her hands on the Formica edge of the counter and hung her head. *I can't get sick again. I just can't.* Only even as she lectured herself, she knew from experience how powerless she might be. As a kid, she had been taken to several different psychologists by her parents. All those professionals had become a blur in her mind now, and none of them had been able to help her.

Releasing the hem of her shirt, she stared with burning eyes at the red mark on her cheek. *I will not fall apart over a stupid dream*, she told herself. *I will not call my mom and upset her, either.* Her parents already believed she was emotionally fragile, and she refused to cement that conclusion in their minds. Instead, she was going to take a shower and drink some very strong coffee. She'd feel better with a jolt of caffeine in her system, and as she got ready for work, the nightmare would lose its hold on her.

Stripping off the damp shirt, Lane swept aside the shower curtain to crank on the faucet and adjust the water temperature. Just as she was about to step into the stall, she thought she heard something. A knock at the front door? A notification on her cell phone? Or possibly a tall, thin man with wild eyes and a hawk nose? That last possibility had her putting the shirt back on to make sure all her windows and exterior doors were locked. When she was satisfied that her apartment was safely battened down, she stripped again and stepped under the spray, closed her eyes, and let the sluice of warm water ease the tension from her body. As she began to relax, the throbbing places on her thighs and torso hurt less, and by the time she turned off the faucet, she felt more like her usual self.

After drying briskly with a towel, she stood naked in front of the mirror again. The red marks on her skin had faded a bit. Or was it merely that she was flushed from the hot water and the splotches didn't stand out as much? She didn't have time to wonder. On Wednesdays, she worked a thirteen-hour shift and had to be at the restaurant at eleven. By midnight, her feet would be screaming for mercy, but the tips were usually good.

After dressing and doing her hair and makeup, she rifled through her purse for her car keys and noticed that her hands were still trembling. *Maybe*, she decided, *I shouldn't drive.* She didn't mind the walk to work during daylight hours, but she truly hated coming home after dark. She lived and worked in a seedy part of Maple Leaf, originally a small town near Portland that was now practically swallowed by urban sprawl. With that sprawl had come drug use, gang activity, and a rise in other crime. *Maybe Mac will give me a lift home*, she decided. He was a great boss and always glad of extra help at closing time. If she set up the chairs and mopped the floors, he'd probably be happy to give her a ride.

After grabbing her purse and a sweater for later, she set out for the restaurant, which was roughly a mile away. On her days off, she often jogged twice that distance one way. As she moved along the sidewalks that bordered people's front yards, she strove to take deep breaths of the crisp September air and enjoy the scenery. Most of the lawns were patchy and yellow from a hot summer and too little water, but occasionally she saw a well-manicured sweep of green grass and bright clumps of autumn flowers. Residents in this neighborhood were of all different income brackets, some of them retirees on pensions, with a smattering of young white collars who were renting until they could save enough to buy a first home. Lane fell somewhere in the middle, earning just enough with her wages and tips to avoid needing any kind of government assistance, yet never getting far enough ahead to sail smoothly over economic rough patches. Last month when her washing machine had stopped working and her landlord refused to get it repaired, she'd lived on marked-down cans of soup and PB&Js for over two weeks in order to buy a used replacement.

As she drew closer to her place of work, the aged residential area gave way to tired old shops and eateries, the fronts of which all needed face-lifts. Lane had walked this section so many times that she knew all the businesses by heart and didn't look through the smoky windows at the interiors. Three teenage boys stumbled from a video arcade, all of them laughing and elbowing one another off balance. Lane cut them a wide berth, wondering if it was a no-school day. She suspected that the boys were truants and hoped their parents wised up before the kids ended up in serious trouble. Lane had never touched booze or drugs during high school or college, but she knew how easily teenagers could get their hands on illegal substances.

She was midway down the block when she heard masculine voices raised in anger. Glancing up, she saw TATTOO JIM'S emblazoned on the shop window. The next instant, a tall, thin man burst out of the doorway, slammed into Lane, and nearly knocked her off her feet. Staggering to regain her balance, she dropped her purse and sweater. She heard the man snarl an obscene expletive. Then he grabbed her arm, digging in hard with his fingers and making her gasp.

"You!" he cried.

Looking up at him, Lane was stunned into speechlessness. And terror. It was the man from her nightmare. Only he wasn't a figment of her imagination now. He was real, and so was the brutal dig of his strong fingers, which she'd felt so recently on her throat. *Same hawk nose. Same pockmarked face. Same thin and oily brown hair.* What truly horrified her, though, was the crazy glittering expression in his blue eyes.

"I told you!" he roared. "What I'd do if you ran again! Stupid bitch! Now you're in for it."

He jerked so hard on her arm that she lost her right shoe. Then, in a swirl of fear, she realized that he was pulling her toward a rattletrap car parked at the curb. She had no time to think. She only knew she had to break his hold on her and run. When she dug in her heels, he whirled to face her. Remembering snippets of what she'd learned in a self-defense class, she threw her weight onto her right leg and swung up with her left one, driving the toe of her remaining sandal into his groin with all the strength she could muster. He folded onto the sidewalk like a marionette with broken strings, and Lane, free of his grasp, turned to run. She felt his fingernails scrape over her right ankle and knew she hadn't hurt him badly enough to incapacitate him for long.

Run! Run for your life! her brain chanted. The sidewalk blurred in front of her, except for a brown blob that lay directly in her path. *My purse!* She bent low at the waist to snatch up the handbag but missed her mark. *Don't stop*, she thought. *You've got your phone. That's all you really need.* Behind her, she could hear the thud of his shoes on the concrete and the rasp of his breathing. *Three feet behind me? Maybe four?* She increased her speed. Rounded a corner. Darted between parked cars out into the street. Dimly she heard brakes squeal. Then horns honked. Aware through every pore of her skin of the man behind her, she fixed her gaze straight ahead and kept running.

With the sound of city traffic, she could no longer hear the man clomping along behind her, but she was afraid if she slowed down to look back that he'd be on her. So she just kept going. Down an alley. Across yet another busy street. Up two blocks, over three more. She considered going home, but if he followed her, he'd know where she lived. *No, no, no. Not smart.*

When exhaustion finally drove Lane to stop and lean against a building to gasp for air, she saw no sign of the man. A shudder convulsed her body. She closed her eyes, gasped more deep breaths, and wished that she could collapse on the walkway with her back against the bricks until she recovered. But no. She couldn't stay here. She'd lost him, but that didn't mean he'd stopped looking for her.

She set off again even though she wasn't sure where to go. If she called home, her mom would come get her, but then Lane would have to field all of her parents' questions. And how could she possibly tell the truth without her mom and dad thinking that she'd completely lost her mind? No. Telling this story would be a death knell for whatever credibility she still had left. Knowing that, she couldn't bring herself to call the cops, either. What had happened made no sense. She'd been viciously attacked by a man she saw in a dream. Then she had encountered that same man on the street. He'd tried to drag her to his car. A tale that absurd would have even the best of cops raising his or her eyebrows with disbelief.

Skin crawling and heart leaping at every sound behind her, Lane set off walking. Well, hobbling better described it, because she wore only one shoe, which messed with her gait. She considered ditching the sandal she still wore, but since it had come in so handy for the groin kick, she decided to keep it on. *Just keep moving. Worry about the shoe situation later.*

Lane had no idea where she was going, and eventually she had taken so many turns that she no longer knew for sure where she was. She ducked into the recessed doorway of a shop, fished her phone from her pocket, and used GPS to pinpoint her location. Her apartment was nearly a mile away in one direction and the restaurant was nearly two in another. Still fearful that the man might be following her, she discarded the thought of returning to her apartment. She'd be safer at the restaurant with people around her. If that creep followed her there and tried anything, at least then she'd have witnesses who could tell the police that there actually was a man after her, a flesh and blood man, not a figment of her imagination.

She was about halfway to the restaurant when a cold realization turned her blood to ice. Her purse contained all of her identification cards. If that man had circled back and picked up the handbag, he would know her name, where she lived, and even where she worked, because she distinctly remembered leaving her last paycheck stub inside the bag when she'd made a deposit at the bank. She stopped dead on the sidewalk, her mind racing with a dozen possibilities, all of them frightening. *Dear God.* In her wallet, she kept a list of emergency contacts. If that man found it, he would know her parents' names and phone numbers. What if he went online and found their home address?

Lane tried to slow her breathing and talk herself down. Looking at this situation rationally, it made absolutely no sense. Maybe everything, from her nightmare forward, had never really happened, and she had imagined it all. It was an unsettling thought to entertain, forcing her to contemplate the possibility that she really had gone over the edge this time.

Gnawing her bottom lip, she stared down at her phone. *Should I call Mom?* Part of her recoiled at the thought. Her poor mother had already been through a lot, and Lane detested the thought of burdening her with anything more. Even so, when Lane evaluated the facts, beginning with the nightmare and then what followed, she had to admit that it was all too absurd to have actually happened. And that had to mean she had lost touch with reality.

She speed-dialed her mom's cell phone and got no answer, only the chirpy greeting that Ann Driscoll had recorded for voicemail. Ann often left her cell lying here or there around the house and couldn't hear it ring when she got a call. Lane cut the connection and called the landline.

"Hello. Driscoll residence."

Tears stung Lane's eyes, and she almost hung up. "Hi, Mom." Her voice trembled, and she wanted to kick herself. "I, um—I'm okay, so don't panic. All right? I'm just a bit shaken up."

"What's happened?" Ann's voice went shrill. "You

don't sound like yourself. Where are you? What's wrong? Aren't you supposed to be at work?"

Lane cleared her throat and swallowed. "I, um— Mom, I can't really explain it. I had a crazy nightmare about a man attacking me." More words bulleted from Lane's mouth, but she was so upset that she lost track of what she said or might have left out. "Anyway, I'm really scared this time. I mean—well, I never really believed I was crazy, but this time . . ." Lane's voice trailed off, and she squeezed her eyes closed. "This time, nothing makes sense."

"Where are you, sweetie?"

"My GPS says I'm on the eight-hundred block of Park Street."

Ann sighed into the phone. "I'll be there in ten, twenty max, depending on traffic." She paused and then added, "I love you, Lane. Please know that your dad and I will always have your back, no matter what."

"I know, Mom." Lane sincerely meant that. Her folks loved her; she had never questioned that. "If I see him and have to run, I'll text you my new location." She grimaced and hunched her shoulders. "If the man even exists, that is."

Ann made a soft sound of protest. "We'll talk more when I get there. Keep an eye out. Stay calm. I'll be as fast as I can."

Lane disconnected, stared down at the device screen through a blur of tears, and wished, not for the first time, that her parents had never adopted her. They were such good people, and they didn't deserve to have a screwed-up daughter who brought them more worry and concern than joy.

Nine minutes later, Lane saw her mom's white Ford Edge turn the corner onto Park Street. Lane crossed a grass median to reach the curb as her mother pulled the car up in front of her and stopped. Pocketing her phone, Lane opened the passenger door and climbed in. To her surprise, Ann turned off the ignition, moved her seat back, and locked the doors before reaching across the console to grasp Lane's hand.

"Tell me again." Ann's short salt-and-pepper hair shone in the sunlight coming through the windshield. "All of it. About the dream and then what happened when you ran into the man on the street."

Lane released a taut breath and related the entire story to her mother a second time.

Ann unfastened her safety belt, pushed up the sleeves of her lightweight gray sweater, and turned sideways on the seat. "Which arm did he grab, honey? Did he hurt you?"

Bewildered, Lane met Ann's gaze. "You believe it happened? Mom, *I'm* not even sure it really happened."

"Which arm?" Ann insisted.

"My left. He ran into me as he stormed from the tattoo parlor and then turned to face me as I caught my balance. He seemed to recognize me. Grew angry. Grabbed me. He tried to drag me to what I surmise was his car, a banged-up and rusty junk heap with peeling burgundy paint."

Ann drew up Lane's sleeve. "For a man you imagined, he had a strong grip. He left a thumb mark. Lift your arm higher." When Lane did as she'd been asked, Ann said, "There are finger marks on the underside as well." She met and held Lane's gaze. "You didn't imagine the encounter, honey. It really happened. Are you certain you've never seen this guy before, like maybe at the restaurant?"

Lane shook her head. "He isn't the type. Our patrons

aren't wealthy, but they're several steps up from being a gutter rat like that guy is."

"Harvey's isn't that fancy a place. Are you positive you never waited on him?"

"Absolutely positive, Mom. The first time I ever saw him was in my dream this morning."

Ann ran her fingers through her hair and sighed. "Well, you didn't conjure up those marks on your arm, sweetie."

"But it makes no sense, Mom. My dream definitely wasn't real, and yet the guy recognized me. He said in my dream that he'd kill me if I tried to run again, and on the sidewalk, he referred to that warning. He yelled, 'I told you what I'd do if you ran again!' And then he called me a stupid bitch and said I was in for it."

"Yes, well." Ann sighed. "As bewildering as it may seem, honey, there has to be a rational explanation."

Lane could only shake her head. As much as she appreciated her mom's willingness to believe her story, she suspected it stemmed mainly from motherly desperation, because Ann's only alternative was to conclude that her daughter was nuts.

"I love you, Mom."

Ann reached over to pat Lane's cheek. "The feeling's mutual." She restarted the car engine and pressed the seat position button on the driver's door. "Now, where is that tattoo place? Maybe your purse is still on the sidewalk."

"In this part of town?" Lane shook her head. "If that man didn't get it, someone else did."

"It can't hurt to check. I'm uncomfortable with the thought that he has your ID and credit cards, not to mention your checkbook which, I'll point out, will provide him with your home address."

A shiver ran down Lane's spine as she recalled the crazy look in the guy's eyes. If her purse wasn't still on the sidewalk, she'd be afraid to go back to her apartment. Using her phone's GPS, she gave her mom directions to the tattoo parlor. Ann slowed the Ford to a crawl as they approached, and Lane gasped with unexpected delight when she saw her purse still lying where she'd dropped it.

"It's there!" she cried. "I can't believe it!"

Ann double-parked beside an older-model Jeep. Lane panned all the cars lined up along the curb to be certain the burgundy sedan was gone before she opened the passenger door and got out of the vehicle. Slipping between two cars, she gained the sidewalk and ran to get her handbag. Just as she bent to pick it up, the man from her nightmare charged from the tattoo parlor and grabbed her arm.

"I knew you'd come back for it!" he said. "Stupid broad!"

Before Lane could launch a counterattack to get away, he vised an arm around her and jerked her so hard against his torso that the breath rushed from her lungs. Then, in what seemed like the next instant, Ann reached the sidewalk and leaped onto his back. With one arm curled tightly around his neck, she punched wildly at his face with her other hand.

"Let go of my daughter!" she screamed, and then started jabbing at his eyes with her acrylic nails.

The man roared with rage and shoved Lane away from him with such force that she fell. The rough concrete scraped her elbows and knees, but she was so worried about her mom that she barely felt the pain. She scrambled back to her feet, but before she could help her mother, the man managed to break Ann's hold on his neck and pulled her off his back. Ann hit the sidewalk and rolled, landing full-length in the gutter.

The man whirled toward Lane and drew a knife from his pocket. With the press of a button, he ejected the blade. The well-honed steel flashed in the sunlight, and Lane knew she was about to die. Only just as the man started toward her, the scream of a siren pierced the air. His wild blue eyes narrowed.

"Next time," he said, and then he turned to run, grabbing her purse as he went.

"Bastard!" Ann screamed after him.

Lane ran to her mother and crouched beside her. "Mom! Are you hurt? Please, say you're okay."

Ann struggled to stand. Lane brushed mud and debris off her mother's gray slacks and sweater. "I'm a little banged up," Ann said, "but I'll live." She met Lane's gaze. "You?"

"I'm okay," Lane assured her.

Just then the tattooist emerged from his shop. His beefy arms sported so many swirls of ink that it was difficult to tell where the short sleeves of his T-shirt ended and his skin began. A large gold lip ring twinkled just above his black soul patch. "You ladies all right? That dude is totally crazy. I called the cops."

Lane couldn't help but note that he'd done nothing to help them during the physical encounter. She suspected that a lot of people would have been reluctant to interfere, though, more was the pity. The sound of the siren grew louder, and she looked up the street to see the two-way traffic pulling over as the bubbletop sped toward them.

Three hours later, after a grueling conversation with two police officers who clearly hadn't believed her story, Lane was exhausted, and the last thing she wanted was to pack up her personal things in order to stay the night with her parents. Unfortunately, she had no choice. Her attacker knew where she lived, so the duplex was no longer safe. Lane's father escorted her while her mother went to buy packing boxes.

"Just clothing and other necessities," Brent Driscoll reminded Lane as she went into her bedroom. "You can get the other stuff later."

Lane wasn't sure staying with her parents was a good idea. The man who'd attacked her was dangerous and it wouldn't take him long to find out where her mom and dad lived. What if he went to their house in search of her and harmed them in the process?

"Dad, I really don't think my staying with you is a good idea. If I don't go to your place, maybe he'll leave you and Mom alone."

"I understand your concern, honey, but I won't get a wink if you're at some friend's place. Another young woman can't keep you safe. I can."

Ann walked in just then with flattened boxes under both arms. "I got to U-Haul just in the nick of time. They were about to close for the day." She smiled at Lane. "I'll start packing kitchen stuff while you grab clothing and whatnot."

Lane's heart jerked. Her parents seemed to think she was leaving her apartment for good, not just temporarily. "When this blows over, Mom, I'll want to live here again. It's not that far from here to the restaurant."

"You can always get another waitressing job," Ann retorted. "Besides, your father and I miss having you around."

Lane enjoyed the company of her parents; she truly did. But she'd been out on her own too long to happily contemplate living at home again. Little things, like being reminded to take her vitamins, bugged the heck out of her. Her mom fretting about how little sleep she got some nights was another bone of contention. Being a waitress often kept a person out until the wee hours of morning, and at restaurants, there were frequent staffing problems as well, so employees were called in to cover someone else's shift.

"I'll visit more often, Mom, but I'm not moving home permanently. Before we know it, I'll be thirty. How silly would that be?"

"You're only twenty-six, a long way from thirty, and I promise not to remind you to brush your teeth."

Lane sent her dad an exasperated look and went to her bedroom to start packing her clothes. She could hear her parents talking in the kitchen but couldn't make out what they were saying. When Lane emerged, they abruptly ended the conversation. Ann had a stricken look on her face, and tears lined her pale cheeks.

"What is it?" Lane asked, not certain she really wanted to know.

Ann brushed beneath her eyes with trembling fingers. "Your father thinks you should leave town and tell nobody where you are, including us."

"What?" Lane knew she'd heard her mother correctly, but added, "Please, repeat that."

"I think you should get the hell out of town," her father interjected. "Unless you've failed to tell us the absolute truth, Lane—and I don't believe for an instant that you've lied—you have no idea who that man is or why he's after you." He held up his hands like a supplicant. "Just hear me out. According to your mother, the police didn't believe that you don't know the guy. In defense of the officers, your story about that dream is a little hard to swallow. But all of that aside, that creep is after you, and I think he means you serious harm. I don't know why, and without a name so I can track him down there's no way I can find out or protect you twenty-four/seven."

"Dad, I assure you, I left nothing out." Lane gestured toward her bedroom. "I dreamed about him this morning. I was literally terrified when I woke up. Then I ran into him on the sidewalk as I walked to work. He seemed to recognize me, and then I got away and ran. I swear to you, I'm not lying."

"I don't think you're lying, sweetheart. But the honest truth is, it's a farfetched story, and I can't blame the police for thinking you somehow got on that guy's bad side and aren't telling them everything. As long as they doubt what you tell them, we can't count on them to help you or try to find him. They didn't even take you to the station to look at mug shots on the off chance that you might be able to identify him."

"No." Lane slumped her shoulders. "No, they didn't, and if they believed me, I think they would have done that. But having said that, Dad, don't you think my leaving town is overkill?"

"No. In fact, I think it's necessary for your safety. Maybe he has you confused with someone else, but that makes him no less dangerous. He'll find you sooner or later, and when he does, I'm afraid he'll do something terrible. You'll be safer if you get out of the Portland area."

Lane had lived in Maple Leaf all her life, except for when she had attended Oregon State for two dismally unsuccessful semesters. She had no idea where she'd lived prior to being adopted, and she didn't think her parents knew, either. Not that it really mattered. She'd been only three years old at the time.

"But, Daddy, this is home. And even if I leave, he might still find me if I don't change my name."

Brent Driscoll shook his head. "Changing your name shouldn't be necessary. We know next to nothing about the guy, but I doubt he's part of anything large-scale or has the technical know-how to track you on-line." Brent, an accomplished IT professional, knew computers inside and out.

Clearing his throat, he added, "He's obviously crazy, Lane. And somehow he's got you confused with someone else."

Ann interjected, "This does appear to be a case of mistaken identity. He clearly believes you're someone he knows, and to say he's out to get you is an under-statement. It's possible that he thinks you double-crossed him or something. Now he wants revenge. Your father and I truly are worried about your safety." She splayed a trembling hand over her breastbone. "We love you, sweetie. We don't want you to end up dead."

Lane stared incredulously at her mom. "You agree with Dad? You think I should leave town?" She shook her head. "I can't just walk away from my life." She swept out her arm to indicate her surroundings. "This is my *home*. I have a steady job here and a fairly good income. You're here. My friends are here. My whole *life* is here."

Ann darted a glance at her husband. "We aren't suggesting that you leave permanently, only that you take a little hiatus from this area. Only a few months, probably. We'll help you financially." Her mouth quiv-ered and twisted. "Those cops didn't believe you. I saw it on their faces. They listened. They took notes. But in the end, they did absolutely *nothing* to help or protect you!" She flapped her hands as if to rid them of water droplets. "And that *man*. He was crazed, Lane! For whatever reason, he laid in wait for you to come back for your purse. Now he knows your home address, the names of your parents, and even where you work. If you remain here, you're putting yourself in danger. As much as I hate it, your dad is absolutely right. You need to get out of this area."

Chapter One

Jonas Sterling dreaded his annual visit to Simply Sensational, Ma Thomas's overcrowded scent shop. Being surrounded by porcelain figurines, expensive bottles of perfume, frou-frou gift items, and every scent of fancy soap known to women made him feel too big for his skin, and the more he worried about knocking something off a shelf, the clumsier he seemed to be. He also disliked the countless mirrors, at least one in every section, so ladies could see how a pair of earrings might look on them or how a different brand of cosmetics could transform their faces. Almost everywhere he turned, he glimpsed his reflection and was reminded that his hair, the color of toasted bread, needed a trim.

But his mom deserved a special present on her birthday, and she always glowed with delight if he coughed up the money for her favorite perfume, Chanel No. 5. Only he couldn't for the life of him remember which kind of Chanel she liked. There were three choices on the shelf, *Eau de Parfum Spray*, *Eau Premiere Spray*, and *Eau de Toilette Spray*. Why did perfume makers have to make shopping so confusing?

Unfortunately for Jonas, Ma Thomas, who surely knew Kate Sterling's perfume preferences, was busy with another customer, and he didn't want to interrupt her. Grandmotherly plump, she was a sweetheart with short blond hair, merry blue eyes, and a charming manner always enhanced by the ready smile that had become her trademark. When someone wandered into her shop, she rolled out the red carpet. Her prices were high compared to those in Crystal Falls, yet she still managed to do a good business, mainly because she made every single customer feel important. When it was Jonas' turn, he, too, would have her undivided attention.

Jonas picked up the larger square bottle with golden liquid in it. It was the shape he remembered, and the perfume was the right color, whereas the premiere, in a similar container, had clearer stuff in it. *This has to be the one*, he thought. Only he couldn't be certain, and he sure as heck didn't want to get the wrong thing and put his mom to the bother of returning it. He guessed he could just wait. He wasn't busy with clients this afternoon.

Just as Jonas was about to return the spritzing bottle to the shelf, the overhead bell on the front door jangled and a young woman entered the shop. For a moment, Jonas stared at her in astonished disbelief and then he felt as if his whole body went numb. The glass container slipped from his fingers, dived to the floor, and went off like a shrapnel bomb when it struck the tile. At the sound, the young woman turned and fixed her gaze on him, her eyes just as blue and expressive as he remembered. There was no doubt in his mind; it was Veneta Monroe. He hadn't seen her in over six years, not since the night when she'd handed him a Dear John letter to break up with him, but she hadn't changed a bit. Her strawberry blond hair was still cut in a bob. Her eyes, the clear blue of a tropical lagoon, still dominated her heart-shaped face. And, judging by the airy floral dress she wore, her choice of fashion was still vintage Boho.

Startled by her sudden appearance and unable to help himself, Jonas gaped at her, a dozen different thoughts ricocheting inside his mind, none of them pleasant. He'd loved her once—or thought he did at the time. Now he felt nothing but mounting anger. How could she saunter into his hometown, which she'd dissed every chance she got for being nothing more than a spot on the road? *"The most boring place in the world,"* she'd called it. *"Nowhere-ville. Off the beaten path."* And that last description was just accurate enough to anger Jonas even more, because nobody accidentally visited Mystic Creek. The town rested deep in the foothills of the Cascade Mountains, the two-lane highway leading to it a treacherous ribbon of sharp curves with no gas stations, convenience stores, or reliable cell phone service. Not to say tourists didn't visit. They came in droves during the summer to window-shop, patronize the quaint eateries, and see the natural bridge, but they didn't happen upon the town accidentally.

"Oh, my goodness!" Ma Thomas cried out as she advanced on him. "Did it cut you, Jonas?"

Collecting his thoughts and composure with no small amount of effort, Jonas forced his gaze to the shards of glass at his feet. "No, I don't think so." He bent to brush shimmering fragments from the legs of his jeans. "I'm sorry for the mess, and I'll pay for the perfume."

"Don't be a goose," Ma scolded, flapping her hand. "Accidents happen. For me, it's a tax deduction and only a little mess to sweep up, nothing more."

Veneta Monroe. He was certain of it. No two people could look that much alike unless they were identical twins, and he knew for a fact that Veneta had no siblings. And apparently she had no memory, either, because he'd seen no flash of recognition in her eyes when she'd turned to look at him. And *that* pissed him off even more than her sudden appearance in Mystic Creek. She always had been a master of pretense. He didn't know what he'd ever seen in her or how he could have believed he was in love with her.

After explaining to Ma Thomas that he'd return tomorrow to purchase the perfume, Jonas left the shop, his trajectory to the door forcing him to almost brush elbows with Veneta as he passed her. It gave him no small amount of satisfaction to pretend that he didn't recognize her, either. She'd always been vain, certain that she was the focal point of any crowded room. There was no quicker way to tick Veneta off than to ignore her.

Once outdoors on the sidewalk, Jonas paused to take a deep breath of late September air. Hardy flowers in window boxes still lent color to the brick-fronted shops of East Main Street, overshadowing the splashes of orange and black that always heralded Halloween with the approach of October. Studying the town where he'd grown up and hoped to grow old gave him a sense of place and calmed him. Yes, it had been a shock to see Veneta again, but he had matured a lot since his college days, and he realized now that she'd been wrong for him in so many ways that he'd be hard put to count them all. Whatever had led her to Mystic Creek, it hadn't been him, and he was glad of that. When she had ended their relationship, she'd cited many reasons for her sudden change of heart, but it actually all boiled down to one thing, that he was too tame and boring for her taste. *Well, touché, Veneta. You were too wild and unpredictable for me, so we're both better off.*

Jonas took another bracing breath and noticed this time that he reeked of perfume. He glanced down and saw that the legs of his trousers were splotched with wetness. *Damn.* Returning to his apartment hadn't been part of his plan for the afternoon, but now he had no choice but to shower and change clothes. He couldn't have dinner at his parents' house smelling like a French whore.

Palms slick with sweat, Lane rubbed them on the folds of her cotton skirt while waiting for the shop owner, Mary Alice Thomas, to finally have time for her. *Please, God, I need this job.* After three days of applying for waitressing positions at the many eateries in Mystic Creek, Lane was starting to feel just a bit desperate. Unlike in Maple Leaf, where restaurants and cafés had rapid employee turnover, people in Mystic Creek seemed to value their jobs, making it difficult for a newcomer to get a foot in the door. Lane's parents had given her plenty of cash to make a fresh start, but she had been paying her own way ever since she flunked out of college at twenty years old. It grated on her nerves to use their money when she was perfectly able to earn her own. Ann and Brent Driscoll weren't rich, after all, and Lane suspected that they'd dipped into their retirement funds to finance her escape.

This is insane, she thought as Mary Alice Thomas chatted up another customer. *I shouldn't have listened to Dad. Shouldn't have run. What kind of person pulls up stakes and walks away from her whole life? What'll*

I do if I can't find a job? Now that I've signed a six-month lease on that cottage, I'm obligated to pay the rent. When I can finally go back home, I want to be able to pay my folks back, and I won't be able to do that if I'm forced to spend every dime they gave me.

It seemed to Lane that Mary Alice took forever to handle each transaction. In Maple Leaf, business owners and customers were always in a hurry, far too busy for personal exchanges. To pass the time, Lane wandered up an aisle, stopping to admire a stunning jewelry display, a high-end cosmetic counter, and a fashion scarf rack. At the back of the shop there was what appeared to be a seating area, a small round table flanked by three chairs and a child-size table off in the corner where a shelf sported a collection of storybooks and a toy box overflowed with dolls, trucks, and Lincoln Logs. Lane couldn't help but smile, because she liked the feeling she got from this place—definitely swanky enough to draw in customers and yet also homey and welcoming.

"I am so sorry, dear!" Mary Alice said from behind Lane, causing her to give a startled jerk. "Mabel is such a doll, and since her heart attack, I don't see her all that much anymore. When I do, it's such a treat, so I visit with her as much as I can."

Lane ran her gaze over the older woman's pantsuit, a stylish and businesslike ensemble in a shade of blue that matched her twinkling eyes. "Please, don't apologize. I'm in public service myself and understand the importance of good PR."

Mary Alice chuckled, a musical little laugh that made Lane feel warm and welcome. "Public relations, you say? Well, yes, I suppose one might call it that, but in truth, Mabel is a dear friend. Without her support, I don't know how I would have survived when my husband died." She frowned slightly. "But enough about that. I've kept you waiting far too long. How may I help you?"

Lane's mouth went dry. She'd rehearsed what she would say, but now that the moment was upon her, she couldn't remember a single word of her little speech. "I, um—well, I'm looking for a job, and I, um, saw the Help Wanted sign in your window, so I just thought I'd drop by and check it out."

"Oh!" Mary Alice chuckled again. "I'd forgotten all about it. Yes, yes, I am looking to hire someone. Have you any experience with perfume and cosmetics?"

Lane stifled a defeated sigh. "No, I'm afraid not. I'm a great waitress, but there are no job openings available." She glanced around and shrugged. "I wouldn't think that selling stuff like this would be all that different than waiting tables, though. It's all about pleasing the customers. Isn't it?"

Mary Alice smiled. "To a large degree, yes. But there's a bit more to it than that. For instance, what perfume would you recommend if a lady tells you she prefers something flowery and light? Or something sultry and suggestive?" Her wrinkled cheek dimpled. "It takes a knowledge of different perfume brands to direct a customer to a scent that may appeal to her."

Lane felt her shoulders slump. "You're so right. I'm sorry for bothering you. I thought maybe this might work for me."

Mary Alice folded her arms. "As it happens, I'm looking for a bit more than just an employee. I'm over seventy now and tire easily. Ready to slow down; you know? So I'm hoping to find someone interested in managing this place, perhaps even buy in eventually and become a partner." She gave Lane another measuring look. "I can't fancy myself retiring. Not entirely. Coming here each morning and visiting with my customers gives me a reason for being, if that makes any sense. But, like it or not, I'm getting too old for all the physical work." She waved a hand at all the shelving behind her. "Dusting alone is an endless job, and much of it requires me to climb a tall ladder. Needless to say, my balance isn't what it used to be."

Just thinking of this nice older lady falling from a ladder made Lane's heart trip. "You shouldn't be dusting anything up high, Ms. Thomas."

Mary Alice's eyes widened. "Please, darling, just call me Ma. I know it's a silly nickname. Makes me sound like a mother figure for the entire town, but it actually came from the initials of my first and middle name, *M* and *A*. Being in business, I got tired of using my full name in my signature, so I shortened it to M.A. Thomas, and way back when, somebody started calling me Ma. Now almost everyone does. It's much faster to say."

Lane nodded. "Well, Ma, thank you for your time."

The older woman touched Lane's arm. "Don't hurry off. Let's talk over a cup of coffee or tea. Shall we? When I asked what you know about scents, I wasn't implying that it takes a degree in aromachology to do this job well. With time and a lot of sniffing, almost anyone can learn the ropes." She went to a small corner shelf where a black Keurig held court on the top shelf. "Coffee for me, but what would you like? I keep a nice selection of teas, too."

"Coffee will be lovely," Lane replied. "French roast if you've got it. Anything black if you don't."

Ma filled the air with her delightful laugh again. "Take a seat, dear. I'll join you in a moment."

Lane lowered herself onto a chair. "Having a play area was a brilliant idea. If the children are entertained, the moms can shop in peace."

"Yes, and in our little town, a smart business owner realizes that little people will one day be big people who may become regular customers. Some of my teenage regulars now were once toddlers who played in that corner."

Minutes later, Mary Alice joined Lane at the table and placed at its center a tray laden with filled coffee mugs, packets of sugar and creamer, and a plate of delicious-looking pastry.

"From the Jake 'n' Bake," she explained. "I stop by there every morning for fresh bakery items to go with treats I make at home. It's nice to have an area where people can sit and reenergize. Sometimes, with a dose of good conversation, a hot beverage, and a snack, the ladies can shop for another couple of hours." Her expression grew serious as she met Lane's gaze. "They don't always shop here afterward, mind you, but I believe the hospitality brings them back in, and that's my ace in the hole, so to speak. In Crystal Falls, a woman can sometimes save as much as twenty dollars on a single bottle of perfume. In order to compete, I had to offer something more than the Crystal Falls stores do."

Lane took a sip of coffee and said over the rim of her cup, "So you offer conversation, beverages, and snacks?" She smiled as she returned the mug to its saucer. "That's fascinating. I'm from the greater Portland area. A place like this would be rare there. Shopkeepers are normally all business, saying only what's necessary during a transaction. Most don't attempt to have any form of personal conversation. No matter how many times I go to one particular place, I've never been greeted by name."

She smiled. "This is a nice touch. Very personal and—well, welcoming, I guess. You've created a lovely small-town, neighborhood sort of feeling here. I can see why people come back again and again."

"Yes, as I said, my ace in the hole." Mary Alice stirred a packet of sugar into her coffee and took a careful sip. Over the cup, she studied Lane with undisguised curiosity. "How long do you plan to remain in Mystic Creek?" she asked. "Is your move here permanent or temporary?" Lane needed this job, and a large part of her wanted to say she hoped to remain in town indefinitely. After being a waitress for so long, she knew how costly it was for employers to train people, and that was money down the drain if an employee quit soon after she got her bearings. But she couldn't bring herself to lie to such a sweet older lady. "I'd love to say I plan to stay indefinitely, Ma, but the truth is I'm hoping to be in town no longer than six months."

"I see." Ma's brows drew together in a slight frown. "That's disappointing. I was hoping to find someone who might stay on."

Lane took a sip of her coffee and then set down her mug with a decisive click. "I understand. It's a big investment to train somebody and then have them quit. I probably shouldn't have taken up your time. I'm a good waitress, and I'm confident that I'll be a quick study as a new hire in a café or restaurant here. But there are no openings, and I really need a job to keep me afloat until I can return to the Portland area." Forcing a smile, Lane added, "It was worth a shot. Right?"

Ma smiled, too, her blue eyes twinkling as Lane leaned sideways to grab her purse. "Not so fast, sweetie. I didn't say I won't hire you, only that I was hoping you might stay on. I'm looking for an industrious young person, male or female, who might be interested in becoming a partner in the business and possibly even buying me out before I get so old that I'm forced to close the doors. I'm not as young as I used to be, and running this place alone is getting to be too much for me. Unfortunately, I haven't found anyone who's interested in that offer yet. Not even anyone who wants the job." The smile in her eyes slowly moved to her lips. "So, in a very real way, I need someone to help me stay afloat, too." She laughed and flapped her hand. "You'll probably think I'm a crazy old lady, but I firmly believe that God is always up there, orchestrating things. If you like the job and stay on for six months, perhaps this is his way of giving us both a helping hand."

Lane couldn't quite believe her ears. "So you might hire me anyway, knowing that I'll be waltzing out of here in only a few months?"

Mary Alice laughed again. "It isn't only job seekers who are sometimes desperate." She gestured at the shop. "See those top shelves? Every time I scale a ladder to dust up there, I fear for my life. My sense of balance has grown so bad that I can stumble and fall on level ground. It's scary for me to stand on a ladder rung. Even one foot up from the floor, I could break a hip—or worse—if I fell. And, believe it or not, running this place requires a lot of physical work. Lifting heavy boxes of merchandise. Stocking shelves. Cleaning the floors. Dusting. I'm over seventy now, and my butt is dragging by closing time."

"You shouldn't be climbing ladders. My mom is only in her fifties, and she fell from a kitchen stepstool. Broke her arm and was hospitalized for a concussion. It scared my father so badly that he took the stepstool to Goodwill and won't let her buy another one. If something is over her head, she's under strict orders to let him get it down for her."

Ma chuckled. "Good for him. I think I'd like your father. He sounds like my husband, a wonderful man who loved me to the moon and back." Her expression grew solemn for a moment, but then she brightened. "So . . . what do you say? Do you want to give this a shot? I won't color it pretty. I'll work your tail off while I play lady of the manor. I've run out of steam, and I'm barely able to stay open for a full eight hours a day now. It's heartbreaking for me to think about liquidating and selling. After my husband died, I bought this building. Gutted it, remodeled. It's my baby, something I dreamed of and made into a reality. Maybe God sent you to help me last another six months, and during that time, another younger woman will walk in who'll be delighted for a chance to own it herself one day."

Lane glanced around them and almost blurted that she would be on cloud nine if she ever got an offer like that. But she'd never worked in a scent shop. She'd never even owned a bottle of expensive perfume except when her parents bought her some as a gift, which happened rarely because, out of necessity, she had grown to like vanilla. As a waitress, it was a complementary smell that coupled well with food. Or so she assured herself, because buying a bottle of it didn't overload her budget.

After setting aside her musings about one day being a business owner instead of a worker, Lane said, "I'd *love* to give it a shot. Like I said, I really need a job. Without going into details, a sticky situation developed for me in the Portland area, and I needed to get away for a while. My parents are helping me financially, despite the fact that they really can't afford to. The sooner I'm back to work and able to pay my own way again, the better."

Mary Alice dipped her chin in a nod. "So, when can you start?"

Lane thought of the small U-Haul trailer parked in front of her rental cottage. It was still stuffed with her belongings, and she needed to unload it. She also needed to buy a bed, a kitchen table, and at least one comfortable chair. As it was, she ordered fast-food takeout and stood at the kitchen counter to eat. She'd found a rickety lawn chair on the back deck and dragged it inside, but every time she rested her weight on it, she feared it might collapse.

"I still have some unpacking to do—and I need a few pieces of furniture." What an understatement that was. "But I could start tomorrow if I can work only mornings and part of the afternoons for a week. That way all the shops won't be closed for the day, and I can finish getting settled in after my shifts."

Mary Alice chortled. "Can you show up at eight and work until three?"

"Done," Lane agreed.

"You haven't even asked about the pay," the older woman said.

It was Lane's turn to laugh. "What about *desperate* did you not understand?"

Mary Alice sighed. "It'll be minimum wage, plus ten percent commission on sales. You'll make a comfortable wage if you're quick to learn the ropes and how to cater to the customers."

That sounded more than fair to Lane.

*   *   *

Soon after, when Lane parked in front of her rental, she couldn't help but feel excited about her new job, not so much about the offered wage, but more about the possibilities. As a waitress, Lane had little hope of ever owning a restaurant or even being part-owner, but such an opportunity might be hers for the asking if she learned the ropes at Simply Sensational and enjoyed the everyday challenges of working there.

Taking a deep breath, she mentally scolded herself for dreaming and took a moment to just stare out the windshield. Unfortunately, she couldn't tamp down her excitement. The cottage she now rented was lovely. Lane had liked it on sight, but she hadn't allowed herself to think of it as being permanent. Now, with Mary Alice's job offer at the forefront of her mind, she was suddenly brimming with excitement. The little house sat along Mystic Creek, offering fabulous views of the waterway and the mountains. It came with a huge yard, a back deck for sunbathing, swimming, and barbecuing, and featured a bay dining nook off the kitchen that overlooked the stream. It was nicer than anything Lane had been able to afford in the past. She especially liked the master bath, appointed with a deep garden tub, plus a nice tiled shower.

For a very long time, Lane had wanted to get a dog. Now, if she liked working with Ma Thomas and decided to stay in Mystic Creek, why couldn't she have a pet? When she'd been looking at an Oregon map to find a place where she might escape, one of the most attractive aspects of Mystic Creek had been the plethora of outdoor opportunities the town offered. She was a runner, but she loved hiking even more, and this whole area was honeycombed with trails. A dog would be a fabulous outdoor companion and would provide her with company at night. Even snowboarding with a dog might be fun. She'd seen videos of people doing that with their canine sidekicks and couldn't see why she couldn't do the same.

Kate Sterling's new kitchen clock ticked louder than the old one, and Jonas wasn't used to it yet. *Tick-tock, tick-tock*. His mom hated digital timepieces and had found this one at a yard sale. The damned thing drove him bonkers. This room had always been his go-to sanctuary when life threw him a curveball. Except for the new clock, he always found it soothing. Just hearing his mother rattle around in her kitchen seemed to put his world back to rights.

As usual of an afternoon, Kate was baking. Today the offering was chocolate chip peanut butter cookies, which smelled like heaven and made his mouth water.

"So, to what do I owe the honor of your presence this afternoon?" Kate asked, dimpling a cheek at him. A slightly built woman with shoulder-length dark hair and gorgeous brown eyes, she looked at least a decade younger than she actually was. "Or dare I ask? You look troubled."

Jonas tried to relax the frown he felt wrinkling his forehead. "You won't believe it, but here goes. I saw Neta in Mystic Creek today."

Kate froze with a spatula lifted in one hand. "Neta, the girl you went with at university?"

Jonas nodded.

"The one who dumped you in a letter and broke your heart?"

Nodding to that went against his grain. "She didn't break my heart, Mom. It was only a little bruised."

"You sulked around this house all that spring break," she countered. "I know the signs of a broken heart when I see them."

"I was young, disillusioned. I think it hurt my pride more than it did my heart. And, honestly, I felt absolutely nothing when I saw her today." He shook his head. "And you wanna hear the weirdest part? She acted as if she didn't recognize me."

Kate resumed her task of transferring hot cookies onto a ceramic platter. "That *is* weird, but it must have been only an act. Didn't the two of you argue about one day living in Mystic Creek, you in favor of the idea and her against it?"

Sometimes Jonas was flabbergasted by his mother's sharp memory. "I don't remember telling you about that."

"You didn't. You were home for a weekend from school, and I overheard the two of you quarreling over the phone. You had her on speaker."

Jonas imagined his mom hovering outside his bedroom. "You eavesdropped?"

"If you're implying that I deliberately listened, I'm offended. I was putting folded laundry in your dad's bureau drawers and couldn't help hearing the conversation." Kate winked at him over her slender shoulder. "I may have stayed longer than necessary to tidy up the stacks. I'll admit to that much. She was a selfish little bitch. I was relieved when you got rid of her."

Jonas rarely heard his mom use the B-word, which startled him. "It was the other way around. *She* got rid of *me*."

"Whatever." Kate set the platter on the table and gave him a dessert plate. "You were well rid of her, and I was glad to see her go. According to her, you'd never be successful as a psychologist in a tiny town like Mystic Creek, and, forgive me for letting it piss me off, but she referred to me and your father as 'ignorant hayseeds.'"

Jonas got a piece of cookie caught in his throat and coughed. "Neta thought anyone without a college education was an ignorant hayseed, Mom. It probably wasn't personal." He quickly added, "Not that I'm defending her."

"You'd better not be. I'm your dad's helper and a housewife, and I don't resent being referred to as such, but I've been an invaluable asset to him and deserve credit for that. And your father is an intelligent, self-taught, successful man who put all his children through college. He deserved her respect. Her calling him names earned her no points with me."

Silence fell as Kate spooned more dough onto the baking sheet and put it back in the oven. The ticking of the new clock began to drive Jonas batty again. When she joined him at the table, taking a seat across from him, she reached across the surface to touch his hand. "I'm sorry. I'm not being very sympathetic. Let me start over. I know it must have been a shock for you to see her."

Jonas nodded. "I brought her to visit only once, and she couldn't wait for the weekend to be over. Absolutely hated it here. It gives me cause to wonder why she would come back."

"Maybe she hoped to see you again and find some kind of closure. As reluctant as I am to say anything nice about her, I must concede that she was fond of you at some point. Sometimes we can't completely put feelings like that behind us. We need to confront the person and gauge our reaction in order to know, beyond a doubt, that all the fond memories are only that, memories."

Jonas sighed and shook his head. "But she didn't confront me. She acted as if she didn't recognize me."

Kate chucked him under the chin. "You're too wonderful and handsome for any woman to forget you, so I call baloney on that. She only pretended not to recognize you, sweetie. Maybe it was nerves. People do strange things sometimes"

"I call baloney on the wonderful and handsome part," Jonas said with a grin. "But thanks for the compliment."

"What'll you do if you see her again?"

He thought for a moment. "I guess I'll pretend I don't remember her. That made the first encounter nice and easy, and I honestly don't have any desire to talk with her. The most troubling part of this for me is that I ever fell for her in the first place."

"You were young, Jonas. And love is a mystery, but you'll know when you find the real thing. As you said, you've matured. When the right lady comes along, you'll feel a zing of awareness that you've never felt with anyone else, and when she smiles, it'll light up your whole world."

Lane ate what would serve as her dinner in town late that afternoon at Taco Joe's and then went shopping for a bed, an expenditure she had dreaded making only that morning. How strange it was that her outlook could change so swiftly and so drastically. Now, as she sat in her late-model Hyundai hatchback in front of her rental cottage, she found herself imagining all the little things she could do to make the house into a real home. Because she was staring straight at the front veranda with a white railing that lined all but the stairway, she thought about how darling and welcoming it could be with pots of trailing flowers hanging from the eave. And a birdhouse! Back when she'd still lived at home and had a real yard, she'd always wanted to put out wild birdseed. But her mom had always nixed the idea, saying the seeds blew in the wind and peppered a lawn and flowerbeds with weeds. Lane preferred being able to watch the robins and swallows over having perfect grass, for in her mind, green sod was only a backdrop for the truly beautiful things, sort of like gorgeous jewelry displayed on black velvet. And to Lane, the truly beautiful things were birds and butterflies, little bunnies, and maybe even deer. Oh, how fun it would be to have a doe and her baby fawn grazing near her windows.

Grabbing her purse, Lane thought, *I can make this place into a real home. Heck, with the money I earn, maybe I can even buy this cottage one day and have my very own house. Mom and Dad could come visit, and I could drive back to Maple Leaf often to see them, too.* As she climbed from the car, a new resolve seemed to pulse in her veins.

Adirondack chairs, she decided as she moved toward the porch. *The old-fashioned kind, made of real wood, so I can paint them the same color as the trim on the cottage.* The house had been left to weather for years, its once white siding now almost gray. Lane knew she'd have to scrape and sand the dwelling's exterior before she could change its color, but instead of discouraging her, the prospect only energized her. *I'm going to make a partnership with Ma Thomas work!* she thought. And her mind was off to the races as she bounced up the steps.

Once in the house, she hurried to the kitchen, where she'd left the trailer rental paperwork and the keys. She needed to shift the packing boxes around in order to find the one marked SHEETS AND BLANKETS. Her bed would arrive in less than an hour, and she wanted to make it up as soon as the deliverymen left so she would have a proper place to sleep that night. The twin-size air mattress she'd been using under her sleeping bag had developed a slow leak, and she awakened each morning lying on the floor.

An hour later, Lane stepped back from her newly made-up bed. She'd even found her floral spread and pillow shams. Rubbing her arms, she sighed and smiled. It felt good to see something familiar, even if it was the only thing in the house that reminded her of the apartment she'd so hastily left just a few days ago. She sat on the edge of the mattress, gave a little bounce, and broadened her smile. For the first time since coming here, she would have a comfortable place to sit while she called her folks and gave them an update.

Moments later, Lane was no longer smiling. "What do you mean, your house was ransacked?" she asked her parents, who had her on speaker.

Her father answered. "We don't know why he came here. We only know that it must have been your attacker. The majority of the damage occurred in your room."

Lane squeezed her eyes closed and clenched her fingers over the edges of her cell phone. Her old bedroom had been exactly as she'd left it at age eighteen, a shrine of sorts that shouted "teenage girl." A burglar would have known with only a glance that it wasn't the room of an adult.

"Recent pictures of you were stolen," Ann interjected. "Others were—damaged beyond repair. The police officers who answered our call believe that the intruder acted out of rage, that he may mean you harm."

"But *why*?" Lane heard her voice go high-pitched and quivery. "I swear to you, Mom. I don't know why that man has it in for me. None of this makes any sense."

"What *does* make sense," her father replied, "is exactly what you're doing now, keeping your head down and your whereabouts a secret. Whatever you do, don't slip up and tell us where you are."

A cold chill shot up Lane's spine. "Why? Surely you don't think your phones are being tapped—or that the house is bugged. That's crazy, Dad. You said you strongly doubted that he has the technical know-how to do any of that stuff."

"And I did strongly doubt it, Lane. But I didn't take into account who the guy might work for."

Lane's heart caught. "Did you learn something new that I'm not aware of?"

Her father sighed, the sound drawn out and reflecting his sense of helplessness. "After the break-in, let's just say the police began to take the matter more seriously and took your mother to the station to look at mug shots. She saw one man who resembled the fellow who grabbed you on the sidewalk. Not a positive ID, but a strong maybe. The guy she believed was him—well, the cops say he's not just a neighborhood pusher, Lane. They have reason to believe he's connected to a drug ring. So far, they just haven't been able to prove it. If they're right, he's far more dangerous than I initially thought. A well-organized crime operation will have technical personnel who could track you."

Lane's skin pebbled with sudden fear, and she glanced uneasily over her shoulder. "Do you think I'm in danger?" she asked, when all she really wanted to do was scream, *How can this be happening to me? I've done nothing to be on anyone's bad side.* Instead, she knotted her free hand into a tight fist that made her knuckles throb.

"We can't rule out the possibility," Brent replied. "It's undoubtedly a case of mistaken identity, but until they discover they've made a mistake, they're trying to find you."

"What should I do?" Lane asked.

"Nothing, for the moment. Just keep on keeping on. Cash purchases only. Don't tell us where you are when we speak on the phone. If you contact friends, don't tell them your whereabouts, either."

Lane didn't have as many close friends as her father believed, but her stomach knotted with anxiety anyway. "I bought a bed today, Dad. Paying with that much cash—well, these days it raises eyebrows. So I paid with a check."

"To some degree, that can't be avoided for large purchases. Writing a check is probably safer than using a credit card. Your personal bank accounts should be more difficult to access. I can't access mine anymore without responding from my phone to a verification text."

Ann excused herself from the conversation to take a dinner casserole from the oven.

Lane let out a breath she hadn't realized she'd been holding. She'd been religious about not using her credit cards even while traveling to Mystic Creek. And her dad had gotten a friend of his to rent the U-Haul under his name so it couldn't be linked to her in any way.

"That's good to know." She caught her lower lip between her teeth. "Dad, the break-in. How much damage was done to the house? Was Mom horribly upset?"

He sighed. "She was upset, and so was I. However, as ugly as it was to have our privacy invaded, we're both relieved that you're safe. That was our silver lining. The rage he was feeling when he destroyed your photos—well, seeing the evidence of his violent feelings unnerved us both. And knowing that he took some of the more recent pictures—well, that was alarming. We're both so glad you left. The cops will have an eye out for him—although your mother says he looks much different now. In the mug shot, he was cleaner cut. Wore a shirt with a collar. Clean-shaven, too."

After ending the conversation, Lane tossed her phone onto the bed and hunched her shoulders to rest her elbows on her knees. Hearing her parents' voices made her wish she were back home. She supposed that every adult occasionally wished they could be a kid again, and right then, she would have loved to feel her dad's strong arms around her.

She went to the kitchen for a glass of wine to help her relax. So far, she wasn't completely unpacked, but she'd found a couple of kitchen boxes and unearthed two goblets. It felt nice to drink wine—or anything else, for that matter—from a proper glass. After taking one sip, she circled the house to make sure the exterior doors were locked, not because she was nervous, she assured herself, but just to be on the safe side. Because her new bed was the only piece of furniture in the house, she returned to it, plumped up the pillows against the wall to create a backrest, and groaned as she sat back and lifted her legs onto the mattress.

After finishing her wine, Lane forced herself back to

her feet. As of tomorrow, she had a job, and her time wouldn't be her own any longer. She needed to unload the small trailer so she could return it without a penalty. After throwing on jeans and a T-shirt, she began the arduous task of hauling in boxes. She'd marked all of them to indicate the nature of the contents. Some went to her bedroom, others to the kitchen, living room, and master bath. She had no intention of unpacking all of them tonight. Just getting them into the house was her main goal. Even so, she was tired by the time she finished at a little after nine. And, with all the exercise, she was hungry. She found a can of lentil soup, drew a glass mixing bowl from one of the kitchen boxes, and heated her snack in the microwave. While standing at the counter to eat, she promised herself that she'd find more furniture soon. Not new stuff. She would shop in the secondhand shops to find good buys.

She decided on a luxurious bath and a second glass of vino before she turned out all the lights and slipped into bed. *Ahh*. She smiled into the darkness. This mattress was much more comfortable than the one she'd had at the apartment. She snuggled down, bunched her pillow to support her head and neck the way she liked, and closed her eyes. Her last thought before she drifted into the black softness of slumber was that she'd look for furniture tomorrow after work.

Chapter Two

On some level, Lane knew she was dreaming, but no matter how hard she tried, she couldn't force herself awake. *The windows are boarded up.* She pressed her hand against the rough wood and tried to pry a slat loose, but it was nailed to the interior window frame and only a pry bar would loosen it. She peeked through a crack and saw that the window had been boarded over on the exterior of the house, too. The realization filled her with building panic. *I can't get out! They're going to kill me. Somebody needs to help me.* Given to claustrophobia, Lane couldn't breathe and began tearing at the wood with her fingernails. *I have to get out!*

Lane's growing panic jerked her awake, and she sat straight up in bed. For a moment, she didn't know where she was, and that added to her terror. Her breath came in shallow pants. Sweat beaded on her face and tickled her skin as cool rivulets trailed down her cheeks. Then her gaze landed on the French doors where moonlight bathed the panes of glass, and she remembered where she was. *No boarded-up windows.* It had been no more than another nightmare. Only just like the last time when she'd dreamed of that man attacking her, this dream had seemed so real. Even the tips of her fingers stung from clawing at the wooden planks.

Feeling shaken, Lane crawled out of bed and crouched by an electrical outlet where she'd plugged in her phone and left it to charge on the hardwood floor. The screen said it was 4:43 a.m. *Almost five in the morning.* Lane didn't routinely get up so early, but even if she'd feel tired all day, she didn't wish to go back to sleep. The nightmare waited for her in the far reaches of her mind, and she wanted it to stay there. It couldn't be a part of her reality today, not when she was about to start a new job. That had to be her focus— learning more about the shop, schooling herself on all the different scents and how the cash register worked. Ma's register kept a running tally of her inventory.

She took her phone with her into the master bath. Even though she'd bathed last night, she wanted a hot shower to wake herself up and get the salty perspiration off her skin. She turned on the faucet, sliding the indicator over to the sweet spot where the water temperature was exactly right. Then she stripped off and stepped under the spray, sighing as the jets prickled her flesh. Holding her breath, she tipped her head back to enjoy the heat on her face.

"Please, please, help me!"

Lane jerked and gasped as the voice went off like a bomb inside her head again. Water went up her nose and down her throat, and she choked.

"They're going to kill me. I know too much. I don't know why they're waiting, but time is running out. Please, help me. Somebody, anybody. Please!"

Still coughing, Lane shoved open the shower door and staggered out onto a faded blue bathmat that she'd brought from her old rental. Her body convulsed as she cleared the last of the water from her airway. *That voice.* It was as familiar to Lane as her own, and yet hearing it terrified her. *I won't fall down into that rabbit hole again*, she assured herself. *The voice isn't real. You know it can't be real. So just block it from your mind.*

With trembling hands, she grabbed a towel and wrapped it around her head. Then she dried off with its rack mate. *New towels. I need to buy new towels.* After slipping into underwear, she stood at her open closet, determined to think only about what she should wear her first day on the job. *Nothing too fancy, nothing too casual.* She wanted to strike just the right note. Her wardrobe was mostly Bohemian, or as her father called it, hippie-style. Lane was a comfort lover, and loose, flowing attire not only appealed to her on that level but also satisfied her need to maintain her own look. Not to mention that she could dress herself for pennies on the dollar compared to the prices she would encounter in ladies' apparel shops where everything was brand-new and priced accordingly.

Lane grabbed blindly at clothing, jerking it from the hangers and slipping it on. *Coffee.* She needed a cup— or two or three. She hurriedly dressed, checked herself in the mirror, and dashed to the kitchen where she'd done her best last night to get organized. She found the coffee grinder. Pulverized some beans. Filled a reusable, knockoff K-Cup. Brewed a first serving. Bypassing sugar or creamer, she stood by the bay window to drink it black. Stared at the empty deck. Tried to imagine it with a barbecue and furniture. A lounge. Some comfy chairs. Outdoor planters filled with flowers. Only no matter how hard she tried to focus on those things, the voice still rang inside her mind, as real to her as hearing herself talk.

Her cell phone suddenly rang. She leaped and sloshed coffee onto the window ledge. Swearing under her breath, she reached into the pocket of her skirt and withdrew her phone. The caller ID read MOM. She released a taut breath and answered the call.

"Hi, Mom."

"Good grief! You're up? I was just going to leave a voicemail, asking you to call me."

"I—um, woke up early." Lane wanted to tell her mother about her dream, but another part of her wanted to pretend it hadn't happened. "Is everything okay there?"

Ann sighed. "No more break-ins, if that's your question, but it has made me worry about you. I just needed to hear your voice to set my mind at rest."

"I'm fine, Mom." *Liar, liar, pants on fire.* Lane wasn't fine. She was scared.

"There's something wrong, Laney. I hear it in your voice."

Mothers. Lane didn't know if all moms were as intuitive as hers, but she figured most of them were. "I'm really a-okay," Lane tried.

Ann's voice sharpened. "Please, Laney, don't shut me out, not when I'm so edgy about your safety, don't know where you are, and worry about you every second of the day."

Lane's shoulders slumped. "All right, all right. I had another dream. It was a doozy and jerked me awake from a sound sleep."

"And?"

Squeezing her eyes closed, Lane said, "I'm hearing voices again."

Ann sucked in a sharp breath, the sound echoing in Lane's ear. "Is it Nita?"

Nita had been Lane's imaginary friend when she was little. At least that had been the explanation of a number of psychologists over the years when Lane had been forced by her parents to get counseling. Eventually, when Lane grew tired of seeing counselors, she'd just stopped telling her parents if she heard the voice. It had been easier that way.

Lane felt suddenly exhausted. Drained of all energy. "She never went completely away, Mom. For your sakes and my own, I stopped telling you when I started to hear her again. It was making you and Dad crazy. Making me crazy. Nothing we tried ever made it stop. That's the bottom line. When I got older, I just couldn't see any point in worrying you."

"Lane, you'll never be so old that your father and I will stop caring about you."

"That isn't what I meant, and you know it. Worrying you wasn't making me better. Talking with professionals never helped me. I just got tired of all the hassle, the drain on your finances—just all of it."

Ann clucked her tongue. "We never begrudged a dime we spent trying to help you."

"I know that, but did I really need help? So what if I'm a little nutty? Isn't everyone? What's normal?"

"Lane, don't try to snow me. You're upset."

"Yes, a little. It interferes with my concentration, and it's unnerving to hear a voice inside my head. Sometimes it scares me. I wonder if I'm totally losing it. If I'm one step away from being in a psychiatric ward, strapped to a bed. Of *course* I'm upset. But it bothers me even more to burden you with all that."

"You need to see someone, Lane, and this time, let down all your barriers. Don't go into it tongue-in-cheek. Don't hold stuff back."

Lane grabbed a paper towel to clean up the mess on the windowsill. "It wouldn't do any good. I don't have any deep, dark secrets that I've been holding back."

"You can't let this continue to destroy your life," Ann popped back.

"It hasn't destroyed my life, Mom. It's just made me a little different from other people. And, you know me. I kind of like being just a little different."

"It destroyed your college aspirations. It's prevented you from challenging yourself with a decent job that promises you a future."

Lane tossed the wet wad of paper into the trash can with an angry flick of her wrist. "I'm sorry that I got poor grades. I'm sorry if it embarrassed you and Dad. I'm sorry you have to tell your friends I'm only a waitress at a glorified café who lives off tips and has to pull double shifts in order to make it. Oh! And I mustn't forget that I lived in a dump in the seediest part of town."

"That isn't fair."

Lane knew her mother was right. She swallowed hard. Took a deep breath and slowly released it. "I'm sorry, Mom. I know you guys love me. That you worry about me. And I totally get it. I'm pretty much a mess, and I'm sorry for that. But no matter how hard I've tried, I can't change things. I can go for months without hearing anything, but it always comes back eventually. I just have to learn to live with this."

"That's the craziest thing I've ever heard you say. How can you just live with it? Please, promise me that you'll see someone, Lane."

"I'm in a little town. I doubt there's a psychiatrist or psychologist practicing here. I'd have to drive clear to—"

"Don't say it—the name of the closest large town, I

mean. I don't want to know where you are, what part of the state you're in. Your dad is being very smart to insist upon that. I'm terrible at keeping secrets, Lane. You know that. Without thinking, I might tell someone where you are."

Lane rolled her eyes, and then a smile tugged at her lips. Her mom really was awful at keeping secrets. "Right. I almost slipped up. The drive to the nearest larger town is not an easy one. I honestly can't see myself going there twice a week to tell some shrink all my problems."

"I understand," Ann replied. "But promise me you'll make the drive if it gets bad."

"I promise to look into it, and if it gets bad, Mom, I'll give counseling one more try. But not unless it's really bad. Does that satisfy you?"

"I guess I'll have to settle for that," Ann conceded. "And call me, too. It might help if you have someone to talk with."

Four hours later, Lane recalled making that promise to her mother and had to admit, if only to herself, that she could barely think straight. The voice that she'd heard since childhood was growing relentless. *Please, somebody help me.* Only there was no way that Lane could determine where Nita might be—or even if she was real. And if she wasn't real, what did that say about Lane's mental stability?

"Are you all right, dear?"

Lane glanced up from the open cash register and hoped her confusion wasn't mirrored on her face. Ma Thomas stood at her elbow, her normally cheerful and smiling countenance creased with concern.

"I'm fine," Lane blurted, which she knew was a knee-jerk answer. But how could she tell her new boss that she was hearing voices without getting fired on the spot? "It's just—well, I keep forgetting the department codes, and I'm afraid I'll ring up a sale under the wrong inventory key."

Ma Thomas flapped her hand. "Stop worrying so much. It's your first day, and it's hard to keep everything straight. I know how that goes, and I'll be astounded if you make no mistakes. And the more nervous you feel, the harder it is to remember stuff and the more mistakes you'll make."

Lane knew that might be true of most people, but what was going on with her was worse than a mere case of first-day-on-the-job nerves. Her brain felt like a cluttered computer hard drive that needed a defragmentation. She couldn't focus. Not with all the yammering inside her head. At moments, like right now, she felt like a moron. A lady had just purchased something in a white box with gold lettering, and Lane hadn't even been sure what it was. She read the words, but they couldn't sink in. All she could clearly determine was the price of the item, so she'd rung it up under *Variety*. That wasn't right; she knew it wasn't right.

"I'll do better tomorrow," she promised and hoped it wasn't a lie. She absolutely had to do better, or Ma might decide to let her go. "I'm excited about this job. It's a dream come true for me. Really, it is. And normally, I catch on really fast."

Ma patted Lane's arm. "Stop fretting. You'll do a little better with each passing day."

Lane hoped Ma was right. Even as distracted as she presently was, she was falling in love with the shop. Ma was a brilliant businesswoman, but what truly impressed Lane was her ability to focus on each and every customer to make them feel special. Her grandmotherly appearance and sweet disposition was a charming combination that people found hard to resist. On top of that, Ma offered everyone a cup of coffee or tea to go with their choice of fresh pastry, which made the shop seem more like a second home to them than a mere store. Even the kids loved coming in. At their small table in the play corner, they got to enjoy a donut and hot chocolate that Ma made sure had cooled enough not to cause burns if it were to spill. Sometimes, in order to let a frazzled mother relax and enjoy browsing, Ma sat on an impossibly little chair in the play area and read the kids a story. *Just like at Grandma's house.* The children knew they were welcome. Ma never fretted about them breaking anything. Moms and kids alike could relax at Simply Sensational in a way that Lane doubted they could anywhere else.

But as much as Lane appreciated having a job and as excited as she felt about the possibility of staying on, she couldn't silence that voice. It was like being on one end of a phone line, listening to a stranger talk and being unable to reply or end the call.

During her lunch break, Lane walked nearly the full length of Main Street to eat at Taco Joe's again. Instead of tacos, she ordered a burrito and salad, only to discover that she had no appetite. The mere thought of filling her mouth and trying to swallow made her feel as if she might gag.

She liked Joe, the owner. He was an attractive fellow with dark hair, a dynamic grin, and a warm, down-to-earth manner. Ball caps with different silly sayings hung on the interior walls of his establishment, which Lane tried to read, but her concentration was still just as fractured as it had been at the shop.

Joe approached her table with a concerned expression on his sun-bronzed face. "Is something wrong with the food?"

"What?" Lane struggled to make sense of the question. "Oh, no. It's fine. I just thought I was hungry and now I'm not."

"If you'd like something else, I can whip it up for you in no time."

Lane shook her head and tried to smile. "This is absolutely fine. I've just lost my appetite."

At that exact moment, Lane got the horrible feeling that someone had grabbed her around the throat. Suddenly, she couldn't breathe. Panic flared within her. Startled, she leaped to her feet, knocking her chair over backward. Joe caught her by the shoulders. Looking up at him, she felt her face growing hot. An airless pounding began in her temples. Black spots danced before her eyes. She felt as if she might lose consciousness.

"Are you all right? Are you choking?"

Joe's voice seemed to come from far away. Struggling to breathe, Lane pressed her palms to her chest and broke his hold on her by bending forward at the waist. Then, as suddenly as the pressure on her throat had begun, it stopped. She gasped for air.

"Easy, easy," Joe coached. "Slow, deep breaths." He placed a palm on her back. "Is it asthma? I've heard that difficulty breathing can come on really fast."

Lane couldn't answer him. Her need for oxygen overruled all else. As her head began to clear, she slowly straightened, her body trembling and weak. Joe ran behind the counter and got her a glass of water. She accepted it and took a hesitant sip, fearful that trying to swallow liquid might cause her to choke.

It was then that she heard another voice, the voice

of a man, only it was inside her head. *"Next time you try that shit, I'll kill you."*

Lane grabbed her purse. "I'm sorry. I have to go," she told Joe as she hurried for the door. "I'll stop by and pay my tab tomorrow."

After exiting onto the sunny sidewalk, Lane leaned against the brick front of a building, closed her eyes, and dragged in several more deep breaths, hoping that it might clear her mind and help her focus. *What's happening to me?* Even as Lane asked herself that, she accepted that she had no answers. She only knew that her earlier reluctance to seek counseling had flown out the proverbial window. This was too crazy for words, and she needed help.

With shaking hands, she fished her phone from her purse and did a Google search for psychiatrists and psychologists in the area. She didn't expect to find anyone in Mystic Creek and was surprised when a local practitioner popped up. Jonas Sterling. Before she could change her mind, she brought up his contact information and pressed CALL.

She expected a receptionist to answer, but instead a man with a deep, friendly voice said, "Hello. Jonas Sterling here. How may I help you?"

Lane almost ended the call. Just the thought of seeing yet another counselor and spilling her guts made her stomach knot. "I—um—I think I'm losing my mind."

He chuckled. "Don't we all sometimes?"

Lane wished he wouldn't make light of her predicament. She was hearing voices. Hands she couldn't see had just clenched around her throat. She was losing it. "I think I need to see someone, the sooner the better, if you have any openings."

"I have a four o'clock," he said.

Lane's heart sank. "I don't get off work until three, and I've got errands to run." In truth, she just needed a few pieces of furniture, and it struck her that being comfortable in the cottage wasn't nearly as important as retaining her sanity. "Never mind. I can run errands another time."

"No, no. Honestly, five or shortly thereafter will work just as well for me. I have a six thirty dinner engagement, but if I run a little late, it'll be okay."

Lane nodded and then realized he couldn't see her. "I—yes, that sounds good."

"May I have your name, please?"

For an instant, Lane had to rack her brain to answer the question. "I, um—Lane Driscoll." She took a breath and slowly released it. "Where is your clinic located?"

He chuckled again. "Nothing as fancy as a clinic yet. I have an in-home practice right now. My apartment is above the Straw Hat. As you enter the restaurant, you'll see a flight of stairs off to the right. The door is at the top."

Lane stood just across the street from the Straw Hat. "Got it. I'll see you shortly after five, then."

"That works. I'll see you then."

Jonas spent the rest of the afternoon running errands and helping his dad out at the family farm. When he got back to his apartment at half past four, he took a quick shower and threw on clean clothes before going into the living room, where he'd set up a makeshift office. *Someday I'll have a proper clinic*, he promised himself. *And a front desk receptionist who'll remember to ask a potential patient if he or she has health insurance.* He had to laugh at himself, he supposed. As a psychologist, he was good with people, but he wasn't, by any stretch of the imagination, an organized guy. He needed to work on his professionalism.

After quickly combing his damp hair, he settled at his desk with five minutes to spare. While he waited for a knock to come at his door, he tidied the top of his desk. He'd just started to write a check to pay his electric bill when he heard the light tap of a fist.

"Come in!" he called out.

The next instant, his new patient stepped over the threshold, and all Jonas could do was gape at her. It was Veneta Monroe. She wore a V-neck wraparound dress that sported a floral pattern in blue and a calf-length, jagged hemline. It was so typical of Veneta's fashion sense—or the lack thereof—that his surprise swiftly turned to anger. It was one thing for her to show up in his hometown and act as if she didn't know him, but it was absolutely outrageous of her to book an appointment with him under a fake name.

Without any forethought, Jonas said, "You've got to be kidding me. *Really?*"

Veneta appeared to be genuinely bewildered by his greeting. Jonas didn't know what her game was, but he refused to play.

"I'm sorry?" Her questioning tone outraged Jonas even more. "You are Jonas Sterling. Right?"

"I think we both know the answer to that question," he shot back. "Just leave. I've moved on. You've moved on. We have absolutely nothing to say to each other."

She stepped closer to his desk. "I'm sorry, but you must have me confused with someone else. I'm Lane Driscoll and I called earlier for an appointment."

Jonas ran his gaze over her and was relieved that he no longer felt even a hint of attraction. "Well, Miss

Driscoll." He snarled his lip as he emphasized the last name she'd just given him. "I'm canceling on you. Please leave."

She sank onto the chair facing his desk, met his gaze, and said, "I don't understand. I need your help. Do you think I'd even be here if I weren't desperate?"

Jonas had always been cursed with a tender heart. And even though he knew she was playing him—or trying to—he couldn't quite ignore the dark circles that underscored her blue eyes. Her face was also pale, and her posture indicated that she was not only tense but also nearly beside herself. Maybe, he decided, she truly did need help.

"I'm afraid that isn't possible," he told her. "Given the nature of our past relationship, I can't possibly act as your counselor. It would be unethical. You should find another psychologist. There are plenty in Crystal Falls."

"Our past relationship?" She repeated his words with an edge of incredulity. "I've never clapped eyes on you in my life."

Jonas picked up a pen, stared stupidly at it, and then tossed it back on the blotter. "Look. I don't have time for this. And whatever your game is, I'm not going to play."

Tears welled in her eyes, and her facial muscles began to quiver. But even as convincing as she was, Jonas knew it had to be an act. Although he was no longer emotionally invested in Veneta, he could have described every detail of her face in his sleep. She even had the dark mole he remembered on her cheek.

Clinging to his composure, he modulated his voice to calmly say, "Please, just go. I don't know why you're here. What you hope to gain. But I'm not interested."

She shot to her feet. Jonas saw that her whole body was shaking. Her hands, clenched over the strap of her brown purse, were white at the knuckles. An odd little sound came from her lips, and then she whirled away and scurried toward the door.

Jonas' shoulders jerked when it slammed closed behind her. The sound reverberated through his apartment like a rifle shot. He whooshed a breath past his lips. Made a fist in his hair. Tried not to think about the tortured expression he'd seen in her eyes. If she truly did need help, he had just done the equivalent of throwing her to the wolves. While it was true that he couldn't, in good conscience, offer her counseling because of their history, he could have at least helped her find another practitioner—someone he knew personally and trusted.

Decision made, he came to his feet and crossed the room in three long strides.

Chapter Three

Once downstairs, Jonas walked directly to the exit doors without making eye contact with any of the restaurant patrons. He knew if he did that someone would try to strike up a conversation with him, and he didn't have time to linger. If this wasn't some stupid game Veneta was playing, he had to put the past behind him and assist her in any way he could.

He saw her on the sidewalk. The evening breeze whipped her floral skirt around her legs with each step she took and toyed with her reddish-blond hair, making it flash like burnished gold in the fading sunlight. "Hey, Veneta!" he called. "Wait up!"

She acted as if she didn't hear him. He muttered a curse under his breath and quickened his stride to catch up with her. "Lane!" he tried. "Hold up for just a second."

She abruptly stopped and whirled to face him. "You told me to leave, and I left. What more do you want?"

Jonas slowed his pace and studied her tear-streaked face as he closed the remaining distance between them. "If you'll return to my office, I'll get online and find someone else who can help you."

Her blue eyes sparkled with anger, and she lifted her chin in a gesture of defiance that he remembered all too well. "I'm perfectly capable of finding someone else by myself, Mr. Sterling. I was just hoping to see someone quickly, and since I think I'll need more than one session, I wanted to avoid the long drive to Crystal Falls two or three times a week."

"I understand," Jonas settled for saying. "And I'm sure you're quite capable of going online to find someone else. It's just that—" He broke off and raked a hand through his hair. "I overreacted. I guess seeing you again had more of an impact on me than I thought. I shouldn't have asked you to leave. I attend meetings in Crystal Falls every couple of months and personally know several psychologists who practice there. I can probably get you in to see someone faster than you can manage on your own, and I also have the added advantage of knowing who's good and who isn't."

She rolled her eyes, another gesture of hers that he remembered. "Why do you persist in saying we know each other? I'd remember if I ever met you, and I haven't."

Jonas met and held her gaze, and he saw no trace of guile or recognition in her eyes. She honestly didn't remember him. How that could possibly be, he wasn't sure. "Maybe I've just got you confused with someone else." He didn't believe that was the case, and it galled him to pretend it was. But that was a worry for later. "Please, let's put that on a back burner for now. If you'll come to my office, I'll help you get an appointment. There's a female practitioner in Crystal Falls that I like and admire. She might be a perfect fit for you."

She sighed and folded her arms at her waist, a defensive body posture if ever he'd seen one. "All right," she finally agreed. "If you can get me in to see someone quicker, I'd be foolish to pass on the offer."

Jonas fell into step beside her as they returned to his office. Inside the restaurant, Tim and Lynda VeArd waved him a friendly hello. He smiled to acknowledge them and led the way up the stairs. Once inside his apartment, Veneta resumed her seat on the chair facing his desk and pressed her fingertips to her temples.

"Headache?" he asked. "I've got some ibuprofen."

"I wish I could just swallow a pill and get rid of it," she replied. "But it's a voice inside my head. I can't make it go away. And it gets so loud sometimes that I can barely think."

Jonas swiveled his chair toward his computer screen. *A voice?* That didn't sound good. Auditory hallucinations could be caused by schizophrenia, which was serious. On the other hand, though, hearing voices could also be caused by a host of other things.

"Are you getting plenty of sleep?" he asked over his shoulder as he waited for his computer to boot up.

"With a voice shouting inside my head?" Her tone rang with sarcasm, but there was also an edge of desperation. "Her name is Nita. That's what I used to call her, anyway. She was my imaginary friend. Or should I say she *is* my imaginary friend. She certainly hasn't left."

Jonas froze with his hands poised over the keyboard. A tingle of alarm ran up his spine. His pet name for Veneta had been Neta, and a lot of her friends had called her that as well. He turned to look at this woman who claimed her name was Lane Driscoll, wondering for the first time if he was wrong about her. As weird and outlandish as it seemed, what if she was actually telling the truth? She was a dead ringer for Veneta Monroe, but there were subtle differences as well. Her voice was a little softer, for one. Her manner was also more refined. But what really stood out to Jonas was that she seemed far more diffident. Veneta had been self-confident to a fault, always barreling into situations with no thought of the consequences.

Studying her, he gave himself a hard mental shake. It was crazy to think she might not be Veneta. No two people could look so alike unless they were identical twins. Jonas resumed his search online for a psychologist. "To be on the safe side, I'd like to look at the patient reviews before I decide who might be the best choice for you. If you have time, that is."

"You're the one with a time crunch," she replied, still rubbing her temples. "A dinner engagement, you said."

"It's just dinner at my parents' place." He shrugged. "They'll cut me some slack if I show up a bit late."

As he quickly scanned the reviews, Lane began telling him more about herself. He really didn't want to hear her personal information, but he couldn't think how to cut her off without being rude.

"I know it sounds crazy when I talk about having an imaginary friend. Adults aren't supposed to have them. But Nita has been around for as far back as I can remember. Not to say she's with me all the time."

"Huh," Jonas said. It was his standard response when he wanted to convey disinterest.

"I didn't mind hearing the voice when I was little. I guess you might even say I drew comfort from it. Maybe it made me feel less alone or something. It's just that now, it's frightening and insistent and I don't want it inside my head."

Jonas abandoned his online search and turned to regard the young woman with a thoughtful frown. "This may seem like a really dumb question, but is there any chance that you were adopted as a very young child?"

Her eyes widened. "How do you know that about me?" she demanded. "It's not something I share with others very often. My parents are wonderful people, and the fact that they're not my biological parents doesn't seem important."

"I didn't *know* that about you. I was just venturing a guess." Jonas studied her heart-shaped face, trying to spot some tiny difference in her countenance that would tell him she wasn't Veneta. Only there was nothing. "How old were you when you were adopted?" he couldn't resist asking.

"Three," she replied without hesitation.

"Do you remember your birth mother?"

"No," she answered. "All I actually know about her is that she stipulated prior to giving me up that my first name could never be changed. My adoptive parents honored that request even though my dad dislikes it. He says Lane sounds like the name of a county."

Jonas couldn't help but smile. "Well, there *is* a Lane County in Oregon. I attended college there." He sighed and slumped back in his caster chair. Her story about being adopted at three was almost identical to the one Veneta had told him. Even the request that her first name never be changed was the same. "Do you remember having a sister?"

Her lashes fluttered, feathering momentarily over her cheeks. She was beautiful, he decided, with delicate features and big blue eyes that a man could get lost in. He suffered a distinctly uncomfortable moment of déja vu, because it was Veneta's face, right down to those soft, full lips that he'd kissed countless times.

"A sister?" She shook her head no. "I recall very little of my childhood prior to being adopted, only hazy snatches of memory. A woman's face sometimes.

A sense of great loss. But mostly my memories are comprised of stories my parents told me. Things I did when I was very young. Funny things I said." She pushed a strand of hair away from her eyes. "I have no actual memories. Isn't that pretty normal, though? Or do other people remember being only three?"

"Some people do, and some people don't," he told her. "I can remember falling off a slide at the park and breaking my arm. I was three when it happened. It's a clear memory, but I recall nothing else. Not who I was playing with or even who took me to the park. It's just a blip."

She shrugged and pushed at her hair again. "Well, I don't even have blips. Maybe the woman's face is a memory. She might have been my birth mother. But I'll never know for sure."

Jonas sat forward and braced his arms on his knees. "Think carefully. Is it possible that you had a twin sister?"

She arched her eyebrows. "Why do you ask?"

Jonas held her gaze. "Because I know you. Or at least I thought I did. You look exactly like an old girl-friend of mine."

She scrunched her shoulders again. "You mean I resemble her? I can't possibly look *exactly* like her."

"Oh, but you do. And I do mean exactly. That's why I asked you to leave my office earlier, because I thought you were her and were playing some kind of head game with me."

Her brow pleated in a bewildered frown. "I look *exactly* like her?"

"Right down to the mole on your cheek. Even more interesting, Veneta's story about her adoption is almost exactly like yours. Unlike you, she did have vague memories of her birth mother, but nothing definitive. Her first name was never to be changed. You're either Veneta and messing with me, or you're her identical twin."

She held up a hand. "Not possible. Adoption agencies refuse to separate twins."

"I know," he retorted, "but that isn't to say it never happens in independent adoptions."

She closed her eyes and pressed her fingertips against her temples again. "I have absolutely no memory of having a sister. My only memory is of Nita, my imaginary friend. I always felt as if Nita was a part of me. I can remember"—a distant expression entered her eyes—"I was about five, I think, and my mom grew angry with me for talking about Nita. She told me Nita wasn't real and I had to stop talking about her. It made me angry, and I threw a temper tantrum. Looking back, I think I frightened my mother because I didn't normally act out that way."

"Little kids get angry," Jonas told her. "And whether your imaginary friend was real or not, your mom probably shouldn't have told you she wasn't. According to the research I've read, most children know that their imaginary companions aren't real."

"I didn't. To me, Nita was as real as I was."

Jonas printed out the information on the female psychologist he knew in Crystal Falls and handed it to Lane. Or was she actually Veneta? Until he knew the answer to that question, he needed to watch his step. "That's the therapist I told you about. I think she'll be a perfect fit for you."

Her eyes darkened with shadows. "I thought you were going to pull strings for me to get an appointment faster."

"I will," he assured her. "It's after hours now. I'll

give her a call in the morning to see if she can work you into her schedule."

She folded the paper and stuck it in her handbag. "Thank you for that. Needless to say, I can't sleep well. Maybe talking with her will help, and I'll be able to get a full eight."

"What does she say to you? The voice, I mean." The instant Jonas asked that question, he knew he shouldn't have. The less he knew about this young woman's personal problems, the better off he would be.

Lane's face drained of color. "She says someone is going to kill her and she's begging for help."

Jonas' stomach knotted. "Sweet Christ."

"It gets worse."

He held up both hands to forestall her. "I shouldn't have asked. Even if you're telling the truth and actually aren't the Veneta I know, I shouldn't counsel you. In the strictest sense, it isn't really illegal for me to treat someone with whom I am or have been personally involved, but it's strongly discouraged."

"Except we aren't personally involved and never have been. I think I'd remember something like that. Don't you?"

"One would think so, but by your own admission, you're pretty upset right now."

"I am *not* that Veneta person." She drew her wallet from her purse, opened it, and tugged her driver's license from one of the card slots. With a flick of her wrist, she tossed it on the desk blotter. "Explain *that*."

Jonas studied the state-issued card. Her photo. Her name and address. And lastly, her birthdate. "I'm trying really hard to wrap my mind around this."

She plucked the piece of plastic from his grasp. "I'm trying really hard to retain my sanity."

The note of recrimination in her voice didn't escape him. Jonas couldn't think of anything more he could say in his own defense. Regardless of her identity, she was an exact replica of a woman with whom he'd once been emotionally involved. If he allowed her to confide in him, he'd be breaking his personal code of ethics.

After putting her wallet away, she drew the strap of her purse onto her shoulder. Jonas tried not to notice how her slender fingers trembled. She looked like a person who was holding on to her composure by a thread.

"Could you possibly prescribe a sleep aid for me?" she asked.

Oh, how Jonas wished he could do that. He had experienced sleep deprivation back in college, and he knew, at a certain point of exhaustion, that it became difficult to even think straight. "I'm sorry. I'm not licensed to write prescriptions."

She sighed. "Well, it was worth asking. Right now, I'm frantic for a good night's sleep. This was my first day working at Simply Sensational, and I screwed up more things than I got right. If I don't do better tomorrow, Mary Alice may fire me."

She looked so utterly drained that Jonas experienced a startling urge to hug her. The feelings that moved through him were troubling, to say the least.

"Good luck," he said softly, sincerely meaning it.

Long after she left and the sound of her footsteps on the stairs faded away, Jonas sat at his desk, staring at nothing. In his mind's eye, he could still see the front of her driver's license, her birthdate standing out in his memory as if it had been in bold print.

She'd been born on the same day and in the same year as Veneta Monroe. If she actually was Veneta, why would she have let him see that information? Surely, she would have realized it would be a red flag to him. Yet she had tossed the license onto his desk with an air of confident indignation, as if the information on it would prove to him, once and for all, that she was who she said she was. He had no explanation for that except that she might be telling the truth.

That line of reasoning brought Jonas full-circle to his earlier suspicion, that Lane and Veneta were identical twins. As unlikely as it was for twins to be separated for adoption, it was the only explanation that made sense. He hadn't gotten the impression that Lane was lying. Most people had little tells when they lied, some of them unable to look you directly in the eye, others exhibiting a facial twitch or speaking faster, often with a higher pitch to their voice. Rapid hand movements were also common. Lane had exhibited none of those signs. Instead, she had appeared to be mostly distraught and bewildered.

After checking his watch, Jonas leaped up from his chair. He had to run, or he'd be late for dinner. He grabbed his keyless remote from off the desk and went to find his jacket. At this time of year, as summer bumped noses with early autumn, the nights grew chilly in Mystic Creek, and Jonas knew from experience that he'd probably end up outside with his dad at some point during the evening. Jeremiah Sterling always had an ongoing project to work on, with a smattering of unexpected emergencies tossed into the mix to keep him hopping.

Jonas always enjoyed having dinner with his folks. Kate was an amazing cook, one of those people who could create a feast at a moment's notice, and she was also a congenial hostess. Tonight she'd served home-made spaghetti and meatballs with a spinach salad. Feeling satiated after polishing off second helpings, Jonas lifted his wineglass to his mother, who looked lovely in a red top and boot-cut jeans.

"Another amazing meal, Mom. Thank you. I've eaten downstairs in the restaurant so much that I have the whole menu memorized. It's nice to have something different—and better tasting."

Kate's brown eyes twinkled with laughter. "Before you leave the house, do you ever look at yourself in the full-length mirror I bought and hung in your bathroom?"

Jonas glanced down. "Why? Is my barn door open?"

Jeremiah, who was still a handsome man with only a smattering of gray in his tawny hair, threw back his head and laughed. His hazel eyes shimmered like whiskey shot through with sunlight as he settled his gaze on Jonas. "Nope. Tonight you're not indecently exposing yourself, but you do have a sock stuck to the back of your shirt."

Jonas reached around to feel. When he located the sock, it snapped with static electricity as he tugged it off his clothing. "Damn, I hate when that happens." Heat crept up his neck as he recalled walking through a crowded restaurant three times. "Why didn't one of you say something?"

Kate shrugged her slender shoulders. "You seemed preoccupied when you got here, and not in a good way. Besides, it's only us. If you come for dinner with half your underwear drawer on your back, we don't care." Her cheek dimpled in a saucy grin. "Due to your profession, it may behoove you to develop a classier look, but I doubt that'll ever happen. I've told you a hundred times to use laundry softener sheets. They get the static out of your clothes. But you listen to nothing I say."

Half of a meatball remained on Jonas' plate, and he couldn't resist polishing it off. After chewing and chasing the food down with a sip of merlot, he said, "I listen, Mom. It's just that it always slips my mind to buy dryer sheets when I'm at the market."

"That's because you think too much," his mother retorted. "About your patients, of course, and that's a worthy attribute, Jonas, but you should try to at least focus on what you're doing while you're shopping." Kate narrowed her eyes. "So, spill. You're worried about something, undoubtedly about someone you counseled recently. What's the problem?"

"She isn't really a client of mine," Jonas explained.

"Oh, good! That means you can give us the dirty without breaking confidentiality!"

Jonas couldn't help but laugh. Kate Sterling rarely engaged in gossiping, and yet she often pressed him for details if she got wind that he was counseling someone she knew. Jonas wasn't allowed to reveal anything, not even a patient's name, which frustrated his mother to no end. "You're definitely in luck. A woman called while I was helping Dad today. She sounded very upset and said she needed to talk with someone right away, so I agreed to meet with her shortly after five. You'll never believe who walked into my office. I about fell off my chair."

"Who?" Jeremiah asked. "Don't tease me by dangling a carrot in front of my nose. I could die of a heart attack at any given moment and never get the full scoop."

Jonas knew his father was in good health for a man

in his sixties. He occasionally experienced arrhythmia, but he went for regular checkups and the doctors said his heart was still in fair shape. "It was Veneta Monroe. If you don't remember—"

"How could I forget?" his father asked. "She was that snarky little twerp you brought home for a weekend back when you were in college. Longest two days of my life."

"She wasn't *that* bad." Jonas took another swallow of wine. "Although, I have to admit, she wasn't trying to win a popularity contest that weekend. She hated everything about Mystic Creek. Called it Podunk, USA."

Kate leaned across the table to refill Jeremiah and Jonas' wineglasses before topping off her own. "Ah-ha!" she said. "I nailed it. She came here to seek you out and get some closure, and when you didn't engage with her, she decided to beard the lion in his den."

Jonas shared the actual story, leaving nothing out. "It was an unsettling situation for me. She said she was hearing voices. That she could barely think or sleep, and she needed help. At first, I thought she was playing games and told her to leave. After she stormed out, I had a change of heart, thinking that the very least I should do was help her find another therapist."

"So she doesn't remember you. Not at *all*?" Jeremiah sat back in his chair with the stem of his wine goblet resting on his paunch. "That's weird."

"So weird it's unbelievable," Kate interjected. "She must have been lying."

Jonas shook his head. "Initially, I thought so, but then I started to change my mind. I'm good at reading people—not only because I'm trained to do so, but also because I have a knack for it. I don't think she was lying."

"So, let me get this straight." Kate held up a finger. "She looks exactly like Veneta." Another finger went up. "She even dresses like Veneta and wears her hair in a similar style, and yet you don't think she's Veneta? What have you been smoking?"

Jonas met his mother's gaze. "Don't jump up and check me for fever. I know it sounds crazy—all of it. Two people can't look that much alike unless they're identical twins. There were small differences, not in appearance but behaviors. Her voice is softer, and her manner is more refined. Veneta had a rough childhood, and she could be crass at times. This gal has a ladylike demeanor." Jonas swirled his merlot and gazed at the burgundy haze of its legs on the curvature of the crystal. "That got me to thinking. What if she actually is?"

"Is what?" Jeremiah asked.

"Veneta's identical twin." Jonas set down his glass. "This woman even showed me her driver's license to prove she is who she says she is."

"People can get fake ID, Jonas," Kate pointed out.

"Yes, they can, and they do. But if she's really Veneta, why would she go to all that effort to get a fake ID in order to fool me and then not change her date of birth? I can see her not changing the year, but using the same month and day? If I were pretending to be someone else, I wouldn't leave my birthdate the same on a counterfeit license. It'd be too big a red flag, especially to someone like me, who knows so much about her."

Frowning thoughtfully, Kate smoothed away a wrinkle in the tablecloth. "I see where you're going with this, Jonas, but don't you think the identical twin explanation is a little farfetched?"

"At first, yes. But her adoption background was eerily the same as Veneta's. Both of them were three at the time, and the adoptive parents in both cases had to agree that they would never change the girls' first names."

"Well, of course the story would be nearly the same if this gal is actually Veneta. The question in my mind is what can Veneta hope to gain by deceiving you?"

"Good question," Jonas replied. "And there was nothing to be gained, Mom. My first reaction was anger."

Jeremiah scratched below his ear, a habit of his when he was thinking. "Normally, twins can't be separated during an adoption."

"But what if the adoption was arranged outside the usual channels?" Jonas asked. "Adoption attorneys are mostly ethical, but there's a lot of money to be made in baby trafficking, and some attorneys may not hesitate to pull some fast ones. Some childless couples will cough up their last dime in order to get a kid."

Kate nodded. "One of my friends and her husband spent a small fortune in order to adopt their baby boy."

"An independent adoption, most likely," Jonas inserted. "They're normally legal, but sometimes they're the equivalent of a child being sold to the highest bidder."

Kate's expression went from thoughtful to concerned. "Babies aren't commodities on a market shelf. In the case of my friend, I know the baby boy found a wonderful home, but if potential adoptive parents aren't properly vetted, just the opposite could easily occur."

"Yes," Jonas agreed. "But in Lane's case, I don't think she landed in a bad place. She seems to deeply love her adoptive parents."

"You just referred to her as Lane," Kate observed. "Does that mean you actually believe her story? Be careful, Jonas. If she's Veneta, she's up to no good."

"I appreciate your concern, Mom, but caution is my middle name," he said. "I just don't want to jump to conclusions and discount everything this woman said when there's a chance she may be telling the truth."

"How will you check her out?" Jeremiah queried.

"I'll start by Googling her. If I can find a Lane Marie Driscoll online, it'll be a good start."

Two hours later, Jonas sat in front of his computer, staring at the screen. He'd not only found evidence that a Lane Marie Driscoll existed, but he'd unearthed details about her life. Where she'd attended high school. A picture of her performing in a church choir at Christmas. The address of her childhood home. It wasn't particularly fascinating research, but it proved, at least to his satisfaction, that Lane Driscoll was exactly who she said she was. Though taken when she was much younger, the likenesses he viewed of her were definitely of the same person he'd met earlier in his office. *Mind-boggling.* Though Jonas had heard it said that everyone had a double somewhere in the world, he didn't believe such a thing was really possible. A remarkable resemblance, yes. He could buy into that. But it was a much bigger leap for him to think that two people who weren't genetically identical could look exactly alike.

Even though Lane had a terrific headache and was so sleep-deprived that her whole body felt heavy, she pasted on what she hoped was a bright smile as she entered Simply Sensational the next morning. The mingled scents of different perfumes greeted her, as did Mary Alice, who was at the back of the shop dusting merchandise.

"Good morning, sweetie!" she called. "I'm so excited today about having you onboard! I couldn't believe how much less tired I was when I got home last night. I even had the energy to work outside for a while and put one of my flower gardens to bed for the winter."

Lane hung her coat on a wall hook behind the cash register. "That's awesome!" She walked the length of the shop to where Ma stood. "I can do that unless there's something else you'd like me to tackle."

"I'm good doing this if you can get the sitting area prepared. I picked up pastry, but I haven't gotten it put out yet. And the coffee center probably needs tidying."

"Consider it done." Lane hurried to the back of the shop and went to work, putting out the baked goods on a tray, quickly rearranging all the K-Cups, and then straightening the children's bookshelves. "Would you like a cup of coffee, Ma?"

"I'd love one!" she called back. "Will you join me?"

Lane definitely needed more coffee. After an almost sleepless night, she'd slept in as long as she could this morning and had downed only one cup while she'd showered and gotten ready for work. Doses of caffeine throughout the day might be all that would keep her going. "I'd love that. Maybe we can even steal a couple of minutes to sit and actually enjoy it."

Ma abandoned her dusting task and came to sit at the table, where Lane served her a mug of joe. "I'm all for that."

"Two sugars and one French vanilla creamer. Right?"

Mary Alice laughed, her blue eyes twinkling. "You see? Your memory is still alive and well."

Lane could only hope that her memory served her as well when she had to ring up customer purchases later. "You mean there's hope for me?"

"More than a little." Ma smiled as Lane sat across from her at the table with her own mug of coffee. "I'm very pleased so far, Lane. It makes me feel so positive about everything. For so long, I kept hoping I'd find someone to help me here, but it just never happened. I have no idea why." She shrugged in apparent bewilderment. "It's a great opportunity for a young woman, but nobody I mentioned it to seemed all that interested. I hope, over time, that you grow to love Mystic Creek and decide to stay on. Maybe you'll even decide you'd like to work out a partnership arrangement."

"I can't make any promises at this time," Lane said, "but I have to admit that the possibility interests me."

Mary Alice leaned sideways to grab a donut from the serving case. "It's early on. You aren't sure yet if this is your cup of tea, and I'm not sure yet that you're right for the position. I have a good feeling about you, though, and I can't help but hope."

Lane was so disappointed in her own performance the previous day that she asked, "Do you really have a good feeling about me? That I may be the right person, I mean."

"Absolutely. You're bright. You're ambitious. You're good with the customers. If you should decide to remain in Mystic Creek, I'll be beside myself with delight."

Tears burned at the back of Lane's eyes. She quickly blinked them away. "Thank you for that. I know I totally screwed up a number of times yesterday."

"How would any of us learn without totally screwing up?" Mary Alice popped back. "Lighten up on yourself, honey. You were wonderful with the customers and the kids. That's the most important thing to me. Screw-ups can be rectified. People are pretty understanding when cash register mishaps occur, especially here in such a small town where the pace is slower. Women aren't in a rush when they shop here. If they have to wait a few minutes while we iron out a wrinkle, they don't really mind."

"I'm glad to hear it, because I didn't sleep well last night, and my brain feels like mush." Lane helped herself to a bear claw. "I'm pretty sure we haven't seen the last of my screw-ups."

"Why couldn't you sleep?" Ma asked.

Lane didn't feel comfortable sharing the truth, that she'd been plagued with bad dreams all night. "Just nervous, I guess. All keyed up. I'm very excited about working here, for one."

Ma took a bite of her pastry. Cheek bulging, she added, "I know it sounds silly, but this shop truly is my baby. Now that I'm over seventy, I know my days as a business owner are numbered, and it would break my heart to sell this place and watch it be turned into a pizza parlor or something. It's my dream. You know? One I worked so hard to make come true. I want nothing more than to eventually turn it over to someone who will love it as much as I do."

Lane glanced around. "It's a fabulous shop, Ma. If I'm lucky enough to be the person you've been waiting for, then I'll be over the moon." A wave of guilt swept through Lane as she regarded the older woman. Ma had no idea that her hopes rested upon someone so messed up in her head that she heard voices. "Let's just take it slow and see how it all pans out. Maybe I'm the right person. Then again, maybe I'm not."

Ma got up and put her mug in the small corner sink. "I trust in my instincts, Lane."

As Lane rinsed out their coffee mugs, she heard the familiar voice again. *"They're waiting. Holding off for some reason. They can't let me go. I know too much."* Fingers dripping water, Lane squeezed her eyes closed and pressed the heels of her hands against her temples, hoping if she applied enough pressure that the voice would go away.

"Honey, are you okay?" Ma asked from directly behind her.

Lane jumped with a start and turned to face the other woman. "I'm—uh, I'm fine. Just a slight headache."

"Would you like some ibuprofen? I keep some under the counter up front."

Even though Lane knew the tablets wouldn't help, she did have a headache. "Awesome. I'll go grab a couple."

Minutes later, two women with kids entered the shop, and Lane grew so busy helping the customers find a scent they liked that she forgot all about her problems. Working at Simply Sensational, she decided, was like hosting a day-long tea party. Ma offered every visitor baked goods and hot tea or coffee. With Lane there to help, the older woman could now sit at the round table in back and chat with her guests. She often had a child on her lap. In a very real way, Ma was a grandmother figure to nearly every youngster in town.

In Maple Leaf, where Lane had so recently lived, running a business the way Ma ran hers would be regarded by other entrepreneurs as crazy, but Lane was already a huge believer. The people of Mystic Creek visited the shop not only to buy soaps and scents and novelties but were also coming for the gestures of affection that Ma made toward each and every one of them. She dispensed hugs and gentle pats. She kept clean tissues in her pocket to wipe runny noses. And she was such a warm and down-to-earth person.

Lane worried that Ma would be a very hard act for her to follow. For one, she wasn't old enough to pull off the grandmotherly thing, and for another, she hadn't been around young children very much. She guessed that she'd be better off developing her own business persona, and maybe over time, she could assume the role of a surrogate aunt to all the kiddos. For now, she was hard pressed just to remember people's names, a worry that she pondered in between customers as she took advantage of breaks to start decorating for Halloween.

"You are so clever!" Ma said several times as she admired Lane's decorative displays of cobweb-draped branches, jack-o'-lanterns, and a scarecrow. "This place has never looked quite so festive."

Lane smiled. "I love decorating for the holidays. Maybe, if I don't mess up so badly that you fire me, I'll still be around for Christmas. That's when I really get into gear."

Chapter Four

Lane hadn't felt like eating lunch, so when she got off work at three, she was starving and wanted only to grab a quick meal somewhere before she headed home to crash. Preoccupied as she left the building with deciding what kind of food sounded good, she walked right into Jonas Sterling, who was standing just outside the door. With a laugh, he caught her by the shoulders to right her balance.

"Whoa!" he said. "Where's the fire?"

Lane pushed at her hair and retreated a step to put space between them. She'd been so distraught when she saw him last night that she hadn't really noticed how good-looking he was. His chiseled facial features were sun-burnished to a caramel richness, and his tawny hair, which lay over his forehead in a lazy wave, complemented his complexion. "Mr. Sterling! What brings you here?"

His eyes shimmered like golden beryl in the slanting sunlight. "Let's just say I've been doing a lot of thinking. I did make that call this morning to get you in quickly to see the psychologist I recommended, but now I'm questioning the wisdom of that. You may be better off just seeing me."

"Oh." Lane groped for something to say. "What brought about the sudden change of heart?"

His lips slanted into a crooked grin that creased his lean cheek. "Now that I've had time to think it over, I believe you are who you say you are, and if my suspicions are correct, I may be able to help you in ways no other psychologist can." He held up a hand. "Please, will you have an early dinner with me and hear what I have to say?"

Lane shifted her purse strap onto her shoulder. "I, um—actually, Mr. Sterling, I think I may be more comfortable with a female counselor." Now that she'd really *looked* at Jonas, she couldn't imagine telling a man so handsome all of her deepest and darkest secrets. "No offense or anything. I just think it may be easier for me to speak candidly with another woman."

His eyes began to twinkle with mischief as he focused on her face. "No offense taken. I understand. But can you at least have dinner with me and hear me out?"

Lane was too tired to be coy. "The truth is, I'm starving. So I guess I can do that."

He glanced up the street. "What sounds good? All our best restaurants are within easy walking distance, and I'm open for anything except Mexican food at the Straw Hat. Not that the food there isn't good. I just eat there more often than not because I live upstairs, and I've become weary of ordering the same things over and over."

"Chinese?" Lane suggested.

"A woman after my heart," he said. "I've been craving some good Chinese food, and Chopstick Suey always delivers."

As they fell into step together, it didn't escape Lane's notice that Jonas moved around her to walk between her and the street. *A gentleman*. That could be a devastating attribute in a man so attractive. Just walking beside him made Lane's skin tingle. Such a strong reaction to a male was completely atypical of her, and she filed the feeling away in her memory banks as a red flag. The last thing she needed in her life right now was another complication, and a romantic relationship could often grow complicated.

When they entered Chopstick Suey, a tall, attractive young man with pitch-black hair and brown eyes greeted them near the entrance. "Jonas! Hey, man, good to see that ugly mug of yours again. It's been a while."

Jonas smiled and touched Lane's elbow. "Lane, I'd like you to meet Hunter Chase, the owner of this fabulous establishment and my longtime friend. Hunter, this is Lane Driscoll. She's new in town, so don't scare her off with your usual obnoxious behavior."

Hunter winked at Lane. "In case you can't tell, we went to school together and never outgrew ribbing each other mercilessly." As he spoke, he grabbed two laminated printouts and led them to a booth. After Lane slid into a seat across from Jonas, Hunter handed her one of the menus. Gesturing over his shoulder, he said, "There's a full bar, and before you ask, it's fine to order a margarita. We won't be thrown off our stride if you don't want the traditional green tea."

Lane surprised herself by laughing. "As it happens, I love margaritas."

"On the rocks, frozen, or straight up?" he asked.

"Oh, I'm not ordering one," Lane replied. "Only dreaming."

"Aw, come on. I know a margarita attack coming on when I see one, and I mix one of the best ones you'll ever taste."

Jonas spoke up. "I'll join you, Lane. A margarita sounds like just the thing."

Lane sighed. "Okay, you guys have me convinced." To Hunter, she added, "I prefer crushed ice, whizzed in a blender until I barely notice it's there. And, please, make it a double. If I'm going to imbibe, I may as well go for broke and get a decent night's sleep."

Hunter arched one black eyebrow. "Got it. Two doubles, coming up."

As he walked away, Lane offered Jonas a smile. "Your friend is very nice."

"So am I," he replied with a wink. "Just give me half a chance to prove it."

Lane nodded. "I can do that, but I'll warn you right now that I didn't sleep much again last night. I'm running on empty, and once I get a margarita and a hot meal under my belt, I may pass out from exhaustion."

"In other words, I should get right to the point and make it short."

"Pretty much," Lane admitted. "I honestly can't remember ever being quite this tired."

"Okay. Here's the straight-to-the-point version." Jonas leaned slightly forward, as if he feared someone might overhear what he was about to say. "I think you have an identical twin. In fact, I'm almost positive you do."

Lane's earlier edginess mushroomed into what felt almost like a panic attack. "That simply isn't possible because twins are never separated for adoption in Oregon."

"It's a frowned-upon practice in adoption agencies across the country," he agreed, "but not all adoptive parents go through accredited agencies. People can also hire an adoption attorney who can find them a baby outside the regular channels."

"What are you saying?" Lane heard her voice go shrill. "That my mom and dad *bought* me?"

"No, not at all. Sometimes the adoptive parents support the young mother throughout her pregnancy. And she might have a wish list for things like financial help with college tuition and other stuff after she has the baby."

"How is that any different? You're splitting hairs."

He puffed air into his cheeks. "Lane, try not to take any of this personally."

"They're my parents, and I love them. They would never resort to *buying* a baby."

He sighed. Just then Hunter returned to the table with their drinks. Her stomach knotted with nerves, Lane latched on to her glass like a woman dying of thirst. She took a huge gulp.

"Have you made a menu choice yet?" Hunter asked.

"We're moving slow tonight," Jonas replied. "We'll order in just a few."

"No hurry."

As Hunter walked away, Lane gazed after him. Then she focused on Jonas again. "They would just never stoop to that."

He nodded. "I get that. I really do. But for the sake of discussion, can you set those feelings aside for a moment and consider the possibility that sometimes adoptive parents are so desperate to have a child that they'll go to any length?"

Lane tightened her fingers around the glass stem. "We should order. I didn't eat lunch, and on an empty stomach, this margarita may knock me for a loop."

He opened his menu to study the choices. Lane followed suit. After a moment, he said, "I think I'll go for the Sichuan pork."

"Vermicelli rolls sound fabulous to me."

Hunter stopped at their table just then to take their orders. As he walked away, Lane cocked her head sideways to question Jonas with her eyes. "Why the sudden change of heart, Mr. Sterling? Last night, you were dead set against helping me."

"True, but only because I thought you might be lying and were actually Veneta Monroe."

"What changed your mind?"

"You're her exact double, but I've noticed little differences. You're a more reserved person than Veneta is. Veneta also liked to show off her figure."

"I could still be Veneta. Maybe I've just changed."

He held up his hands. "Okay, I have to come clean. I Googled you last night. Please note that I did so only after I was already halfway convinced that you weren't Veneta. And I found you. I didn't come across a lot of information, but I found enough to prove that you are who you say you are. Pictures of you when you were younger. What high school you attended. Later what college you chose." He winked at her. "You're a damned Beaver, of all things, and I'm a Duck. If we watched a Civil War game together, we'd probably kill each other before it was over."

Lane couldn't stifle a laugh. "You're assuming that I'm a football fan and that I'm loyal to my alma mater. But you're wrong on both counts. When I started college, I began hearing the voice again. Can you imagine how hard it is to concentrate on much of anything, let alone college coursework, when you're afraid you're losing your mind?"

Jonas took a sip of his margarita. "Oh, but if you actually have an identical twin named Neta, maybe you're not crazy after all."

He spoke with such certainty that Lane straightened her posture and willed him to keep talking.

"Think about it," he told her. "If you and Veneta were separated at only three, doesn't it make sense that you might have been unable to say her name correctly, thus Veneta being shortened to Neta?"

Lane couldn't argue that point, so she remained silent.

"You also look exactly like her," he went on.

"As I pointed out before, maybe you're just misremembering what she looks like."

Jonas shook his head. "I was once romantically involved with Veneta, Lane. I haven't forgotten what she looks like. You even wear your hair in a similar style to hers. That's why I asked you to leave my office." He gestured with his hand. "I'm still walking an ethical fine line, but if you're telling the truth, which I'm convinced you are, I can help you without a true conflict of interest."

Lane fiddled with the condiment rack, which sported trendy serving bottles of soy sauce and tamari. "I haven't agreed to have you as a counselor as yet, and I probably won't, so you're worried about nothing."

"Oh, but I think you will agree, not because you feel as comfortable with me as you might with a woman, but because I'm looking at this situation from a whole new angle. You may think I'm a little nuts at first, but play along with me during dinner, and then we'll see where we're at."

"That seems like a harmless enough request. I can play along with anyone for an hour, especially when it means a free meal and drinks."

He chuckled and nodded. "The bill is definitely on me." With his smile, the deep crevice in his cheek reappeared, leading Lane to wonder if he'd once had a boyish dimple that had lengthened and deepened over time. "So humor me with your life story insofar as it pertains to the voice in your head."

Lane breathed in deeply and slowly exhaled. "My parents say that I was a difficult little girl to understand. When I played, I talked almost incessantly to someone they couldn't see. Eventually, they figured out that my invisible little friend was named Nita. They were initially amused. Then, as time wore on, they started to worry that I needed Nita because I was lonely. They decided to just let the situation ride in the hope that I would outgrow it.

"When I was four, I fell asleep on the living room carpet while watching a cartoon. Apparently, I had a terrible dream. I began screaming and looked as if I were fighting off an attacker. After my mother woke me up, I was terrified and cradled my right arm as if it were either broken or badly bruised. When my mom examined me, she found red marks on my body, and my arm appeared to be swelling. She called my dad at work, and they took me to the ER. The doctor took X-rays of my arm and rib cage. He could find nothing really wrong with me physically and couldn't explain the red marks."

He sat across from her with his glass poised before his mouth, staring at her.

"What?" she asked.

He set down his drink with a loud click. "Which arm was it?"

"My right, I believe."

"Oh, my God, this is incredible."

"What's incredible?"

"Veneta told me a lot about her childhood. Her

adoptive father was an abusive alcoholic, and Veneta suffered a broken arm from a beating, but she wasn't taken to the ER. Her adoptive parents were afraid they'd be charged with child abuse. To this day, she still has a bump on her right forearm where the fracture never healed properly."

She saw him flick a glance at her right arm. With a sigh, she extended it toward him. "Go ahead. Feel for it. I have no lump."

He ran his fingertips along her forearm and then withdrew his hand. "Sorry. I'm a doubting Thomas, I guess. Please, go on with your story."

"I don't really remember much about it. According to my mom, I favored the arm for a few weeks. She and my dad grew so concerned that they decided to take me to a child psychologist."

"Wise choice," he said. "But I'm guessing the sessions didn't help."

"No. The psychologist determined that I had an imaginary friend, which was common in children my age, and he wasn't concerned. He said I would outgrow it as I got older. Only I didn't. I think I became less dependent on Nita for companionship as I got older, but she never completely went away. And as I matured, I became increasingly aware that other kids my age didn't have imaginary friends. That upset me and made me feel like an oddball."

Just then, a waitress brought their food to the table. Once they began eating, Lane continued with her story between mouthfuls. "My mother decided that more counseling for me was in order. They found a different child psychologist—a better one, they hoped—and I began seeing him regularly. Instead of calling Nita my imaginary friend, he referred to her as my alter ego.

His theory was that I was too unassuming to act out when I grew upset, so I invented Nita, another version of myself, who encouraged me to behave more boldly."

Jonas splashed a little tamari on his fried rice. "Not knowing about a possible identical twin, I would have probably said pretty much the same thing. I've dealt with a couple of kids with alter egos. It's very liberating for a child to switch personalities, going from being afraid to do something to not thinking twice about it."

"Only I'm no longer a child, Jonas. My formative years are far behind me."

"You're assuming that I believe you have an alter ego, but I don't. You hear a voice and have violent dreams that seem so real you actually wake up with red marks on your person. That isn't the work of an imaginary friend."

"It's happened more than once," she confessed. "The last time was just recently."

She went on to tell him about the man in her dream, how she'd seen him hours later on the street, and how she was essentially now in hiding to prevent him from finding her. "It was surreal. When he saw me, he seemed to recognize me. He even referred to threats he'd made to me during the dream. It was almost as if he was actually in that dream with me or something. I was totally freaked out."

Jonas set aside his chopsticks and rested his arms on the table. "That would freak anyone out."

"The only explanation I can think of is that he mistook me for someone else that he knows—someone who's double-crossed him or something. Even weirder, he was so convinced I was that person that he lurked inside the tattoo parlor, waiting for me to return for my handbag."

Jonas nodded. "Only what if it wasn't as simple as that, Lane? All of this, everything you've told me, has me thinking that we're dealing with something else entirely. Something scientists have not yet been able to prove even exists: a telepathic link between identical twins."

Lane's heart squeezed. She could see the glitter of excitement in Jonas' eyes. Did he view her as a possible rung in his ladder to success? If he could prove that telepathic communication between identical twins did exist, wouldn't that make him a star in the world of psychology?

"Wow," she mused aloud. "If such a link between twins exists, that would be quite a feather in your cap. Wouldn't it?"

His hazel eyes darkened, and his jaw muscle began to tick. "I didn't go looking for you, Lane. You somehow found me. And I'll remind you that when you came to my office asking for help, I initially refused to counsel you." He let that hang between them for a moment. "I *chose* to return to Mystic Creek and set up my practice knowing that I'd never set the world on fire here or be famous in the world of psychology. All I want is a small, manageable practice. A good quality of life. I hope to make a decent living at it, but beyond that, I have no aspirations or expectations that I'll ever get rich. I enjoy helping people." He paused again for what she guessed was effect. "I'd like to help you. But if you're suspicious of my motives, I'll happily bow out."

Lane could tell from the expression in Jonas' eyes that he sincerely meant that, and she felt awful for questioning his motives. "I'm sorry. I didn't mean to offend you, and I'm certainly not asking you to bow out. I'm just dubious—no, let me say *extremely* dubious—about having an identical twin. In all the times that I've asked questions of my parents about my adoption, they've never mentioned that I may have had a sibling. On top of that, they're both law-abiding people who would never consider adopting a child illegally."

He sighed and pushed his platter aside. "Let me just say what I came to say, and then I'll pay our tab and leave you to finish your meal in peace."

Lane had lost her appetite, too, so eating no longer felt like a priority. She sank back against the cushions, met his now accusing gaze, and said, "Okay, shoot."

"I don't think you're losing it when you hear what you refer to as the voice. What I do think is that your parents took you to psychologists who never thought outside the box, meaning that they were limited by what they believed to be proven fact. With all the studies ever done on identical twins, no scientist has ever proven that an emotional or mental link may exist. There have been studies that suggest the possibility, but never any absolute and irrefutable conclusions to support it. Therefore, until it's proven, the average psychologist doesn't entertain the possibility while counseling a client. They would never think that the voice you heard in your head might be the voice of your identical twin."

"But you do?"

"I'm not one of those psychologists. Call me fanciful, if you like. But I'm a guy who reads the studies with an open mind and also looks at all the information that contradicts the studies. The reputed phenomena between identical twins is one of those issues for me. I've read news articles about identical twins who were separated at birth or during early childhood who never knew, for most of their lives, that they had an identical twin." He straightened his arms slightly and pressed his palms against the table between them. "Then, by some fluke of chance, they meet. Maybe they're looking for their birthmother. Maybe a relative lets the big secret out of the bag. But such people have actually met later in life, and they are blown away by how similar they are. Not just in looks. That's pretty much a given. But they dress similarly. Wear their hair the same. I recently read about two guys—identical twins, of course—who drove the same model of car, had similar homes, wore the same style of clothes, and had a wife and kids with the same first names. I could go on. But it's enough for me to look at those similarities and believe a telepathic link may exist. I've also read stories about twins who have experienced things similar to what you have. Those twins did grow up together, which may have strengthened the bond between them. But there are reports that one twin, in a different location, experiences empathetic pain when the other twin is sick or injured. As a psychologist, I have to look at those instances without bias and ask myself, what if those twins are telling the truth? I also have to ask myself why they would lie. The fallout can't be much fun for them, with doctors submitting them to a battery of tests and grilling them for hours."

Lane felt out of her depth. "Let me make sure I understand. You think the voice may be real?" If she hadn't felt so emotionally off-kilter, she might have laughed. "That it's my sister, communicating with me telepathically? I have to admit, it's pleasanter to believe that than to doubt my own sanity, but I can't jump to conclusions just because it's easier."

Jonas inched one hand farther forward to grasp hers. The strength and warmth of his grip sent a surge of awareness up her arm. "You aren't crazy. If you don't have an identical twin, there are other conditions that could be causing your symptoms, many of them treatable. You could have a chemical imbalance, for instance. But for now, my gut tells me to investigate the most obvious possibility. Remember that I once had a close relationship with Veneta, doomed from the start though it may have been. I *know* you have a double, and the way I see it, I'd be foolish to disregard that knowledge."

"Well, as crazy as this conversation seems, at least I can take a small measure of comfort in knowing that you no longer believe I'm Veneta."

"The only thing that really bugs me now is that you somehow landed in Mystic Creek. I understand that coincidences can occur, but what were the chances that you would gravitate toward the hometown of Veneta's ex-boyfriend?"

Lane shrugged. "I can't explain that. I was looking for a small, out-of-the-way town, for one, and Mystic Creek met my criteria. I also felt a sense of familiarity when I saw the town's name on the map. Other than that, this area offers things that I love to do. Hiking, for one. I enjoy outdoor recreation. I didn't think I'd be here for that long, but I saw no harm in picking a place where I could at least enjoy my stay."

"Fair enough." His brow knitted in a frown, and then he gave her an inquiring look. "Did you ask your parents if they brought you to Mystic Creek at some point, maybe for a sightseeing trip? Back when you were little and you don't consciously remember it?"

"One thing my father insisted upon is that I not tell them where I am. When it's safe for me to go home, I'll ask them, but for now, he doesn't even want to know what part of the state I'm in."

He nodded. "Well, however it happened, I'm glad you came here, and I'm even gladder that you came to my office. We got off to a rough start, I admit, but now that we're clearing the air, I think I may be just the person who can help you." He held up a hand. "Not because I'm *the* best psychologist on earth, but because I'm willing to forget the studies and explore the possibilities."

"Even though you have to be entertaining another possibility, that I'm just nuttier than a fruitcake?"

He chuckled, relaxed his shoulders, and took a generous swallow of his margarita. "Even though. But I honestly don't think that's the case. That you're nuts, I mean."

He signaled a waitress that he was ready to pay their tab. After he had calculated a tip and signed the receipt, he stood and gazed down at Lane for a long moment. "I'll leave you to think about that. If you'd like a counselor who'll be more inclined to believe you than not, give me a call."

With that, he waved farewell to Hunter and left the restaurant.

Jonas decided to spend the remainder of the evening just chilling at home. After a couple of hours on his computer, he settled back in the recliner with a cold beer to read the latest issue of *Monitor on Psychology*. He was starting to grow drowsy when a light but insistent knock came at his door. Sighing and blinking himself fully awake, he tossed aside the magazine, set his glass on the end table, and strode across the living room–office area to see who had come calling so late. A glance at his Fitbit told him it was nine thirty.

He jerked open the door, half expecting to see one of his brothers on the landing. Instead, he had to drop his gaze nearly a foot to focus on Lane Driscoll's pale, tear-streaked face.

"Lane?"

She barreled over the threshold so fast that he had to fall back a step to allow her entry.

"What's wrong?" he asked as he closed the door. She was clearly upset, and it looked as if she'd dressed in a rush, one of her slender shoulders bared by a peasant top that had slipped down her upper arm. "Did something awful happen?"

Without waiting for him to offer her a seat, she perched on the edge of a sofa cushion and rested her head in her hands. "It was a series of something-awfuls. I'm sorry. I shouldn't have come here, but I need to talk to someone." She lowered her palms to meet his gaze, her blue eyes shadowed with emotion. "I hope I didn't wake you. It's been a bad night from start to finish."

Jonas could see that she was wound up. Her pillow-tossed hair lay in loose ringlets over her forehead. She wore no cosmetics that he could see. But what alarmed him was her pallor. He crouched in front of her, resting his elbows on his bent knees.

"I can see that you're upset." He no sooner spoke than he wanted to kick himself. That was a line he might use during a therapy session—a leading observation to encourage a patient to talk, and Lane hadn't come to him for counseling. "We're sort of friends, I wasn't asleep yet, and I'm a fairly good listener."

She clasped her hands on her lap, her grip so tight

that her fingers became splotched with red against pressure points of bone white. "I, um—I called my parents to ask them more questions about my adoption. That was the first awful thing when I got home."

"Only guessing, but apparently that didn't go well?"

She shook her head. The corners of her mouth quivered as she began to speak again. "All I did was ask if it was possible that I had a twin sister. My father got angry and defensive." She leaned forward and poked out her chin. "And my mom grew evasive." Tears welled in her eyes. "Oh, Jonas, I think they were lying!"

Jonas stood and crossed into his small kitchen at the back of the apartment. She needed something to calm her down, but he didn't think a beer would be enough to settle her nerves, so he bypassed his fridge and went to the wine rack instead. "What kind of red wine do you prefer?" he asked over his shoulder. "I've got a shiraz, a merlot, and a cab."

"I like all three, but I probably shouldn't."

"I disagree. You're pretty upset. One glass might help you to relax." He grabbed a bottle of cabernet and quickly pulled the cork, silently patting himself on the back for not getting floaters in the liquid. He and corkscrews had never gotten along.

He poured them each a glass of wine and hunkered down in front of her again as he passed one goblet to her. "Cheers. Take a couple of big gulps. It'll take the edge off."

She did as he suggested and then wiped her mouth with the back of her hand. "They were lying, Jonas. My dad *never* reacts that way to a simple question. And my mom is—well, she's normally honest to a fault, and I could tell that she felt cornered by my questions." A tear slipped over her spiky lower lashes to trail down her cheek. "I wasn't being accusatory. Honestly, I wasn't. It was just a simple question. 'Is it possible that I had a twin sister when you adopted me?'" She waved her hand. "With my dad, it was like lighting the fuse on a stick of dynamite. Before it was all over, he said I was insinuating that they'd done something illegal. How could I believe that he and my mother would ever be a part of something like that?" Her face twisted. "I didn't believe that of them at the beginning, but I did at the end of the conversation. There's no other explanation for my dad's immediate defensiveness and outrage."

Jonas' stomach tightened. He hated that Lane was losing faith in her parents. She obviously loved them deeply, just as he did his own mom and dad. Learning that one's folks weren't perfect could be a difficult pill to swallow, even for adults. "Like I said before, Lane, I imagine sometimes childless couples become desperate. For one reason or another, they can't adopt, and in the end, bending the rules or ignoring state laws may be their only alternative."

"They aren't like that."

"Anybody can be like that in the right situation. Lots and lots of people who can't have kids are going to great lengths to get a child." He took a sip of his wine. "I'm not saying they're evil people or criminals. They ache to hold a child in their arms, and nothing else can fulfill that need."

"How do you know? You've never been in a childless marriage. Or have you?"

Jonas bit back a smile. "No, I've never been married, but I have counseled couples who can't have children. Trust me. Their pain is real, and their yearning for a child pretty much eclipses everything else. They get on waiting lists. They open up their homes to caseworkers. They go through background checks. They'll do almost anything to be approved, but even then, they must wait, and sometimes they wait until they become too old to adopt."

She sighed and shook her head. "I know now that there are details about my adoption that my parents haven't told me. Why would they deceive me about something so very important?"

Jonas had no real answer to that question. "When you've calmed down, I think you should talk with your parents again, keep an open mind, and let them know you won't be judgmental. You know how much they love you, and you clearly love them. One thing my parents have always done to make it easier for me to be honest with them is to remind me that they'll always love me, no matter what. Maybe that can work in reverse for you. It's up to you, of course. If you don't mean it, you shouldn't say it."

She pushed her hair from her eyes. "Of course I would mean it. Even if my dad murdered someone, I'd still love him. That doesn't mean I would approve of his actions."

"Adopting a little girl and loving her with all his heart isn't exactly on a plane with murder," he reminded her. "Maybe they did bend a few rules to get you. Maybe you had a twin sister, and they knowingly separated you. We don't know the circumstances, and we shouldn't judge them without first knowing all the facts."

"I think I did," she said, barely above a whisper.

"You think you did what?"

"I think I had a twin sister. Have a twin sister, I mean."

Again, Jonas' stomach clenched. Somewhere along

the way, he'd become convinced of the same thing himself, but he hadn't expected Lane to come around to his way of thinking so swiftly. "What changed your mind?"

"I was exhausted after the conversation with my folks, so I went to bed early. I had another awful dream, only it was different."

Jonas' legs were tiring in the crouched position, so he shifted his weight to sit cross-legged on the floor. "Tell me about it."

She stared at something behind him for a long moment and then, without ever refocusing on his face, she said, "I was trapped in that room with the boarded-up window again." Her voice softened. "It was very dark." She hugged her waist and continued to stare at what he guessed was the wall, the look in her eyes so distant with introspection that he knew she was lost in the nightmare again. "I was afraid. So very afraid. Then I heard footsteps in another part of the house. My heart started to pound. I was so terrified I could barely breathe. And then I heard someone sobbing inside my head. A woman. In my dream, I tried to see her, but it was so dark I couldn't make her out. Only I—" She pressed a palm over the base of her throat. "Only I felt her there. Near me, maybe within arm's reach. I remember wondering if it was Nita."

Jonas kept silent, not wishing to jerk her back to the present with his voice.

"Just then the door to the room swung open, and this long rectangle of light fell over me. I saw a man's silhouette in the opening. I thought, 'This is it. The boss man told him it's time to kill me.' It scared me so badly that I jerked awake."

Jonas' skin had pebbled, not so much from hearing

her words, but more from seeing the fear in her expression.

She finally looked him straight in the eye again. "I couldn't make out the man's face, but he was tall and thin, like the man in my first nightmare. I told you about him. How I dreamed that he attacked me and then ran into him in town."

Jonas recalled most of the details. "Did he start to attack you in this dream?"

"No, but I believed he might. Jonas—please, don't think I'm crazy, but I think Nita gets inside my head somehow, that my thoughts and fear during the dream were actually her thoughts and her fear."

Jonas swirled his wine. "I don't think you're crazy at all—I think you might be experiencing a telepathic link."

"Afterward, when I woke up from the dream, that was my first thought. I'm not *really* in that room when I dream, but it feels as if I am."

"Okay."

"Okay?" Her voice rose to a shrill pitch. "How can you act as if that's a perfectly normal thing for someone to say?"

"Because, for you, it may be perfectly normal. Have you ever read about the genetic likenesses between identical twins, Lane? They aren't only identical on the outside; they're mostly identical on the inside. I read about a murder case in which one identical twin committed the crime but got off, not because he wasn't guilty, but because his brother's DNA matched his, and the authorities couldn't prove which man did it."

"How does that relate to me having a voice inside my head?"

Jonas set his wine aside to get up and then sat with

her on the sofa, leaving the center cushion empty as a buffer zone between them. "I'm just driving home to you how identical you and Veneta probably are. As you age, epigenetic drift can occur. That's when the gene sequences of identical twins are altered by environmental influences. Like, say, cancer and chemo treatments. Or one of you being an alcoholic or an overeater with obesity issues. There is supposedly a new test now that can pick up on those differences caused by epigenetic drift, but I don't know if it's being routinely used yet to solve crimes. The point I'm trying to make is that your heart, at birth, was exactly like Veneta's. Same goes for your brain. When you imagine that, doesn't it make it easier for you to accept that you and Veneta can communicate by thought?"

She downed the rest of her wine. "Am I truly exactly like her?"

Jonas thought carefully before replying. "In appearance, yes. Not so much in other ways." He paused to search for the right words. "Veneta was more exuberant and always in the limelight. If she wasn't the center of attention, she'd do something outlandish to get everyone's focus on her. You seem more reserved, a person who thinks before she speaks or acts. But don't let that throw you. Some scientists theorize that a power play of sorts occurs within the mother's womb between identical twins, with the stronger fetus imposing its will over the weaker one. Imagine, if you will, jockeying for position in close quarters. It stands to reason that the stronger and larger baby would get the most comfortable resting place. Other scientists believe that the differences in personality take place when the ovum splits, giving one twin certain traits that the other one lacks and vice versa. It's a really fascinating topic, actually. Imagine being so alike genetically that you—"

Jonas heard a soft sound and broke off talking to discover that Lane's chin had dropped to her chest. The empty wineglass lay sideways on her lap, loosely grasped in her limp fingers. *Damn*, he thought. *I've put someone to sleep again. Not everyone thinks all this stuff is fascinating. Why can't I remember that?*

Chapter Five

Perturbed with himself, Jonas took comfort from the fact that he'd helped Lane relax enough to fall asleep. Judging by things she'd said, he didn't think she'd gotten much rest for several days. Easing off the sofa so as not to wake her, he got a pillow and quilt from his linen closet. Then he set himself to the task of laying Lane down full-length on the cushions with her head cradled on a crisp cotton pillowcase. When she was in a reasonably comfortable position, he covered her with the blanket and then crouched beside her. She looked so exhausted and yet peaceful that he couldn't help but smile.

Against his better judgment, Jonas allowed himself to study Lane's countenance with masculine appreciation. She really was quite lovely. He liked the way her finely bridged nose tipped slightly up at the end. Her lashes, a reddish brown that was a shade darker than her strawberry blond hair, feathered her cheeks like delicate folding fans—the pretty kind that women had once used to cool their faces on hot afternoons. In sleep, the perfect bow of her lips seemed fuller and shone in the lamplight, a pale, natural pink that struck him as being far more kissable than a mouth smeared with lipstick.

He pushed quickly to his feet and forced himself to take a seat at his desk, where he could spend time on his computer. *Lane is off limits*, he warned himself. *Don't let yourself get sideswiped by physical attraction. You were involved with a woman who looks exactly like her.*

Jonas decided to search for any mentions of Veneta online. If Lane's dreams actually stemmed from a telepathic link, then it sounded as if Veneta was in serious trouble, possibly held against her will by a man who intended to kill her. Jonas couldn't imagine how his ex-girlfriend had managed to land herself in such a fix.

Resigned to a long evening because he couldn't very well go to bed when a woman he barely knew was asleep on the sofa, he began his search by just typing in the name Veneta Monroe. He expected to find very little, if anything, so he was startled when he got a hit right off the bat.

Lane surfaced from thick blackness to a state of sleepy awareness. Delicious softness and warmth cocooned her body. Fluttering her lashes, she recognized the painting of a stream above the sofa and realized she had fallen asleep in Jonas' apartment. Embarrassment washed through her, but then she saw him through a drowsy haze and couldn't hold on to her sense of humiliation. He sat behind his desk, his gaze fixed on the computer screen. She blinked to bring him into sharper focus and took advantage of the opportunity to study him. In profile, he was decidedly masculine, with a high, straight forehead that complemented his chiseled brow bone and the sharp bridge of his nose, which sported a small knot that did nothing to detract from his rugged appeal. He had a thick, muscular neck, a square jawline, and a strong chin. The one shoulder within her view was, she decided, well-padded with muscle, judging by the way his shirt skimmed the contours instead of hanging loose.

At the sight of him, an unwarranted feeling of safety enveloped her. She didn't really know him well enough to trust him, but on some level, she did. Otherwise she wouldn't have raced over here tonight—and she definitely wouldn't have felt relaxed enough to fall asleep on his couch. She started to sit up, but a delicious languor stole over her and kept her anchored to the sofa.

"Ah, you're finally awake."

The sound of Jonas' voice jerked Lane from her musings, and she sat up so suddenly that her head went a bit dizzy. She grabbed for words. "Yes. I—um—I'm so sorry. I didn't mean to drift off on you. That's so rude."

He chuckled and pushed up from the chair. "Actually, *drifting off* doesn't describe it. It was more like passing out. You were with me one second and gone the next. And I didn't think it was rude at all. Just the opposite. You finally lost the battle with sleep deprivation. It was as simple as that."

Lane pushed the quilt off her legs and swiveled to place her feet on the floor. "What time is it?"

"Nearly two in the morning."

"Oh, God, I've kept you up until all hours. I'm so sorry."

"Don't be. I was glad to see you get some much-needed rest." He strode around the desk and leaned back against its edge, which hit him midway up the back of his thighs. "And I have no early morning appointments, so I can sleep in, no damage done."

"Doesn't the restaurant downstairs get noisy early in the morning?"

"Not normally. At about ten, they start prepping for the lunch hour, but as a rule, not before that."

Lane stood and began folding the quilt. "This is lovely." She ran her palm over the neatly stitched pattern. "My grandmother was a quilter, and the wedding ring was her favorite."

"Ah. Is that what it's called? When my mom asked which of her quilts I liked best, I just said the one with the loopy circles all over it."

Lane bit back a smile. "She does beautiful work."

"She does; doesn't she? It's so pretty that I stopped using it on my bed. Afraid I'd wear it out." Standing with his ankles crossed, he bent his head and studied the toe of his boot, which he moved back and forth. When he looked back up at her, Lane knew from his expression that he was about to say something she might not want to hear. "I have to tell you something that may be a little upsetting. Because you're so tired and in need of more sleep, I promised myself I'd wait until tomorrow. But I honestly don't think I should."

"What is it?" Her voice rang in her ears like a whine coming from the bottom of a barrel. She swallowed hard. "I probably won't sleep much more anyway."

He nodded and then his broad shoulders slumped as he released a heavy sigh. "I did an Internet search on Veneta and found news of her right away. She was last seen in Plover Bay, Oregon."

"Last seen?" Lane repeated. "That doesn't sound good."

"It isn't. Not good at all, Lane. She just disappeared. No one knows where she is—or what happened. She just dropped off the face of the earth."

A cold feeling swept over Lane. "You're talking about her as if she may be—dead."

He lifted a hand. "I think that's the general conclusion, but both of us know she isn't. Not yet, anyway. She went missing two weeks ago, according to the news articles."

"Missing," Lane repeated, her voice shaky. "When people go missing, how often are they typically found alive?"

He apparently clenched his teeth, for his jaw muscle began to bunch and then relax. Finally, he said, "Sometimes people resurface. Other times they don't. But I'd rather not focus on that. Instead, I'd like to think positively—that she's alive, because you're still getting signals from her."

Lane hugged her waist and stared at the floor. "*If* it's actually her voice. It's a pretty farfetched explanation, Jonas." She met his gaze again.

That dimple in his cheek reappeared, creating a deep slash that ran from just below his high cheekbone to the corner of his mouth. "I don't believe you're crazy." He held up his hands. "Honestly, I don't. I do have some experience under my belt, and the thing about you that stands out to me is that you're completely aware of how off the charts all of this is. And you're willing to accept that it may mean you're emotionally unstable."

"That's a good thing?"

He laughed, but the sound was devoid of sincere humor. "Do you know how many people come to me with the idea cemented in their brains that they're normal? It's the rest of the world that's nuts, not them." He sighed. "That isn't to say they're happy with how they feel or even with their own behaviors. They realize their world is clear off its axis. But only with repeated counseling sessions can they reach a place of understanding that maybe, just maybe, they're the ones with the problem and they're creating their own misery."

For as long as Lane could remember, she'd had an achy spot deep within her chest that grew more pronounced whenever she heard the voice. Each time, it made her question her sanity. Each time, it filled her with a sense of hopelessness. Now she felt that dull pain inside her splintering apart. Her vision went blurry with tears, and her chin started to quiver.

"What?" Jonas looked alarmed. "Don't cry. If I said something wrong, I take it back."

A wet giggle pushed up her throat. "Please, don't. You're the first person, ever, who knows I hear voices and doesn't think I'm nuts."

He rocked back on his heels. "And that's making you cry?"

"Happy tears," she informed him. "Tears of relief, maybe. I'm twenty-six, and for twenty-three of those years, everyone I confided in made me feel like I should be locked away in a loony bin."

He smiled slightly. "You're not headed for the loony bin. The only fly in the ointment for me is that Veneta never mentioned hearing a voice, and that seems odd. I think she would have mentioned it to me, given my major, but she never did."

"Wouldn't telepathic communication go both ways?"

He nodded. "One would think so. But maybe you're more open to it than she is, or she's not telepathic and you are. No study done has ever proven that telepathic communication between twins actually exists, so how it works is uncharted territory. But *if* it exists, I suppose it's possible that one twin may have more telepathic ability than the other one."

Lane realized her blouse was hanging off her shoulder and straightened the gathered neckline. When she met Jonas' gaze again, she said, "With her missing, I feel like I should try to find her, but I have no idea where to start."

"In Plover Bay. That'd be my vote, anyway. It's where she was last seen. The news report didn't give a lot of details, only that she seemed upset, left her place of employment in the middle of a shift for a lunch break at home, and hasn't been seen since. The police suspect foul play, because she left all of her belongings behind in her apartment. And her car was there, too. She didn't just pack up and leave town without telling anyone. Something must have happened. The general assumption is that she's probably dead."

"But you don't think so," Lane observed.

"Do you?"

She shook her head. "I think she's being held against her will in a boarded-up room. That's what I see in the dreams, anyway. And I think she's either in Maple Leaf or a community near there, because that's where I ran into her captor."

"Do you feel compelled to try to locate her?"

Lane thought about it for a moment. "I wouldn't even know where to start. And I can't just up and leave town. I just started a new job, and Ma Thomas has offered me a really great opportunity. I don't want to blow that."

Jonas stared at her for so long that Lane was pushed to ask, "What?"

"I'm just thinking. If your dreams—or visions—are accurate, her life may be in danger. How are you going to feel if the voice inside your head suddenly stops? Are you going to blame yourself?"

A cold feeling washed over Lane. "If the voice suddenly stops, that would mean she's dead."

Lane had wished a thousand times that the voice would go away and never return. But that had been before she met Jonas. "I don't want her to die. I just don't know how to help her. And I have a lot at stake here if I let Ma Thomas down. She could fire me on the spot. As for a weekend trip, I just moved here, and I've only worked a couple of days. I can't afford a road trip."

"Don't worry about the costs." Jonas pushed erect and walked in a circle, his boots making little sound on the carpet. "If we go over the weekend, you won't even have to miss work."

"We?"

"Yes, *we*. You don't think I'd let you go to Plover Bay alone? It could be dangerous."

"Protecting me isn't your job. And if I don't worry about the costs, I may not be able to pay my rent next month."

"I'll cover the expenses," he said.

"I can't let you do that, Jonas. Really, I can't."

He laughed and shook his head. "I may not be the richest man in the country, Lane, but I can afford a weekend trip to the coast without missing the money."

"Why Plover Bay?" she asked. "I saw the man in Maple Leaf. Doesn't that indicate that he's holding Veneta near there?"

"It does. But who is he? What is he mixed up in? How did Veneta get on his radar? Why was she in Plover Bay? Who did she associate with there? What kind of people would she have met while doing her job?"

Lane held up a hand. "Okay, I get it. We may be able to learn some, if not all, of that stuff in Plover Bay, whereas we probably can't in Maple Leaf. Unless she has lived there, too, which I find hard to believe. The population has exploded there, and I probably never would have run into her, but it stretches my imagination to think nobody who knew me wouldn't have encountered her at some point. If she looks as much like me as you say, wouldn't they have said something to me?"

With growing alarm, Lane contemplated taking a trip with Jonas and being alone with him in a vehicle for hours. And what about the cost of lodging? Would he expect her to share a room with him? He seemed like a nice guy, but in reality, she barely knew him.

"Try to see this from my standpoint," he continued. "I knew Veneta. And if it's all the same to you, I really don't want to live with the regret of doing nothing and then learning that she turned up dead."

"But we barely know each other," Lane inserted quickly. "I'm not sure I feel comfortable about taking a road trip with you."

He arched an eyebrow, and then a smile stole slowly over his face. "I've lived here most of my life, and in Mystic Creek, there are no secrets. If you're worried about my character, take a walk along Main Street tomorrow and ask anyone you meet about me. People also have long memories. You'll hear about every bad thing I ever did. But one thing I'm certain you won't hear is that I've ever gotten out of line with a woman."

Some of the tension eased from Lane's shoulders. "I intended no insult."

"None taken. I have two younger sisters, and if one of them told me she was going on a road trip with some guy she barely knew, I'd be all over it. So I totally get where you're coming from. How about if we sleep on it and revisit the situation in the morning?"

Lane liked that idea. She had no reason to distrust Jonas, but on the other hand, she had no reason to trust him, either. "There's another wrinkle. Simply Sensational is open on Saturdays. Ma will expect me to be there."

"If anyone in this town has a heart of gold, it's Ma. Can't you just ask for Saturday off? You don't have to tell her why. Just say you've got some business to take care of."

Lane straightened the quilt and placed the pillow on top of it. "I can give it a shot. All she can do is say no. Right?" She scanned the room in search of her purse and saw it on the floor near his desk. As she went to retrieve it, she asked, "How do you get out of the building after the restaurant closes?"

"No worries. I'll let you out."

Jonas led the way out onto the landing, punched in a code on a keypad to disarm the security system that protected the building, and then walked Lane downstairs to the restaurant's street-side doors. After he unlocked them, she turned as if to say something to him, but then she only gazed up at him, her lips slightly parted. He hadn't bothered to turn on the lights, and in the moon and lantern glow coming through the glass, her eyes shimmered like polished silver. He got an almost overwhelming urge to run his hands into her coppery hair and tip her face up to his. Only his inner alarms saved him from being totally stupid and kissing her. He couldn't allow himself to do that when she was already worried about going on a trip with him.

"Were you able to find a parking place nearby?" he asked. "It's the middle of the night. I don't mind walking with you to your car."

She drew the strap of her purse over her shoulder. "It's just a few spaces away. I should be fine."

Jonas held the door open for her and then followed her out onto the sidewalk. The crime rate in Mystic Creek was low, but that didn't mean nothing bad ever happened. "I'll sleep better if I see you safely inside your vehicle with the doors locked. Not to say you wouldn't be fine, but I'd rather be safe than sorry."

Her car was only a quarter block away and under one of the old-fashioned sidewalk lanterns. Jonas hung back while she opened the driver door and slipped inside. Before starting the engine, she poked her head back out.

"Thank you for all you did tonight," she called. "And let me apologize again for keeping you up so long. I'm really sorry about conking out on you."

"No worries. Drive safe."

Jonas watched as she backed the car out onto the street. Then he gazed after her as she drove away. Long after her car's taillights were swallowed by darkness, he still stood there, wondering what the hell had come over him inside the restaurant. He had almost kissed her.

Lane felt nervous about trying to sleep again. She hadn't dreamed at Jonas' place, but maybe she had been subconsciously aware of his presence and that had held the nightmares at bay. After slipping back into her nightshirt, she climbed into bed and drew the blanket up to her chin, thinking how much more comfortable she was on a mattress and box springs than she'd been on that leaking air mattress. That led her to think about the fact that she hadn't yet bought any other furniture. She had hoped to spend the latter part of Saturday afternoon shopping. Always having to eat standing up was getting old, for sure.

Guilt flooded through her at the thought. How could she be worrying about ordinary things when her sister might be in danger? *If I have a sister*, she reminded herself. In a weird sort of way, Jonas' theory made sense, but that didn't mean he was right. She recalled the expression on his face when they'd stood looking at each other before she exited the restaurant. For a moment, she'd thought he might kiss her, and now she was almost sorry that he hadn't. He was a very attractive man, and as she was coming to know him better, she couldn't deny that she liked him. A woman could do a lot worse, for sure. Only how could that ever work? Did Lane really want to mess with her sister's ex-boyfriend? The idea didn't sit well.

If I even have a sister, she reminded herself again.

And with that thought, she slipped into a black and blessedly dreamless sleep.

The following morning, Jonas felt compelled to keep searching online for Veneta. He hoped to find evidence that she'd resurfaced somewhere after leaving the Oregon coast, but all he found was a DMV record on her in Florence and then an arrest record in Plover Bay for driving under the influence. Both documents were a few months old.

Jonas searched his phone records to find Lane's call to him when she'd been searching for a counselor. He dialed her number.

"Hello?" she answered.

"Hey, it's me, Jonas. Have I caught you at a bad moment?"

"No. I'm on my break. What's up?"

Jonas told her what he'd been able to learn. "Plover Bay is where she was last seen, and nothing else on her is popping up. I still think our best bet is to start asking questions there. Maybe we'll dig up some information about where she may have gone or who may have had it in for her."

"I asked Ma for Saturday off," she told him. "She says it isn't a problem."

Jonas was glad to hear that and smiled. "Ah. Can I take that to mean you've overcome your wariness about traveling with me?"

Long silence, and then she said, "I wouldn't go as far as to say that."

He laughed. "I'll be a complete gentleman, I swear."

"I hope so. I'm a black belt, and I'd hate to have to hurt you."

"Warning heeded." Jonas tried to imagine her in a *karategi* or *judogi*, but the picture wouldn't gel. Then again, he probably wasn't the first man to underestimate a woman's strength. He leaned back in his office chair and put his feet up on the desk. "What do you think about leaving Friday when you get off work? That way we can spend the night in Plover Bay and get an early start on Saturday, talking with people."

She sighed. "Okay. I slept like the dead last night. You said that I won't hear the voice anymore if she dies. The sudden silence worries me."

"So you're starting to believe it's Veneta getting inside your head?"

"I'm waffling back and forth. One minute I think you're right, and the next I wonder who's crazier, you or me."

"I understand," Jonas replied. "And if it's any comfort, I don't know what to think myself."

She sighed again. "And I'm along for the ride. What you said—about how I might feel if I do nothing and then I never hear her again? I've wished a thousand times for that voice to get out of my head. Even now, I want it gone. But not that way."

Jonas felt a pang of guilt. "I took a pretty hard line with that. I wish now that I hadn't said it."

"I'm glad you did," she countered. "Just like you, I don't want to live with that kind of regret."

Jonas hoped their visit to Plover Bay might spare them both a lot of grief. "Friday, then? What time will you get off work?"

"Three. If I pack the night before and have my stuff in the car, we can leave as soon as my shift ends."

The following afternoon, Lane planned to shop for furniture, but as she left Simply Sensational at three, it was such a sunny and beautiful day that she got a wild urge to enjoy the outdoors even though her time might be better spent getting her rental livable. *I'll be gone this weekend*, she assured herself. *So what's the big rush to buy a kitchen dining set and comfortable chairs for the living room? I've had a headache all day. Why not ditch responsibility and do something really fun that may help me sleep tonight?*

Decision made, Lane drove toward the cottage, plotting her outdoor adventure as she navigated the curvy country road. She truly enjoyed running, so that was her first thought, but then she remembered her mountain bike, which she'd unloaded from the U-Haul trailer and parked on the veranda. Atop a bicycle, she could attain greater speed, and just the thought of feeling a fresh mountain breeze in her hair was irresistible. She loved the smells here. There was no overlay of au-

tomobile exhaust. No traffic noise. A long bike ride
would be amazing.

Once at the house, she quickly changed clothes,
choosing to wear a navy blue skort instead of jeans,
topped by a pink knit shirt with three-quarter length
sleeves. White running shoes completed the ensemble.
She knew it wasn't a trendy outfit for biking, but she
doubted anyone would see her. It was a weekday afternoon, after all, and most adults were still at work. Besides that, she'd never allowed current fashion to
govern her. Looking exactly like everyone else had
always bugged the heck out of her, so much so that she
was almost phobic about it.

As she pushed off on her bike and skirted the potholes in the graveled driveway, she smiled so hard her
cheeks ached. *This is what I need*, she thought. *Good
old-fashioned exercise. No wonder the dreams are inter-
fering so much with my sleep patterns. I start to feel fid-
gety and edgy when I don't push myself physically.* She'd
always been a high-energy person, and since coming to
Mystic Creek, she hadn't even gone jogging, which had
been a necessary part of her routine back home.

Her plan was to enjoy an intense and physically
punishing ride, so as she turned onto Mystic Creek
Lane, she began pumping her legs to attain a safe but
exhilarating speed. If she rode long enough and hard
enough, maybe she could have a can of soup for dinner,
take a lovely bath in the garden tub, and fall exhausted
onto her new mattress to sleep like a baby all night.
That sounded so good that she angled her body forward over the handlebars and began pedaling as if her
life depended on it.

It truly was a glorious afternoon. Lane knew from
talking with Ma Thomas that winters were harsh in

Mystic Creek, and September was about to slip behind the curtain to offer October center stage. It was entirely possible that warm and sunny afternoons might soon give way to snow and frigid temperatures. In order to exercise then, she'd have to bundle up and go skiing, snowshoeing, or boarding. There was also a nice gym in town. If she made enough in commission at the shop over the winter, she might be able to afford a membership, she supposed, but indoor activity had never appealed to her. Stale air. The smell of sweat. She greatly preferred being outside. Dragging in a deep breath of the sun-warmed and pine-scented air, she reveled in the feeling of being one with nature.

The landscape passed by her in a blur of deep forest green splashed with autumn colors, aspen and cottonwood leaves turned golden, bushes that dotted the woodlands with scarlet, and berries flashing in the sunlight like polished red marbles. As she rode, Lane promised herself that she'd go hiking after work the following day to truly enjoy the scenery as she exercised. She'd never seen any landscape more beautiful, except in photographs.

She navigated a particularly sharp curve, the momentum of her bike carrying her out into the middle of the road. Because she'd seen no cars, she wasn't worried. The residential area lay behind her, and she doubted that she would meet any oncoming traffic. She was alone in a multicolored wilderness that stretched as far in all directions as the eye could see.

Except for a horse.

A *horse*? As she executed the sharp turn, it had popped up in front of her like an apparition. Lane grabbed for the handbrake and felt the mountain bike go into a sideways skid on the soft dirt peppered with gravel and larger rocks. For an instant, all she could see was the equine, which loomed ahead of her like a reddish-brown wall. Aware that she might injure the animal if she couldn't stop, she made a snap decision to lay the bike down and go into a home-base slide, hoping that she could come to a stop before the bike and her body struck the animal's legs.

Thankful for the soft dirt—and not so thankful that she'd chosen to wear a skort as jagged pebbles and rocks grazed her bare skin—she dimly registered the sound of a man's voice. From the corner of her eye, she glimpsed the horse rearing onto its hind legs to swing sideways. *Thank you, God*, she thought as she and the bike skidded past the animal without a collision.

Moments later, Lane found herself sprawled like a rag doll on her back as fluffy, white cumulus clouds drifted across the powder-blue sky above her. She blinked and struggled to catch her breath.

"Lane? Are you okay?"

She batted her eyelashes again, wondering why her eyes stung. Then Jonas Sterling's burnished face came into focus. She stared stupidly up at him, still so stunned from the crash that she couldn't figure out how he'd come to be there.

"Jonas?"

He grasped her shoulders and drew her to a sitting position. "Hallelujah, we're on a first-name basis." Despite the forced note of levity, she also heard an edge of concern in his voice. "Seriously, Lane, are you all right? Do you hurt anywhere?"

Lane felt tears welling, not from a wave of emotion or because she was in pain, but because, as her head cleared, she realized she had dirt in her eyes. She reached up to rub them, but Jonas caught her wrists. "Don't do that. I've got water. It'll be safer if I wash it out." He leaped to his feet. A moment later, he returned with a canteen. Hooking a finger under her chin, he said, "Open wide and look straight up."

Lane did as he said. Water sluiced into her eyes, streamed over her temples, and drenched her hair.

"Better?" he asked.

As she blinked away the water, she realized that the burning had mostly stopped. "Yes, much better."

He stripped off his blue plaid shirt, moistened it, and dabbed at her cheeks. When Lane saw the dirt that came away on the cloth, she had a purely feminine thought. *I must look an absolute fright.* Then she scolded herself for being an idiot. What truly mattered was that both she and the horse hadn't been seriously injured. Her right thigh stung, most likely from a scrape, and she also felt a burning sensation on her elbow, but other than that, nothing hurt. Well, if she counted the twinges here and there, she guessed she might have a few bruises, but nothing serious.

"How did you get here so fast?" she asked.

He chuckled as he swabbed at something on her neck. She guessed that he was attacking more dirt, which was possibly mud now that he'd splashed her face with water. "I was on the horse. I like to go riding at least once a week, and Rascal enjoys taking breaks by the creek. I trailered him over from the family farm."

Lane's head was finally clearing. She glanced at the horse, which was now chomping on grass at the edge of the road as if nothing had happened. "Is his name indicative of his temperament?"

"Naw. He's a great horse. Mischievous as a colt, though. Hence the name. Everyone who met him said he was a little rascal, and it stuck."

Lane glanced at her bike, which lay on its side about three feet from her. As far as she could determine, it had suffered no damage that a good hosing-off wouldn't fix. "I'm so glad I didn't hit him."

"Me, too," he said with another chuckle. "It wouldn't have been a fun experience for either of you. Or me. I'm pretty sure both of you would have been badly hurt, and the cell phone service out this way totally sucks. I wouldn't have been able to call for help."

Lane sighed. "Note to self; go slower on country roads. I wrongly assumed that nobody else would be out here."

He sat back on his bootheels, the damp shirt dangling from one hand. He wore a white undershirt, similar in cut to a woman's tank top, only with narrower shoulder straps. Lane had seen men in films wearing them, but never in person. Her dad wore regular, short-sleeve T-shirts under his clothing. She noted that Jonas' muscular arms and shoulders were as tanned as his face, which led her to wonder how a psychologist managed to be in the sun enough to have a burnished torso.

"You about ready to try standing?" he asked.

Lane nodded, grateful when he pushed to his feet and offered her help up. His hand was large, hard, and incredibly warm, his thumb and fingers encompassing her own and even partially encircling her wrist. The contact sent a jangle of awareness up her arm. His mouth tipped into a crooked grin that displayed straight white teeth that could be featured in a toothpaste commercial.

She wobbled slightly before she caught her balance. When her stance felt steady, she offered him a smile. He loosened his hold on her hand and moved back a step. "All good?" he asked.

Lane nodded. "Probably far better than I deserve." She pushed at her hair, felt the drippy shanks near her ears, and nearly groaned. She undoubtedly resembled a mud wrestler who'd just lost a match, which wasn't a pleasant feeling for a woman when a handsome man was studying her. "It was stupid to go that fast on a road where I might encounter traffic."

He shook out his shirt and rolled it up. "Actually, there aren't a lot of cars out here at this time of day. It gets busier at night."

"At night?" Lane heard the ring of incredulity in her voice. "What's the attraction? There's nothing out here."

He laughed and gestured with one hand. "To kids, that's the beauty of it. There's the creek, dozens of old logging roads and landings. It's teenager heaven. Skinny-dipping. Bonfires. Drinking some beer. Bringing picnic baskets full of food. A perfect place to hide from their parents and do forbidden things."

Lane nodded as if she'd once been a teen who'd walked that path, even though her psychological issues had pretty much prevented her from having very many friends. "I see."

"Speaking of picnics . . ." His voice trailed off, and he raked a hand through his hair as he regarded her with a question in his eyes. "I don't suppose you feel up to an impromptu meal along the creek. I have a favorite spot not far from here where Rascal enjoys taking a break. He grazes while I devour the lunch my mom always packs for me when I go for a ride. I told her I'd already eaten lunch, but when it comes to providing her loved ones with food, she never listens and packs me meals big enough to feed two men and a boy. I'd be happy to share if you're game."

Lane almost said no. She barely knew him, after all. But then she backed up mentally and reminded herself that she'd be traveling with him over the coming weekend. If she spent some time with him this afternoon, it might make their trip a little less tense. Plus, she had burned off more than a few calories while riding the bike, and she was hungry. Pushing at her hair again, she said, "I'm not at my best after that crash."

He ran his gaze over her face. "You look just fine. If you're not uncomfortable from the spill, you should take me up on it. My mom fixes fabulous saddlebag lunches, and they're always more than I can eat, especially today, I'm guessing, because I took my midday meal at one. I'm starting to feel a little empty, but I'm definitely not hungry enough to do her offerings justice all by myself." While Lane considered the suggestion, he narrowed an eye at her. "Soft, chewy chocolate chip cookies for dessert, and she makes the best ones this side of the Great Divide."

Lane told herself it was the mention of chewy chocolate chip cookies that became a deciding factor for her, but the truth was she'd never shared a creek-side meal with a gorgeous cowboy, and today seemed to be her time to make stupid choices. A woman couldn't *always* play it safe, after all. Sometimes she needed to throw caution to the wind and embrace the moment.

"Sure. That sounds fun. Plus, it will mean no trip into town for food later. All I have in the house is canned soup. I still haven't gotten my kitchen organized enough to cook, and there's also nowhere but my bed to sit while I eat."

"We're on."

He strode over to collect her bike, which Lane was pleased to see had no dents in it. She couldn't in good conscience afford to pay for any repairs, not while she was still dependent upon her parents for money.

As he pushed the bicycle over to her, he said, "We can park this on the side of the road and come back for it. Or you can ride it down to the landing."

She gave him what she feared was a vacuous look until she determined that he was offering to let her ride double with him on Rascal. There were two problems with that suggestion. First, she'd never been on a horse, and the prospect of doing that now made her stomach clench with anxiety. Second, she'd have to sit behind him, her spread legs flanking his and her arms around his waist to hang on. She wasn't sure which was more unnerving, the animal or the man.

"I'll ride my bike," she settled for saying. Then, not wishing to let him know she felt wary of him and his horse, she added, "It's an expensive bicycle, a birthday gift from my folks. If I left it behind and one of those teens you mentioned drove by and grabbed it, they'd be very upset with me. I think they dropped close to a grand to buy it for me."

Jonas nodded. "Makes sense. The kids around here aren't normally into thievery, but there are a few rotten apples in every barrel." His high forehead creased in a frown. "Can you ride slow? I can't trot Rascal over the road. It's got too many potholes."

"Will I be able to navigate it on a bike?"

He chuckled. "I saw how you took it down and into a slide." His arched one eyebrow. "Impressive stuff, lady. I'm pretty sure you can pick your way through the rough sections without batting an eye."

Seconds later when Lane tried to adjust her riding speed to accommodate Rascal's lumbering pace, she was giggling and Jonas was hooting with laughter. The slow progress had her wobbling on the bike like a newbie.

"This makes me feel like I suddenly need training wheels!" she cried.

"Go a little faster and cut circles around us to stay within my sight. I doubt anybody's down there, and I doubly doubt there would be anyone who might harm you, but I try to be extra cautious when the safety of a lady is on the table."

Jonas steered Rascal over to the center of the road, and Lane began riding slow circles around him and the horse. When they reached the logging road that led to the creek, cutting circles was no longer an option, because the thoroughfare narrowed to one lane. When Lane jumped off the bike and started pushing it, Jonas shook his head.

"Nope. I'm not letting you walk all the way down. We can hide the bike in the brush if you're worried about it being stolen, but you need to climb on with me."

Lane took stock of Rascal and the man astride his back. "Nope. I've never been on a horse, and I'm not going to be on one now."

"*Why?* He's a perfectly good mount, one of the best."

"He may be the most trustworthy horse on earth, but I'm afraid I'll fall off."

"You can't fall off if you're holding on. Unless, of course, I fall off, and that hasn't happened since I was in diapers."

To Lane's dismay, he swung off the horse, strode over to grab her bike, which he hefted so easily it could have been a tricycle, and carried it off into the manzanita bushes that lined the road. "There," he said as he scrambled back onto the rutted and narrow byway, "it's all hidden and safe." He moved in close to Rascal and motioned her over. "Trust me."

Lane decided that nervousness made every challenge seem bigger. Rascal suddenly looked twenty feet high at the shoulder, and Jonas looked half again as tall. And strong. In nothing but an undershirt to hide his torso, he sported muscles that she'd seen only in beefcake photos.

"Come on. I don't bite."

She refused to act like a schoolgirl, so she walked toward him, determined to be a sane, mature woman who didn't get all fluttery around a handsome man. She expected him to swing up into the saddle and then pull her up to join him. Instead, he drew her over and said, "Left foot in the stirrup."

"Oh, no. I can't be in the driver's seat."

He laughed and said, "Darlin', I'd never be so foolish as to let a greenhorn drive. Come on. Foot in the stirrup."

Lane made a stab with her running shoe and fell short of her mark by about a foot. "It's too high."

"Damn, girl. I didn't realize how vertically challenged you are."

The next second, Lane felt his hands at her waist and she was airborne. She squealed as he deposited her on the saddle. Once she was balanced, she grabbed the saddle horn with both hands, squeezed her eyes closed, and breathed out, "Oh, my God. Please, Rascal, don't buck."

She jerked as Jonas swung up behind her. He hooked one arm around her waist and grabbed the reins with his free hand. Every muscle in her body snapped taut.

"Lane, just relax. I won't let you fall off, and Rascal

definitely won't try to unseat you. He likes pretty ladies as much as I do."

Lane decided that she should have insisted on walking. Having Jonas' rock-hard palm pressed against her
rib cage just below her right breast was far more unnerving than what she'd imagined it might be like to
ride behind him with her arms around his middle.

She guessed that it took fifteen minutes for them to
reach the creek, and when they did, she forgot all about
worrying where his hand was at. During her hikes,
she'd stumbled upon some beautiful stream terrain,
but normally, the trails were groomed and frequented
by dozens of outdoor enthusiasts. This old landing was
nature in the raw, with flowing expanses of green grass,
ponderosa pines crowding the edge of the clearing,
and a gently sloping bank to the water. For Lane, it was
like entering a photograph, only here she could hear
the song of the stream and the birds.

"Oh, Jonas, it's beautiful."

"Yep." He loosened his hold on her. "Hang tight while
I dismount."

Lane grabbed the saddle horn as he swung off the
horse. Then he held up his arms, a clear indication that
he wanted her to fall into them. When she hesitated, he
said, "You can do it the traditional way, but the drop
from the stirrup down might be a bitch. You're too
short to grip the horn for support."

Lane decided she was being silly and leaned sideways. He caught her and swung her down the rest of
the way, not releasing his hold on her until she had her
balance. Then he drew a small wool blanket and a
zip-up cooler from the saddlebag. Down by the stream,
he created a picnicking area with a hard snap of his
wrists. A moment later, he was seated on the blanket and

drawing food from bag. Lane spent a moment brushing away the rest of the dust on her clothing and body. Then she knelt by the stream to wash her face, arms, and hands. The water was so cold that she shivered when it flowed over her skin.

She shook her arms dry as she ascended the slope to join him on the blanket. She counted four sandwiches, all protected in ziplock bags. Chips. A small container of dip. A quart-size bag of cookies and an equal amount of raw vegetables.

"How much can one man eat?" she couldn't resist asking. "Did your mom expect you to winter out here?"

"I have a big appetite." He handed her a sandwich. "I'd offer you a choice, but they're all roast beef."

"I decided to be vegan once. I missed beef so much that I only lasted a month."

He laughed as he began opening the bags of veggies and treats. "In college, I tried being a vegetarian. I caved in less than a week. The carnivore in me is alive and well, too."

Grabbing a sandwich for himself, he peeled back the plastic and took a large bite. Fascinated by the way his jaw muscle bunched and relaxed as he chewed, Lane caught herself staring. Frustrated with herself, she focused on her own meal, which was, by "impromptu picnic" standards, pretty amazing. The roast beef was moist and tender, and the lettuce had retained its crispness.

After swallowing, she said, "Kudos to your mother. This sandwich is amazing."

He nodded. "She's got a knack when it comes to food. Probably out of necessity. On a farm, you have lean years, and she had a large family to feed. That's a pretty way of saying we were sometimes as poor as church mice, and it fell to her to make sure we didn't go hungry. She's pretty creative in the kitchen." He flashed a grin. "You'll think you've died and gone to heaven when you bite into one of those cookies."

Lane realized that she had gone from being nervous to feeling relaxed. Jonas had a laid-back, no-pretense air about him that soothed her. That trait would probably serve him well in his chosen field. She doubted most psychologists were as down-to-earth as he was. His clients undoubtedly felt as if they were confiding in a good friend.

"You didn't tie up Rascal," she said. "Aren't you worried that he'll run away?"

"He won't go any farther than the next clump of green grass." He glanced over his shoulder at the horse. "We come here a lot. He enjoys it."

"He's a beautiful animal," Lane observed, and she truly meant it. The horse was big, powerfully muscled, and glowing with good health. "Have you really been riding since you were in diapers?"

"My dad says he had me on a horse at six months of age." He shrugged. "He was holding me, I'm sure. I can't remember back that far, of course, but I know I was riding by myself at four. We had a lazy old pony that had been conditioned to kids by my older brothers. Dad would saddle her for me, and I used a mounting block to climb on. When I got older, I rode her bareback a lot. Riding comes as naturally to me as walking."

Lane couldn't imagine a child of four being allowed to go riding. Growing up, she'd never even had a dog. "I can't picture myself ever being an equine enthusiast," she admitted, "but I have to give Rascal high marks for offering me a wonderful first and last experience on horseback."

He chuckled. "Not your last. We've still got to ride back to your bike."

Lane groaned around a mouthful of food, which made Jonas bark with laughter.

With most people she didn't know well, Lane felt compelled to keep a conversation going, but she didn't with Jonas. Maybe it was the serenity of the setting or the fact that he gazed thoughtfully at the creek as he ate. She only knew talking didn't seem necessary.

When it was time for dessert, Lane moaned with delight at the first taste of his mother's cookies. "Oh, my *stars*. Do you think she'd give me her recipe?"

He nodded. "She'd probably be flattered if you asked. She bakes every afternoon without fail."

"Who eats all of it?"

He shrugged. "My brothers all live in town, and they're raising families now. She also has plenty of other people dropping by. Neighbors and friends. Plus, she takes goody plates to a couple of old people on their road. And my dad is like a vacuum when it comes to sweets."

Lane's father was always trying to diet. "Is he overweight?"

"My dad?" Jonas grinned and shook his head. "Not an ounce of fat on him. He works hard. Calorie intake has never been a concern for him."

They chatted intermittently while they polished off the cookies. Then they tidied up, Jonas stowing the canvas cooler and refuse in the saddlebag while Lane shook out and folded the blanket.

Moments later when they were back on the horse, Lane felt relaxed enough to lean back against his chest. "That was nice," she told him. "It's such a beautiful spot! I had no idea there was a creek-side picnic area like that so close to my house."

"Over the winter, it's not as accessible, but it's a great place to enjoy during the warm months."

Silence fell between them, and Lane gave herself up to the rhythmic movements of the horse. The muted clomps of his hooves and his occasional chuffing soothed her almost as much as being in the clearing had.

"Lane?"

There was a faint note of alarm in Jonas' voice, so she straightened her spine. "What?"

"Do you remember where I hid your bike?"

Lane peered at the thick underbrush. "You're having me on. Right?"

"No. I wish I was. I honestly don't remember exactly where I stuck it."

After moving forward a few more feet, Jonas suggested that they dismount and execute a search. Lane couldn't help but laugh as they walked along the rutted road, peering into the thick brush for a glimpse of blue metal.

"What's so funny?" Jonas asked. "It's a thousand-dollar bike."

"I'm just imagining the conversation with my folks when I tell them I've lost it."

"Somehow I don't think they'll see the humor."

"Oh, yeah. Once they get over being upset, they will. Two mature adults hiding a bike to keep it safe and then not being able to find it? Come on, Jonas. Who wouldn't see the humor in that?"

"Me."

That set Lane to laughing again, and Jonas finally joined in, saying that he would find the damned bike even if it meant renting a metal detector. Fortunately, that didn't prove to be necessary. Jonas began searching the ground for their tracks and eventually located the spot where he'd carried the bicycle off the road.

"Whew!" Lane pretended to wipe sweat from her brow. "Saved by Davy Crockett!"

"Oh, hell, no. I grew up on Grizzly Adams reruns, and I love raccoons. I could never get into a guy who made one into a hat."

Lane could see his point. As she reclaimed her bicycle, she said, "This was fun, and your mom's sandwiches were delicious. Thank you for inviting me."

His amber eyes shimmered like cognac shot through with sunlight as he held her gaze. "It was my pleasure, and Mom will be delighted to think I ate four sandwiches and a dozen cookies for lunch. It's her mission in life to feed up her guys." He thumbed away something on her cheek. Startled by the unexpected contact, she gave him a questioning look. "Just a smudge of mud you missed when you washed off."

"You let me eat dinner with mud on my face?"

Shoving his hands into his pant pockets, he grinned and shrugged. "I didn't want to make you any more nervous than you already were, so I just let it slide. It was only a little splotch."

As Lane rode her bike home, she couldn't stop smiling. He'd known how nervous she was about being alone in the woods with him, and he hadn't been put off by that. She was glad that she had accepted his invitation to picnic with him. Friday afternoon and their departure to Plover Bay was coming soon, and she didn't feel nearly as apprehensive about traveling with him now.

For Lane, Friday still came on winged feet. She was on edge about going to Plover Bay with Jonas. What on earth would they find to talk about while stuck inside a car together for hours? And what if they couldn't find a motel with two vacancies? She hoped he'd had the forethought to book them rooms. People flocked to the Oregon coast in the autumn to go crabbing, because the meat of the crustaceans was less likely to be contaminated with Red Tide toxins in months that contained the letter *R*. Not all of those crabbers arrived with travel trailers or campers. Lane's dad had always gotten a room anyway, and she figured a lot of other people did the same.

By early Friday afternoon, Lane had tortured herself by imagining every possible thing that might go wrong over the weekend and decided enough was enough. According to Ma Thomas, Jonas was a great guy and came from a wonderful family. If Lane ended up having to share a room with him, she would just deal with it somehow. It wouldn't be the end of the world.

At precisely three o'clock, he entered the shop. Dressed for the coast, he wore a blue terry polo shirt, wide-fit linen pants, and canvas espadrilles. Lane couldn't help but give him an appreciative once-over. Jonas had the good looks to pull off nearly any style, and the clothes suited him almost as well as the western jeans and boots that he normally wore. Not for the first time, she marveled over how handsome he was.

"Am I too early?" he asked.

"No. Right on the dot." Butterflies fluttering wildly in her stomach, Lane went behind the checkout counter to grab her purse and sweater. "I park my car around back. It's better for business not to use up the street parking. Ma's in the storeroom, going through stock. I can tell her I'm leaving on the way out."

He flashed what she was coming to think of as his trademark grin, his straight teeth gleaming white in contrast to his sun-bronzed skin. "I figured where you probably park. I grew up here, remember. I parked out back, too, right behind you, but then I found the alley door locked, so I had to walk around."

"Oh. Sorry." Lane hoped he couldn't tell how rattled she was. "Ma keeps it locked. She says it startles her when people come in from the back. And that's probably just as well. She keeps her extra stock in that room, and most of it is fairly expensive stuff."

She led the way to the rear of the building. They found Ma elbow deep in a box filled with packaged perfume. She pushed to her feet and dusted her hands on her slacks. "Hello, Jonas. It's lovely to see you again." She trailed her twinkling gaze over his outfit. "You look ready for the beach. I hope both of you have a lovely time."

He glanced down at himself and shrugged. "It can't hurt to be comfortable."

As Lane exited the building with him, he said in a whisper-soft voice, "You apparently didn't tell her why we're going to Plover Bay. She seems to think we're off for a romantic getaway."

Lane felt heat crawl up her neck to pool in her cheeks. "I tried saying what you suggested, that I have business to take care of, but when she figured out that we were driving to the coast together, she decided the business was of a romantic nature. I tried to disabuse her of the notion, but she didn't buy it."

"Ah, well. Ma's not a gossip. She probably won't mention it to anyone else, and even if she does, it'll do no harm. We're both adults."

Uncomfortable with the turn of their conversation,

Lane unlocked her car to get her suitcase from the back seat.

"I hope you brought a light jacket, preferably water resistant," he said. "The forecast predicts sunny weather, but over on the coast, you never know when it'll cloud up and rain."

Lane held her luggage in one hand while she re-locked the car with her keyless remote. "Yes, I packed a jacket, a winter scarf, a shawl, *and* practical walking shoes."

He winked at her as he relieved her of the suitcase. "Sorry. Old habit. I come from a big family, and when we went on trips, somebody always forgot something. My dad and mom started going over a list of must-haves before we left, and half the time we kids delayed our departure by at least thirty minutes while we ran back into the house for things we forgot."

As an only child, Lane had always envied other kids who had large families. "I'm super organized," she assured him.

"That's good to know. Maybe some of it will rub off on me. I'm probably the most unorganized person you'll ever meet."

"Did *you* remember to bring a jacket?" she asked.

"Yep. I drew up a list of everything I might need and checked off items as I packed. If I've forgotten anything I absolutely need, I can buy it."

"I haven't been using my credit cards since leaving Maple Leaf."

"Wise decision. Credit card purchases are pretty easy to track if you have the right computer software."

After getting in the car, Lane wasn't sure what to expect, but it wasn't a shopping excursion at Flagg's

Market for road trip snacks and drinks. Jonas insisted that travel was less boring with treats to eat. "Driving that far without food would be like going to a double-feature movie and not buying popcorn."

Lane preferred to eat jelly beans during a film, but she got into the spirit of things after they entered the store. Jonas acted like a kid, grabbing all his favorite munchies and encouraging her to do the same. When they got in line to check out, both of them had their arms full, she was laughing, and for the first time since Jonas had suggested they go to Plover Bay together, she thought it might turn out to be fun. *Well, given the reason for this trip, not fun, really*, she decided. *But at least he's good company.*

As soon as they got out of town and onto the highway, Jonas uncapped his first bottle of Coca-Cola. When Lane left hers in the bag at her feet, he encouraged her to follow his lead and have a drink. In response, she said, "I remember this highway. There'll be no rest stops or gas stations until we reach the turnoff heading west, and I can't just stand alongside the road in an emergency like a guy can."

He chuckled. "Ah. I'm assuming that you've never used a two-door outhouse."

Lane could tell by his tone that he was teasing. "No, I can't say I have. What, exactly, is a two-door outhouse?"

"That's when you park alongside the road, open both doors on the passenger side, and take care of business between them where nobody driving in either direction can see you."

She gave him an incredulous look. "Do you plan to wear a blindfold?"

"Nope. All the guys in a car have to get out, too, and stand with their backs against the driver's side." He shrugged. "That's how my family handled emergency stops, anyway."

Lane thought that it might be interesting to meet his relatives. They sounded delightful. "If I drink both these bottles of pop, do you have any idea how many emergency stops you might have to make?"

"Don't tell me your father is one of those guys who turns road trips into driving marathons and gets in a grump if he has to pull over and let all the traffic he's passed get ahead of him again."

Lane couldn't help but laugh. "He's the absolute worst."

"Well, I don't mind stopping. It'll give me a chance to stretch my legs, and we have plenty of time to eat a nice evening meal somewhere and get settled in at a motel before it's too late."

Lane conceded the point and opened one of her drinks.

Jonas turned out to be quite a talker and kept her entertained for the next hour with stories of his childhood. At certain points, Lane laughed so hard that tears streamed down her cheeks.

"I always wished that my parents had adopted at least one other child," she confessed. "You are so lucky to have grown up in a family of six. I had nobody to fight with or to have fun with, and when you're the only kid, you can't get away with much of anything."

"It wasn't all fun and games," he assured her. "But, yeah, I guess I was lucky. Fighting with your siblings teaches you a lot about life and how to get along with others. When my older brothers weren't punching me behind our parents' backs, they were teaching me how to throw a punch. When I found a snake in my bed, I learned really fast to not scream like a girl, because they teased me unmercifully for weeks if I did. When I went on my first date, each one of them took me aside to give me advice and slip me a condom, which my dad relieved me of before I got out the door. I tried just handing over one, but he was too savvy to fall for that."

Lane started laughing again. "Your poor father!"

"Don't get me started. He says raising four boys gave him half of his gray hair."

"What gave him the rest?"

Jonas grinned. "Raising two girls when he knew exactly what the boys dating them had on their minds."

Lane succumbed to helpless mirth again.

Before they reached the Highway 20 junction, Jonas stopped to top off the gas tank, which allowed Lane to use the restroom before they began the long drive from there to Eugene. By the time they reached Eugene and got on the Randy Pape Beltline, which swung right onto Highway 126, Lane was far more relaxed than she had expected to be. Jonas was easy to be around, kept her engaged in conversation, and seemed not to care about their timeline.

"Would you like to eat now or wait until we reach the coast?" he asked.

Lane had just finished off a bag of jelly beans. "Are you hungry?"

"Hell, no. Maybe road trip snacks were a bad idea."

"We can save the rest for when we drive home, I suppose. On the other hand, the thought of fresh seafood may revive our appetites."

"True." He rifled through his snack bag and handed

her a bag of caramel corn. "Will you open that for me? Once I'm in a restaurant smelling deep-fried seafood, I won't care how full I am. I'll eat anyway."

Lane opened the bag and gave it back to him. Then she retrieved her roll of SweeTarts and began munching on those.

"Do you *like* those things?"

"Mmm." She smiled at him. "I take it you don't?"

"When I eat sweets, I'm into pure sugar, no sour stuff." He crammed another handful of caramel corn into his mouth. After swallowing, he said, "I noticed a bandage on your elbow. Are you pretty banged up from the bike wreck?"

Surprised that he'd noticed the Band-Aid, Lane shook her head. "I have a few superficial scrapes, but nothing too bad. I'm thankful I crashed on dirt instead of asphalt. If not, I'd be singing a different song."

Eventually, after Lane seemed to have relaxed, Jonas steered their conversation back to their reason for the trip: finding Veneta. "She may be working as an accountant by now if she got her degree. That was her major, anyway, but she made a few noises about ditching that to become a nurse. Your dreams of her don't indicate that she has settled down at any long-term job, though." He told Lane about Veneta's dependency on prescription sleep aids and later her shift to buying narcotics on the street. "My best guess is that she continued to pop pills and somehow landed herself in hot water. If she didn't get her degree, she's most likely a waitress somewhere, at a restaurant or bar. During college, she worked at high-end places to pay for her education. If she's down on her luck, she could even be bartending in some dive. Either way, it seems to me that we should start this search by making inquiries at eateries. The nicer restaurants may not be open in the morning and most bars aren't, either, so maybe we should start out with cafés and hit the other places in the afternoon and evening."

"Sounds like a plan," Lane agreed.

Chapter Six

When they arrived in Plover Bay, it was nearly seven in the evening. Jonas wanted to secure their rooms before they went out to eat. Most of the motels looked pretty full, and his fear that he wouldn't be able to find them lodging began to mount. *Why didn't I call and make reservations earlier this week?* he asked himself. Then he wondered why he was even bewildered. Forgetfulness was his MO, always had been. His mom said he had too many things on his mind, but the truth, as Jonas saw it, was that he tended to hyper-focus on one thing to the exclusion of all else. Normally, that trait caused him very few issues, but he had a bad feeling it might tonight.

"Are you saying that you didn't get reservations somewhere?" Lane asked.

Jonas' stomach lurched. "I, um—sort of forgot."

She glanced over at him. "This is crabbing season, you know. That's why all the motels have so many cars out front. What will we do if we can't find rooms?"

"We'll find rooms," Jonas replied with far more confidence than he felt.

After striking out at the motels in town, Jonas stopped at a gas station to ask an attendant for guidance.

"There's a beachfront inn out Highway 101. I can't

remember its name. Really classy. Great views of the ocean. But I hear it's pretty expensive."

At this point, Jonas didn't care how much the rooms might set him back. He absolutely had to find lodging. If he didn't, Lane was bound to think he was scheming to get her into bed with him by finally finding only one room where they'd be forced to share a sleeping space. And no amount of denial on his part would likely change her mind.

"Thanks, man. Much appreciate the advice."

As Jonas walked away, the guy called out, "If it's too rich for your pocketbook, call around in the morning to find other lodging. Even though it's our busy season, most of the motels have a few un-booked rooms early in the day."

Jonas gave the fellow a thumbs-up before climbing back into the car. "He says there's a really swanky place farther out of town. Maybe they have vacancies."

"Swanky?"

"Expensive." He flashed her what he hoped was a confident smile. "It'll be fun. The rooms have great ocean views and beach access. Maybe we can get in a walk on the beach before we call it a night."

An hour later, after paying for a three-bedroom suite, which was the only size unit vacant, Jonas was determined to take a walk on the beach in order to get his money's worth. When he opened the door to their quarters, Lane gave a startled gasp of surprise.

"Oh, my goodness, this is amazing, Jonas. Are you sure you can afford it?"

The cost wouldn't send him into bankruptcy, but that was about as positive as Jonas could be. "No worries. It wasn't that pricey." Only almost as much as a month's rent for his apartment. He set their luggage down in the well-appointed living area and pivoted on his heel to take in the décor. "It really is nice. Isn't it?"

Lane stepped over to the French doors that opened out onto a small beachfront deck. Jonas headed straight for a bedroom, praying to God and all His angels that he'd find a lock on the door. His knees went weak with relief when that was precisely what he found. Over his shoulder, he said, "Perfect. We can make this work. You'll have your room, and I'll have mine."

She turned from admiring the ocean view. "Just so you know, I won't come unglued tomorrow night if we end up having to share a room. I know you better now. I'm no longer worried that you might try to take advantage of the situation."

Jonas could only hope he deserved that measure of trust. After being with Lane for hours, he thought she was far lovelier than Veneta had ever thought of being, and he couldn't deny, even to himself, that he was attracted to her. She had a quick wit. When she laughed, she did so with abandon, and it was a natural, unaffected sound that was easy on the ears. She was also an interesting person to converse with, intelligent and spontaneous. He had thoroughly enjoyed her company during the drive.

"There's a restaurant," he said. "Shall we just eat here?"

She wrinkled her nose. "It'll be expensive here. Besides, we had our hearts set on some amazing fresh seafood, and it's been my experience that the best seafood is usually found in ocean-side diners. They stay in business by serving consistently good dishes that not only bring in tourists, but also the locals."

Jonas was more than happy to find a less expensive

place to eat. They drove along the coastline and stopped at a faded little eatery called the Crabby Old Man. Lane thought the name was a clever play on words, and, judging by the building in need of fresh paint, Jonas hoped the cost of their meals wouldn't give him sticker shock.

It turned out that Lane was right about the quality of the food. Jonas ordered the captain's platter, which turned out to be amazing. Lane had deep-fried calamari that she said was the best she'd ever tasted. Jonas ordered a bottle of white wine, which they shared. Between them a short pillar candle flickered inside a seablue hurricane lamp, and the light played over her delicate features, making her seem to glow and illuminating the lagoon-blue of her beautiful eyes.

After taking a sip of her second glass of wine, she said, "Tell me more about Veneta. What was she like?"

Jonas took a moment to collect his thoughts. "Mercurial," he settled for saying. "She'd be on top of the world one minute and depressed the next."

"And you found that attractive?"

Jonas had to laugh. "Actually, no. But her mood swings weren't apparent to me in the beginning. I guess we went through what you might call a honeymoon period when she was putting her best foot forward. Then the real Veneta started to emerge."

"And you didn't like what you saw?"

Jonas drew his napkin off his lap and laid it on his platter. "I thought I was in love with her, so when she grew depressed, I tried to cheer her up. When she cried, I wiped away her tears. I didn't really . . ." Jonas let the sentence trail away. "It's difficult to explain. It was kind of like when you're wading on a river's edge, feeling your way with bare feet. You can feel the water getting deeper, but not alarmingly so. And then, bang, you take one more step and go under, taken off guard by a sharp drop-off." He met her gaze. "Does that make any sense? In a way, I truly did wade in over my head. So it was never a case of me liking or disliking what I saw. It was more me wondering what the hell happened."

An expression of sadness played over her face. "It makes perfect sense. Relationships are tricky. I suppose all of us hope to present ourselves to a potential partner in the best light, but some people are masters of deception. When they finally decide to let the other person see who they really are, it's a shock. You aren't expecting it."

"The voice of experience?"

Her cheeks went pink. "In a way, yes. And I like your analogy about it being similar to wading along a riverbank. You do start to notice little things. Nothing alarming. And you tell yourself they don't matter, because they *are* such *little* things. Only suddenly all of them together become big, and you do feel as if you stepped in over your head."

"Exactly." Jonas picked up his fork and pushed at a lone French fry he hadn't eaten. "And to draw a clear picture and be fair to Veneta, she must have realized we weren't a good fit, because she was the one to break it off."

"Were you devastated?"

He sighed. "For a bit. But then I snapped out of it. I realized how wrong she was for me and accepted that maybe the same was true in reverse. Two perfectly nice people may not be good for each other. I'm a pretty laid-back person, but being with Veneta exhausted me. She had extreme highs and extreme lows, with no middle ground in between. She was either deliriously happy or in the depths of despair. I just wasn't geared for that. In many ways, I knew she was wrong for me. But she had a sweet, almost shy side that lured me in, and it took a while for me to see her less attractive traits. Imagine pieces of a jigsaw puzzle and how you try to form a complete picture with them. That was how it went for me. Little glimmers of realization, but never the whole picture—until the end. By then, she was drinking way too much and buying sleeping pills off the street. She seemed to have no stop button with booze or drugs, and sometimes when she mixed them, she grew almost manic."

"I'm sorry it ended badly."

He shrugged. "Don't be. It's the bad relationships that don't end that you should be sorry about. I dodged a bullet, and so did she."

When they got back to their suite, Lane wasn't quite ready to sleep, so she was secretly pleased when Jonas invited her for a walk along the beach. She grabbed a sweater to drape over her shoulders and set off beside him. It had grown quite dark, but the moonlight helped illuminate their way. As they descended a steep dune littered with rocks and driftwood, Jonas grasped her hand. His grip was strong and radiated warmth up her arm. She sneaked a glance at his profile and admitted, if only to herself, that she wished she'd met this man before Veneta did. There was something about him that was inexplicably attractive to her.

They set off for a rock formation that loomed in silhouette against the star-studded night sky. The sound of the surf played gently in the background, and the waves sent up a salty mist that moistened her cheeks and tasted wonderful when she licked her lips. Occasionally a diehard seagull called out in the darkness. Jonas hadn't released his hold on her hand, probably only because the visibility was poor, but for a moment, she allowed herself to pretend they were lovers out for a moonlit stroll. Then she realized where her thoughts were taking her, and she banished them from her mind.

"I've always loved the Oregon coast," she told him.

"Yep, me, too. To visit, anyway. I don't think I could handle the wind and rain over the winter."

"Me, either," she confessed. "But if I were rich, I wouldn't turn up my nose at a summer home."

"Great idea. Says me, who hasn't even bought his first house yet."

She laughed and spun away from him, letting the hemline of her handkerchief dress whirl around her legs. "And says me, who hasn't bought a house yet and possibly never will. I'm doing well just to pay my rent. Every time I think I'm getting ahead financially, something happens to drain my savings. Last winter, it was my car breaking down. This summer, the washing machine croaked, and my landlord refused to replace it. It only took a couple of laundromat visits to convince me I'd spend more doing that than I would buying a used replacement."

He chuckled. "You sound like me. Before I buy a house, I want to set up a proper clinic, maybe even bring in a partner. I set money aside monthly in a savings account, the amount starts to look impressive on paper, and then, bang, something happens. Tires for my truck. Those things cost the earth. And then—"

"You have a truck?"

"I do. Any self-respecting man in Mystic Creek absolutely *must* have a truck. The car dates back to my last year of college. It was free and clear when I moved back to Mystic Creek, so being the idiot that I sometimes am, I went into debt again for a four-wheel-drive muscle truck."

She laughed and grasped his arm as they ascended the sandy slope to the inn. Once back in their suite, Jonas sat on the sofa, rested his hands on his knees, and said, "You aren't going to believe this, but I'm not sleepy and the long walk made me feel a little hungry again. Laugh if you like, but if my stomach feels even slightly empty, I toss and turn."

"I'm with you. Maybe the lounge has a bar menu."

Together, they set off to locate the lounge. The inn was quite large. At one point, they wandered into the pool area, where a young couple was necking in a hot tub, which set them both to snickering. When they finally found the lounge and settled at a private table, Lane couldn't help thinking about how right it felt to be with Jonas. Unlike all the blustering boys she'd met in college, Jonas apparently felt comfortable in his own skin and had no urge to impress her with his masculine prowess, money, or career prospects. He was one of the most candid people she'd ever met, revealing himself to her in ways other men probably wouldn't.

They settled on ordering a cheese plate with delicious aged cheddar, raw vegetables, black olives, rounds of sourdough bread, and dip. For drinks, they each enjoyed a rich, dark beer and had fun trying to pick up on the different subtle hints of flavor. "Coffee," Lane offered. "A hint of chocolate," he countered. Burnt grain. Tar. They bounced their impressions off each other like two combatants slamming balls the length of a ping-pong table. It was the perfect way to chase away mild hunger and also relax before retiring.

In the dim light of the lounge, Lane couldn't help but admire Jonas' chiseled features and the masculine set of his shoulders. His tawny hair gleamed like polished oak, and his hazel eyes, sometimes green and sometimes amber, were expressive and compelling each time he met her gaze. She glanced at his firm mouth and couldn't look away, wondering how it might feel if he kissed her.

No sooner did that thought enter her mind than Lane rejected it. She absolutely couldn't entertain such a notion. They were here to search for Veneta, and regardless of how attractive Jonas was, she couldn't allow herself to forget their purpose.

Feeling suddenly flushed and pleasantly buzzed, she waved a hand in front of her face. "I'm not normally a three-drink person," she revealed.

He grinned. "Don't rain on my parade. I'm trying to ply you with alcohol for a big seduction scene."

"No, seriously," Lane said in a stage whisper. "I think I'm tipsy. What if I stagger all the way back to our rooms?"

He narrowed an eye at her. "You are so very different."

"Different from what?"

"Veneta. It was nothing for her to down two bottles of wine. Did she get tipsy? Yes. Did she worry about it? No." His burnished brows drew together in a frown. "Dear God," he added, his voice dipping to almost a whisper. "Oh, man, where was my head at?"

"What?" Lane asked, her pulse accelerating because she could tell Jonas had just thought of something terrible.

"Veneta. All the symptoms. Her lack of a stop button. Always worried about her weight and rarely eating very much. Her dependency on narcotics and alcohol. Her moodiness and depression. How could I know her so well and not see what was right in front of my nose?"

"I'm sorry. I'm not following." Lane held his gaze. "What was right in front of your nose?"

"All the symptoms of a person who's messed up because she was abused as a child. Veneta presented so many of the symptoms, and it never came together for me until right now. Why? I knew her father had broken her arm. That he beat on her and her mother all the time." A shadow of emotion deepened the hue of his eyes to brown. "She even grew violent a couple of times. It was all there, Lane, all the signs. And now, I'm kicking myself for not putting it all together back then. I might have been able to help, not in an official capacity, but by getting her in to see a counselor."

Lane felt blindsided by her own sense of regret. She'd been feeling resentful of her parents ever since talking with them about her adoption, and now, suddenly, she was reminded of how very lucky she'd been to have them as her mother and father. Unlike Veneta, Lane had never been mistreated, and despite her recurring emotional issues brought on by hearing voices, she was otherwise a fairly stable person. Thanks to the unflagging love she'd been given all her life, she'd never been one to drink too much alcohol, had never touched illegal drugs, and wasn't prone to violent outbursts driven by either sadness or anger.

With that realization, Lane's mood took a downward turn, and she hoped Jonas didn't think she had the propensity to be mercurial in temperament like her sister. If she truly had a sister. It was still difficult for her to wrap her mind around that.

"I know why I'm wanting to kick myself, but what's wrong with you?" Jonas asked. "Did I say something?"

She forced a smile. "No. Sorry. I'm just woolgathering, I guess."

"About Veneta? We'll do our best to track her down and help her. If we fail, it won't be your fault."

"I didn't dream of her last night, and I haven't heard the voice all day. What if—?" Lane broke off and shook her head. "How can I worry about someone I'm not even sure is real?"

"Oh, she's real." Jonas leaned forward over the table to get closer to her. "Lane, no matter what happens, you're here. You're going the extra mile for someone it's hard for you to really believe exists. Do you know how extraordinary that is? No matter what happens, I don't want you to ever feel that you didn't do enough."

When they got back to their rooms a few minutes later, they both retired to their separate chambers. Lane's had a lovely bath with a deep, jetted tub. She decided to enjoy the amenity and save herself the trouble of a shower in the morning. Before disrobing for her plunge into chin-deep ecstasy, she stepped back to the door that opened onto the common area she shared with Jonas.

Then she turned away without locking it.

The next morning Lane awakened at ten after six, decided to take a shower even though she'd bathed last night, and dressed for the day, pairing a denim skirt with an airy blouse and slipping into sandals with a supportive sole in case the day ahead called for a lot of walking. With her hair blown dry and drawn back from her face, she wore only a touch of cosmetics. In the moist sea air, her makeup tended to dissolve and run. She didn't want to look like a raccoon by mid-afternoon.

Jonas stood in the small kitchenette making coffee. When he heard her bedroom door open, he flashed a grin over his shoulder. "Hey, you. I thought you were still asleep."

"When I don't work a late shift, I tend to be an early riser." She sniffed the air. "Oh, that coffee smells good!"

He offered her the first cup.

"No, you go ahead. I can make my own." Lane elbowed him away from the coffeemaker and began making another serving. "So what's our game plan for today?" she asked. "Any new ideas come to you overnight?"

He sat at the tiny breakfast bar, elbows braced on the counter, coffee mug cradled in his big hands for easy sipping. "For one, I think we should check out and leave ourselves open to staying somewhere else tonight. This has been fun, but it's a little too pricey for a psychologist trying to build up his clientele. Secondly, we don't know what we may learn today about Veneta. These little coastal towns aren't that far apart. She may have worked in another community as well. If we get a lead and have to head to another town to broaden our search, we'll be free to do that."

Lane appreciated his honesty about his finances. "I have no problem with less opulent lodging, Jonas. In fact, all we really need is a room with two beds, as long as it's clean."

He took a swallow of coffee and whistled at the heat. "I can swing two rooms as long as we can find vacancies, and if we can't, we can always come back here." He arched an eyebrow. "I don't think this place attracts people who come over here to go crabbing. They want cheap lodging and food."

She stirred a packet of sugar into her coffee and went to stand across from him at the bar. "If we have to return here tonight, I will happily cover half the cost."

He pulled a face and squinted one eye at her. "No way. I said I'd cover the expenses, and I will." When she started to protest, he held up a forefinger. "No point in fretting about it now. Come tonight, we may be in Coos Bay or Brookings."

"Where we will surely find more crabbing enthusiasts. It may be difficult to find less expensive lodging there, too."

"Possibly." He turned the conversation to another topic. "Most of the bars and fancy restaurants won't be open until around noon. What do you think of the plan I came up with yesterday about spending the morning visiting little cafés where Veneta may have worked?"

"I think that's a great plan."

He nodded, and a slow grin slanted over his mouth. "Breakfast in a greasy spoon, my dream come true."

She laughed and set herself to the task of drinking the coffee.

The day turned out to be an emotional roller coaster ride for Lane. Unbeknownst to her, Jonas had brought a photograph of Veneta from one of his college albums, and at the first café while they were eating breakfast, he drew it from his shirt pocket when their waitress returned to their table to refill their coffee cups.

"Do you recognize this woman?" he asked while displaying the snapshot. "She's a good friend, and we're trying to locate her. We'd appreciate any help we can get."

The waitress, a plump redhead with freckles and a friendly smile, cast a sharp glance at Lane. "I—um—is this some kind of joke? Or a test? I've got it!" She laughed triumphantly as if she'd just solved a mystery. "You're here from the university to do a study on whether or not people in tourist towns pay any attention to the strangers they serve."

Jonas got a blank look on his face and lowered the hand holding the picture back down to the table, allowing Lane to see the image. The moment she looked, she felt as if a boxer had just rattled her brains with a knockout punch. Leaving Jonas to deal with the waitress, she escaped to his car, only to realize when she got to it that she couldn't get inside without a key. She leaned against the fender and tried to focus on her breathing. *In and out. Slow and deep.* Her whole body was trembling, making her grateful for the vehicle's solid support at the small of her back. She hadn't recognized the background in the photograph, but the likeness of the woman in it had been an exact replica of Lane herself. It had been the eeriest feeling she'd ever experienced, seeing someone who looked so much like her that she might have been looking in a mirror.

On some level, she had understood that she and Veneta were doubles, but it hadn't seemed real until now. *I have a sister. No, not just a sister. I have an identical twin.* There was no question in Lane's mind of that now. She and Veneta looked exactly alike. Lane even dressed similarly to the other woman and wore her hair in an easy-to-maintain bob.

Hearing footsteps on the gravel, she glanced up and saw Jonas striding across the parking lot toward her.

He wore a worried expression that became even more apparent to her as he got closer.

"I am so sorry," he said after closing the distance between them. "I shouldn't have sprung her picture on you like that. I just didn't stop to think."

"It's okay," she pushed out. "I'm going to be okay."

He groaned, settled in beside her against the car, and looped his arm around her shoulders. Despite the little warning signals that went off in her brain, Lane pressed closer to his strength and warmth, feeling suddenly chilled even though the morning was balmy.

"I really am sorry," he said again. "I didn't stop to think that you've never seen Veneta. Or at least you don't remember ever having seen her. I know it must have been a shock."

She turned her face against his shoulder and breathed in the clean smell of his cotton shirt. "It's not your fault. You told me. Remember? You said we look exactly alike. Only somehow it didn't sink in, not all the way. I didn't comprehend that she looks so much like me that I would think it was me in a picture."

He released a long sigh. "I'm an idiot. Bringing a photo of her is probably the stupidest thing I've ever done. Anyone who sees you is seeing Veneta. I guess grabbing the snapshot was a knee-jerk impulse."

"It's all right, Jonas. I needed to see that photo, you know. As recently as last night, I was still dubious about having an identical twin. Now—well, all my doubts flew out the window."

"I'm sorry I didn't ease you into seeing that."

Lane straightened away from him and took a bracing breath. "It's fine. I've got my head wrapped around it now. Veneta exists. And now, more than before, I know I have to find her. Before something happens.

You know? Because—well, there are lots of reasons, but the selfish one is, I'll feel robbed if I never get to meet her."

Jonas pushed erect and settled his hand on her shoulder. The weight and warmth of his touch sent a zing of awareness down her spine. When he quickly broke the contact, she wondered if he had felt it, too.

"Yeah. I get it. I really do. You haven't met my dad and my older brothers, but we all look alike. People say we even talk and act alike. When I look at them, I see myself in them in so many different ways, and if I'd never met one of them and was informed of his existence, I'd be hell-bent to find him. With siblings, it's like—I can't find the right words—but you want to see them, know them, pal around with them. I can't imagine never knowing my brothers. My sisters, too, of course, but they take after my mother more, and it isn't quite the same."

Lane mustered up a smile. "Now that I've seen her picture, I've got to agree with you. There's no need to show it to anyone else. All people have to do is see me, and they'll know what she looks like. *Exactly* what she looks like."

He circled the car and slid in under the steering wheel just as she fastened her seat belt. As he started the engine, he said, "I guess we should just drive around and stop at every little diner we see. What are your thoughts?"

"You're probably thinking a bit more clearly than I am right now. I'll let you decide."

He nodded and shifted into drive. At their next stop, they entered a place called Emma's Diner. From the outside, it looked like an old house except for the wheelchair ramp that angled up to the front porch and the neon signs that flashed in the windows, advertising brand-name drinks. The interior of the structure had been gutted and remodeled at some point, for it was spacious with colorful red-cushioned swivel stools at the bar, red-and-white-striped booth seats flanking red Formica tabletops, and a checkerboard floor. *Vintage sixties*, Lane thought, and half expected to hear Elvis singing "Return to Sender" on the old jukebox that sat along the end wall.

Before Jonas could guide her to a booth, Lane saw a large-busted and broad-hipped older woman rushing out from behind the service counter. Dressed in blue uniform pants and a smock, she looked like a barge bearing down on them. "Neta!" she cried. "Oh, honey, you're a sight for sore eyes. I've been worried *sick* about you!"

Before Lane could form a logical response to this effusive greeting, the woman's beefy arms gathered her into a crushing hug that stole her breath.

"Don't you *ever* do that to me again. You hear?" She grasped Lane's shoulders and moved back a step to give her a once-over. "I swear, I didn't sleep well for an entire week after you just up and vanished."

Lane couldn't think of a single word to say and was glad when Jonas broke in. "This isn't Neta. I know she looks exactly like her, but that's because Neta is her identical twin."

"Oh." The woman shot a skeptical glance at Jonas. "If this is a joke, I'll not take kindly to being the butt of it, young man. I love this young lady like a daughter." She gave Lane's shoulders a light squeeze and moved back a step. "I was picturing her dead in a ditch somewhere."

Lane's stomach knotted at the image that revelation

formed in her mind, and the grimness of it cleared her head. "This truly isn't a joke, ma'am. My name is Lane Driscoll, and I've come to Plover Bay to track down my sister, Veneta." She indicated Jonas with a sweep of her hand. "And this is my friend Jonas Sterling. If you aren't too busy, would you mind sitting with us for a few minutes and answering some questions?"

"Emma," the woman said, holding out her right hand. "Emma Savage. And like I said, I love Neta dearly. If anyone else came around asking questions about her, I'd give them the boot. Not the cops, of course. I cooperated as well as I could with them, hoping the information I provided might help them find her. She just up and vanished. Left everything behind, even her car."

"She took none of her personal belongings?" Jonas asked.

"Not even her clothing. The only things the police couldn't find at her apartment were her purse and cell phone. And they say her phone hasn't been used since she disappeared. I don't know how they know that. Some kind of tracking device, I guess. Or maybe her cell phone service provider gave the police that information."

Emma gestured toward a booth, and Lane and Jonas preceded her to the dining compartment, sliding in next to each other to sit facing the woman. Emma squeezed in across from them, her bosom billowing over the table edge to rest on its surface.

"Can you tell us about the day she disappeared?" Jonas asked. "Anything you remember may help. Did she seem distracted? Upset? Nervous?"

"Lord, yes." Emma nodded emphatically. "Only I think a better way to describe it is to say she acted scared.

Normally she was a vivacious person, always joking and laughing with the customers. She got great tips; I can tell you that. But that day, she seemed as nervous as a cat on a hot tin roof. Every time the bell over the front door jangled, she jumped with a start. You know what I'm saying? I got the impression she was afraid a particular person might come in looking for her, and she didn't want to be found."

Lane studied Emma's round face. She wore no cosmetics, and her gray hair was drawn back into a ponytail at the nape of her neck. She was also overweight, probably from eating mostly diner food. But she had lovely eyes, the color of a summer sky on a clear, hot day. Lane could see her as being the sort who would grow fond of a younger woman and take her under her wing.

"Neta never mentioned having a sister," Emma said, her tone laced with suspicion. "In fact, she told me she was adopted and had no siblings."

Lane nodded. "That's true. At age three, we were adopted out to different parents, and until just recently, I didn't know Veneta existed. I doubt that she knows I exist, either."

"You look amazingly alike," Emma mused aloud. "In fact, it's still hard for me to believe you aren't Neta."

"I understand," Jonas interjected. "Back in college, I dated Neta, and when I first met Lane, I didn't believe her when she told me she was someone else."

Emma relaxed her shoulders slightly and smiled at Lane. "No one here ever called her Veneta. Just Neta. She worked here for almost a year. One of the best waitresses I ever had. Only then something happened. She grew distracted. Nervous. A little cross sometimes with the customers. There at the last, she'd come to work reeking of vodka." She held up a hand. "I know they say you can't smell vodka, but I sure can. She wasn't drunk, mind you, but I knew that she'd been drinking. I could tell she was troubled about something, but even though I asked, she wouldn't tell me what was wrong." Her eyes sparkled with unshed tears, and she gave Lane a sympathetic smile. "I have a bad feeling about her disappearing the way she did. I just don't think she'd willingly do that. She was never one to call in sick or be late, because she knew what a hardship that would be for me. Then she just quit during her lunch hour without any notice? That just doesn't ring true to me."

A lump of anxiety rose in Lane's throat. "Jonas and I believe she's in serious trouble of some kind. If she left here of her own volition, Emma, do you have any idea where she might have gone? Back to her hometown, maybe? Did she mention any friends by name—people she might have gone to for help?"

Emma shook her head. "Neta wasn't one to talk about herself much. I do know, for sure and certain, that she wouldn't have gone home. She didn't get along well with her parents."

Jonas angled a questioning look at Lane and then settled his gaze on Emma again. "Please don't take offense at this question. You're obviously deeply fond of Neta. But did you see any signs that she might have been doing drugs?"

"Neta?" Emma rolled her eyes. "She drank. I'm certain of that. But I never suspected that she was doing anything else."

"People who are on drugs can be distracted and jumpy, just as you say Neta was before she disappeared."

Jonas repositioned the condiment rack sitting at the center of the table. "Not saying that was the cause of her behavior. But it might have been."

Emma sighed. "It's possible, I suppose, but I really don't think she was into drugs. I've been down that road more than once with employees—and they miss work, steal from my till, and get customer orders all screwed up. Neta did none of those things."

Moments later as they left the diner, Jonas said to Lane, "Maybe we should focus the rest of our morning on visiting places where Veneta may have worked or frequented. Judging by the records I dug up online, she lived here for two years. She only worked at Emma's for half of that time. I'm guessing she must have been employed somewhere else before she got the job here."

Lane was recalling how weird it had felt when Emma thought she was Veneta and raced out from behind the counter to hug her. "Sure," she agreed. "Whatever you think."

Jonas stopped beside the car to gaze down at her. "You're upset. Care to talk about it?"

She scrunched her shoulders. "It's just—such a strange experience. Seeing that photo. Then Emma's reaction when she first saw me. It's finally starting to feel real to me. You know? And it's a lot to take in. We see ourselves in a mirror our entire lives, believing that we're one of a kind. It's mind-boggling for me to realize that I'm actually not."

The salty breeze caught Lane's hair and trailed it over her eyes. Jonas reached out to tuck the strands behind her ear. "Not true. You're still one of a kind. A person with your own likes and dislikes. Your own personality. Your own life experiences and memories. Looking the same doesn't mean you are the same."

"True, I suppose." Lane turned to open the passenger door. "Full speed ahead. In order for me to ever meet her, we need to find her."

After Jonas was inside the vehicle and had started the engine, he said, "It's a quarter after ten. By eleven, some of the bars will probably be open, and early in the day like this, business should be slow. It should be a great time to chat up some bartenders to see what they know. After we hit a few of those places, we can visit cafés after the lunch-hour rush."

"We aren't going to find her here in Plover Bay." Lane fastened her seat belt. "Whether she left of her own volition or was kidnapped, she's definitely no longer here."

"True, but that doesn't mean we can't gather some helpful information," Jonas pointed out. "Like what kind of trouble she might have been in."

Chapter Seven

As the day wore on, Jonas found himself growing increasingly worried about Lane. They visited several eateries and bars, and each time they entered a new place, he could feel the tension rolling off her. He guessed that she was expecting a repeat of what had happened at Emma's Diner, with someone thinking she was Veneta. Jonas hadn't stopped to think how difficult that might be for her, and he felt bad about not anticipating her turmoil. He also felt a little guilty, because at each stop, he hoped Lane's appearance *would* cause a stir. If no one recognized her as being Veneta, this whole trip would be for nothing.

By three in the afternoon, he had just about lost hope. Weary and more than a little hungry because they hadn't eaten lunch, he suggested that they stop somewhere for a meal.

"Sure. I'm hungry, too." Lane glanced over at him. "Where would you like to eat?"

"Anywhere that serves hot food."

She smiled. "That'll be easy. We can find a restaurant, I suppose. Or maybe we'd be smarter if we just go to another bar and grill. That way, we can check it out while we eat and kill two birds with one stone."

"Brilliant idea."

Driving along Highway 101, Jonas pulled over at a place called the Pirate's Den. It sat on a bluff above the ocean and had probably been trendy at some point, but the passage of time and the constant battering of coastal winds had stripped away the building's paint and left only gray plank siding. A boardwalk on stilts led to the double swinging doors of the establishment. Cupping Lane's elbow in one hand, he guided her up the steps and along the walkway.

When they stepped inside, Jonas' first impression was of a dark and gloomy place, but as his eyes adjusted, he saw that it wasn't as seedy as he'd first thought. Crosscut plank flooring, as gray as the exterior siding, gleamed in the overhead lighting. An L-shaped bar sported stools with high backs for comfortable seating. It looked like a clean, well-maintained place, even though it was obviously old.

Three men sat at a corner table, chatting over a pitcher. An older couple occupied another table and were eating either a late lunch or an early dinner. Jonas led Lane to the bar, where they could each take a seat and talk with the bartender, a tall, beefy fellow with thinning blond hair.

When he turned to greet them, his friendly smile vanished the instant he saw Lane. "Well, well, well," he said. "You finally decided to **resurface**. Good to see that you're okay."

Jonas could see Lane was **trying** to think what to say. Her lips were parted slightly, but no words were coming out. He decided to take over. "She isn't who you think she is," he said. "Her name is Lane Driscoll. We're here looking for her sister, Veneta Monroe."

"Bullshit. What do you take me for, an idiot?"

Jonas tried a smile. "It's true. Lane is her identical twin."

The man stared intently at Lane's face. He clearly didn't believe Jonas, and a slight smirk played over his lips. Glancing at Jonas, he asked, "What'll ya have?"

Jonas ordered a light beer and twisted on the stool to reach for his wallet. The bartender didn't ask Lane for her order. He just drew Jonas beer from a tap and mixed Lane a drink. When he set both glasses on the counter, he smiled.

"That's your *sister's* favorite," he said. "But, of course, you already know that. Right?"

Jonas heard the challenge in the bartender's voice and glanced at Lane to assure himself she was okay. Her cheeks high with color, she lifted the tumbler, took a swallow of the drink, and then made a face. She set the tumbler back on the counter and pushed it away. "My sister can have it. That's straight vodka. Isn't it?"

"Not straight. I cut it with some water," the man told her. "It's got one hell of a kick. Your *sister* can drink them all night."

The guy clearly wasn't convinced that Lane wasn't Veneta. Jonas placed a hand on Lane's back. Due to the ever-present coastal breezes, she had donned a light sweater earlier, and through the cotton knit, he could feel each of the delicate vertebra in her spine, like tiny marbles beneath his fingertips.

"What would you like instead?" he asked.

"Just a soft drink, please. Diet Coke if you have it." She nudged the glass even farther away. "If my sister drinks those all night, she's a better woman than I am."

Jonas smiled. "I've had vodka on the rocks a few times. It's more for sipping than gulping."

"Huh." Gaze still fixed on Lane's face, the barkeep frowned thoughtfully. "You really aren't Neta, then?"

Lane drew in a long, shaky breath. "No, I'm really not."

As the bartender rifled through an under-counter fridge for a can of chilled soda, he said, "I apologize. You look so much like her, I thought you were having me on. She can be quite the jokester, Neta can." He transferred the rejected tumbler into the sink, popped the can tab, and then poured Lane's drink, which he set in front of her. "Always a laugh a minute when she came in."

Jonas knew exactly what the bartender meant. When Veneta was on a roll, she'd been fun to be around. Sadly, her happy moods nearly always ended with depression. Jonas recalled times when she'd cried herself to sleep after a lively night out with friends.

Resting his bent arms on the bar, the other man gave Lane a long study. "Wow. I've only ever met one set of identical twins, and I couldn't tell them apart, either. It's hard to believe two people can look so much alike. Kind of mind-blowing."

Lane took a sip of the Coke, then cleared her throat and managed a smile. "Do you know Neta well?"

The bartender shrugged. "After pulling beer taps for over forty years, I can't honestly say I've ever known a bar patron all that well. I *think* I know them, but over time, you learn that even drunks have their secrets."

"Ah. And do you think my sister was hiding anything?"

"At first, yes. Right before she disappeared, no. At least not as much." Pausing, the bartender glanced at his other customers before continuing. In a lowered voice, he added, "The drug use—she got a little sloppy about trying to hide it."

"Drug use?" Lane sat straighter. "Neta was doing drugs?"

"The drugs were doing her, not the other way around." He sniffed and rubbed under his nose with his shirtsleeve. "She'd come in here higher than a whirl-wind kite, and more than a few times, I caught her snorting coke right here at my bar. That last night—right before she went missing—I had to eighty-six her." He pulled a face. "I felt really bad about that when I heard she disappeared the next day. Like maybe I should have tried harder to help her. But, hey. This bar is all I've got. I couldn't afford to get shut down, and letting somebody snort cocaine in here is a surefire way for that to happen."

"I understand," Lane assured him. "I'm sorry she was so thoughtless."

He sighed and wagged his head. "Not thoughtless, honey. At that point, she was pretty much brain-dead. Seriously messed up. And, if I was reading things correctly, that was the least of her problems."

Jonas leaned closer. "What do you mean?"

"I think she got in over her head with a dangerous crowd," the bartender revealed. "She said a few things. You know?"

"Like what?" Jonas pressed.

"That she had enemies. People she wanted to put behind bars. Said they'd killed her best friends." He sighed. "Nothing too detailed. But it was enough to worry me." He glanced at Lane. "I tried talking to her. You know, just the usual stuff you say when you think somebody's off on a bad path. That maybe she needed counseling or drug rehab. That maybe she should back off on the drinking. With her, it was in one ear and out the other. She said she was on a mission, that paybacks were hell. That last night, she got so wasted that she fell off her barstool. A little later, when I caught her snorting, it was the straw that broke the camel's back. She was a regular, and I was fond of her, so I called her a cab. Sure as hell didn't want her driving home in that condition. But she got pissed when I said she was eighty-sixed and refused to wait for a ride. Said she'd be perfectly fine behind the wheel. That was the last I ever saw of her."

"Did you tell all this to the police?" Jonas asked.

"Oh, yeah. All of it. Neta's a nice gal. I wanted to help her if I could. But what I knew—well, it wasn't all that much, really. The enemies she mentioned? I never heard any names. No particulars. Same went for the best friends she said they murdered. Essentially, what I told the cops was pretty useless."

Lane, apparently shaken by the bartender's revelations, shifted her weight on the barstool and looked to be collecting her composure. "You did all that you could. And I appreciate that you tried to help her."

He nodded. "I'm really sorry. That she went missing, I mean. When you walked in, I was so relieved, thinking you were her. I never expected to see her alive again." He winced and puffed out a breath through his lips. "Sorry. That's a shitty thing to say to her sister. But it's the truth."

Minutes later when they had returned to the car, Jonas waited to start the engine. "You okay?" he asked Lane.

She fiddled with her seat belt and then pushed back her hair. "I'm all right. I think I should be more upset that he said she's probably dead."

"You don't know her," he countered. "Or love her. Try not to beat up on yourself about that."

"She *is* my sister. Surely I should feel something more."

Palming away some dust from the dash, Jonas said, "What you're feeling or not feeling right now is normal. Once you meet Neta and get to know her, it'll be different. But right now, she's a complete stranger to you."

"How about you?" she asked. "You know her."

Jonas considered carefully before he spoke. "I thought I loved her once upon a time, but all those feelings died a long while back. I don't wish her any harm. I hope that we can track her down and help her. But other than that, I mostly feel bewildered by that whole conversation."

"Bewildered?"

Jonas nodded. "Neta didn't have a stop button. I've told you that. She was a pretty heavy drinker, even back then. Mostly wine, occasional mixed drinks. So I wasn't surprised to hear that she got pretty smashed that last night. What bothers me is the drug use. In college, she only took sleeping pills. Not to say that was okay, but it was all she ever did. No weed, no meth or coke. It's hard for me to picture her snorting white powder up her nose anywhere, let alone in a public place."

"If she was addicted to sleeping pills, maybe she got hooked on other substances later."

"Possibly," he conceded. "But I keep circling back to what Emma told us this morning. She was pretty adamant about Neta not being on drugs. She basically described a responsible, bright, cheerful waitress who never missed work, showed up on time, and never got the orders mixed up."

"Maybe Emma only thinks she can recognize a user," Lane suggested.

Jonas shook his head as he started the car. "She seems like a pretty sharp old gal to me. And I'll bet she's been running that diner for years. That means she's probably dealt with dozens upon dozens of employees. She picked up on the fact that Neta was drinking, but she seemed certain she wasn't doing anything else." At the highway, Jonas turned north to drive to another bar that he'd seen earlier. "And, according to that bartender, the night before Neta worked her last shift at the diner, she was combining cocaine with booze, so smashed that she fell off a barstool. How does someone get that messed up and show up for work early the next morning looking and acting fine?"

"Maybe the effects of cocaine are short-lived."

"Maybe. I've never tried the stuff. But I have experienced a booze hangover, and trust me, I wasn't bright and bushy-tailed the next morning. Something feels off to me."

"Something feels off to me as well," Lane said. "We went into the last bar to eat, and we got so sidetracked that we didn't order food. Now I'm starving."

He threw back his tawny head and barked with laughter.

Over the next three hours, Jonas and Lane visited every remaining bar in Plover Bay and then began hitting the higher-end restaurants. Two more bartenders recognized Lane, and both of them told pretty much the same story about Veneta that the first man had.

Feeling sad as they retreated to the car after leaving the last restaurant, Lane said, "Well." It was all she could think of to say.

Jonas put a hand on her shoulder. "Don't be discouraged or feel that we've failed."

"How can I not?" She glanced up at him. "We've gotten some information, yes, but it isn't nearly enough to help us find her."

"True," Jonas agreed. "But what we've learned can give us some direction."

Lane was so tired that she felt as if she'd put in eight hours of heavy labor. She wanted to find Veneta just as much as Jonas did, but she couldn't help but feel overwhelmed by the thought of a repeat performance. "Her life may be on the line. We didn't learn very much today, but I can't just turn my back on her."

"I know you're tired. It's been an emotionally draining day. And it's true that we've failed to learn very much. But from small acorns, big trees grow. We did gather some acorns today. We know, for instance, that Veneta no longer gravitates toward fancy restaurants, so we won't waste our time with them again. We also know that she frequented drinking establishments, all within fairly short distances of each other. So the next time you're recognized in a bar, we'll know to canvass all the bars near there. *And* we learned that she's mixing drugs with booze."

Lane gazed up at him with a heavy feeling in her chest. "We may not find her in time."

"Maybe not," he conceded. "But we'll know we did our best. As for today, I think we've done everything we came here to do. We can probably just head home in the morning." He started the car and flashed her a grin that gave her butterflies. "For tonight, I think we should reward ourselves by staying in that suite on the beach again."

"It was too expensive, Jonas. I'll be perfectly happy at a cheap motel."

He chuckled as he edged the vehicle toward the highway. "I can swing it for one more night. We're here. We put in a long day. What better way to end it than listening to the waves come in as we fall asleep? I *love* hearing the waves. Even better, I really enjoy a walk along the shoreline before calling it a night."

Since he was paying, Lane felt it was his decision to make. "Okay. It's a very nice inn. If you're sure you can afford it, I certainly won't complain."

He laughed and headed in that direction. This time, Lane went into the office with him while he booked their accommodations. Glimpsing the in-house restaurant at the end of a wide hallway, she left Jonas to fill out the paperwork while she went to check it out.

"It's a really classy restaurant," she told Jonas minutes later as they took a luggage cart out to the car. "We should find another seaside diner tonight. Eating here might cost an arm and a leg."

"The gal at the desk recommended a French restaurant a few miles south of here. She says it's fabulous."

"Sounds expensive," she countered.

Jonas rolled his eyes. "Would you stop? Where's your sense of adventure?"

"Trapped inside my wallet," she popped back.

He laughed and put their suitcases on the cart. "Why are we using this monster? I could just carry our luggage to the suite."

"When in Rome . . ." She cast him a sidelong glance. "We don't want to look like a couple of country bumpkins."

"Why not? I *am* a country bumpkin."

Helping him pull the trolley behind them, Lane said, "A well-educated bumpkin. You handled yourself well today, asking all the right questions and getting people to open up. I was impressed."

"Yeah, well, I watch a lot of cop movies."

Lane was delighted when they entered the suite. "Oh, wow! We're a lot closer to the water in this unit." She stepped over to the French doors to admire the view. "I think we could sit on the edge of the deck and let the waves tickle our toes."

Jonas moved in behind her to look out over her shoulder. And in that moment, she felt as if his near-ness electrified every cell in her body. The sexual attraction was suddenly so strong that Lane closed her eyes and silently scolded herself for even entertaining the thoughts she was having. And she knew that it would be complete madness to act upon them. Jonas had once believed himself to be in love with a woman who looked exactly like her, for one thing. Even if he was experiencing the same feelings she was, how could she know for sure he wasn't confusing her with Veneta?

Despite her warnings to herself to tread cautiously, Lane found herself completely captivated by him when they reached the restaurant and were seated near an ocean-view window. Their table looked like a work of art, draped in crisp white linen, appointed with clev-erly folded burgundy napkins, and boasting a blown-glass candleholder at its center that was shaped like a dolphin jumping over the water.

"Oh, Jonas!" she whispered as the maître d' walked away. "This place is gorgeous."

He had already opened his menu. "Uh-oh."

"What? Is it frightfully expensive?"

He angled her a loaded look. "The prices are the only thing I can read."

Lane opened her own menu to see what he meant and let loose with a giggle. The entire list of offerings was in French. "We can wing it," she assured him. "Where's your sense of adventure?"

"In my wallet."

Lane perused the menu a moment longer. "In small print under each French heading, they've written a description in English. We've got this!"

Jonas ordered a bottle of French red wine that was one of the best Lane had ever tasted. After enjoying an escargot appetizer, they both chose *soupe à l'oignon* as a starter. It was fabulous, made with caramelized onions and beef stock with crunchy chunks of French bread and melted gruyere cheese on top. Lane ate only half of hers in order to save room for her main course, duck confit. Jonas settled on the beef bourguignon, and they opted to divide a creamy leek *flamiche*, a puff pastry with filling that was divine.

"Dessert?" Jonas asked as their table was cleared away.

Lane groaned. "I honestly don't think I can take another bite."

"Ah, come on," he urged. "We could share one."

Lane hated to discourage him from enjoying a bit of sweetness after his meal, so she agreed with a dip of her chin. Jonas chose *café liégeois*, a concoction layered with coffee, ice cream, chocolate, and cream that looked so tempting she couldn't resist dipping into the parfait glass with her long-handled spoon. When she moaned while savoring the first bite, Jonas chuckled. After she settled back, he finished the dessert.

"I'm amazed at how much food you can put away," she commented with a smile.

"I was born with one hollow leg," he retorted, his hazel eyes twinkling with mischief. "At least that's what my mother always says. My dad was always a big eater. Now that he's older, not so much, but he still has a healthy appetite."

Studying him, Lane wondered what it was about Jonas that made her feel so relaxed while in his company. She guessed it was because he was so laid back himself that his attitude rubbed off on her.

After polishing off the *café liégeois*, he glanced out the window. "It's getting late. We need to head back to the inn. If you don't mind, I'd like to sit on our deck and watch the sunset."

"I won't mind at all. It'll be beautiful."

It was a balmy evening, so Jonas rolled down the front windows of the car as they drove. Lane enjoyed the smells of the ocean and having the wind in her hair. It was the perfect way to end a long and emotionally draining day.

Once back in their suite, Lane changed into sweatpants, a T-shirt, and a pair of sandals that she could kick off if Jonas wanted to take a walk on the beach later. She joined him on the deck, where he was stretched out on one of the two lounges. She settled on a chair, afraid she might grow drowsy if she got too comfortable.

His gaze fixed on the horizon, which was already streaked with deepening hues of red and gold, he asked, "You got your phone handy for pics? It's going to be a stunner."

She patted her pants pocket. "Yep. I'm a lousy photographer, though."

She joined him in watching the golden orb of the sun inch closer to the water, and Jonas proved to be right; it was a spectacular sunset. She snapped several pictures and then showed them to him.

"They're beautiful," he said. "You're not lousy at it."

"Anyone can take a decent photo with a subject like that. It's gorgeous from every angle."

He sprang to his feet and drew her up from the chair. "Care to join me for a walk?"

"I'd love to. But I think I'll grab my shawl first. Now that the sun has gone down, there's a nip in the air."

"Good idea."

They each went to their rooms and emerged into the common area a moment later pulling on their respective garments. After they stepped back out onto the deck, Jonas took hold of her hand, and she was mildly alarmed by how right that felt. His grip was strong but not punishing, and the heat of his touch, magnified by the coolness of the breeze, sent tingles of awareness up her arm. Glancing at him, she wondered what was happening between them.

He caught her looking at him and smiled slightly. "Are you feeling the same way I am?"

If another man had asked Lane that question, she might have played dumb, but with Jonas, she just couldn't. Sidestepping the slide of an incoming wave, she pressed closer to him. "I'd be lying if I said I wasn't."

He nodded and sighed. "My pragmatic side is warning me that this is crazy, but another part of me wonders if meeting you isn't the best thing that's ever happened to me." Then he added, "It's funny, actually. When Veneta broke up with me, she did it in a letter, what I now think of as my Dear Jonas letter. She said that I'd fallen in love with the wrong part of her—the nicer part of her. She also said she couldn't picture herself being happy with someone as controlled and levelheaded as I was. She needed to take risks, and I wasn't a risk taker. She wanted to be crazy sometimes, and I lacked spontaneity. Looking back on it now, I don't know why I was hung up on a woman who was so wrong for me. I guess sometimes we fall in love with what we believe someone to be and not with who they really are. If I had truly loved her, I'd still have feelings for her, and I don't."

Lane gently squeezed his fingers to let him know she was listening and understood how he felt. "There's an attraction building between us. I won't deny that. But at the same time, I don't think it's wise for either of us to be feeling this way." She wanted to ask if he'd been in another relationship since being with Veneta, but she couldn't think how to phrase the question without seeming nosy. "Your memories of Veneta could be messing with your head."

He laughed. Then he sobered. "Trust me, Lane. I'm not the least bit confused. If anything, the more I'm around you, the more I realize how different you are from her."

Having said what she felt needed to be said, Lane decided to change the subject. "My mind has been heavy with thoughts of her all day, but I'm ready to forget about her for now so I can enjoy what's left of the evening."

"I'll second that," he said. "It's an evening that's too beautiful to waste, and it isn't as if there's anything more we can do to find her, not tonight."

Farther along the shore, they came upon a driftwood log that provided them with comfortable seats. They sat only inches apart, their arms almost touching, and as if by mutual consent, they both gazed in silence at the ocean. In the moonlight, the swell of each wave shimmered like molten silver. A cool breeze toyed with her hair. Beneath her bare feet, the gritty sand still felt warm.

"This is perfect," she mused aloud.

"It sure is." He turned to look at her, his gaze moving slowly over her face. "But, at risk of appearing to be confused, not even this gorgeous evening is as perfect as you are."

Lane rolled her eyes. "I'm not perfect, Jonas. Far from it."

"I didn't mean in the broad sense, only that right now, in this moment, I can't think of a single other person I'd rather be with."

"Aw, thank you," she said with notes of amusement and levity, hoping to lighten the mood.

"I'm serious," he said. "You're an amazing lady, Lane Driscoll. I know how difficult it was for you today. I felt you tense up every time we entered a new building, not knowing if someone inside would think you were Veneta or how it might play out. She obviously made some enemies along the way. If we'd encountered the wrong person, someone who had it in for her, it could have gotten ugly."

Lane had worried about that possibility more times that day than she cared to admit. "It was stressful," she admitted. "But I wasn't really scared or anything. I knew you would step in if things went south—that you'd protect me."

Even with only the light of the moon playing over his face, she saw his expression grow pensive. "Thank you for the vote of confidence, but how could you know for sure that I'd protect you?"

She couldn't help but smile. "Because that's just who you are. Or who I think you are, anyway." And even though she knew it was unwise, she added, "You're not boring, Jonas. Not at all. You're solid and steadfast. You make a woman feel safe."

His firm mouth tipped into a reciprocal grin. "Ah, but some women find safe guys boring. They prefer to walk on the edge. An unpredictable guy is more exciting."

"Women who find safe guys boring must be a few cards shy of a full deck. Romantic relationships are unpredictable enough without someone being a loose cannon."

"The voice of experience?" he asked.

She braced her hands on the log and leaned slightly forward. "Yes, only I was the loose cannon each time, not the other way around."

"I hear a story coming."

She groaned. "It's not a very interesting story, I'm afraid. Have you ever heard of a woman who won't stay the night at a guy's house because she snores?"

He chuckled. "Where did that come from?"

"Trust me, there are women out there who are horribly embarrassed about their snoring and believe they might lose some guy they really like if he finds out. So they avoid situations where they might fall asleep and snore."

"You snore?"

It was her turn to laugh. "No, thank goodness. At least I don't think I do. But my problem was far worse. I never knew when I might hear the voice, and when I did, I was frightened, because hearing it made me believe I was insane. I needed to be alone. Had to hide it. And that was when I was wide awake. It was always there in the back of my mind that I might fall asleep and dream, which would have been even worse."

He gave her a long study. "Are you trying to tell me that you've never spent the night with a man?"

Lane narrowed her eyes at him. "I'm trying to tell you that I pretty much avoided relationships. I gave it a whirl twice. Both times I chickened out before things began to get serious, because I knew it all might blow up in my face if and when the truth came out."

"You never could trust even one guy enough to believe he would accept you for who you are?"

"I hear voices, Jonas. You're the first person I've ever told who didn't immediately write me off as being nuts. Even my parents believe I'm an emotional basket case. They love me anyway, but still. And that's how it's been for as far back as I can remember, always having to hide that side of myself, many times even from my mom and dad. I hated seeing the pain and worry I caused them. Hated making them feel sad. Hated when they began to harp at me to get more counseling. They always paid for me to go, it never helped me, and I knew they couldn't really afford it."

"Ah. There's a mystery solved. Now I know why you worry so much about the cost of things when I'm paying the bill."

Lane stared at him. "Until now, I never made that connection, but I suppose you could be right. Even as a young teen, I knew my seeing a counselor was hurting my parents financially. So eventually I began hiding it when I heard the voice."

He sighed and resumed gazing out at the ocean. "I'm so sorry you had to go through that."

"Me, too. But it is what it is. People who hear little

voices in their heads are considered to be crazy. A schizo. I never even told my friends. I was afraid to."

"You aren't crazy, Lane. I hope you realize that now."

She nodded. "Yes. For the first time in my life, I'm starting to believe I'm not nuts."

She joined him in admiring the ocean, which stretched like an undulating silver blanket as far as the eye could see. After a long period of silence, Jonas turned toward her again, his hazel eyes shimmering in the faint light.

"You've never been with a man, have you?"

"Once, kind of, sort of."

"Kind of? Sort of?"

"He was drunk. I didn't mention it was my first time. He penetrated and realized. Then he swore at me and passed out. For me, it was—well, I'll just say it was far less than enjoyable and wasn't an experience I cared to repeat. So I didn't."

He studied the craggy rock off to their left, watching as the waves crashed against it and spouted upward. "Talk about rotten luck."

She laughed. "My luck is like that of a bald man winning a comb as a prize."

He laughed and bumped his shoulder against hers. "Good one."

As they walked back to the inn, Lane half expected Jonas to ask more questions about her one time in the sack with a guy. But, Jonas being Jonas, he didn't. As they neared their small deck, he rested his hand over the back of her neck, his palm warm and firm above her shawl, his fingertips lightly caressing her skin. His touch so delighted her that she almost shivered.

Once they were inside with the French doors closed behind them, he withdrew his hand and stepped away from her. "I'll lock up. You can go ahead to bed if you like."

Even as keyed-up as she was, Lane couldn't deny that she was tired. "I think I'll do just that." She paused outside her bedroom door. "Thank you for all you did today. I couldn't have done it without you being there for moral support."

"No problem. I was happy to help."

Lane stepped inside her suite, and for the second night in a row, she didn't lock the door.

Thirsty, so thirsty. Lane tried to work her mouth, but her tongue was so dry that it was stuck to her teeth. When she swallowed, her throat felt as if it had been painted with craft glue. If he doesn't bring me water soon, I'm going to die. *Feeling as if she couldn't breathe, she struggled to sit up and couldn't. Her hands were bound behind her back. She stared into the blackness that surrounded her, straining to see something, to see anything, but she couldn't.*

Then she heard footsteps. It was him, coming toward the room. Every muscle in her body knotted with tension. Would he kill her this time? She almost hoped he would. Then, at least, this would be over. She heard the doorknob rattle. The next instant, bright light flared, stabbing into her eyes like icepicks. She blinked. Tried to clear her vision. Slowly, the man who stood over her came into focus. Tall, rail thin, hair hanging over his shoulders in oily ropes. Above his scraggly beard, his sunken cheeks were pockmarked from repeated bouts of meth rash. As he bent over her, the rank smell of his body made her nostrils burn.

He grasped her by the shoulders and drew her to a sitting position. "I'm gonna untie your hands so you can eat and drink. But fair warning. You try anything, and I'll kill you." He laughed softly. "Gonna happen soon anyway. Only reason the boss hasn't already offed you is because of that broad I saw that looks just like you. That's got him all nerved up. He's afraid she knows stuff—that you told her everything. He's trying to find her. Needs to get rid of you both." He laughed softly. "That'll be my job. I'm good at making problems disappear."

Lane felt the ropes fall away from her wrists. The instant her blood could move freely again, her hands exploded with pain. She gasped. Tried to move her arms. They hung from her shoulders at a backward angle like dead weights. The man set a plate on her lap and held out a glass of water. She stared at the clear liquid, yearning for it, needing it, imagining how wonderful it would be to moisten her mouth. But she didn't have the strength to move her arms.

"Don't play games with me, bitch," the man warned. "I always win. You know that."

"You tied my hands too tight." Her voice was so hoarse that it resonated through her head like a frog croaking. "I can't make my arms work."

"Bullshit," he said with a hiss. "Drink it, or I'll pour it down your throat."

He caught her chin in his hand, tipped her head back, and shoved the glass against her lips. Water slopped into her mouth. She tried to swallow, but her throat felt paralyzed. She choked. Began to cough. He shoved her head farther back and sloshed more water into her mouth. It went down her windpipe, burned in her lungs. She felt like she was drowning.

Lane jerked awake with a gasp and sat straight up in bed, one hand clamped over the base of her throat.

Her shoulders jerked convulsively. She struggled for breath. *Only a dream. I'm not really choking.* But she felt as if she were, and the line between dream and reality no longer existed.

Veneta. Always before, Lane had questioned her own sanity after dreaming of her, but now that feeling had vanished. She was afraid for Veneta, who was obviously in danger, but she was no longer worried about herself.

Chapter Eight

Knowing she wouldn't be able to just go back to sleep, Lane drew a sweatshirt on over her sleepwear and left the bedroom. Jonas had left a floor lamp on dim to serve as a night-light. She tiptoed to the French doors and silently let herself out onto the deck, bypassing the lounges to sit on the step that led down to the beach. The cool ocean breeze penetrated her pajama bottoms, slightly chilling her skin. In order to feel warmer, she looped her arms around her bent knees.

Then, and only then, did she allow herself to dwell on the nightmare that had awakened her. Prior to the man's arrival, the room had been so dark that she could see nothing. The lack of natural light told her that Veneta was still being held in the same house with the boarded-up window. That was good news. *Kind of, sort of.* At least Lane knew her sister hadn't been moved to a different location. The problem was that Lane had no idea where that boarded-up house was. Somewhere in or near Maple Leaf, but city sprawl had expanded the residential areas to nearly three times the size of what had existed a few years ago. Searching for Veneta would be like looking for a needle in shag carpeting.

The planks beneath Lane's buttocks suddenly began undulating behind her, as if giving under someone else's weight. She threw a nervous look over her shoulder and recognized Jonas' lofty silhouette against the star-studded night sky.

"You okay?" he asked in a low voice.

She nodded and scooted over to make room for him to sit beside her. "I'm good. Just another Veneta dream." She sighed. "The dream was awful. I don't mean it wasn't. But I'm relieved to know she's still alive."

He lowered himself onto the step beside her. He'd thrown on a jacket to shield himself from the night air. "That is a big relief. I was starting to worry, too. Such a long silence wasn't a good sign."

Lane turned to look at him. He sat with his arms braced on his bent knees, his broad shoulders hunched slightly forward. In the moonlight, his honey-gold hair shimmered as the breeze ruffled the strands. "No, it really wasn't a good sign. So for the very first time, I actually felt glad about getting my sleep interrupted."

"Did you learn anything from it?"

Lane shrugged. "I'm not sure, but this was the first time I could hold myself apart from it and not feel so frightened. Staying calmer helped me to pick up on stuff I might have otherwise missed."

"Such as?"

"Well, for one thing, I think she's dangerously dehydrated. During the first part of the dream, she was desperate for a drink of water. Her mouth was bone dry, and so was her throat. Later in the dream, she was so weak that she couldn't move her arms to take the glass of water the man brought to her."

"So you think time is running out."

Lane's heart squeezed. "Yes, I'm afraid it is. If she doesn't start getting more food and water, she'll be dead before we can find her."

Jonas went quiet and then asked, "What else did you pick up on?"

"That they're actively looking for me."

"What?"

"I know," she said with a humorless laugh. "On the surface, it makes no sense. But during the dream, the man said they're afraid Veneta has told me everything she knows. From the start, I couldn't figure out why they were after me. Now it makes more sense. We look exactly alike, so they've probably deduced that we're identical twins and must be assuming that we know each other. Veneta has knowledge of something that they don't want to get out. Apparently it would mean big trouble for them—whoever they are. In their eyes, I'm a loose end."

Jonas went back to gazing out at the ocean. "Which means you're in danger even though you don't actually know anything."

Lane shivered and hugged her sweatshirt closer around her torso. "Yes—if they can find me. I thought it was complete overkill when my father insisted that I leave town. But he made the right call. If I had stayed in Maple Leaf, I might be dead by now—or being held in the same house with Veneta."

Jonas looped an arm around her shoulders. "Not getting amorous," he said. "You're cold. Just trying to warm you up."

She leaned closer, relishing the heat that radiated from his body. "Why are they holding her? I'm certain they intend to kill her, so why would they wait?"

"Good question." Jonas swept his hand up and down her arm. "Given what we learned from the bartenders, I'm assuming they're drug runners. Maybe they're holding off because they believe you're in the know and can rat them out. Until they have you in their custody, you could go to the police and accuse them of murder. If they can find you and shut you up, they must think they can get away with getting rid of you both." He tightened his arm around her and gave her a gentle jostle. "I need to get you back inside. You're shivering from head to toe."

They stood simultaneously and hurried back to their suite. After securing the French doors, Jonas turned a questioning gaze on Lane. "Do you think you can sleep now? If not, I don't mind staying up to keep you company."

"Thank you for the offer, but now that I've had time to calm down, I realize how tired I still am. I'll be miserable company tomorrow during the drive home if I don't get some more rest."

He drew off the jacket and draped it over the arm of an easy chair. "I could do with catching a few more Z's myself."

The following morning, Lane awakened early and found Jonas in the kitchenette again, already making coffee. This morning, he wore a pair of jeans with a blue plaid shirt tucked into the belted waistband, and the beachy espadrilles had been replaced by western boots.

"You've dressed to return inland," she observed.

"Good morning to you, too," he retorted with a smile. "And, yes, thought I might as well." He gave her a quick once-over. "You look nice. That's a pretty dress."

Lane glanced down at the burnt orange and brown floral print that she wore. It was vintage Bohemian with silky layers that drifted gracefully when she moved. She'd brought along a rust-colored shawl to go with it. "It's almost October. Time for fall colors."

"Actually, today is October fourth."

"It is?" Lane frowned. "How did that happen?"

He chuckled. "You were pretty stressed out last week. Maybe you just lost track of the days."

Lane sat at the small bar and allowed him to give her the first cup of coffee while he made another for himself. She smiled when she tasted hers. He had added one packet of sugar, just the way she liked it. *He'll make some woman a fabulous husband*, she decided and then immediately wanted to kick herself for allowing the thought into her head. Jonas was a great guy, but even though she was attracted to him, she didn't think it was wise to spin any romantic fantasies yet.

"Penny for your thoughts," he said, catching her by surprise.

"Oh, nothing important. My thoughts at the moment aren't worth a cent." She glanced at her phone. "It's not even seven. Shall we check out and head over the pass to get home early?"

He winked at her over the top of his mug as he took a first sip of coffee. "I'm not in any hurry. Are you?"

Lane thought for a moment. "I need to do a load of laundry tonight so I have clothing for work tomorrow, but that's no big deal. Why?"

He took another swallow of coffee. "It's just that I rarely get over to the coast, and I was toying with the idea of driving south on 101. It'd mean more driving to get home. But I've got a friend—an old college buddy named Jeff—who's now a cop. It might be interesting to get his take on this whole mess. Also, since he works on the coast, maybe he's heard scuttle from other officers that hasn't been publicized."

The thought of meeting one of Jonas' friends made

Lane feel a bit nervous. She wasn't sure why. And then it came to her. "Does he know Veneta?"

"He was around when she and I were dating. I don't think he particularly cared for her, to be honest. I don't think most of my good friends did."

"Was she *that* bad?"

"It wasn't that." He took another pull from his coffee mug. "She wasn't bad. It was more that we just weren't good together, and my friends saw that right away." He set down his cup and lifted his hands in feigned bewilderment. "Like I said, I had blinders on. So did Veneta, I guess. Only she came to her senses before I did."

The inn had supplied them with a fruit bowl, and Lane grabbed a banana. She wasn't really hungry yet. She just wanted something to do with her hands. "So, you think this Jeff might have heard something to help us pinpoint where Veneta is?"

"I'm hoping." He shrugged his shoulders. "If not, it won't be a complete waste of our time. It's a beautiful drive, which may turn out to be our lull before the storm."

Lane chewed a bite of fruit and swallowed. "Meaning?"

"When I get back to Mystic Creek, I'll be searching the Internet for any clues I can find on the events in Veneta's life that may have gotten her mixed up with bad actors. If I find something, we'll need to move quickly. If she's already dehydrated and malnourished, the clock is ticking."

"We could do that right now instead of visiting Jeff. This place has Wi-Fi, and we needn't check out until eleven."

Jonas shook his head. "I honestly believe that picking Jeff's brain is more important. We should leave the

Internet search for later. Maybe you can do a little sleuthing on your phone during the drive."

Lane couldn't argue the point. After the dream last night, she felt the same sense of urgency that Jonas apparently did, and it was entirely possible that his friend might know something that could help them. "Okay. I'm game. Have you spoken with Jeff to make sure he'll be available?"

"No. I wanted to check with you first. But I can call him right now."

Listening to Jonas' side of the conversation with half an ear, Lane quickly finished eating the banana and then went to her bedchamber to make sure she had packed everything and was ready to leave. When she emerged a moment later with her suitcase in tow, Jonas already had his luggage sitting near the interior exit door, where all the check-out information was displayed.

"Jeff has the day off," he informed her. "He's got a new girlfriend and is eager for me to meet her. And he's looking forward to meeting my lady friend." He shrugged. "I saw no point in feeding him any details. Time enough for that when we get there."

Lane guessed it was silly, but the thought of having another stranger mistake her for Veneta rattled her nerves.

Practically everyone who lived in Oregon occasionally drove along Highway 101 to enjoy the beautiful coastline, but Lane hadn't been on that scenic route for at least five years and her memories had faded. She thoroughly appreciated all the gorgeous views, marveled over the many rock formations, and managed to relax in a way she hadn't yesterday. Unfortunately, her attempt to search for information about Veneta online went badly, because her phone kept losing its signal.

"The cell service along this highway is strong one second and gone the next," she complained.

"No worries. I'm a whiz at Internet searches, and it can wait until we get home."

Jeff, a Coos County sheriff's deputy, lived on the outskirts of Bandon, a small coastal town with a spectacular golf course, according to Jonas. Jeff lived in a less opulent neighborhood, but it was a nice area, nevertheless, with ranch-style ramblers on large lots with plenty of yard space. Jeff's home was lovely, with gray plank siding and forest-green trim that had weathered well. In the driveway, a county police vehicle was parked abreast of a white Nissan.

"I can't wait to see him," Jonas said as they got out of the car. "In college, you make a lot of friends. You know? But only a few of them are special friends, the kind that you can picture yourself hanging out with into old age. For me, Jeff Stanton is one of the latter." He grasped Lane's elbow to guide her along the walkway to the covered front porch. "I never had to worry when I went out with him. One of us always kept a clear head." He leaned forward to ring the doorbell. "He wasn't one to get into fights. Before going anywhere, we knew which one of us would be the DD. It worked for us."

Lane was about to respond when the door opened. Jeff, tall and broad-shouldered like Jonas, filled the doorway. He wore a gray sweatshirt over faded blue jeans. A shock of curly black hair fell lazily over his forehead. His brown eyes lit with happiness at seeing Jonas and then went deadpan when he looked at Lane.

"Veneta." He said the name in a flat, give-nothing-away tone. "Good to see you. Jonas didn't mention that—oh, never mind. What am I thinking? Come in, come in."

"This isn't Veneta," Jonas quickly informed him. "Lane, may I present Jeff Stanton. Jeff, this is Lane Driscoll, Veneta's identical twin. Or so we believe."

Jeff nodded. "I can see why." He smiled at Lane. "Wow. I'd swear it was Veneta standing there. Good to meet you."

"The same, I'm sure." Lane had a strong urge to flee back to the car. "Thank you for having us over with so little warning."

Jeff gestured them into the entryway and then closed the door. "I've got the day off." He started to shake hands with Jonas, but then grabbed him in a guy hug instead, which ended almost as quickly as it began. "Man, it's good to see you."

He led them into a comfortably appointed living room, with a tan, overstuffed recliner sectional creating an arc opposite a sixty-inch flat-screen television hanging on the wall. Two separate recliners flanked each end of the sectional to create a comfortable conversation area. Lane and Jonas sat next to each other on the larger piece of furniture. Jeff went to the kitchen to grab a few beers, which he set on a rectangular oak coffee table.

"Lane, do you like yours in a glass?"

She did, but she chose not to tax him with another trip to the kitchen. "From the can will suit me just fine."

The snap and spew of cans being popped open filled the room. Jeff sat forward on a recliner, elbows braced on his knees, his beer cupped in his hands. After giving Lane a long study, he said, "You really aren't Veneta. You look exactly like her, but you're totally different in personality."

Lane forced a laugh. "You can tell that in so short a time?"

Jeff nodded. "Oh, yeah. She rarely drank beer and never from a can. With her, it was mostly wine. She was also—how do I put this?—louder. Loud voice, loud laugh. Always the life of the party even when there was no party."

"Jonas mentioned that you didn't care for her."

He waved a hand back and forth as if he were cleaning a blackboard. "No, no. I liked Veneta just fine. She's a nice person. Just not right for Jonas." He glanced at his friend. "I may have been more critical of her to Jonas than I should've been, but it was nothing personal. I was just trying to make him see what I saw, namely that she was totally wrong for him."

Jonas winked at her and smiled, as if to say, *This story must sound familiar.*

"I saw that," Jeff teased with a grin. "I'm guessing you've already told her everything I just said."

"Pretty much," Jonas admitted.

"I'm also guessing you're here because Veneta has gone missing. When I saw Lane, I thought she had resurfaced, but I was guessing wrong, apparently."

Jonas nodded. "That isn't to say I wouldn't have dropped by anyway, just to see you. But Lane and I came to the coast searching for clues, basically. We'd very much like to find Veneta before it's too late."

Jeff's smile melted away into a concerned expression. "She's been missing almost two weeks."

"Over two weeks, actually," Jonas corrected. "And if you're about to tell me she may already be dead, we know she's still alive."

Jonas went on to fill Jeff in on everything, including Lane's lifelong telepathic communication with her sister.

"Seriously?" Jeff looked incredulous. "You've heard her voice and had nightmares all your life? I find that hard to believe."

"Most people do," Lane replied. "Jonas is the only person who didn't automatically assume I was nuts."

"Mostly because, like you, I noticed how different Lane's personality is from Veneta's," Jonas interjected. "And also because I've always been fascinated by the possibility that some identical twins may be so alike genetically that they can actually pick up vibes from each other even when they're separated by great distances."

Jeff took another sip of beer and nodded. "I watched a documentary several months ago—heck, maybe even over a year ago—about identical twins who discovered each other and met years after they were separated."

Jonas chuckled. "You and half the country. I watched that, too, and it was pretty amazing how alike those twins were, even though they'd never met until they were middle-age adults."

"It sure blew my mind," Jeff agreed. "There were two men that really boggled my brain. Older, settled into good marriages, and—"

Jonas interrupted with, "They had wives with the same first name. Kids with the same first names. Wore their hair the same. Dressed the same."

"You *did* watch it," Jeff affirmed.

"I did, and at the time, it was mostly for the entertainment aspect. But I have done a lot of reading about the possibility of a telepathic—or maybe I should call it a genetic—link between identical twins. Some scientific researchers adamantly deny there's any possibility of it. Others argue that too many things indicate that there *is* a strong possibility. Heck, some researchers even believe some fraternal twins may have an uncanny form of telepathic communication going on. And I've counseled two different sets of identical twins whose experiences led me to believe it does occur, and we just haven't proven it yet."

"My friend Jonas, the imaginative shrink." Jeff made a token toast to Jonas by lifting the beer can. "Now I remember why I enjoyed hanging with you, man. When a conversation lagged, you always had something intriguing and mind-boggling to say." He glanced at Lane. "None of what you guys have told me could have been easy for you, Lane. You must have thought you were nuts half the time."

Tears burned at the backs of Lane's eyes, because Jeff seemed to believe her story. *Another person who doesn't think I'm certifiably insane.* For as far back as she could remember, she'd wished for just one person to take her at her word. Now, suddenly, she seemed to have two individuals who didn't think she was wacko.

"I didn't just *think* I was nuts, Jeff. I *knew* I was." Lane stared into the hole left behind by the pull tab on the top of her drink can. "I spent a lot of my life trying not to get sick again—meaning I didn't want to be crazy again. I tried really hard to block the voice out. To not hear it. Sometimes, weeks or even months would go by without any disturbances inside my head. I'd think I was finally well. And then, *bang*, I was a basket case again."

Looking pensive, Jeff nodded. "I can't begin to imagine what that must have been like, how you must have felt." He gestured with his empty hand. "Everybody knows people who hear voices are crazy. Right?

I would be pretty worried and shaken up if I all of a sudden started hearing things."

Lane nodded. "The day I met Jonas, I was at my wit's end. The voice was distracting me during the day, and the dreams wouldn't let me sleep at night. So I called him for an appointment."

"Which didn't go well," Jonas inserted with a laugh. "When she walked in, I thought she was Veneta. Things got a little ugly before they got better."

"He thought I was Veneta and pretending to be someone else just to mess with his head," Lane added.

Jeff let loose with a deep, rumbling laugh. Just then, his front door opened, and a young woman with wind-blown blond hair and an armload of grocery bags stepped into the entry. "Oops! I hoped I'd get back before you guys got here."

Everyone in the living room stood for introductions, which made the blonde smile and shake her head. "Oh, no. I'm not going through all the niceties when I'm holding what feels like a hundred pounds in my arms."

Both Jeff and Jonas hurried forward to assist her and collided with such force that they almost knocked each other off their feet. Then they both burst out laughing. While the two men caught their balance, Lane circled them to relieve the other woman of two grocery bags.

"I'm Carla," the blonde called over her shoulder as she led the way to the kitchen. "Just put everything here," she said, indicating a long island countertop. "Mostly it's for you guys anyway." She flashed a saucy smile. "Jeff wanted snacks. So he tidied the house while I went shopping. Seeing Jonas is a big deal to him. Chips and dip are his idea of putting on the dog."

Lane couldn't help but like Carla. There was no pre-tense with her, no posing or fluttering of her hands to show off her gorgeous fingernails, which were ruby-slipper red. She quickly drew items from the bags. Lane glimpsed a plastic tray of fresh vegetables and dip. Bags of chips. Assorted dips. A sausage and cheese platter with dividers and a clear plastic lid.

"My goodness! You got way more than chips and dip!" Lane exclaimed.

"Yeah. I hope you like to nibble." Carla raised a penciled eyebrow. "I didn't get your name."

"Lane Driscoll."

Just then, the guys walked in. Jeff gravitated toward the island like metal shavings would to a magnet, and Jonas was right on his heels. Within moments, all four of them were sitting on barstools with plates in front of them, which quickly became laden with snack items. Lane couldn't remember when, if ever, she'd felt so at ease with people who were still all but strangers to her. Jeff was as unpretentious as Carla was, and between the two of them, they made Lane feel as if she'd known them for years.

Carla was a cosmetologist licensed to do both hair and nails, but she confessed that she preferred doing nail art. "It allows me to be creative," she explained. "An art form of sorts. After Jeff and I get married and pool our incomes, I may quit doing hair altogether."

Jeff tucked a piece of broccoli inside his cheek to say, "Everyone should be able to love their job, so I'm all in on that." He met Carla's gaze and winked at her. "Besides, married guys say, 'When mama ain't happy, nobody's happy.' So I'll really, *really* want my wife to be happy."

Carla giggled and selected some cheese from a tray. "Happy or not, I'll still have to fly on my witch's broom once a month to keep my pilot's license current."

After several minutes of getting-acquainted chit-chat, Jeff steered the conversation back to Lane's revelation about the telepathic connection she might have with her identical twin.

"Oh, my *God*!" Carla cried, feigning a shiver. "I love to hear about stuff like that. It always gives me goose bumps." She took a sip of canned soda. "My friend has an identical twin. Some of the stuff that's happened with them over the years is downright spooky."

Intrigued, Lane asked, "Like what?"

"Well, when my friend got pregnant, she held off on telling anyone in her family until she was safely through the first trimester. When she finally called her twin, who wasn't married, the sister burst into tears and said she thought she might be pregnant, too. She'd missed two periods and had felt queasy in the mornings. But every time she went to buy a home-testing kit, she chickened out at the last minute. She wasn't certain her boyfriend would be supportive, so she basically decided to ignore the situation and hope it would go away. My friend insisted that her twin get tested, so the twin went to town, bought a test, and stayed on the phone with my friend while she waited for the results. It was negative, and that night, the twin finally got her period. They decided it was a case of Couvade syndrome of sorts, with the other twin experiencing the symptoms of pregnancy even though she wasn't actually pregnant."

Jonas thumped the counter with his fist. "You *see*?" He directed the words at Lane. "Explain *that*. The other twin didn't even know Carla's friend was pregnant! That's definitely a sign of telepathic communication or a genetic link or *something*."

Lane laughed and shook her head. "You no longer need to convince me, Jonas."

"I know, but still. Even now, I think you worry that you're losing it. You haven't totally eliminated your doubts."

Lane gestured with a piece of celery. "True. But I don't agonize for hours about it now. I just remind myself that she exists and the voice I'm hearing may be real."

The conversation became a volley of comments, going back and forth, ending with Jeff saying, "This is really interesting stuff." He glanced at Jonas. "And here I always thought psychology was boring."

Jonas grinned. "I'm glad it's of interest to you, because I'm really hoping that you'll do some research to see if you can dig anything up that may help us find Veneta. As a law officer, you have better access to online files. Right? Like, for instance, Veneta's arrest records. I found evidence that she'd been charged with a DUI up in Plover Bay, but only a mention. I sure would like to see the details—like maybe the arresting officer's report."

"Your brother Barney's a cop," Jeff said. "Not to say I wouldn't be happy to help. I'm just wondering why you haven't asked him to do it."

Jonas swallowed a bite of food and said, "I'm sure Barney would be glad to help, too. But he doesn't live and work on the coast. You do, and you'll have kept abreast of the news over here. Maybe remember things. For instance, a bartender in Plover Bay told us that Veneta said someone murdered her best friends. I got the impression that Veneta was bent on avenging the friends' deaths. Do you recall anything like that over—

hmm—let's say over the last three years? A young woman or women dying? Possibly a suspicion of foul play? Surely something like that would be all over the news."

"How do you know Veneta's best friend wasn't a guy?" Carla asked.

"Good point," Jonas conceded. "My first thought was another woman, though. Most of the time, don't women reserve the title of *best friend* for someone of the same gender?"

"Mostly," Carla agreed. "But not always."

Jeff's forehead pleated into a pensive frown. "I'll give it some thought and see if anything comes to me. Off the top of my head, no suspicious deaths are coming to mind."

"I've got it!" Carla cried. "Julia Foxglove. No, wait. Jillian. Her first name was Jillian. She died of a drug overdose, and the circumstances were suspicious. That happened a couple of years back in Plover Bay. A heap of heroin was found in her bloodstream. The coroner found the needle track on her arm. But officers at the crime scene were unconvinced that her death was accidental."

Jeff snapped his fingers. "You're right. I remember that now. They found her body in her car, way to hell and gone out in the woods. The crime scene officers saw no sign of a struggle. On the surface, it looked like an unintentional OD. Only there was no drug paraphernalia anywhere in the vehicle, and the coroner said it would have been virtually impossible for her to have driven the car that far out into a forest with that much heroin in her system. Fed directly into a vein, she would have felt the effects within seven to eight seconds, according to him. No way could she have driven that far."

Lane said, "Maybe she didn't shoot herself up until she was already out in the woods somewhere, and she tossed all the paraphernalia out the window."

"The cops thought of that," Carla inserted. "They got volunteers to help them search all along the roads she drove in on, but they found nothing."

Jeff held up a finger. "And there were other tire tracks near her car, which was parked in a clearing at the end of the road. Investigators speculated that someone in another car had followed her into the woods, done the drugs with her, and then grew panicky when she stopped breathing. In that event, all the drug paraphernalia could have been in the other car."

"In the end, though, the case remained unsolved." Carla opened a bag of corn chips and grabbed a handful. "Some of her friends came forward, screaming to high heaven that she'd been murdered. They said she'd gotten clean and hadn't touched any drugs for over a year."

Jeff sneaked one of Carla's chips off her plate, and she playfully slapped his hand. Jeff was laughing as he told Jonas, "I'll do some digging online. Maybe I'll find the names of her friends that came forward and learn that Veneta was one of them."

"That's *exactly* why I thought you could help us," Jonas replied. "You think like a cop."

"I want in," Carla said with a whiny edge to her voice. "I love a good mystery, and I've never gotten to help solve one."

Jonas told them about the grueling day that he and Lane had spent visiting bars, cafés, and restaurants. "Trust me. It wasn't all fun and games. It was particularly rough on Lane."

"Oh, I can't wait!" Carla said. "I can help cheer her up if she stresses out again."

"They haven't invited us to go along," Jeff reminded her.

Carla shot an accusing look at Jonas, who immediately turned to Lane with his brows arched in query. Lane had liked Carla right off the bat, and she could already see why Jonas valued Jeff as a friend. "Why not?" she said. "If we have to go into another town and do all that again, it might be a lot less stressful with a little comic relief."

"Ah-ha!" Carla exclaimed, pointing a finger at Lane. "Are you saying we'll make you laugh? My grandma made me read every Nancy Drew mystery ever published. I'm an investigative genius. The comic relief will just be icing on the cake."

Jonas sighed and glanced at the time on his Fitbit. "It's getting late. We really need to go. But I'll definitely give you a call if we go on another sleuth-a-cation. It'd be fun to do it together. If you can get the time off, that is."

Jeff rocked back on the barstool. "I've got so much vacation time saved up. They keep hounding me to take time off, but I can't think what I'd do. I'm not much for sightseeing. I can't really afford a stay in the tropics. I'd end up just staying at home and wearing out my TV remote, changing channels. I can definitely get time off for a sleuth-a-cation."

"And I work for myself," Carla added. "To take time off, I only have to reschedule my appointments."

"I really like your friends," Lane told Jonas later in the car. They were still on Highway 101, going north to Plover Bay to take the same route back to Mystic Creek that they'd come over on Friday night. "I felt relaxed with them almost instantly."

"Jeff's a good man," Jonas said. "And I think he got

lucky when he found Carla. She's awesome. Isn't she? I can see her being really interested in discussing his cases with him. He'll be able to bounce ideas off of her."

Lane agreed. "She's really a nice gal. I don't know them well, but they seem like a perfect match."

He signaled a lane change to pass a sedan in front of them. "I felt put on the spot when she started pushing to be included in our next sleuthing trip. I wasn't sure how you'd feel about it."

"Normally I'm pretty private. People treat me differently when they find out about hearing voices and having such vivid dreams. But I didn't get that feeling with Jeff and Carla. They seem really interested, and neither of them looked at me as if I'm weird. Maybe having them come along will lighten things up, and there's also a possibility that they'll be a big help. Four minds are better than two."

During the drive, Lane tried to do searches for any mentions of Veneta, but once again, the cell phone service was spotty. She finally loosened her seat belt a bit so she could sit sideways in her seat to look at Jonas without getting a crick in her neck. Until they drew close to Eugene, they chatted about Veneta and all that they'd learned or hadn't learned over the weekend. Then, after exhausting that topic, Lane shared some of her childhood memories, as did Jonas. Again, most of his stories made her laugh.

He was an extremely handsome man with a great sense of humor, a sharp wit, and a gift for reading between the lines. It puzzled her that such a man had managed to stay single.

Jonas chuckled when she made that observation aloud. "I've been in a few serious relationships, but none of them felt completely right. I hope to one day have what my parents do, not only a love to last a lifetime but also a strong friendship that allows them to truly enjoy each other's company. I can't count the times I've walked into their home to find them talking over coffee at the kitchen table or sometimes playing a game. They never watch television in separate rooms like so many couples do. They find programming that they can enjoy together. They even read in the same room, sometimes aloud to each other, other times snuggled in their recliners next to each other as they enjoy different novels."

"I hope you find that someday."

"What do you hope for?" he asked.

"In a relationship, you mean?" Lane sighed. "I'm not even sure I want to be in one. I was too confused and conflicted in my late teens and early adulthood to yearn for a serious relationship. That kind of emotional involvement requires the sharing of one's most private feelings, and I just couldn't go there. It was easier to keep my secrets to myself. Even my parents worried that I wasn't strong enough mentally or emotionally to be in a serious relationship."

Jonas reached across the console to grasp her hand. "You're stronger emotionally and mentally than your parents could ever imagine."

For Lane, Jonas' words were a gift that fortified her and worked like a balm to soothe the wounds deep within her. It felt incredibly liberating to have someone like Jonas believe in her. "Thank you for saying that. It means a lot to me."

"It's only the truth." He gave her fingers a quick squeeze and then withdrew his hand. "That's how I see you."

Except for one fuel stop, Jonas drove straight through to Mystic Creek. They arrived around seven, both of them were hungry, and Jonas suggested they grab a meal at the Cauldron.

"I've never come here," Lane revealed as she walked with Jonas to the café entrance. "Is the food good?"

"To die for. I tend to eat at the Straw Hat, mostly for convenience. It's right downstairs. But on evenings when I'm not that tired, I'll come over for some variety and hopefully see my brother Ben. The owner, Sissy Sue Sterling, is his wife." He leaned forward to hold the door open so Lane could enter and then followed her inside. Lane slowed so he could take the lead. He took her to a table near the fireplace on the west wall, and they sat across from each other. "She inherited the place when her aunt died, and it was a rough go for her in the kitchen at first. She'd worked in diners and had been training to be a cook, but her main job was waiting tables. Cooking and ordering supplies was mostly uncharted territory for her. She says she called her former boss a lot—apparently he was a great cook—and he got her through the rough spots."

Lane took an appreciative sniff of the air. "Judging by the smells, I'd say she knows what she's doing now."

"She makes the best beef bourguignon I've ever tasted, but it's only offered as a special. I count myself as being very lucky if I come in when she's serving that."

"Given that she's your sister-in-law, why don't you just ask her to text you a heads-up when it's a beef bourguignon night?"

Jonas rolled his eyes. "My mom gets weirded out about all of us coming in too often. There's six of us kids, plus her and Dad. And my brothers are all married with kids. She doesn't want all of us to become pests. Plus, Sissy insists on either giving us a discount or letting us eat for free. That's not good for her bottom line."

"Maybe you could just insist on paying the regular menu prices," Lane suggested.

Jonas grinned. "You obviously haven't met Sissy. She's a tiny little thing. Looks like a pixie. But she's got a gigantic attitude. If we tried to insist, she'd get her back up."

Just then Lane glanced up and did a double take when she saw a man who looked like Jonas approaching their table. He was tall with a lean but muscle-packed body, honey-gold hair, chiseled features, and hazel eyes. He carried a little girl on one hip who looked to be about two or three. She sported a mop of hair that was almost black and had the most striking blue eyes Lane had ever seen.

When the child saw Jonas, she threw her little arms wide and shrieked, "Unka Donut!"

Moving quickly, Jonas got out of his chair and was able to catch her as she jumped from her father's arms. "Hey, Peanut. You've grown again. I'm gonna have to stack a bunch of books on your head."

Apparently glad to be relieved of his burden, Ben settled on an empty chair to Lane's right and thrust out his hand. "I'm Ben. We may as well get the introductions underway ourselves, because Katie will demand all Jonas' attention for at least the next five minutes."

Lane laughed and glanced over to see Jonas back in his chair, his tawny head bent to hear something Katie was saying. Once again, the thought occurred to her that he was going to make some lucky lady a fabulous husband. She turned back to Ben and grasped his prof-fered hand. "Lane Driscoll."

"I already know who you are," Ben said. "Our mom could speak of little else all last week. She's still half-way convinced that you're Veneta and back in Jonas' life only to do him wrong. *Again*."

Lane raised an eyebrow. "I hope you don't believe that, too."

"Jonas filled me in. It's a fascinating story, identical twins separated at birth. Great fodder for the tabloids, anyway."

"We were three, actually. Possibly younger. But I was adopted at three. I don't know if I spent time in an orphanage or foster home before that occurred."

"And over your lifetime, you've heard your sister's voice. If it's not all in your head, that's an interesting phenomenon."

Lane wasn't sure she was going to like Jonas' older brother. He definitely wasn't one to pull his punches. She decided to direct the conversation away from her and back at him. "Katie calls Jonas Unka Donut. Where did that come from?"

Ben chuckled and relaxed on the chair. "She couldn't say *Jonas* when she first started talking, and somehow it came out as donut. Now Jonas will probably be Unka Donut forevermore, because it seems to have stuck, and all the kids call him that."

Lane forced a smile. Jonas glanced up just then, lev-eled his gaze on his brother, and said, "Don't stick that size-twelve boot in your mouth, Ben. No matter what Mom's told you, she's not Veneta."

"I sure can't tell it by looking," Ben replied. "I met Veneta, remember. In all my life, I've never seen two people who look so much alike."

"That happens with identical twins, bro, thus the term *identical*," Jonas retorted.

Lane sensed tension building and wished Jonas had taken her to eat next door. Just then, Katie said, "I gotta go potty."

Ben straightened on the chair and reached for his daughter. "Hold on, honey. It's not that far to the bathroom."

And just that quickly, Ben left with Katie. Jonas gazed after them for a moment and then met Lane's eyes. "I'm sorry. It's a close-knit family, and everyone tends to circle the wagons when one of us may be under fire. My mom and dad didn't take well to Veneta." He held up a hand. "They aren't snooty people, my parents. She just got off on the wrong foot with them, mostly her doing. When I brought her home for a weekend to meet my family, she seemed to be on a mission to point out to me every bad thing she could think of about Mystic Creek. Too small. No career opportunities here. Too isolated. I'm not saying she was completely wrong. It was more the way she went about it, being so negative about every little thing. But the worst part of it was her attitude toward my parents, which she made no attempt to conceal. On the surface, my mom seems angry, but the truth is, her feelings were badly hurt."

"I'm sorry Veneta was unpleasant to them."

"Not your fault, no apology needed." He settled back in his chair. "It's just that my mom is worried—fearful, I guess, is a better word. You show up in Mystic Creek—a dead ringer for Veneta, and yet you claim you're someone else."

Lane surprised herself by laughing, and some of her agitation abated. "It is a pretty farfetched story. I can't really blame your mother for being suspicious."

He chuckled and said, "She'll come around once she meets you. So will my dad." He glanced in the direction Ben had gone with his little girl. "We haven't ordered yet. We can go somewhere else if you like. It truly doesn't matter to me, one way or the other."

Lane picked up her menu. "He wasn't *that* unpleasant. Besides, Sissy is offering the beef bourguignon. If it's truly the best you've ever tasted, I want to try it."

He held her gaze for a long moment. "You're a good sport. Thank you. Ben really is a great guy. You'll like him."

"I'm sure I probably will."

Chapter Nine

Lane was beyond exhausted by the time she and Jonas finished their meal and he drove her back to Simply Sensational to get her car. After wrestling her suitcase from the trunk, he deposited it on her back seat and then turned to look down at her. For Lane it was one of those moments she wanted to remember. Moonlight shimmered down through the pine boughs above them, limning his hair with a silvery halo. His eyes, hooded by prominent brow bones, still glistened in the darkness. But what fascinated her most was how the moon glow cast his chiseled features into stark relief by outlining them with shadow.

"Well," he said. And then he fell silent.

Lane's feet suddenly felt as if they'd been glued to the ground, and her pulse quickened. He looked as if he wanted to kiss her, and she hoped he would. Instead, he merely pressed his bent forefinger against the underside of her chin. It was a simple gesture—but the combination of the contact and the warmth of his touch still jangled her nerves and made her stomach feel quivery.

It seemed to her that they both stood frozen in place and only stared at each other for a small eternity. No words passed between them. He just gazed down at her as if he were making love to her with his eyes.

Then, as if an invisible hand gave him a light shove, he retreated a step. "Goodnight, Lane. I hope you can get some rest and have a good day tomorrow."

"I hope the same for you," she managed to reply.

He climbed into his car and started the engine, but he didn't put the vehicle into reverse to back away. With a start, Lane realized he was waiting for her to get safely inside the Hyundai. She hurriedly slid under the steering wheel, locked the doors, and pushed the START button. When her backup lights flared, Jonas drove away, tooting his horn twice in farewell.

"Whew!"

Lane pressed her forehead against the steering wheel and took deep breaths. What on earth was happening to her? She didn't do relationships and had no desire to give romance another whirl. So why was she getting all in a dither over Jonas Sterling? Yes, he was walking, talking eye candy, and he was also a genuinely decent guy. That was a powerful and tempting combination. But she'd met lots of good-looking men who were nice, and not a single one of them had ever made her heart go pitter-pat. *You've got to stop this, Lane. Getting involved with him would be a huge mistake.* Intellectually, Lane knew that was true, only her body didn't seem to be receiving the message from her brain.

At five minutes before eight the next morning, Lane unlocked the storage room door at the rear of Simply Sensational and found Ma once again rifling through a box. With her usual winning smile, Ma straightened from her task.

"Good morning!" she chirped. "I hope you had a marvelous weekend."

Lane wanted to say the weekend had been wonderful and let it go at that, but she truly liked and admired Mary Alice Thomas. It wouldn't be right or fair of Lane to pretend her trip to the coast with Jonas had been all fun and games. It was time for her to tell Ma the truth and let the chips fall where they may.

"Actually, there were a few enjoyable moments, but mostly it was emotionally draining."

"Oh, I'm so sorry." Ma frowned. "Jonas is such a nice young man. I truly hoped you'd have a marvelous time."

Lane began helping the older woman to locate the scented body lotion that she was looking for. "It wasn't a pleasure getaway. Jonas and I were trying to find my sister. She's my identical twin."

When the lotion had been found, they restocked the shelf up front. As they worked in tandem, Lane continued to fill Ma in on the true reason for her visit to Plover Bay.

"You have an identical twin you've never met, and now she's gone missing?" Ma sounded truly horrified. "Oh, honey. How sad is that?"

"Pretty darned sad. Jonas has a picture of her. She looks exactly like me. I'd like to meet her someday, but that may not happen if Jonas and I can't find her."

After years of hiding so many personal things about herself, Lane felt as if a weight had been lifted from her shoulders now that Ma knew the truth. And she had Jonas to thank for that. By believing in her, he had somehow imbued her with enough confidence to believe in herself.

After they had the place ready to open, she and Ma adjourned to the back of the shop, where they sat across from each other at the adult table with steaming mugs of coffee and a paper plate laden with fresh pastry from the Jake 'n' Bake sitting between them. As Lane picked up a glazed donut, she thought of Katie, who called Jonas *Unka Donut*. She shared the story with Ma.

"Oh, what a cute name for an uncle!" Ma said. Then her smile faded. "I'm so sorry for all you've gone through, Lane. And I can't wait for you to find Veneta. It'll be interesting to see if it actually has been her voice that you hear."

Lane questioned the older woman with her eyes. "So . . . the jury is still out? I know it's a weird story, and you probably think I'm crazy."

Ma shook her head. "I don't think you're crazy. Not at all." She took the last bite of her maple bar and wiped her fingertips on a napkin. "My husband had a twin, not identical, fraternal. But they had a thing going on between them, too. Nothing as impressive as telepathic communication, but sort of like that. When one of them got sick, the other one sensed it somehow and just had to call to make sure all was well. My husband fell off a ladder one year while putting up Christmas lights and broke his arm. His brother called within an hour." Ma shrugged. "It was weird, but I grew to think nothing of it over time. For them, it was normal." She smiled at Lane. "Maybe that's why I'm so quick to believe your story."

"Thank you for telling me about your husband and his brother. It makes me feel slightly less abnormal."

Ma chuckled. "Sweetie, we're *all* abnormal. You're not alone in thinking that everyone else is normal and you're not, though. It's the human condition. We'd all like to fit perfectly into the model of what we believe is normal, but *normal* doesn't exist, so it's an impossible-to-achieve aspiration."

Lane joined her in laughing. "I guess maybe you're right. Maybe I should say I'm *weirder* than most."

Ma sighed, and all signs of levity left her expression. "I want you to know I understand that finding Veneta has to be your number one priority right now. If you need to leave again, I'll manage just fine. You needn't worry that your absences will impact our agreement, not even if they're long absences."

Lane wanted to hug the older woman. "Thank you, Ma. I always dreamed of becoming an English teacher, but now, with partnership in Simply Sensational possibly on the table, I'm no longer certain I want to do that. You've given me an opportunity to make a good living here, and I really like the town. Even though people here work hard to make their livings, just like everywhere else, the pace seems slower and more relaxed. I also enjoy the country feeling and the casual interactions between people on the sidewalk. The thought of making Mystic Creek my forever home is very appealing."

"It is a wonderful place to live." Ma stood and brushed crumbs from her pant legs. "I've always loved it here."

During her lunch break that day, Lane got takeout from Taco Joe's and sat on the fender of her car out behind the shop to enjoy the beautiful autumn weather for a few minutes. After taking her first bite of food, she was rather surprised when Jonas' car turned into the alley. Moments later, he parked behind her Hyundai and climbed out, holding a takeout bag from Taco Joe's in one hand.

"I saw you going in for lunch from my apartment window. I decided it was a good plan."

She laughed. There was something about Jonas that allowed her to relax and laugh more frequently. "How did you know I'd have my lunch outside?"

"We've got a telepathic link," he teased as he lifted a hip to sit on the adjacent fender of the vehicle. "If you'd gone inside, I could have joined you there. Ma wouldn't have minded, and I could have gotten her help with the perfume for my mom."

Lane remembered how he'd dropped a bottle of expensive perfume the first time she saw him. Only now, as she looked back on that moment, did she comprehend that he'd been startled into clumsiness when she walked in. "That's right. You never got any perfume."

"Nope, and I'd better get my act together. Her birthday is on Saturday."

"Ma knows her favorite brand, and you still have a few days to pick it up."

Jonas unwrapped a taco and consumed a third of it with one bite. "I'll feel better if I take care of it right away. I'll just have Ma gift wrap it for me, and then I'll drop it off at their house. That way, no matter where I am on Saturday, she'll know I didn't forget her big day."

Lane sent him a curious look. "Are you going somewhere?"

He polished off the rest of that taco and reached into the sack for another one. "Actually, I think we both are. When you get off work today, would you mind coming to my place? I'll order some takeout for dinner, and after we eat, I'd like to spend the evening looking at an Oregon map."

"Why? What do you hope to accomplish?" Lane took a bite of her food while she waited for his answer.

"I keep going back to the fact that you ended up in Mystic Creek. You said you felt a sense of familiarity when you saw the town's name. I know there were other reasons you thought this area would be a good fit for you. The hiking opportunities and other outdoor recreational activities. Also the fact that this town is off the beaten track. But I can't get the coincidence out of my head. Of all the towns in Oregon you could have chosen, you picked the one where I live. Doesn't that seem weird to you?"

Lane dabbed at the corners of her mouth with a napkin. "It is, I suppose, but I still don't see how studying a map of Oregon is going to accomplish anything."

He smiled and winked at her. "I'm hoping you'll see something that you key in on again. If I'm correct that you felt a connection to my hometown because you once tuned in to Veneta's thoughts, maybe that can happen again. In the greater Portland area, there are lots of little communities that bleed together. Right? Veneta may be in Maple Leaf, but it could just as easily be another small municipality near there. Maybe the name of one of them will ring a bell with you. Help us narrow our focus and not waste time in only Maple Leaf, if that isn't where she is."

Lane crumpled the taco wrapper and stuffed it back in the bag. "I doubt that'll happen, but I'm game to give it a try."

"Great. I'll see you shortly after five, then?"

"Sounds good. What kind of takeout are you thinking?"

"Chinese?"

"Yum!"

Jonas followed Lane back into the shop to get his mother's birthday gift. While Ma assisted him and then wrapped the perfume box, Lane waited on customers. She was helping an elderly lady find a perfume she liked when Jonas left.

Waving goodbye, she called, "I'll see you later!"

Jonas had the Chinese food sitting on the kitchen table when Lane arrived at his apartment. He led the way to the back and motioned for Lane to take a seat while he poured them each a cup of green tea. Instead, she busied herself with taking the food cartons out of the sacks and then found his flatware drawer to get some serving spoons.

"It smells divine," she told him as they sat across from each other and began serving themselves. "Oh, sweet and sour pork! One of my favorites."

He nodded. "I went a little overboard. You'll have to take some of this home."

"Yum. That can be my lunch tomorrow. Ma has a microwave in the coffee area, thank goodness."

When they'd both eaten their fill, they adjourned to the living room and sat across from each other at his desk with an Oregon map spread out between them. Lane felt a little silly as she studied the names of towns near Maple Leaf.

"No sense of familiarity is coming to me," she told him with a smile.

"You may be trying too hard. Sometimes it can help to just empty your mind. Look at some other area for a while and then come back to places around Maple Leaf."

Lane decided to trace the squiggly red line of Highway 126, the road they'd taken to Plover Bay. Her fingertip stopped dead on the name of one town, and a shivery sensation crawled over her skin. "Jonas," she said softly. "Look!"

He leaned closer, stared long and hard at the town's name, and then said, "Veneta? A town named Veneta?" He met her gaze. "We drove right past it twice. It must be more of a spot along the road than an actual town."

Lane grabbed her cell phone and looked it up. "The population is only a little over four thousand. That's pretty small."

He shook his head. "It's not that far from Eugene, which means it's in Lane County. Are you thinking what I'm thinking? That it's some kind of clue?"

Lane didn't know what to think.

"What if you and Veneta were born in the town of Veneta, and your birth mother specifically chose your first names, or even maybe changed them, hoping that the two of you might one day track down your birthplace?"

Excitement built within Lane at the suggestion. "That makes perfect sense!" she cried. "Her one request was that my first name could never be changed by my adoptive parents. I always thought that was weird, but if she hoped we'd find her someday, it isn't so strange after all."

"Or she wanted both of you to at least stand a chance of finding each other," Jonas suggested. "She may have felt terrible about allowing you to be separated. Maybe that was the only way she could think of to leave you a clue. I wonder if there's a way to see if your first names were legally changed."

Lane's feeling of excitement waned. "It makes sense, I suppose. But even if it's a clue our birth mother left for us, it won't help us find Veneta right now."

Jonas gave a decisive nod. "True enough, so in reality, talking about it is a waste of time."

They bent back over the map, saying the names of Oregon towns near Maple Leaf aloud. Beaverton. Tigard. Milwaukie. Forest Grove. Hillsboro. Lane felt no undue sense of familiarity except for Maple Leaf, where she'd grown up.

"Oh, Jonas!" she said. "This is getting us nowhere. I'm not picking up on anything." She lifted her gaze to his. "And, honestly, I think this is a waste of time. Some of these communities look close on a map, but in reality, in heavy traffic, it takes a lot of time to drive from Maple Leaf to any of them. If that man holding Veneta is working alone and solely in charge, I don't think he would leave her for long periods of time to visit a tattoo shop in Maple Leaf."

Jonas sat back on his chair with such force that the casters carried him backward nearly a foot. "You're right. It was a long shot. But at least now we know none of the other communities summon a sense of familiarity within you as you read their names. That probably means Maple Leaf should be our only focal point."

"So, what should our next move be?" she asked.

"We need to go there. What we'll do to find her when we get there remains to be seen, but if she's losing strength, we need to get up there as fast as we can."

"Tonight?"

Jonas didn't seem to hear her. "I wonder what he was doing in a tattoo shop, anyway. Something on the wrong side of the law, I bet, and it probably involved money. Otherwise he wouldn't have left her alone to go there."

Lane sighed and closed her eyes. "You didn't answer." She lifted her lashes. "Tonight?"

He studied her face. "I know you're emotionally wrung out. I wanted to give you a couple of days to regroup. But I keep getting this sense of urgency I can't explain, maybe because you sense in the dreams that she's swiftly losing her strength."

"So we'll leave tonight, then." This time, Lane didn't pose it as a question.

He grasped Lane's shoulders and drew her to her feet. The warm press of his palms and fingers on her upper arms made Lane acutely aware of him physically, and that made her angry with herself. At this very moment, Veneta could be facing death. What kind of a person could be thinking about sexual attraction at such a time?

He drew his hands from her shoulders, and Lane tried not to reveal how relieved she was that he'd broken the contact. It wouldn't do for Jonas to realize how attracted she was to him. Especially not now, when they were about to go on another road trip together. The knowledge might make him feel uncomfortable. It certainly did nothing for Lane's peace of mind.

"When should we leave?" she asked.

"As quick as we can. We both need to make arrangements to be gone. I'm guessing for at least a week. Even if Veneta is in Maple Leaf, it may take days for us to locate her. For me, preparing to be absent from work is fairly easy. I just need to make some phone calls and postpone my appointments. For you, it won't be so simple. You're newly hired, and Ma is counting on you."

"No, actually. I told her everything first thing this morning—all of it."

"You told her *everything*? I thought it was hard for you to share that stuff. That you rarely do, for fear people will think you're a head case."

"I've always been afraid of that," she admitted. "Meeting you has helped me get past it. Not to say I'd just walk up to any person and tell them I have dreams and hear voices. But I felt that I owed Ma the truth and a heads-up. You know?"

"How did she handle it?"

"Very well. She says she'll be fine, even if I must take an extended leave of absence. She understands that finding Veneta has to be my first priority right now."

Jonas smiled slightly. He trailed his hazel gaze slowly over her face. "I'm proud of you, Lane. I feel like I'm watching a butterfly emerge from its chrysalis. It's a beautiful thing to witness."

While Jonas made a series of phone calls and packed for the trip, Lane drove home to her cottage to call Ma and then refill her suitcase. Jonas would pick her up in only an hour. As soon as she walked into her house, she thought, *Thank goodness I did that load of laundry last night. At least I'll have clean clothing to wear.*

Her conversation with Ma was short and sweet. The older woman assured Lane that she had been running the shop on her own for many years and could certainly do so for another week, even longer, if necessary. After ending the call, Lane dashed to the bedroom and started throwing clothing into her luggage. Normally she drew up a list of things she needed to take and checked items off after she got them in a suitcase. But this evening, her checklist was in her head. *Shoes, check. Underwear, check. Skirts and tops, check. Jeans and T-shirts, check. Sweatpants and her Oregon State jersey.* By the time she had collected everything, she was sweating.

Only a few minutes later, she was once again in the

passenger seat of Jonas' car, only this time they were driving north toward Maple Leaf.

"I'm a little nervous about calling my parents to tell them I'm in the area. How will I explain it to them? They never react well to any mention of my *imaginary friend*. They'll really freak out if I tell them she's real."

Jonas flipped on his turn signal to pass the car in front of them. "I don't see why it's necessary for you to say a word to your parents. You're well over twenty-one, and any familial friction will only distract you. Right now, you need to be focused on finding Veneta."

Lane released a tight breath. "You're right. I just won't call them. Maple Leaf's population has exploded. It's unlikely that I'll accidentally run into one of them."

"Problem solved. That problem is, at least." He readjusted his rearview mirror. "The next problem we need to discuss is the cost of lodging."

Lane reached over to touch his arm. "Before we left for Plover Bay, I had already decided I could bunk with you if it became necessary, and I know you much better now. And, just so you know, I'll reimburse you for the Plover Bay trip and this one as well."

"I didn't mention money in order to be reimbursed!"

Lane couldn't help but laugh at his indignant tone. "We can argue about that later. Right now, we should be thinking about how we might find Veneta. Maple Leaf is pretty much swarming with people now. Just being there isn't going to help us pinpoint where she is."

"True. But I'm hoping, if we talk about your dreams—in detail, I mean—that you may recall details that'll help direct us."

Lane couldn't see how that was going to help, but given that she had no better idea, she decided to run with his. She settled back in her seat and tried to relax. "Which dream should we talk about first?"

"Let's go with the first one you had." He paused. "Well, not the first one you had, of course, because you've been having them all your life. I mean the one you had that morning, right before you encountered Jack the Ripper on the sidewalk."

Lane smiled at the nickname he'd given her attacker. Or, rather, Veneta's attacker. "Jack the Ripper. That totally works. He's creepy. I can tell you that. In my dreams, he seems—God, I don't know how to put it. But I think he's waiting with bated breath to be able to kill my sister. I think he's killed other people and actually enjoys it." She glanced at Jonas. "He terrifies me."

"Yeah." Jonas took an exit that led to the Interstate 5 junction going north. "And being my usual brilliant self, I'm taking you back to Maple Leaf where you might be in danger. If your dad knew, he'd probably kick my ass."

Lane recalled her last conversation with her parents when her father had grown so indignant and angry at her for asking if she'd had a twin sister. After a lifetime of loving him and trusting in him so steadfastly to return that love, she'd been shaken. Her dad had suddenly seemed like a stranger.

Jonas flashed her a grin that was boyishly charming and yet devastatingly masculine. "Just so you know, if anything happens, Lane, I'll protect you with my life."

She managed to meet his gaze for an instant before he had to focus on the road again. "He drew a switchblade on me in front of the tattoo shop. The only reason he didn't run me through, right then and there, was because he heard cop sirens. He's probably armed, Jonas, and not only with a knife."

He glanced back at her. "What do I look like, some idiot who'd show up at a gunfight with a penknife?"

Startled, Lane stared at his profile. "You brought a *gun*?" She had never been around firearms. "People who aren't trained in how to use them can be a danger to themselves and others."

He nodded and braked to a slower speed as a doe and fawn bounded across the road. "Trust me, I'm trained. Remember, I grew up in Mystic Creek and was raised by a rough-and-tumble farmer. He served in the Marines, earned an expert marksmen badge, and brought us kids up knowing how to handle firearms."

"So you can shoot an acorn off a tree branch at a hundred yards?"

"Better than that. No brag, just fact."

Lane gave him a prolonged study. "No BS. How good are you?"

"Well, I'm not as good as my dad; that's for sure. But he took us to the shooting range and insisted on a level of expertise. I became really good with a high-powered rifle and acceptably proficient with a handgun. I'm not an expert by military standards, but I'm fairly confident that I can hold my own against a drug-addicted thug."

"I'm pretty sure he's killed people, Jonas. You haven't. What if you—"

He cut her off with, "I won't hesitate, if that's your worry." He lifted one hand from the steering wheel to gesture. "If you stood a perfectly harmless man in front of me and ordered me to shoot him, I'd have is-sues. You know? But if someone's threatening you or me, all bets are off. Remember, my brother Barney is in law enforcement. You'll never meet a nicer man, but I wouldn't want to be a dangerous criminal in his jurisdiction. Not with the training he got from our dad and then later at the academy."

Lane took in his profile, which she'd already engraved on her memory. A muscular neck. About three inches above his protruding larynx, there was an abrupt shift forward to a strong, squared chin. A jawline that looked as hard as hand-hewn granite. From between his prominent brow bones, his sharply bridged nose jutted like a knife blade. There was nothing feminine about his countenance. Perhaps Jonas spent a good deal of time at a desk, counseling patients, but there was far more to him than just that. She saw in the set of his jawline that he wasn't just blowing smoke. Wasn't trying to impress her with his manliness. If anything, Jonas was a guy who normally understated himself. He was who he was, a farmer's son who'd chosen a sedentary profession but still kept himself in prime physical condition. She had no doubt that he was as proficient with firearms as he claimed to be.

"You make me feel safe," she said softly. "For some reason, you always have. I fell asleep on your sofa. Remember? I barely knew you, but I trusted you."

He grinned at her. "Then relax, darlin'. No son of Jeremiah Sterling's is going to let some drug addict harm a hair on your head. I'll add an aside, of course. If that dream man of yours is hooked up with a stateside drug cartel, that's dangerous stuff. I can blow my own horn all I want, but if a crew of marksmen comes after us with assault weapons, we'll both be toast."

Lane couldn't help but laugh even though it wasn't funny. "Gotcha." She'd also noted that he'd called Veneta's captor Lane's dream man. Not so, she decided. That guy was her worst nightmare. Jonas was her dream man. And the moment she thought that, she knew she was in serious trouble.

During the rest of the drive, Lane struggled to recall details about her visions of the room where Veneta was being held. Jonas seemed to believe that she might remember something important. "My prevailing impression," she finally concluded, "is that the room is dark, partially from the boarded-over window, but also from the walls themselves. I noticed no contrast between the wood—kind of like aged barn wood—and the paint."

"Hmm." Jonas' forehead pleated in a frown. "Most newer houses I've seen have lighter paint on the walls. Maybe it's an old house."

At the beginning of this exercise, Lane hadn't believed she would recall anything of importance. "That makes perfect sense! When I ran into the guy in my dream, I was only a few blocks from my duplex apartment, which is in an old part of town."

Jonas nodded. "Then we should start our search for Veneta in that area. Don't you think? If I were holding a woman against her will, I wouldn't leave her alone for very long. I'd be afraid she might escape. And it also stands to reason that he wouldn't go too far afield from where he's keeping her."

Just then, Jonas' vehicle Bluetooth signaled that a call was coming in. He answered by pressing a button on the steering wheel. "Hey, Jeff!" He grinned broadly. "I was starting to think you might not get back to me."

"Oh, hell, no." Jeff's voice boomed from the dash speakers. "I got your message and immediately phoned Carla. She's so excited about hooking up with you guys in Maple Leaf that I'm surprised she can sit still long enough to call all her clients and reschedule their appointments."

"You're coming, then?" Jonas asked.

"With bells on our toes. Where are you planning to stay? It'd be kind of nice if we're all at the same motel."

Jonas' grin gave way to another frown. "Damn. I haven't given a thought to where we'll stay."

Jeff laughed. "Dear God, you haven't changed a bit."

"You're on my car phone," Jonas retorted. Then he winked at Lane. "Don't start badmouthing me when Lane's listening. She might get a bad opinion of me."

"Hi, Lane!" Jeff boomed. "I hope you don't mind if we crash your sleuth-a-cation."

"Judging from the sound of it, we may be sleeping on park benches," she replied. "But if you're okay with that, of course I don't mind. It'll be good to see both of you again."

"That's Jonas for you. Always flying by the seat of his pants."

Jonas rolled his eyes. "Enough. As soon as we're off the phone, I'll call and make reservations somewhere. We'll be staying someplace cheap, by the way. If you and Carla want something nicer, it's fine. But I need to watch my expenses this trip."

"As long as the bathroom's decent and the bedding is clean, we'll be fine."

"Lane's from Maple Leaf. She should know which motels might be good."

"If it's good enough for Lane, it'll be good enough for us," Jeff said. "We'll be leaving here in a few. Probably roll in about eight thirty."

"Even if I push it, we won't get there until ten. I'll text you the room information. You can go ahead and get checked in. No need to wait up for us."

"Carla will probably be too excited to sleep. She can't wait to see you guys again."

Lane inserted, "Tell her I can't wait, either."

"Good," Jeff replied. "I've been doing some digging, and I'd like to fill you in on what I discovered."

Chapter Ten

As Jonas had estimated, they didn't reach Maple Leaf until almost ten that evening, and both of them were famished, because they hadn't wanted to waste time stopping for a meal along the way. Aware that Jeff and Carla were waiting up for them, Jonas texted Jeff over the hands-free system and invited him and Carla to join them at the Tarnished Spoon, a restaurant with mid-range prices and pretty good food, according to Lane.

After parking the car, Jonas gave Lane a questioning look. "Should we wait in the car until they get here, or just go on inside?"

She smiled and opened the passenger door. "I'm *starving*, Jonas, and I'm fairly certain they've already eaten."

A waitress greeted them when they walked in and guided them to a booth that seated four. Jonas guided Lane onto the bench first and then sat beside her, because their friends would soon join them. Lane immediately opened the menu given to her, so Jonas followed suit. When she said she wanted a hamburger, he narrowed an eye at her.

"I can afford to feed you something better than *that*."

She pushed the menu aside. "I happen to like hamburgers. Besides, it's late, and at this time of night, all the baked potatoes have been under a heat lamp for hours and have probably shriveled inside their skins. The mashed will be dried out, too. I prefer to go with something they'll cook fresh."

"Ah, right. You're a waitress and know about these things."

"I *used* to be a waitress," she said with a smile that dimpled her cheek. "Now I'm a woman with a possible promising future as part owner of a scent shop."

"I'll defer to your experience and have a hamburger, too, I guess." He faked a shudder, hoping to tease another smile out of her so he could see that dimple again. "A shriveled potato sounds disgusting."

Their meals had just been delivered to the table when Jeff and Carla arrived. Lane and Jonas slid from the booth to hug them both hello. Jonas noticed that the ends of Carla's longish blond hair were wet, and her eye makeup had melted a bit, creating a gray shadow beneath her lower lashes.

"Excuse my appearance," she said, as if she'd noticed his assessment. "It's an older motel, but they have a hot tub and pool. I'm like a golden retriever. Just had to jump in."

Jeff and Carla sat opposite them and ordered nachos.

"Please, go ahead and eat before your food gets cold," Carla urged.

Lane chuckled. "I'd be polite, but I'm starving, and if I don't get something in my stomach, it'll be serenading you at any moment."

Everyone laughed, and then Lane tucked into her meal, not taking dainty little bites like many women might have while eating in front of an audience. Jonas liked that about her. She never seemed pretentious. But, then, he found most things about Lane to be attractive, which troubled him. It wouldn't be smart to let himself fall for a woman who didn't feel the same way in return.

Jeff and Carla got glasses of beer with their order. Soon, all four of them were eating. When Jonas had finished his hamburger and fries, he met Jeff's gaze.

"You mentioned on the phone that you've done some digging. I'm dying to hear what you learned."

Jeff popped another nacho into his mouth and didn't swallow before answering. "Veneta Monroe was one of the women who came forward when Jillian Foxglove's body was found. She said her friend hadn't touched drugs in over a year. She insisted there had been foul play. Apparently, Jillian went to a rehab center to get clean, and while she was there, she became friends with another young woman who also ended up dead. When I read the reports on that gal's death, I was spooked to discover that she, too, died in a remote location inside her car from an unintentional heroin OD."

"The plot thickens," Jonas said. "Thanks for digging that information up. So what's your take?"

"At the time Jillian Foxglove was found, I didn't really concern myself with the case too much. I trusted in the investigators to do a thorough job, and when they ruled it to be an accidental overdose, I accepted it. We all know it happens."

"And now?" Jonas felt Lane's body tense beside him as they waited for Jeff's response.

"Now I think there *was* foul play involved." Jeff held up a hand. "I'm not saying the cops working the case didn't do a good job. It was a difficult one to nail down, and if it looks like a duck, and you have no evidence to indicate otherwise, you normally call it a duck. I also remind myself that overdose deaths are one of the saddest things we cops deal with. You stand over young people who just wasted their lives. You know? And you wonder what led them to make such stupid choices. All the negativity of it dampens an investigator's enthusiasm to solve a case." He shrugged. "I'd like to paint a prettier picture for you, but the reality is that drug-related deaths don't get as much focus as they should sometimes. Those cops didn't intentionally write those young women off, but when you've got no evidence to prove foul play, you don't dig as deeply.

"Fortunately, I've got the gift of hindsight in my favor. Two women, dead. And now Veneta is missing, and Lane is hiding out because she's an exact replica of Veneta." He shrugged. "I think it's all connected. Except for Lane, the women all knew each other. My cop instinct tells me that the first two knew something that the killer never wanted to be revealed. I'm only guessing from here on out, but it makes sense that Veneta somehow became privy to some of that information as well, which led to the threatened person kidnapping her, obviously with the intention of getting rid of her. Whoever the head guy is—I'm thinking a local drug network, possibly—he's smart. Instead of getting rid of Veneta in Plover Bay, he had her transported to another area. It would have raised a lot of cops' eyebrows if a third woman—Veneta—died of a heroin overdose on the coast. Taking her inland to Multnomah County to get rid of her was brilliant thinking. Last time I checked, there are about two hundred drug-related deaths in the county per year, a larger percentage of them from meth than heroin, but a heroin death wouldn't surprise anybody. You following me?"

Jonas dipped his chin to indicate that he was. "If he was going to kill her, he needed to move her so the police wouldn't smell a rat and swarm all over him. And taking her to a highly populated region, like the greater Portland area, also makes sense."

Jeff nodded. "Yep. It's not uncommon here for people to OD. One more corpse would go almost unnoticed, if it was made to look like an accidental overdose. And I think his MO is to get rid of people by injecting them with a lethal dose of heroin." He lifted his shoulders again. "It's clean. If you're careful, the cops can't easily pin a murder on you. Wear gloves. Administer the drug. Wait for it to make your victim unconscious. Then leave no trace of any physical evidence."

"And then Lane came along, was Veneta's exact lookalike, and it threw the guy holding Veneta for a loop? He probably believes Veneta told Lane everything she knows."

"Exactly." Jeff took a sip of his beer. "And now, so does the kingpin."

Carla spoke up. "I think the guy that Lane ran into on the sidewalk believed that she *was* Veneta at first—that she had escaped from wherever it is he's holding her."

Jeff sat back and encircled his girlfriend's shoulders with a muscular arm. "Exactly. Only when the dude got back to the house, Veneta was still there. So . . . who in the hell was Lane? That had to be the question he was asking himself. And how was she connected to Veneta, who knows too much? So the kingpin held off on disposing of Veneta, not because he had a change of heart, but because he feared Veneta might have told Lane all about him. In short, our kingpin may think he's in a hell of a fix. If he follows through with getting rid of Veneta, he's afraid Lane knows enough to rat him out and he doesn't know how to find her. He needs to be sure Lane can't come forward before he kills Veneta."

Lane pushed her plate to the center of the table. Jonas hoped she hadn't lost her appetite because of the dinner conversation. Not that he could blame her if that were the case.

"You okay?"

She nodded, but in Jonas' opinion, she looked upset. "So . . ." she said, her voice shaky. "How should we start our search in the morning? I need to find my sister before it's too late."

Jeff and Carla's room was only one door down from Jonas and Lane's. Jonas gave Lane the keycards to open their door while he grabbed their luggage. He froze when he stepped over the threshold. The room was adequate enough, with clean-looking blue carpet, freshly painted white walls, and fairly nice furnishings, but there was only one bed. It looked to be a king-size, which was a plus, but as large as it was, there was *still* only one place to sleep.

"I'm sorry."

Lane had just set her purse atop the mirrored dresser next to a lighted plastic jack-o'-lantern that glowed like an orange basketball. "It's fine, Jonas. Just in case this happened, I brought sweats and a T-shirt to wear as pajamas. No big deal."

He sighed and closed the door. Then he carried their suitcases over to two luggage racks standing against the wall. After ridding himself of the suitcases, he opened the adjacent closet doors. "We've got extra blankets and pillows. I can make a pallet on the floor."

"Don't be a goose." She drew up beside him and opened her carrying case. A moment later, she held up a well-worn Oregon State jersey and a pair of ugly gray sweats. "I don't think my nightwear will drive you into an amorous frenzy."

Jonas suspected she could drive him into an amorous frenzy wearing a burlap bag, but he wasn't about to admit it. "Nice," was all he could think to say.

She giggled. "Do you need to use the bathroom before I call first dibs on the shower? I feel grungy."

Jonas thought she looked perfect. She was wearing the autumn-colored dress with a rust shawl tied in a loose knot over her small breasts. In the glow of the one light that she'd turned on, she looked luminous, her reddish-gold hair shimmering, her deep blue eyes sparkling like a mountain lake at sunset. In all his life, he'd never wanted so badly to kiss a woman.

"I'm fine for the moment. I brought a pair of sweats, too. Wasn't planning to wear them as pajamas, but needs must. I'll get changed while you're rinsing off. When you're done, I'll have a go."

She nodded and stepped into the bathroom. He stared for a long moment at the closed door, waiting to hear the lock click. When he heard the water come on, he smiled slightly. If she were worried that he might burst in on her, she would have locked up. Knowing she trusted him that much made him feel good. At the same time, he worried about how much he was coming to care for her, even without curling up beside her to sleep.

When Lane emerged from the bathroom, Jonas was stretched out on the far side of the bed with two fluffy pillows behind his shoulders and head. As promised, he wore black sweatpants, which was appreciated, but from the waist up, he was nude. Lane came to a sudden stop and stared. His shoulders bulged with hard muscle. When he shifted to look in her direction, his six-pack rippled and looked rock hard. Her mouth went dry, and her heart started to pound. She decided it might not be Jonas who got driven into an amorous frenzy.

"You want me to put on a shirt?" He sat up and swung his legs over the side of the bed to stand. "I planned to after my shower anyway."

Lane's gaze caught on a vertical line of extra pillows that lay at the center of the bed. He'd built a downy barricade, presumably to make her feel more comfortable about sleeping with him. A laugh welled at the base of her throat, and holding it in made her sinuses throb. "What is *that*?" she managed to ask.

"That's a pillow wall. You ever heard that joke about the farmer's daughter?"

Glad for the distraction—because Jonas Sterling was even sexier on his feet than he'd been lying down—she smiled and said, "No, I don't believe I have."

He grabbed a white T-shirt that he'd left on the dresser and put it on, shoving his arms through the sleeve holes first and then yanking it down over his head. Fascinated, Lane watched his every movement. She always pulled a T-shirt over her head first and then worked her arms into the sleeves. With all Jonas' talk about genetics, she momentarily wondered if it was wired into a man's DNA not to give a crap about messing up his hair.

He tugged the hem of cotton knit down to below the waistband of his stretchy pants. "It's a stupid joke. But essentially, the moral of the story is that any man who can't scale a mound of pillows to reach a woman isn't worth his salt." He flashed her a dazzling grin as he gestured at the pillows. "At best, it's a symbolic gesture, but I thought a barrier might make you feel a little more comfortable about sleeping next to me."

Lane was touched by the gesture. "Thank you. It was sweet of you to think of it."

With a loose-hipped stride, he headed toward the bathroom. "My turn to wash up." He stopped to look back at her. "Why don't you see if we can rent a movie? It might be a good way to wind down and fall asleep."

After he vanished into the bathroom, Lane sat down on what he'd designated as her side of the bed and was about to click the remote to turn on the television when a light knock came at the door. Curious, and feeling more than a little cautious, she walked over and went up on her tiptoes to peer out the peephole. What if she'd been seen at the restaurant and it was a bad guy? An eyeball with a dark-brown iris stared back at her. Startled, she retreated a step, imagining Jonas storming out of the shower, gloriously naked and dripping water as he fought another man to protect her.

"Who is it?" she managed to call out.

"Jeff!" A rumble of masculine laughter followed. "Open up. We bring gifts of snacks and wine."

As Lane unfastened the chain lock, she could hear Carla giggling. She drew the door open to allow the couple entry. Carla hugged bags of treats against her chest. Jeff carried two bottles of wine, a corkscrew, and four red Solo cups.

"Oh, my goodness!" Lane couldn't help but laugh. "We only just ate!"

Jeff went to the small round table flanked by two

cushiony chairs that sat in the corner and immediately went to work opening a bottle of the merlot. "There's always room for snacks. We've got party mix, potato chips, chocolate Kisses, and peanut butter cups. If you don't want anything savory so soon after dinner, you can have candy and call it dessert."

"Chocolate Kisses are so yummy with red wine." Carla rolled her eyes. "The peanut butter cups may not be a phenomenal pairing, but I'll manage to choke a couple of them down."

Lane laughed. "Please, make yourselves at home."

Jeff winked at her. "We already have." He sloshed some wine into one of the cups and handed it to her. "Down the hatch. I've got more in the car if we run out."

"Jonas and I were thinking about watching a movie," Lane informed them. "But visiting with you guys will be a lot more fun."

After serving Carla some merlot, Jeff partially filled a cup for himself and went to sit on the bed. When he saw the barrier of pillows, he stared at it for a long moment and then guffawed. "Jonas, Jonas, Jonas. I need to have a talk with that boy out behind a barn."

Lane took a sip of wine, smiling as she swallowed. "I thought it was a very sweet gesture."

Carla plopped down beside Jeff and fixed a questioning gaze on Lane. "You guys aren't—?" She glanced over her shoulder at the useless barrier. "I don't know why, but I just assumed that you were a thing. Maybe because you'd just spent the weekend together when I first met you."

Lane shook her head and plucked at her T-shirt. "No. We're only friends, which is why I'm dressed like a bag lady. My version of modest pj's."

Jeff shook his head. "Well, at least we don't have to

worry that we're interrupting your plans to get cozy later."

Just then Jonas emerged from the bath, his damp hair standing up in spikes. He'd donned the T-shirt again, and Lane was relieved that he had. Seeing him half naked was an unsettling experience for her. "What kind of plans?" he asked.

Jeff chuckled. "Nothing important. We brought wine and snacks. Help yourself."

Jonas, who always seemed ready to eat, strode to the table, his bare feet making no sound on the carpet. "Just what I need, a glass of wine to relax before turning in," he said with appreciation. "And goodies, too." He grabbed a couple of peanut butter cups and sat in a chair by the table. "This is the life."

"It's an apology of sorts." Jeff smiled at Lane. "I was pretty thoughtless at the restaurant tonight. I knew Veneta, but not all that well, and I didn't stop to think that her disappearance and the death of two women she knew might be upsetting for you."

Lane took a chair opposite Jonas. "It was upsetting," she admitted, "but it was also an important and necessary conversation." She took another sip of wine before continuing. "And I deeply appreciate the time you spent looking into it. Now we know for certain that Veneta knew both the women who died. It's all connected somehow."

"So what's our plan for tomorrow?" Jeff asked.

Lane glanced at Jonas. "I don't think we have one. Not really. If Veneta was kidnapped in Plover Bay and transported here, I'm fairly certain she was taken straight to the house where she's being held now. Going around town to ask if anyone's seen her would be pointless."

His brow pleated in a thoughtful frown, Jeff stared into his cup for a moment. "True. But the dude holding her captive has to be going out. For food, at least. We could stake out the grocery stores nearest to the tattoo shop where you ran into him. It's too bad we don't have a picture of the man. Then Carla and I could do surveillance on our own."

Lane sighed. "We could cover two stores at once if both of you knew what he looks like. Unfortunately, there is no picture of him. My mom did see a mug shot at the police station that she thought might be him, but he looks so different now that she couldn't be sure."

"Oh, well," Carla said. "It'll be more fun to do a stakeout together." Her smile faded. "Not that I came to have fun—or that any of us did. I'm sorry, Lane. I know you're really worried."

"What's another place he might go for necessities?" Jonas asked. "If he drinks, he'll occasionally go to a liquor store."

"True, but unless he's a heavy drinker, maybe only once a week," Jeff observed.

"What's our plan if we see him at a grocery store?" Lane asked.

"We'll keep our heads down and follow him," Jeff said without hesitation. He glanced at Jonas. "I think I should drive. I know how to tail someone without tipping him off."

Jonas took a swallow of wine. "No problem." He winked at Lane and added, "Although I am the better driver."

Jeff chuckled. "No ego in your family. You got it all."

They continued to sip wine and chat about possible search strategies. Lane came up with driving around in old neighborhoods in hope of spotting the man's car. She had seen it only once, but the image was still engraved on her brain. If he left it parked on the street or in a driveway, she'd recognize it. Then they'd know where Veneta was being held.

By the time Jeff and Carla left to return to their own room, Lane had consumed two glasses of wine and it was almost midnight. She knew she should be exhausted, but the moment Jonas started turning off the lights, her nerves jangled and she was wide awake. As she walked to her side of the bed, her palms went sweaty. Earlier, she hadn't thought she would feel anxious about sleeping with Jonas, but now that the moment was upon her, she did.

"My offer to crash on the floor still stands," he told her as he strode to his side of the bed. Only the lamp on his nightstand was still on. "I really don't mind."

"No, no. Don't be silly." Lane heard a quiver in her voice and wanted to kick herself. "You won't sleep as well on the floor, and, like you said, we both need to be at the top of our game."

He reached out to draw the covers back on his side. "Okay. We've got the pillows between us. At least I won't be able to roll over in my sleep and do anything stupid."

The pillow barrier had amused Lane earlier. Now she wished it were taller. She flipped back the comforter and top sheet. She'd just gotten situated on her back with the covers tugged up to her chin when she felt his weight depress the mattress. The next instant, darkness blanketed the room. She stared toward the ceiling, unable to see much of anything.

What was it about darkness that sharpened one's

senses? She could hear every breath Jonas took. His slightest movement seemed to shake the whole bed. He smelled of soap, shampoo, and aftershave, a pleasant combination of scents.

"Are you going to be able to sleep?" The unexpected sound of his voice made her jerk. "I don't know about you, but I'm nervous."

Surprised, Lane said, "You are? *Why?* You've definitely got the physical advantage. If either of us has a reason to be nervous, it's me."

He let loose with a long sigh. "I haven't ever slept with a woman. Sex, yes. But I never hung around for breakfast."

"Not even with Veneta?"

"Nope. She had roomies, and I lived at the dorm. When we wanted privacy, we had to time it so nobody was at either her place or mine." He laughed softly. "Doesn't sound very romantic. Does it? But when you're a college student and don't have rich parents, you can't afford to rent a room somewhere. I was on a strict budget back then, and so was she."

Lane closed her eyes, willing herself to get sleepy. Instead she felt electrified by his nearness. Felt him in every pore of her skin. She doubted it was in the stars for her to get very much rest.

Apparently Jonas felt the same way, because he whispered, "Jeff left a full bottle of wine. Maybe if we have another glass, we'll be relaxed enough to fall asleep."

Lane giggled and sat up. "I'm dangerous with a corkscrew. You'd better get it."

He flipped the light back on and swung out of bed. As he opened the bottle and refilled their disposable Solo cups, she looped her arms around her blanket-covered knees. Before returning to bed, Jonas drew the window curtains slightly apart.

"People will be able to look in and see us," she complained.

"Not once the light's turned off again," he told her. "The parking lot lights will give us just enough illumination to see once our eyes get adjusted. Kind of like a nightlight."

He handed her one of the cups, flipped the table lamp off again, and rejoined her on the bed. Lane set her wine aside to fluff her pillows and then leaned back against them with her head pressed against the bedframe. Jonas did the same.

"This is good," he said. "By the time we kill that bottle, we'll be three glasses in. Both of us should be able to sleep. If not, we can turn on the TV. Try to watch a flick. When I'm tired, that always puts me to sleep."

"Really? I'm the same way. I didn't have a television in my bedroom, and when I got home from work, it was always late. I'd watch something to unwind, and I can't count the times I woke up the next morning on the sofa."

"That'll be our next plan of action, then, a boring movie."

After her eyes adjusted to the shadowy light, she could see him again, and she was reminded of just how handsome he was. "I can't believe—oh, never mind."

"I can't believe it, either," he said, which made her laugh. "Here we are, in bed together. It's sort of like getting all dressed up and having nowhere to go. You just look at yourself in the mirror and think, now what?"

Lane smiled as she took a big sip of wine, hoping it might help her relax. "This is silly, you know. We aren't nervous with each other in other situations."

"In other situations, we're not together in bed wearing clothing that can be dispensed with in one second, flat."

The wine caught in her throat, and she choked on it.

"Are you okay?" he asked.

She caught her breath and nodded. "Sorry. It went down the wrong pipe."

"Yeah, I probably shouldn't have said that. When I'm nervous, I lose my filter. I'm attracted to you. No point in lying about it. And I think you're attracted to me. So it's there between us. The possibility. And even though we both agree it wouldn't be smart, I'm tempted."

"Me, too." Lane surprised herself with the admission. "You're right. I'm attracted to you, too, but worse than that, I like you. A lot. But given your history with my twin, I'm hesitant to take our relationship to another level right now. What if we did, and then it all went wrong? If things may not end well, we'd be foolish to go there. Wouldn't we?"

He sighed and grabbed the remote off his nightstand. "It's hard for me to argue your logic. Let's find a movie. That'll help both of us settle down."

He scrolled through the options. Lane rejected a few, and he did as well. They settled on a flick about the Italian mafia in Chicago, which was just interesting enough to hold their attention but not exciting enough to keep them awake to see what happened next. They finished off the wine, each of them drinking two glasses. Then Jonas lowered the television volume so it wouldn't keep them awake when they grew drowsy.

Lane's last thought before she finally drifted off was that she hoped she didn't gravitate toward Jonas in her sleep.

* * *

In the morning, Jonas grabbed clothing from his suit-case and went into the bathroom to change first, leaving Lane to ponder her selection of garments to decide what she wanted to wear. Jonas was glad to just be a guy. No matter what the occasion, he wore essentially the same stuff: socks, boxers, pants, a shirt, and shoes. For special occasions like dinner out, a funeral, or a wedding, the cut of the clothing was more elegant and a jacket might be required, but he still wore the same basics. For women, it wasn't as easy as that. They had oodles of different choices to make—a skirt and blouse versus a dress, slacks or jeans versus shorts, lots of different styles in tops, and what shoes went well with their ensembles. The mere thought of having to make choices like that every morning, sometimes without a cup of wake-me-up first, gave him a headache.

When he exited the bath, he found Lane already dressed, and the sight of her startled him. She was wearing jeans—full-length, skin-tight jeans that show-cased her feminine form in a way that her loose, flowy dresses, skirts, and skorts never would. Her top, a pale-pink cotton knit with three-quarter length sleeves, only enhanced the effect her jeans had started, clinging to her breasts and the indentation of her slender waist. The overall impact on Jonas was mind-boggling. A certain part of his male anatomy went instantly hard. His mouth went chalky. His heart started to pound. He couldn't have yelled, "Fire!" if the entire motel compound had gone up in flames.

"Do I look that bad?" She plucked nervously at her top, drawing his attention straight back to her breasts. "I figured we might end up doing some walking today. Running shoes and jeans seem more practical."

Jonas worked his mouth for some saliva to moisten his tongue. He seemed to be fresh out. "I—um—no. You look great." So great that his own jeans suddenly felt too tight. How could she not realize how beautiful she was? What did women see when they looked in a mirror, a grim altered reality? "I'm—uh—just not used to seeing you in britches. That's all."

"Oh."

She looked unconvinced, and Jonas felt bad for making her feel self-conscious. "Really. The clothing is nice. Way more practical than a dress, at least for today. Even if we don't walk a lot, we may be getting in and out of the car repeatedly. You won't have to worry about flashing your panties at me while you're wearing jeans." The moment he said that, he wanted to bonk himself on the head. How stupid could he get? "I mean . . ." He let his voice trail away, and then he actually did bonk himself. "I don't know what I mean. You're so damned beautiful, I can't think."

Her eyes widened and seemed to turn a darker blue. A lovely flush flagged her delicate cheekbones. "Really? You see women in jeans and T-shirts all the time."

She stared down at herself for a long moment, but Jonas doubted that she could see herself the same way he did. "Yes, really," he assured her.

He glanced at the closed door behind her and wished he were outside, shooting the shit with Jeff. No matter what he thought to say, he only seemed to be making things worse. Sudden inspiration saved him. He pretended that his cell phone vibrated in his back pocket, plucked it out, and looked at the screen, which was blank, but he hoped she couldn't see that.

"It's Jeff. He wants to powwow." He stuffed the

phone back in his pocket. "I think I'll go over and see what's up."

"Okay."

He cut a wide berth around her and almost sprinted for the door.

Lane had never been involved in a stakeout, and it was so boring that she was growing drowsy by ten o'clock. Sitting inside a car to watch the entrance of a grocery store wasn't exactly fraught with excitement. Jeff and Carla got out to stretch their legs several times, but Lane couldn't risk being seen. The man in her dreams might recognize her, even from a distance, so she was stuck inside the car. Jonas, who could have taken short walks, chose to remain in the back seat with her, which made her feel bad. He was much taller than she was, and his bony knees were pressed into the back of the seat in front of him, allowing him no wiggle room.

When Jeff was in the car, he made phone calls to property management companies in the area, trying to get information about homes that had been rented out recently. Most of the people he contacted were reluctant to tell him anything, but a few cooperated when he told them he was a Coos County deputy investigating the disappearance of a young woman. With Lane's help, he described the man they were hoping to track down.

"Nothing," he said after ending another call. "No tall, thin guy with stringy, shoulder-length hair has signed a rental agreement recently at that place."

"Maybe the tall, skinny guy wasn't the one who rented the house," Carla suggested.

Jeff sighed. "If that's the case, we're screwed. If it

was rented by a woman—or some other man—we have no physical description. It'll be like looking for a needle in a haystack with a blindfold on."

As discouraged as he was, Jeff resumed making phone calls, which made Lane appreciate, in a way she never had, the dedication and patience of police officers while they worked on a case. No matter how frustrated he was, Jeff kept his voice modulated to a pleasant tone during each conversation, he thought to ask all the right questions, and he was excruciatingly polite, even when Lane suspected that he felt like yelling.

At noon, everyone was hungry for lunch, so Jeff and Carla walked to a nearby burger joint to purchase each of them a meal. Carla was all abuzz with excitement when they returned to the car.

"We just saw posters advertising the Maple Leaf Harvest Celebration! In February, I think it is. I'd absolutely love to attend one. It's on my bucket list."

Lane couldn't help but smile at Carla's enthusiasm for an event she'd come to take for granted over the years. "It is a fun celebration," she agreed as she opened her sack of food. "They boil down syrup and have a pancake brunch so everyone gets to taste genuine maple syrup straight from the cauldron. They also make candies and stuff. Maybe we can get together again and attend the festival. It's quite a tradition in Maple Leaf. We're proud of our syrup!"

"Oh, I am so *in*. And Jeff will love the pancake part. He's a big fan."

As Lane ate, she tried to keep her gaze glued to the doors of the supermarket, a grimy-looking brick building with a multi-window front that sported so many sales posters that she doubted anyone inside could see out. Occasionally, she had to glance away. It was difficult to eat without looking at her food.

"Hey," Jonas said in a low voice after he'd finished eating. "I can watch for a tall, skinny dude. If I see anyone who even comes close to fitting your description, I'll tell you."

Released from the job of watching the store like a hungry hawk, Lane was finally able to tuck into her meal. She'd ordered a chicken burger, a salad, and water in a thirty-two ounce, super-size cup, because she was thirstier than she was hungry. As she sucked it up through a straw, Jonas gave her a sidelong look.

"Remember the two-door outhouse story?"

Straw still clamped between her lips, she met his gaze and stopped drinking. She didn't relish the idea of squatting in a busy parking lot to empty her bladder. "Good point."

As perverse of her as it was, she wanted the water even more after he warned her not to drink too much. She imagined the cool moistness of it filling her dry mouth and sliding down her throat. It took all her self-control not to gulp down every drop of it. Instead, she ate her sandwich and took tiny sips to wash the bites down.

Over the afternoon, Carla's enthusiasm for sleuthing began to wane. "How do cops do this for days on end?" she asked Jeff. "It was exciting at first, but now it's so boring, I might fall asleep."

"Go ahead and take a nap," Jeff suggested. He swung his head to regard Lane and Jonas in the back. "You guys, too. I've got a general idea of what the jerk looks like. I'll wake you if I see anyone who comes close."

Lane felt drowsy, too. Even though it was October,

the sun was out and bore down on the car. It wasn't uncomfortably hot, by any means, but a let-your-eyes-fall-closed warmth filled the interior, making her bones and muscles feel as if they had melted.

Jonas lifted his arm, inviting her to snuggle close against him and use his chest as a pillow. Lane almost shook her head no, but instead she slid across the leather upholstery, tucked her shoulder under his arm, and rested her head against him as he enfolded her in a loose embrace. For Lane, it was an incredibly wonderful feeling to be surrounded by his strength and warmth.

"You sure you won't hear all of us snoring and get sleepy?" Jonas asked Jeff.

"I don't snore," Carla protested from the front seat.

Lane smiled against Jonas' shirt and closed her eyes. Feeling the vibration of Jonas' voice coming through the wall of his chest was unbelievably sexy, making her wish he would speak again.

"I'll be fine, man," Jeff assured him. "I'm no stranger to stakeouts. They're part of my job. I normally have a partner, and we spell each other to grab some shut-eye. When you guys wake up, I'll take my turn."

Pressed comfortably against Jonas' rangy body, Lane let her muscles go limp. Just as she started to drift off, she thought, *Carla's wrong. She does snore.*

Chapter Eleven

By dinnertime, Jonas was as disheartened by their lack of success as his three sleuthing partners were. The only enjoyable part of the day, at least for him, had been holding Lane. After she'd fallen asleep, he'd shifted on the seat to put his back to the door, lifted her onto his lap, and been able to stretch his legs out. His chest had become her pillow, and as he'd drifted in and out of sleep, he had treasured the feeling of her body draped over his.

And now he was having trouble shoving those thoughts from his mind as he perused a menu to decide what he wanted for a very late evening meal. He knew he was in trouble when item six under the entrees read *sex* until he blinked to clear his vision. He nearly groaned out loud.

"I don't know what I want," Carla said. "What have you decided on, Lane?"

Lane smiled wanly at her new friend. "I'm leaning heavily toward a Bloody Mary with extra vegetables."

Carla giggled and slapped her menu closed. "I'm in!"

Jeff made a growling sound. "You can't drink your dinner, honey. We have to get up early to sit in that parking lot again."

Jonas did groan aloud at that. "Please, don't remind me. On television, stakeouts always look so exciting. Ours was like watching grass grow."

Lane, menu still open, said, "I'm the only one who knows for sure what he looks like. As much as I appreciate all your help, you guys could take tomorrow off, and I could just go alone."

"Oh, no," Carla volleyed back. "If I don't go, you'll see him, and I'll miss all the excitement of tailing him back to where he's staying."

"And if I don't go," Jeff inserted, "no one else knows *how* to tail someone. You'd tip him off, and then he'd be onto us."

Jonas looked up from his menu. "And if I don't go, there'll be only three of you, an uneven number. Everybody knows that's bad luck."

Lane sighed. "I'm sorry it's so boring. But it's the only way, isn't it? Jeff had no luck at all today trying to get any pertinent information from property management places, and that's our only other idea." She set aside her menu. "I think I'll go for the creamy tomato soup and half a grilled cheese sandwich."

"That's one of my go-to dinners when I'm tired," Carla said. With a snap of her wrist, she closed her menu and added, "Only I want a whole sandwich. Jeff likes me with some meat on my bones, and I like to eat. That's why we're such a perfect match."

Everyone laughed. When the waitress came to take their orders, the question-and-answer routine went quickly, and their food was delivered almost as fast. Everyone at the table applied themselves to their meals.

Pocketing a bite of pork loin in his cheek, Jonas said, "You ever noticed how quiet people get when the food comes?"

"I'd keep talking, but I'd have to do it with my mouth full, like you just did." Carla dunked one half of her sandwich into her soup before taking a bite.

Jonas smiled and shook his head at Jeff. "Trade her in for another model. This one's too sassy."

"I can't believe you just compared Carla to a car," Lane said.

Jonas grinned and shrugged. "Hey, men love cars. We've been describing women in car-speak for decades."

"In what ways?" Lane challenged.

Jeff whistled and said, "Hot damn, look at *that* set of headlights."

Everyone at the table turned to look and then laughed when nothing was there. Carla rolled her eyes. "You're so lucky. I had my elbow all ready to jab you in the stomach."

Jeff flashed a grin, but it faded quickly. To Lane, he said, "I'm sorry my property management idea didn't pan out. With this not being my jurisdiction, I can't flash my badge to get information here. We have to be inventive."

"I have it!" Carla cried. "We could walk around the old section of town and knock on doors. Sooner or later, the right guy will answer."

Jeff gave her a long "you've got to be kidding" look. "And then what, Nancy Drew? The man is dangerous, and he's undoubtedly armed. He'd recognize Lane."

"At that point, we'd call the police." Carla looked at Lane and quirked her lips. "Hey, it's better than no idea at all. Right?"

Jeff spread butter on his dinner roll. "I just wish that telepathic link Jonas insists Lane has with Veneta could be controlled somehow." He paused with a glob of yellow on his knife to meet Lane's gaze. "You pick up on her thoughts, apparently, so why can't she pick up on yours? Kind of like talking on a two-way radio. Have you ever tried to communicate with her?"

Lane set what was left of her sandwich on the edge of her plate. "No. For years, it's been my mission in life to block her out, not invite her in." She sat back and shook her head. "You clearly don't understand what it's been like for me, Jeff. Imagine a radio suddenly blaring inside your head. You can't change the channel or turn down the volume. You have no control over when it happens, either. During a college final. When I was trying to take meal orders. When I was counting back change to a customer. One time in high school, this boy I liked was asking me to the sophomore prom. I'd been hoping and hoping that he would. It was, like, the most important moment of my life, or so I thought at the time. And right after he asked, right after he *finally* said the words, Veneta crowded into my brain. I said, 'No! Just leave me alone!' And the boy thought I was talking to him."

"Oh, that *bites*!" Carla gave Lane a commiserating look. "The sophomore prom is so important to a girl that age. I didn't have any one special guy I wanted to ask me, but I remember being so afraid nobody would."

"Did you get a date?" Jeff asked.

"No." Carla pulled a glum face. "A girlfriend and I went stag. Our moms had gotten us prom dresses. They cost a lot, and we couldn't let them go to waste. It was a humiliating night for both of us. All the other girls who went stag wore jeans or shorts, nothing as special as what we wore. We were the quintessential wallflowers, standing there like over-decorated stumps in our pretty gowns and nobody asking us onto the dance floor. Even worse, the other girls without dates avoided us because we hadn't gotten the memo not to dress up."

"Ah, honey." Jeff rubbed her shoulder. "If I'd been around, you would have had a date."

By the time they got back to the motel, Jonas was more than ready to kick back on the bed with a cushiony pillow prop while he inhaled a couple of glasses of wine. When he and Lane entered the room, he stopped dead.

"What happened with our pillow barrier?" he asked, thinking to himself that there was no way, *absolutely* no way, that he should climb into bed next to Lane without it.

"The maid tidied up while we were gone. She probably put them back in the closet."

She went over to the dresser to deposit her purse on top of it. Jonas had always enjoyed watching a woman walk, but Lane's hip action in a pair of tight jeans was enough to make him plop the sack of wine he'd just gotten on the table and open it before he did anything else.

"Where'd the corkscrew go?" he asked.

"I think Jeff grabbed it this morning. It *was* his, after all."

"Great! I bought wine, and we have no opener."

"Just step next door and borrow Jeff's," she suggested.

"If I do that, he and Carla will follow me back like homeless puppies." He waved his hand. "It's not that I don't enjoy their company, but after a whole day in the car with them, I need a break."

"Me, too," she confessed. "Our only activity all day was talking to each other. I need some downtime."

"Now it'll be downtime without wine. I was really looking forward to a glass—or two. Doing a stakeout shouldn't be exhausting, but ours was."

Lane opened her purse. "You can still have some wine if you don't mind straining it through your teeth to get the cork bits out." She fished around in the bag and pulled out a fingernail file. "*Voilà, monsieur.* I am woman; hear me roar."

He grinned and held out his hand. "I can do the honors."

"Not until I scrub it and pour alcohol on it, you can't."

"Until we get the bottle open, we have no alcohol."

"I carry some in my toiletry bag to put in my ears after showering. Otherwise, I get swimmer's ear. And I should probably do the cork excavation. I've got oodles of experience. When I first got my apartment, I didn't have a wine opener and couldn't afford one until payday. My folks bought me several bottles as a house-warming gift, and it just sat there on a counter, calling my name."

When she returned to Jonas with the file, he took it from her hand. "I'll do it. I'm afraid you'll cut yourself."

Minutes later, the cork had suffered multiple stab wounds. Jonas finally pushed down hard enough to shoot the cylindrical stopper into the bottle with such force that the wine spewed upward like a Yellowstone geyser, splattering his cheeks and shirt. He jerked, scrunched his face, and poked his tongue out as far as he could to lick off the droplets.

"I knew I should've been the one to do it." Lane grabbed a hand towel from the bathroom and returned to clean up the mess, starting with Jonas. "Only women understand the fine art of a successful cork attack.

Men try to muscle their way through everything. Sometimes picking at something until it falls apart is the better way."

"I'll make a note of that," he said as she tried to blot the wine from his chest. "We're ruining that towel. Merlot on white. Not good."

"Nah. Before I landed a waitressing job, I was a motel maid for a brief time. People are always spilling wine in motel rooms. They have a special solution to get the stain out."

"What is it? I need some to save my shirt."

She lifted her gaze to his. She wasn't in his arms, but she stood close enough for him to kiss her, and he was tempted. Even after a long day in a warm car, she smelled like vanilla, and her eyes, lightly enhanced by mascara, looked as deep and blue as a diving pool in the tropics.

"They don't share the secret with an ordinary human like you." She gave his shirt a final swipe and stepped away. "But there are some OTC solutions that will work."

"I'll never remember what they are when I go shopping. Anything to do with laundry can't stick in my gray matter when it's competing against food. The shirt will become something I wear to paint or do farm work out at my folks' place."

"It's too nice a shirt to retire it," she told him.

Lane took the stained towel and their cups from the previous night to the bathroom, where she rinsed out both. When she emerged into the sleeping area again, Jonas was ready to pour each of them some wine. And Lane was more than ready to drink it. Being around Jonas was getting to her. On the surface, they enjoyed each other's company and were merely becoming good friends, but beneath said surface, she was struggling with a host of feelings and urges that ran much deeper. She truly liked Jonas. He had a laid-back way about him that helped her relax. She couldn't count the times he'd saved her that day from stifling boredom by making her burst out laughing. He was the *perfect* guy for her, and often when she looked at him, she bemoaned the fact that Veneta had found him first. It just didn't seem fair.

After pouring their wine, he went to the closet to retrieve their pillow barrier. Apparently he didn't feel comfortable about sleeping beside her without it. She wondered if he realized how strongly she was attracted to him. *Maybe*, she thought, *he's afraid I'll be all over him without something to discourage me.* That wasn't very flattering. On the other hand, she couldn't deny the possibility, either. She'd met lots of handsome guys, but never one that appealed to her as much as Jonas did on almost every level.

They settled beside each other on the bed, both of them using the pillows as an armrest, which made the reclining position pretty comfortable. Lane noticed that Jonas was frowning slightly, and she knew him well enough now to realize that normally meant he was troubled about something.

"What?" she asked softly. "Are you upset because I teased you about shoving the cork into the bottle?"

The creases in his forehead eased away, and he chuckled. "No, of course not. I'm not that easily offended."

"Then what's wrong? I know that look. You're upset."

He took a deep breath and slowly released it. "I can't get what Jeff said out of my mind." He looked over at her. "And I know if I mention it again, you may start to panic and get angry with me."

Lane shook her head. "I'm sorry. I'm not following. What did Jeff say that might make me panic?"

"The two-way radio idea."

Lane's stomach clenched. "Oh. That."

"Yeah, *that.* And now I've upset you. It's just that—well, what if, Lane? You've worked so hard all your life to keep her voice or her thoughts, or whatever the hell it is, out of your head. And you've never tried to reverse the dialogue. She's sending out stuff to you. You're trying to dodge it like she's firing bullets. What if, instead, you started firing back?"

Lane swung her feet off the bed so quickly that she almost spilled her wine. "No. You don't realize what you're asking of me. *No.*"

"Don't run off. Can't we just talk about it?"

She puffed air into her cheeks and shifted to look back at him. "No, because you're right. It's making me panic. You don't understand what I've gone through. I thought you did, but you don't. I guess nobody can really imagine it until they've experienced it themselves."

"You're right. I can only try to imagine, and I suspect it's really awful. I'm only bringing it up because it may be the only way for us to figure out where she is. And you've said yourself that time is running out for her."

"Don't pressure me," she warned.

"I'm not pressuring you, Lane. I'm just trying to help you look at a lifelong problem in a different light. You think of this telepathic thing as being a curse. But did you ever stop to consider that it may be a rare gift? If all identical twins had a telepathic link as strong as yours with Veneta, scientists would have already proven in studies that it's possible. You and Neta may be the only identical twins in the world who can communicate with each other this way."

"Hallelujah," she flung back at him, lacing the word with sarcasm. "She's been driving me half-nuts all my life, and now you're asking me to open myself up to even more. I can't do it. I *won't*. And don't you dare remind me that she may end up dying as a result. That's not fair. I'll go to any reasonable length to save my sister. I *will*. But what you're suggesting isn't reasonable."

"Okay." He shrugged his shoulders. "I get it. I won't bring it up again. It was just a thought."

She twisted to sit beside him again and drank her wine in three gulps. "I'd like more," she said, thrusting her cup at him. "And make it a double."

She stared straight ahead at the blank television screen while he poured her a refill. The cork kept blocking the flow, judging by the sound of it, a *gurgle-gurgle*, then a pause. When he handed the cup back to her, she pushed out a thank-you that she knew didn't sound sincere.

"I'm sorry," he said. "I really won't mention it again. I swear."

Lane closed her eyes. She wanted to stay mad at him, but the regret that rang in his voice made that impossible. Lifting her lashes, she gazed into the dark depths of the wine for a long moment. "I'm sorry, too. I shouldn't have gotten angry. You're just trying to think of a way to find her. I understand that."

"Yeah. Tilting at windmills. Isn't that what it's called?"

"No, I think it's more grasping at straws, only that usually means someone is trying to save himself in any way possible. You're not doing that. You're trying to save my sister. I should appreciate that, not get mad at you."

"Yeah, well, it's a pretty harebrained idea anyway."

Lane met his gaze. "I'll think about it," she stated. "No promises, but I will consider it."

He nodded. "I can't ask for more than that. Just promise me one thing. If thinking about it upsets you, just stop. It probably wouldn't work, anyway. I want to find Neta, but not if it means putting you at risk. However she ended up in this mess, she was the one calling the shots. And in a very short time, you've become more important to me than she ever was. In fact, when I think about it, if you doing what I suggested could cause you emotional or mental anguish, I don't want you to. She's made her bed. It's not your responsibility to save her from having to sleep in it."

In that moment, Lane felt the sexual pull she experienced any time he was near grow stronger than ever. Jonas was so different from other men. He didn't come on to her. He didn't grope her. He was more like a good friend—a good friend who could make her stomach clench with a wink or a grin—who could make the feminine core of her tingle and ache with need.

"Who gets the first shower tonight?" she asked, trying to distract herself. "I'm fine with waiting if you'd like to go first."

"You go ahead," he told her. "My hair dries faster. If you get too tired, you may not blow yours dry, and my mom swears going to bed with a wet head is unhealthy."

After finishing her wine, Lane got up to prepare for bed. After showering and blowing her hair dry, she vacated the bathroom so Jonas could have a turn. When he emerged, she was already snuggled down under the blankets with her back to his side of the mattress.

He turned out the lights before joining her. As he slipped into bed, he whispered, "If you're still awake, Lane, I wish you a deep and dreamless sleep."

She smiled into the darkness but didn't respond. If she did, they might start conversing again, and she didn't think a pillow-talk session would help in any way to dampen her desire for him. Instead, she just lay there with her back to him, trying to figure out why her dormant libido had suddenly sprung to life.

They'd all set their wake-up calls for five a.m. the next morning so they'd have time for breakfast before the supermarket opened. Lane jerked awake at the raucous ringing of the room phone, feeling as if she hadn't slept a wink. Jonas' wish for her to have a deep and dreamless sleep hadn't come true. Instead, foggy and shadowy images had disrupted her rest, and she couldn't help wondering if Veneta had grown so weak that she was now barely conscious. Lane had dreamed of trying to move and had felt weighted down. Her throat had burned with thirst and was so dry that she could barely swallow.

She couldn't push the disturbing images from her mind as she dressed for the day and dabbed on a minimal amount of makeup before letting Jonas have the bathroom. She'd been quick; he was even quicker. When they were both ready to leave, they went outside while they waited for Jeff and Carla to emerge from their room.

Sitting beside Jonas in the back seat a few minutes later, Lane didn't engage in the discussion about where they should do breakfast. Her mind was on the dreams she'd had last night and the awful feeling she had that Veneta was close to running out of time. Mostly it was like a premonition, only it was also something more. A sensation within her of being alone, that a part of her was fading away. It was difficult to think about food.

The others decided on a pancake house where they could have a traditional breakfast or pig out on Belgian waffles, crepes, or flapjacks. Lane just wanted coffee, but she knew she needed to eat. For one thing, it would be hours before lunch, and for another, she knew Jonas would notice her lack of appetite and become worried.

During the meal, she dutifully poked food in her mouth even though she was barely aware of what she was eating. Jonas waited for Carla and Jeff to start a conversation between themselves and then turned a troubled gaze on Lane.

"You dreamed of her last night. I can tell."

Lane wanted to deny it. Instead she only nodded.

"Tell me," he said softly.

Lane's throat felt achy, a feeling reminiscent of her childhood when she'd been trying not to cry. "There isn't a lot to tell you, Jonas. It was all kind of foggy and shadowy. In the dream, I could barely move, and my throat burned." Tears did well in her eyes as she pushed those words out. "I think she's dying."

"Ah, sweetheart." Jonas grasped her hand. "We're doing everything we can. No matter what happens, remind yourself of that. You've gone the extra mile. So have I. Jeff and Carla as well."

At the sound of his name, Jeff turned toward them. "We should go to the police." Jeff held up his hand to forestall them from speaking. "I know we're here on nothing more than a hunch. We don't have a shred of proof that Veneta was kidnapped in the first place, let alone that her abductors brought her here. But we can at least *try* to make them listen to us."

Lane tried to keep her voice even. "And tell them what? That I *dreamed* they brought her here?"

"No," Jeff countered. "I don't think you should even mention the dreams or the telepathy thing. Just keep it factual. Tell them that Veneta's gone missing and you *suspect* that she's being held somewhere in this area. Describe the man who accosted you on the sidewalk. Describe his vehicle. If we're lucky, they may even let you look at mug shots. If so, you may come across him. That'd be a huge step forward."

"And if we're not lucky?" Lane asked.

"We're no worse off," Jeff replied. "And at least we've reported it. Even if you're not taken seriously, most of the officers in the precinct will get word of it through the grapevine. They may get a good laugh. They may not believe any of it. But they'll hear about it from fellow officers, and some of the details may stick with them. Let's say some cop is cruising in an older neighborhood and sees the vehicle you described parked in front of a house. He'll probably remember what his fellow officer told him and call it in." He shrugged his shoulders. "It's a long shot, I know. But I'll feel better overall if we file a report. The police can't help us unless we go to them and ask for their help. And even a half-assed attempt on their part to locate Veneta is better than no help at all."

Lane couldn't argue the point. She looked helplessly at Jonas. He knew that her last conversation with the Maple Leaf police hadn't gone well.

"It's your call," he told her. "We understand that it'll be stressful for you. We also know that it may not do any good if we do file a report. We have no evidence to support our theory—no physical evidence, at any rate."

Jeff interrupted to say, "I think we're right, though. We didn't just pick out a town where she might be by drawing a city name out of a hat."

"No," Lane said, her voice taut with tension. "We picked this town because I saw the man in my dream here. How can I possibly tell the police that I'm chasing a dream figure? They didn't believe a word I said the last time."

Jeff scrunched his shoulders again. "And they probably won't this time. You needn't tell them anything about the dreams. The main goal here is to get your sister's disappearance on their radar."

It *would* be beneficial if the police were at least aware of Veneta's possible presence in the area. They'd probably heard about her disappearance through police channels, but Lane felt confident that no mention of it had been on the local news. Pictures of Veneta would have been aired, and people who knew Lane would have noticed the resemblance. Her parents would have received calls from friends. Employees at the restaurant—and even customers there—might have seen Lane's face on television and said something to her.

"What about our stakeout?" Lane tried. "I'm the only one who knows what the abductor looks like, and I can't be in two places at once. Going to the police could take hours."

"We've got a plan." Carla had drawn her blond hair back into a ponytail this morning and wore no makeup. From a distance, people might think she was a teenager. "Jeff and I have a good idea what the man looks like. We can do the stakeout while you're gone. If we see someone who matches his description, we'll take a picture of him to get a yay or nay from you later, and once we've got clear pics, we'll follow him."

"But if it's not the right man and you follow him, nobody will be there to watch the building."

"True," Jeff conceded. "But we saw nobody matching his description yesterday, so it's pretty unlikely that we will today. And in the meantime, we're getting the police onboard."

Lane *really* didn't want to go to the police station. The only person at the table who seemed to understand was Jonas. He still held her hand, and she realized she was clinging to his thick fingers as if they were her lifeline.

"I'll be right there," he told her. "Right beside you. You won't have to do it alone."

Lane nodded. If there was a chance—even the remotest chance—that going to the police might help her sister, she had no choice but to do it. "Okay. I'll go. But I'm not going to like it." She met Jeff's gaze. "It's not that I dislike cops. Please know that. It's just—I don't know—*humiliating*, when you're telling the truth and they look at you like you're a cockroach sitting on their lunch plate."

"A very pretty cockroach," Jonas inserted as he gave her hand a comforting squeeze. "You should finish your breakfast. It may be a while before we get to eat again."

Lane was quivering with nerves when she and Jonas entered the police station. The interior of the building was swarming with people in blue uniforms. Desktop phones pinged with call notifications, the musical pitches reminding Lane of children pounding out tuneless noise on a xylophone. There was also a constant hum of conversation and an underlying smell of food in the air—pizza, donuts, coffee. She couldn't imagine anyone ordering pizza so early in the day, but she guessed law enforcement officers must keep irregular hours, some of them working all night and ending their shifts with dinner, regardless of the time of day.

She and Jonas sat in a waiting area on molded, hard plastic chairs. The floors were multicolor slate and pretty much indestructible. She saw only two magazines on a small table at the end of the chair row. Apparently, keeping people entertained while they waited for help wasn't a priority.

Lane couldn't focus. She hadn't slept well, so part of it was that she was tired. But it was also due to nervousness. She dreaded the interview that was to come. Wanted to run. No matter what Jeff said, they might be pushed into revealing her strange dreams, and if so, she knew from experience how those police officers would look at her.

Jonas curled a strong arm around her shoulders. "I'm here." His voice was husky and vibrant. "Try to remember that you'll probably never see these people again. So what if they think you've lost your marbles? It's no skin off your nose. Right? I don't think that. Jeff and Carla don't think that. When you leave here, you'll be with us, and these clowns can think whatever the hell they want."

Lane pressed her cheek against the hollow of his shoulder and closed her eyes. Drew in the smell of him. Clean cotton, aftershave and cologne, and the musky scent of man. She wanted to just melt into him and disappear. It was childish and cowardly, but that was how she felt. She hated when people thought she was crazy. They got all shifty-eyed. Couldn't look at her, almost as if they were afraid her mental illness might be contagious. Or maybe they were afraid of her. She only knew it made her feel awful—ashamed, embarrassed, angry.

When a female officer came out to get them, Lane was thankful that she was someone new to her. She truly might have run if one of the policemen who interviewed her about the sidewalk attack had come out. She didn't think she could face either one of those men again.

As they followed their escort into the interior office area, Jonas kept his arm around her shoulders. At times, when her knees wobbled, he steadied her balance. When they sat down across the desk from Sergeant Marie Oliver, he began the dialogue, introducing himself and then Lane.

As it turned out, Lane wasn't required to say a whole lot. Jonas just took over. Under other circumstances, she might have resented that, but this morning, she was grateful. Occasionally Sergeant Oliver asked Lane a direct question, and she had to answer, but it wasn't as awful as she'd expected it to be. She kept reminding herself that it truly didn't matter what this woman thought. The goal here was to make these people aware of Veneta's situation and hopefully encourage them to help find her. When the interview was over and Jonas led Lane out of the building, she released a breath she hadn't realized she'd been holding.

"I can't remember anything I said. Did I even sound rational?"

He laughed. "You did great. And I didn't get the impression that she thinks you're nuts. Didn't you hear her say her mother is clairvoyant? We got lucky in that. She believes in the possibility of mental telepathy."

"I don't remember her saying that."

"Well, she did say it, and the minute she did, I wanted to do a victory dance."

"So they'll help us, do you think?"

Jonas unlocked his car with the keyless remote. "Well, I won't go as far as to say that, but she did take down all the information. Right? How she'll handle it, I have no idea. But now it's on file. She did say we hadn't given her much to go on. That there's no proof Veneta is here or that she's even still alive. But she seemed willing to share the information with other officers. That was the best we could hope for."

As they drove back to the supermarket to participate in the stakeout for the remainder of the day, Jeff texted that they were ready for lunch and asked if they would mind doing Subway sandwiches. Lane didn't object to that, and neither did Jonas. After picking up sandwiches, soft drinks, and several giant-size chocolate chip cookies, they drove to the market and parked beside Jeff's car. Jonas delivered their friends' food to them, because Lane might be seen if she left the vehicle.

When Jonas joined Lane again, he said, "This is kind of nice. We can see better, sitting up front. And it'll give us a break from one another. I enjoy both of them. A lot. But sitting in a confined space for hours on end with little to do but talk—well, it gets old kind of fast."

"I'm sure they feel the same way." She reached over to pat his arm and then immediately wondered why she'd touched him. It had come naturally to her, though, and Jonas didn't seem to think it was too forward. "Nobody can carry on an entertaining conversation for nearly twelve hours without running out of stuff to say."

"True." He glanced over at her. "And, to be honest, Lane, I'm a little worried about you."

"Why?"

"I know going to the police station was really difficult for you, and I totally understood how upset you felt, but I can't shake the feeling that there's something else, something really serious, that's also troubling you."

Lane was only half surprised by his observation. Jonas was a very perceptive person, and they had become very close. It seemed to have developed too fast, this understanding of each other that they shared, but it felt natural to Lane. Neither of them had forced it; it had just happened, and now she felt as if he were the best friend she'd ever had.

"You know me too well," she replied. Pressure built in her chest. She knew if she went on talking that, at least for her, it would be the equivalent of jumping off a cliff. But she'd been holding it in all day, and she was no closer to making a decision—possibly the most important decision of her life. "In the dreams, I've never actually seen Veneta. It's more like I enter her body and see through her eyes. In the past, everything was clear. Like I was actually seeing it myself. Now, the dreams are—I don't know how to explain, but what I see is blurry and distant. I think she's very sick. That she's about to drift away." She waved her hand at the supermarket. "And all we're doing to save her is watching a store on the off chance that we'll see her captor."

"We've brainstormed it to death. This is all we could think of. Tonight, maybe, we can drive around the neighborhoods, looking for his car. We haven't done that yet."

Lane shook her head. "There's another thing we can try." She met his gaze, battling against an almost overwhelming urge to break the eye contact and drop the subject. "You know what I'm talking about. I can try to communicate with her."

Chapter Twelve

At Lane's words, Jonas' brow pleated in a frown, and judging by the expression of regret on the rest of his countenance, it was a frown of self-consternation. "I shouldn't have pushed you about trying to communicate with her. You have every right to protect and preserve your own sanity, and deep down, you're afraid you'll lose your mind if you ever open that door. Nobody knows us better than we know ourselves, honey. Trust your instincts."

Turning to gaze out the passenger window, Lane took a deep breath and slowly released it. "If I trust my own instincts, I'll be a coward who let my sister die." She forced herself to meet his gaze again. "I don't think I can live happily with that opinion of myself. Yes, breaking down all the mental walls I've built to keep her out of my head is very scary for me. Once I lower those barriers, she could be inside my head twenty-four/seven. You know? It could destroy my life. I know I haven't done anything all that great with it yet, but it is my life. And it's been hard enough to focus on what's important without opening up a channel of communication with nothing blocking her."

Jonas cupped her chin in his hand, and the moment she felt the gentle warmth of his grip, she had a wild urge to tell him how much she cared about him, how much she longed for more with him.

Instead, she said, "But in reality, Jonas, what better time is there? I'll have you with me. If it's awful, you'll be able to talk me down." She forced a smile and felt it wobble. "It's sort of the same as feeling fortunate when you have a heart attack in the ER waiting room. Someone will be there to save me."

He ran his thumb along her jawline, and the sensation tempted her to crawl over the console into his arms. "Thank you for having that much faith in me. But the truth is, honey, this is uncharted territory for me. Probably for any psychologist or psychiatrist, it would be. I have no idea what the outcome may be for you. If your gut tells you not to do it, don't."

"If I don't, my sister is going to die, Jonas."

"Maybe so." He tightened his hold on her chin, not with enough force to hurt, but enough to convey to her how important she was to him. "But, like I said before, Veneta is an adult. For whatever reasons, she made the decisions that landed her in this mess. That doesn't mean that you're obligated to also pay the price. Putting your own sanity at risk may not help Veneta at all. It could even backfire. And then how will you help her?"

Nobody knew that better than Lane. She could remember so many times when she hadn't been able to hear or understand what someone right in front of her was saying because Veneta's voice inside her head had been so persistent and loud. "It's still something I have to do," she pushed out. "If I don't, and she dies, I'll always hate myself for not having the courage to at least try. I just need a promise from you."

His voice turned husky as he asked, "What's that?"

"When I try to contact her, promise you won't leave

me, that you'll be right there." *With your arms around me*, she wanted to add. "Don't leave me, even for a second."

"Aw, sweetheart." He leaned forward to press a light kiss against her forehead. "I'll be stuck to you like glue."

After texting Jeff of their change in plans, Jonas drove Lane back to their motel where she could lie down and rest in preparation for a long night on the streets. Lane wanted to be in the old neighborhoods as she tried to telepathically communicate with her sister. Her reasoning was simple. Veneta had been largely silent for days, with only hazy and weak signals being the exception. Lane believed her sister was losing her physical strength, and she feared that was impacting her mental acuity as well. If Veneta was sending out weak signals, Lane might not be receiving them. She wanted to be as physically close to Veneta as possible while she tried to connect with her, and the best place to start was on the old side of town.

Jonas wasn't about to argue with Lane's decision. First of all, it made sense, and secondly, it went hand-in-hand with Lane's last dream of Veneta. *Hazy, confused, misty, weak*. Thinking back to his childhood illnesses, Jonas recalled how crazy his thoughts had been when he'd had a high fever. All jumbled, with occasional apparitions of things he was afraid of. Spiders on the wall, sometimes. Snakes at the foot of his bed, at other times. Veneta might be battling far worse things than a fever. *Illness, starvation, and dehydration*. Her thought processes had probably become very muddled.

All Jonas knew for certain was that he needed to look

after Lane. He knew it would be safer to take her walking in old neighborhoods during the day, but they would run the risk of Lane being seen and recognized. He saw no choice but to take her out when it was dark. Unless she was spotted walking directly under a streetlight, she could probably pass through different sections of town without detection.

Jeff and Carla had agreed to remain on stakeout at the supermarket. If they saw a man matching the description Lane had given them, they'd snap several pictures and then tail him when he left the store. Once they could pinpoint where the guy was holing up, they would return to the motel to see if Lane recognized the individual in their photographs. The plan, in Jonas' opinion, had its holes. Jeff and Carla would have to leave the stakeout on a possible wild-goose chase. But it was the only plan they had.

In the meanwhile, it was Jonas' chosen job to make sure Lane lay down and got some sleep. Years ago, when Jonas' brother Barney had been a rookie cop and had just joined a big-city police force, Jonas had gone to visit him and walked a beat with him one night. He'd been exhausted by the time Barney's shift was over. Burning for a drink of water. Sore feet and an empty belly. No matter how physically fit Lane believed herself to be, a whole night of walking would be a lot harder than she imagined.

Once Jonas got Lane settled on the bed, he lay down on the other side of the pillow barrier, hoping to get some rest himself. He'd just closed his eyes when Lane tossed away the pillows and scooted over to lie next to him.

"Hold me, Jonas. I'm not coming on to you. Honestly, I'm not. I just need to feel your arms around me."

The thought flitted through Jonas' mind that she might get more than she bargained for if he drew her against him and held her close. On the other hand, she obviously needed the comfort of his nearness. Only a sorry excuse for a man couldn't offer a woman comfort without being overcome by physical urges.

He slipped an arm under her shoulders and rolled her against his chest—and against other parts of him as well. The feeling that washed through him was amazing. It was as if he'd been waiting all his life to hold only this woman. The dips and curves of her body fitted against his as if they'd been molded just for him. He'd hugged a lot of females close, and he'd never felt this way with any of them. Like he'd finally come home.

The feeling reminded Jonas of something Veneta had said to him just prior to breaking up with him. *"I think you've fallen in love with the wrong part of me."* At the time, her words had made no sense to him.

Of the two women, Lane was the gentler and more thoughtful one, a person who held herself in check before she spoke or acted, a person upon whose mind mistakes weighed heavily. Veneta had been just the opposite, a confetti thrower who boldly filled the world with color and didn't trouble herself over the mess she left in her wake. Looking back on it now, Jonas finally understood Veneta in ways he hadn't been able to back then, because she'd been unable to explain to him what she hadn't been able to fully comprehend herself. *That there were two of her. That she was half of something instead of a whole. That he didn't belong with her. That he'd fallen in love with the wrong side of her.* Lane was the woman he'd been looking for, and he'd found a reflection of her in Veneta. But *only* a reflection.

Jonas had heard so many happily married men say that they'd known, the instant they saw their wives, that "she was the one." That feeling those men spoke of had been based upon looks alone. Before even meeting the women, those men had somehow known. And if it was possible for a man to recognize on sight the woman who would become his everything, didn't it make sense that Jonas had done the same when he'd seen Veneta? That he'd gotten that feeling. *She's the one.* Only he'd had no way of knowing that she had a double, one of them meant for him and the other one not.

Jonas snuggled Lane closer and forced his muscles to relax. He couldn't be thinking about his relationship with Lane right now. His first priority had to be getting some rest so that he'd be at the top of his game tonight in order to protect this woman who'd come to mean so much to him. What if they came upon the man while they were out there? Lane may have not considered that, but Jonas had.

He possessed a concealed carry permit that was recognized statewide. He'd tuck his handgun under the back of his belt and wear a lightweight jacket to hide it. Fortunately, it was now October, the nights were starting to get nippy, and a jacket wouldn't make him feel too warm while walking. It wasn't that he felt it necessary to hide the weapon from Lane. He'd already told her he planned to be packing. He just saw no point in adding to her stress by reminding her that they might stumble into a dangerous situation.

Jonas didn't believe that Veneta's captor had any compassion. If Lane's dreams of her sister were accurate, the guy holding her wasn't feeding her properly or giving her enough water. What kind of man could imprison a woman and then fail to give her food and drink? *Not much of a man*, Jonas decided. Anyone who could do that to another human being had more than one screw loose, and he was dangerous, simply because he had no limits or common decency.

Feeling well-rested and satiated after a restaurant meal with Jonas, Lane thought she was ready for anything. As they left the eatery, Jonas got a text from Jeff, saying it was nearly dark, and the supermarket had closed for the evening, so he and Carla were going to find somewhere to eat. Afterward, they'd text and try to hook up with Jonas and Lane to walk with them through neighborhoods. He and Carla had been able to nap during the stakeout by spelling each other and weren't as tired as they had expected to be.

"I'm sorry," Jonas told Lane. "I'll understand if having them with us tonight is too much. Just say so. I'll explain that this is going to be upsetting for you and you'd prefer not to have an audience."

Lane weighed the situation before replying. "They've become my friends, too, now. As long as they don't distract me, I don't care if they're there to watch me possibly make a fool of myself."

He looped an arm around her shoulders and didn't remove it until they reached his car. Lane was aware of him in a way she'd never been aware of a man. How well they moved together, her hip bumping his muscular thigh, the V where his right arm met his shoulder providing her a perfect place to tuck in close to him. The swing of his stride, loose and well-oiled, affected her walk, forcing her to flow with his lead, very much like dancing. A smooth, rhythmical joining of their bodies.

Once in the car and in the vicinity of where they planned to search, Jonas said, "Just relax and close your eyes. If you sense anything, tell me, and that's where we'll pull over to start walking."

Lane did as he suggested, but she felt nothing coming to her from Veneta. For a full minute, the only sound inside the vehicle was their breathing. Finally, he said, "If you can't pick up on her signals from the car, maybe we'll have more luck walking. You game?"

Lane nodded and unfastened her seat belt.

Two hours later, Jonas was growing increasingly worried about Lane. He'd long since lost track of how many city blocks they had covered. Tucked securely under his arm, she walked with her eyes closed a lot, her expression one of fierce concentration. Jonas was relieved that Jeff and Carla had changed their minds about joining them in favor of kicking back in their room for a couple of nightcaps while they watched television. Lane didn't need people talking to distract her. She also didn't need to feel pressured by anyone around her.

Jonas was about to ask if she was okay when she suddenly jerked to a stop, covered her face with her hands, and started sobbing. Jonas grasped her by the shoulders, acutely aware of how delicate her bones felt beneath his hands. He'd seen Lane get tears in her eyes several times, but he'd never witnessed her giving way to her emotions like this, with violent sobs racking her slight frame.

"It's going to turn out okay," he murmured as she pressed closer against him. He felt her tears dampening his shirt and didn't care. Hell, she could use the garment as a handkerchief as far as he was concerned.

"You're doing everything you can, sweetheart. No one can ask for more than that."

"It's just so frightening not to *feel* her anymore. I can't explain it. But it's as if a part of her has always been there within me somehow, and now that's suddenly gone. A feeling of aloneness and emptiness."

Jonas' heart broke for her. He was close to his own brothers and sisters, and although he honestly couldn't imagine being able to feel their presence when they were apart, he had always been aware of their existence, thinking of them at odd times and just happening to call when one of them most needed to talk. What Lane felt was obviously much stronger than that.

"Listen to me," he told her. "Are you listening?"

"Yes." She nodded and looked up at him. She'd stopped in between streetlights, thank goodness. In the moonlight, he could see her tears glistening on her cheeks, but no one would be able to recognize her from a distance. "I'm listening."

He rubbed his thumbs over her shawl, trying to soothe her. "When people are starving or thirsting to death, they go in and out of consciousness. At times, Veneta may be completely out of it. At other times, she may come awake. When she does, and if you're in her vicinity, maybe you can pick up on her thoughts again."

She nodded and wiped beneath her eyes with trembling fingertips. "You're right. She isn't dead. She's just out of it right now. I'm being a drama queen. I *hate* drama queens."

Jonas couldn't help but smile. "You're not a drama queen. My younger sister, oh, yeah, she can be a drama queen sometimes. Trust me. I know one when I see one, and you aren't."

"Thank you, but I'm not exactly staying calm."

As they set off walking again, Jonas thought to himself that she was one of the strongest women he'd ever met.

Lane and Jonas walked until nearly dawn and then hurried back to his car so she'd be safely out of sight when the sun came up. Lane felt emotionally drained, but her feet didn't hurt the way Jonas claimed his did.

"I was waitressing until only recently," she told him. "It was common for me to be on my feet for twelve hours at a stretch. It's one of those things we get conditioned for, I guess."

Once back in their room, he plopped down on the side of their bed and jerked his shoes and socks off. His ankles didn't look swollen, but his feet were red at the stress points where they'd connected with the cement countless times.

"Okay," Lane told him. "It's time for a long soak. Nice, hot water first. Then cold. Otherwise you'll be hobbling when we go out tomorrow night."

Grumbling about how he hated to be babied, Jonas followed her into the bath and rolled up his pant legs as she filled the tub. When he sat down on the tub's edge with his feet in the hot water, he groaned and said it felt so good he might never take them out.

"I can't believe my feet gave out on me," he said. "I played football. I worked every summer and every day after school on our farm. Now I *still* help my dad out at the farm and go to the gym for a workout on the days that I don't. Only on weekdays, of course. I refuse to push my body seven days a week."

"Jonas?"

"What?" he demanded, his voice sounding more than a little cross.

"Getting sore feet isn't related to your gender or body strength. People who get jobs working on concrete and suddenly must be on their feet for hours on end normally experience foot pain. I certainly did. Your feet just aren't used to it. If you did it every night, your feet would adjust and no longer hurt after a shift."

He sighed. "I just feel like such a wimp." He shot a glance over his shoulder at her bare feet. "Just look. Yours are half the size of mine, and you've got little, tiny bones. How can such dainty feet outperform my snowshoes?"

Lane realized too late that he was making a big deal out of nothing just to make her laugh. And she obliged him. And as she did, she realized that a bit of levity was exactly what she needed. How was it that Jonas always managed to lighten her heart?

"Okay, give me the real scoop. How badly are they hurting?"

He narrowed an eye at her. "I'm dying. I think I need a foot massage."

"Dream on."

She joined him on the edge of the bathtub, her back resting against the wall so she could face him. He cut her a sideways glance, his hazel eyes sparkling with mischief. "What? You're staring at me like I just grew a third eye in the center of my forehead."

In that moment, there were so many things she wished she could say. This man, who presented himself without pretense to the world, had helped her find her center tonight and had been her anchor in the storm. Only how could she put all those feelings into words? Instead, she said, "Thank you for sticking it out with me tonight."

He dragged a hand through the water, creating a

musical chord with the pinging of droplets as they fell from his fingers. "No problem, and you needn't say thank you." All signs of levity departed from his expression. "I was so"—he shrugged—"I want to say I was so proud of you for how you handled yourself tonight, but that seems dumb. I didn't raise you and can't take any credit for making you into the incredible women that you've become."

Lane could scarcely credit her ears. "Incredible? Jonas, I had a major meltdown on a sidewalk in a quiet neighborhood in the middle of the night. It's a wonder I didn't wake someone. They might've called the cops."

He wiped his moist fingers on his rolled-up pants leg. "It was an awful night for you. The silence on her end is tearing you up." He let that hang between them for a second. "You have a strength of character that I don't often find in people. A sense of loyalty, as well. And you don't let yourself off the hook when the going gets rough. Which it definitely did tonight."

Lane felt instantly uncomfortable. Over her lifetime, nobody had ever told her that she was strong. Or loyal, for that matter. Her cheeks went hot. To conceal her discomfort, she bent sideways to test the water temperature and then busied herself with adding more heat.

"It's difficult for you to receive compliments. Isn't it?"

She glanced up. "It makes me uneasy, yes."

"Why?"

He fired back with that question so quickly that she didn't have time to weigh her words and blurted, "Because I don't deserve them."

He reached past her to shut off the hot water. "It's getting a bit too warm." In the sudden hush when the faucet stopped gushing, she heard him release a nearly inaudible sigh. "Ah, Lane. You mean that, I know, and I guess you must have your reasons. But hearing you say it—well, that just makes me sad. I think you've been looking into the wrong mirror."

It seemed an odd thing for him to say, and she gave him a bewildered look.

"Do you know how we humans develop our own self-image?"

She shook her head no.

He smiled slightly. "Good answer, because we don't develop our own self-image. Other people do it for us. The things they say to us. The way they treat us. They create the reflection that we see in our personal mirrors. And sometimes, Lane, that reflection is distorted."

Lane could think of nothing to say.

"You're a strong, caring, and courageous person." He flashed her a smile. "I'm sorry if hearing that makes you uneasy. But I'll keep saying it anyway, because you need to hear it. Apparently, your parents failed in getting those messages across to you."

"My parents love me," she protested. "And they've always, *always* been good to me."

He braced his elbows on his knees and bent his head to gaze into the water. "I know they love you, and I have every confidence that they were the best parents to you that they knew how to be. But yours wasn't a typical childhood because you weren't a typical kid. Your mom and dad were probably bewildered by you. Definitely confused and worried about you much of the time." He fell silent and then, in low voice, said, "Lane, please look at me."

She met his gaze and then couldn't look away, because she saw so many different emotions reflected in his eyes. Pain, regret, a yearning to help.

"Your parents didn't purposefully give you a faulty self-image, and even more important, you were three when they adopted you. By then, you had already developed your categorical self-image. I know you remember very little about that period of your life, but as an adult, look back on it now and try to imagine what you went through. You were a tiny little girl who had a mother and a sister, and at some point, your whole world was blasted apart. As an innocent child, how do you think you perceived all the events that took place? Did you think your mom stopped loving you? That she just gave you away? Were you frightened? Did you feel betrayed? You most certainly must have missed Veneta. Identical twins in the same household can be traumatized if they're suddenly separated. How must you have felt afterward? Your home and all that was familiar, gone. Your mother, gone. And even worse than all of that, your twin, the other half of yourself, suddenly gone."

"Why are you saying all this?" she asked.

Jonas fixed his gaze on the water again. "It's hard to put into words, Lane. Mainly, I'm trying to make you look back and internalize the fact that your life experience has damaged your self-esteem. I think that's why it troubles you when you receive compliments. It pushes new images into the reflection you see of yourself, and those new images don't fit. Imagine a beautiful painting of a virgin wilderness with a computer sitting smack dab in the middle of an untouched forest. What would your reaction be?"

"That the computer didn't belong there."

He smiled and winked at her. "Exactly. Your image of yourself is like a painting that's been engraved on your brain. Dozens of times a day, all of us refer to that image of ourselves. It's familiar. Even if we don't really like our self-image, it troubles us when someone else tries to alter it. Our self-image is who we think we are, and it's unsettling, even disturbing, when we get feedback that makes us question our own identity."

It was Lane's turn to sigh. "I see where you're trying to take me, Jonas."

"Ah, *damn*. A good psychologist never shows his hand."

Lane surprised herself by laughing. "You're a wonderful psychologist." She paused, not sure she should continue. "You're also a wonderful friend. I feel so lucky that I met you. I'll try to work on improving my self-esteem, but it may not be as easy as you think."

"Changing how we see ourselves is never easy." He bent to pull the drain plug. "I'm ready for the cold soak. We need to hit the sack so we can walk the old side of town again tonight. Only I'm hungry. Do you think any restaurants are open this early?"

A half hour later, Jeff and Carla tapped on their motel room door. Jonas had just gotten his socks and shoes back on, and his feet no longer ached as he went to answer the summons. *Lane's a miracle worker*, he thought.

Jeff boomed, "Good morning, kiddos!" as he entered the room. Carla merely smiled at Jonas behind her boyfriend's back and rolled her eyes.

"Good morning!" Lane called from the bathroom. "Be out in a sec. Jonas is *starving*! You want to go out to eat with us?"

Carla went to lean against the doorframe to chat with Lane while she finished brushing her hair. Jeff turned to Jonas and asked in a half whisper, "How'd it go last night?"

"It was rough on her," Jonas replied, matching his volume with Jeff's. "Veneta has gone silent."

Jeff drew back his lips against his teeth, a habit of his when he was thinking that Jonas remembered well. "Shit," he said. "That's not a good sign. Do you think she's dead?"

"I'm not sure what to think, but that's definitely where Lane's mind went last night. For her sake, I *pray* that isn't the case. I'm afraid she'll take it really hard." Head bent, Jonas toed the carpet. "Keep your fingers crossed," he said, glancing back up.

Jeff nodded, his expression going deadpan.

"Stay positive around her, please," Jonas whispered. "I know the odds aren't good, but Lane won't be able to focus if she's all wigged out."

Jeff gave Jonas a thumbs-up and went to stand behind Carla at the bathroom door. Peering over the top of his girlfriend's head at Lane, he said, "I'll never get why it takes a woman so long to do her hair. I'm done in three seconds."

Jonas heard a hair spray can spew, and then Lane said, "Don't test me, buster. I've got excellent aim."

Lane directed her friends to a truck-stop restaurant at an I-5 exit where the food was excellent and served in generous quantities. She wasn't hungry, but she knew Jonas was and that he had a large appetite. She'd been to eateries with him enough times now to know that he sometimes didn't get enough food to make him feel satisfied. That wouldn't be an issue at Jack's Place. Flapjacks stacked a mile high. What looked like a half pound of bacon on a plate. Omelets so large that only a platter provided enough room for side dishes. Twenty-ounce tumblers, filled to the brim with milk or juice.

"Oh, man. This is my idea of a great breakfast," Jonas said as he tucked into golden hash browns and a liberal mound of sausage links. "Reminds me of the spreads my mom used to put out. With a hardworking husband, four growing boys, and two girls at her table, she realized the importance of wholesome food and plenty of it."

Jeff's stack of pancakes was so tall that it leaned slightly, reminding Lane of the Tower of Pisa. He drenched the pile of buttered cakes with maple syrup. Watching him dig in put a metallic taste of nausea in her mouth. She looked down at her own plate, which held two eggs over easy, a Belgian waffle, cottage potatoes, and bacon. She didn't want to take a single bite, let alone try to eat even half of it. Rationally, she knew she should be starving after walking for so many hours, but she felt no hunger pangs.

"You okay?" Jonas asked.

Lane nodded and mustered up a smile. "Just not really hungry."

"Can you swallow a few bites anyway?" He trailed his gaze over her face. "We put in some miles last night. I'll worry if you can't eat."

Lane stared down at her food, remembering how thirsty Veneta had been in the last dream. It didn't seem fair that Lane should have so much while her sister was possibly starving to death.

The meal passed in a blur for Lane, and soon they were all in Jeff's car, Jonas sitting beside her in back. Jonas grasped Lane's hand as his friend navigated his way back to the motel in Maple Leaf.

"We're off to do stakeout duty again," Jeff said as he dropped them off. "Sleep well, you guys. Remember to put out a Do Not Disturb sign. You don't want a maid waking you up. You have a long night ahead of you."

"Thanks for the reminder." Jonas leaned down to wave farewell to Jeff. "I would've forgotten, sure as the world."

Lane walked ahead of Jonas to the motel room. Somehow Jonas had taken to being the one who carried their keycard. With any other man, Lane could be sensitive about things like that, feeling as if men tried to establish dominance over women by doing all the little things that traditionally had been performed by males—driving, paying the dinner tab, registering at a motel. Oddly, she'd never felt that way with Jonas.

Chapter Thirteen

After Jonas unlocked the door of their motel room, he pressed it open for Lane to enter before he did. She was tired, but after emerging from the bathroom dressed in her makeshift jammies, she stared at the bed with mounting dread. Jonas had thrown on his sweats and a T-shirt while she was changing, and he was already stretched out on his side of the mattress, the pillow barrier neatly dividing their sleeping spots.

"What is it?"

Lane couldn't think how to explain and just blurted, "I'm afraid to fall asleep."

He appeared to mull that over. "Because you may dream of Veneta?"

Lane shook her head. "No. Because maybe I won't."

"Oh, honey."

Tears sprang to Lane's eyes. She hated for Jonas to see them. Didn't want him to think she was one of those people who cried at the drop of a hat. "I need to wind down, I think." She glanced around the room. "I can't believe I'm asking this so early in the morning, but do we have any wine left?"

"There are still a couple of bottles in the trunk." Jonas swung his legs off the bed and stood up. "I'll go get them. My sleeping outfit looks more like streetwear than yours does."

When he returned a moment later with the wine and a corkscrew that he'd bought, he began opening a bottle while Lane washed out the Solo cups they'd saved. Soon they were sitting across from each other at the table, talking as they sipped a tasty merlot.

"How are you feeling right now?" Jonas asked.

"A little frantic," Lane confessed. "And scared."

Lane was finally starting to feel the effects of the alcohol, but she didn't feel drowsy yet. Eventually, they ran out of things to say and just sat there, staring at each other as they dutifully finished their wine as if it were doctor-prescribed sleep medication. The silence in the room suddenly seemed loud against her eardrums, and she became acutely aware of Jonas' studied perusal of her person. He didn't take her measure in a rude way that made her feel uneasy. It was more as if he were studying a painting, trying to find a picture within a picture.

When they'd emptied the bottle of wine, they both rose to go to bed. Jonas checked to make sure the door was locked and engaged the security chain before he began turning off the lights. As the room darkened measure by measure, Lane was pleased to note how well the drapes blocked the sunshine.

"Almost as good as nighttime," she observed.

"And it shouldn't get too noisy outside our room until around five when travelers start checking in for the night."

Simultaneously, they both drew back the covers and slipped into bed. Jonas settled in quickly and Lane thought she heard his breathing change. She struggled to keep her eyes closed. Each time her upper lashes lowered of their own accord, she jerked wide awake again.

After a long while, Jonas startled her by curling an arm over the pillow between them and resting his hand on her shoulder. "You're not asleep. I can tell. Wanna talk about it?"

"I don't think talking will help."

"Snuggling worked once. Would you like me to hold you again?"

Lane smiled against her pillow. "Would you mind?"

"Well, it's a hell of a job, but somebody has to do it."

She giggled and turned over to face him. Holding her gaze, he slowly dispensed with the pillows between them. Then, still maintaining eye contact, they scooted toward each other until they met at the center of the mattress.

Lane wasn't sure how it happened, exactly, whether he moved in to kiss her or if she moved in to kiss him. She only knew nothing had ever felt so right to her. The silky moistness of his lips on hers. The gentle probe of his tongue to coax her mouth open. The strength of his arms around her. *This is where I belong*, she thought. *Where I've always belonged.*

The kiss ignited all her nerve endings, and a tingling ache of need pooled low in her belly. She'd never really *wanted* a man. The only time she'd been with anyone, she'd been driven more by her need to fit in with her peers than she had been by desire. But that other guy—she couldn't even remember his name, at this point—hadn't kissed her like Jonas was now, taking her breath away with every caress of his lips.

For just an instant, Lane thought how crazy this was and that she might regret it later, but he was nibbling just below her ear, and the sensation was so delicious, she didn't want to make him stop. And in the next second, she no longer cared how crazy it might be. It felt wonderfully and beautifully *right*, as if she'd been moving all her life toward this moment, and she gave herself up to the magic of it all.

Jonas. He trailed his lips over her skin in places Lane never imagined a man might kiss her. Up the inside of her arm. Down her rib cage. Around her navel. Dimly, she realized her sleepwear had vanished and had only a faint recollection of tugging off her shirt and bottoms, but she didn't feel embarrassed.

"You are so beautiful," he whispered.

And for the first time in her life, Lane felt beautiful. When he finally rose over her on braced arms, she ran her gaze over him, taking in the rock-hard bulges of his biceps, the ripple of muscles in his shoulders, and the contours of his well-padded chest. Even in the shadows, his tawny hair gave off a muted gleam of gold.

"You're the beautiful one," she whispered back. "Make love to me, Jonas. Make this a moment I'll never forget."

"Are you sure? I shouldn't have started this, and I can still stop."

Lane could feel his turgid staff throbbing against her thigh. If he left her now, she might never know how it felt to be with someone who felt so absolutely right for her.

"Don't stop," she said. "I want to be with you this way."

He reared away from her, and she thought he was leaving her. But he only leaned over to grab his wallet from the nightstand. He drew a foil packet from the fold of leather and held it up, flashing her a grin. "Protection."

After putting on the condom, he lowered himself over her again. Looking into his eyes, she saw a glitter in those hazel depths that she'd never seen and realized it was borne of passion. It aroused her, knowing that he wanted her so badly. It made her feel beautiful, desirable, and powerful.

He pushed slowly into her, testing his way, and the resulting fullness she felt, along with a burst of pleasure deep within her, made her cry out. He bent his head closer to hers and held himself still for a moment. "Are you okay?" he asked. "Am I hurting you?"

Lane couldn't find her voice to respond and looped her arms around his neck, trying to tell him without words that she wanted this as much as he did. When he pushed full-length into her, she gasped at the surge of sensation.

He began to move then, establishing a rhythm she instinctively tried to replicate, and soon she was meeting his thrusts. The little explosions of sensation, each stronger than the last, made her breathing come fast and hard. Her vision glazed over, so she could barely see as he increased the tempo. Still hugging his neck, she arched up to meet him, her mind seeming to swirl through darkness, with bright little lights going off inside her head like tiny camera flashes.

Higher and higher he took her, until she reached a pinnacle of sensation that gripped her entire body, snapped all her muscles taut, and robbed her of breath. And then it happened. She lost control completely. Her body went into orgasmic spasms, and she was aware only of him and the eruption of pleasure that he was creating inside of her.

Afterward, he held her snugly against him, stroking her hair and trailing his fingertips lightly down her spine. The way he touched her made her feel treasured. Too drained to move, Lane just melted against him, enjoying the feeling of being one with him, their damp skin sticky, their hearts hammering, his a strong, pounding beat, hers light and rapid.

"That was amazing," she finally said.

"Incredible," he said with his face pressed against her hair. The rumble of his voice vibrated within his chest. "*You're* incredible. I've never felt like this with a woman. Never once."

Lane snuggled closer, loving the masculine smell of him. "Me, either," was all she could think to say in reply. It seemed a silly thing to say, because she'd already told him that she'd been with only one guy and it hadn't gone well. "That's the most special thing that's ever happened to me."

"I'm glad," he whispered, his voice husky with emotion. "I wanted it to be special for you."

"It was," she assured him. "Now that I've experienced it, I'll be hoping to do it again."

Jonas chuckled. "Give me a couple of hours to recharge, and pray I have more prophylactics in my travel shaving case."

Lane fell asleep in his arms with a dreamy smile on her lips.

Lane wasn't sure how long she dozed, only that she awakened in Jonas' arms. He slept with his face pressed against the side of her neck, and each time he breathed out, the downy growth below her hair line shifted, tantalizing her with a tingling sensation on her skin. It felt so good to lie with her back pressed against his chest and abdomen. So good to have all that relaxed muscle and strength wrapped around her. Almost afraid to move for fear of waking him, she thought about how lovely it had been to make love with him. There'd been no awkward moments, no hesitations. She hadn't been at all nervous, even though her first and only other experience with a man had been both humiliating and painful for her. She'd felt entirely safe with Jonas, completely focused on Jonas.

She released a soft, dreamy sigh and closed her eyes, feeling thankful that she had met this man, who had wrought such changes in her life, not only supporting and helping her, but making her feel, for the first time in her recollection, that she was a perfectly sane and normal human being. Over her lifetime, she had encountered myriad reactions from people to her "strangeness," including confusion, concern, and sometimes anger from her parents. Her teachers had always tried to help her, but in the end, most of them had thrown up their hands in helpless frustration.

Jonas was the only person who had ever tried to understand her instead of trying to fix her. And he had done it in such a calm and thoughtful way that it resounded within her like a soothing melody. For the very first time, instead of feeling like a freak who needed to conceal her oddities, she was coming to believe that she was just a normal person with fascinating little quirks. Jonas never made her feel weird or crazy. Instead he made her feel special.

That was a totally new experience for Lane. And it was a gift that only Jonas had ever given to her. She loved that he encouraged her to embrace what had always been forbidden to her by her parents, the inexplicable parts of herself that baffled and alarmed most people. In short, being around Jonas was teaching her that she was okay. She didn't have an *imaginary* friend.

The voice she heard in her mind wasn't a sign that she was nuttier than a fruitcake, either. It was a real voice, that of her identical twin.

My identical twin. Lane stiffened. The delicious languor of just having had fabulous sex fell away from her in a rush. She opened her eyes and stared at the wall, registering that the drapes let in just enough light to tell her the sun hadn't gone down yet.

"What is it?"

The murmur of Jonas' voice next to her ear made Lane jerk with a start. "Nothing. I'm sorry. I didn't mean to disturb you."

She felt him come completely awake, the slackness of his muscles going suddenly hard and vibrant, his lax fingers curving over her rib cage, his breathing shallower and faster. "Tell me."

She realized that he thought she'd had another horrible dream about Veneta. But the actuality was far worse. "I didn't dream of her. Nothing, Jonas."

He sighed and snuggled her up even closer to his body. "It doesn't mean she's gone, honey."

Lane had clung to his reassurances last night, but now they no longer made her feel better. "My mind is so silent now," she whispered. "So very silent, Jonas."

"If she's gone, Lane—and I pray to God she isn't— none of what's happened is your fault. You didn't make any of her choices for her. And most important of all, you never wished her any harm."

Lane felt as if a steel band had tightened around her chest. "I did wish her out of my head, though. At least a thousand times, I wished for silence. Prayed for it. And now I'm finally getting my wish."

With a strength and speed that startled her, he gently flipped her onto her back and moved to canopy her body with his. "Anybody would have wished for that. You only wanted to feel at peace." He bent his head to kiss the tip of her nose. "You never wished anything bad upon Veneta. How could you? Until you met me, you didn't even know she existed. Remember? And Veneta had already been kidnapped by then. It wasn't and still isn't your fault."

Lane released a shaky breath. "Somehow, you always make me feel better."

"Stick with me," he whispered against her cheek. "Maybe the best is yet to come."

Lane turned her face to his. "I hope so."

"No hoping to it. Let me show you," he said, and then he kissed her.

Chapter Fourteen

Jonas had his cell phone alarm set to awaken them at six p.m., but they were both so drained by making love twice more when they were supposed to be sleeping that Jonas kept resetting the app to make it give them another ten minutes of slumber. When the app finally refused to cooperate, he sat up on the edge of the bed, looked at the time, and said, "Oh, shit!"

Lane sat erect behind him. "What?"

"I should have asked for a regular wake-up call. We overslept. It's already six thirty. If we hope to have time for breakfast—or is it still dinner?—we need to get a move on."

Lane raked a hand through her hair. It felt like a rat's nest, stiff from yesterday's hairspray and spiked from perspiring. "I absolutely have to shower, no matter what."

She grabbed the floral bed scarf that the motel kept on the counterpane to lend a touch of color and clutched it close around her body before standing up. Being naked with Jonas in bed hadn't bothered her, but she wasn't about to dash from the room now with nothing to cover her body.

She turned on the tub faucet, adjusted the water temperature, and pulled the curtain closed behind her as she stepped under the spray. She'd just gotten her hair wet, with reddish-blond ropes hanging over her eyes, when she heard the curtain grommets rasping again. She blinked and rubbed her lids, trying to see, and then Jonas' arms came around her.

"What're you—?" Her voice came out in a squeak. "Not in the *shower*."

"Why not?" he asked with a laugh.

"Because I'm *naked*, and the *lights* are on." Lane started to feel a bit cross. "And because I don't do sex in the shower."

He started nibbling her neck, and she felt her knees go watery. "Sex in the shower is phenomenal, and in this case, it's a timesaver. We can both freshen up at once."

Lane couldn't think when he nibbled on the sensitive skin just below her ear, and she could barely focus on what he was saying. Her head went all swimmy. Dimly she realized that he'd vised an arm around her waist to hold her up because her legs were no longer doing the job.

Eventually, when he had her begging for more, he lifted her against the tile wall and gave her more. And, just as he had promised, it was phenomenal.

After grabbing breakfast, which was served 24/7 at Jack's Place, Jonas drove Lane to another old section of town to begin a second night of walking. They both agreed that Lane might be more likely to pick up on signals from her sister without the engine noise of the car to distract her. As they covered their first block on foot, Lane saw that this section of old-town Maple Leaf was going through a slow transformation into its former glory, with beautifully renovated homes of yesteryear standing elbow-to-elbow with ramshackle structures that hadn't yet gotten a face-lift. It was a neighborhood that reflected both the hope for new beginnings and the sadness of decay.

Jonas kept his arm looped loosely around Lane's waist, and as they walked and their bodies bumped gently as they swayed, she was reminded of the blazes of passion that had instantaneously combusted between them in their room. Jonas could be a tender, romantic lover, but he could also be a playful one. This evening in the shower, he'd given her a crash course on how to use soap as a body lubricant that intensified the sensations his touch evoked.

As they passed a renovated home that sported a pumpkin and scarecrow display on the veranda, Jonas said, "It's a beautiful evening, barely even cold enough for a jacket. Hard to believe that it'll soon be Halloween."

"From what I gathered in only a short time in Mystic Creek, the weather there is quite a bit different. Not to say it can't get nippy around Halloween here, but it's not as likely as it is in central Oregon."

"Well, for your sake, I'm glad. If it were colder, a shawl wouldn't be enough to keep you warm. Not to say I don't like your style. But how do you stay warm when the weather does go cold?"

Lane smiled up at him. "I have heavier clothing for winter. Wools and denim. Thick sweaters. And when it's *really* cold, I blend Bohemian with a parka."

"Smart choice, and I'm glad to hear it. In Mystic Creek, you'd freeze to death in the wintertime wearing only a shawl. It's a dry cold, but trust me, with any breeze behind it, it cuts right through you. And we get our share of wind."

Lane leaned more heavily against him, enjoying how the fluid motion of his body carried her along, directing her footsteps. *"Help me. Someone. Please. I don't want to die."* At the sound inside her head, Lane jerked so abruptly to a stop that Jonas' arm, propelled by his forward momentum, jolted her from behind and nearly knocked her off her feet.

He quickly grabbed her by the shoulders to keep her from falling. "What's wrong? Are you all right?"

Joy burst inside Lane like an incredibly beautiful firework. "Oh, Jonas! She's alive!"

He tightened his grip on her upper arms. "Okay. You heard her. Thank *God*! What did she say?"

"She's just asking for help, saying she doesn't want to die." Lane made fists on the front of his jacket. "I can't believe it! I'm so happy!"

Jonas, always the levelheaded one, nodded and then said, "That's wonderful, sweetheart, but we still have to find her."

Hearing that undeniable fact being spoken aloud lessened Lane's joy. Jonas was right; hearing Veneta again wasn't going to help them locate her. "True. So true. Only what more can I do?"

Jonas held her gaze for a long moment. "Talk to her," he said softly. "Just try to get inside her head."

Lane's heart rate accelerated. She'd prayed for this moment all last night, but now that it was upon her, she didn't feel quite as brave as she thought she'd be. "Okay. Okay. I can do this."

Keeping a firm grip on Jonas' jacket, Lane closed her eyes, and for the first time in her memory, she tried to project her thoughts into her sister's mind. *"Veneta, this is Lane. Can you hear me?"*

Lane waited for a response, but instead she got, *"I'm dying. Please. Someone find me. Please, help me."*

Looking up at Jonas, Lane said, "It's almost like a mantra now." She repeated Veneta's litany. "She didn't hear me. I can't break through."

Jonas firmed his hold on her arms. "I'm right here. Try again. No need to stop to give me updates. Just keep trying."

Lane closed her eyes again, the better to concentrate, and pushed out another thought to her sister. *"I'm close to you, Veneta. I've been trying to find you, and I know you're near me. I just don't know where you are exactly."*

She waited for a response, but again, all she received were more disjointed pleas from Veneta for help. *"Please. I need water, just some water, please. Help me. Somebody help me. I don't want to die."*

Lane decided to try a different tact and imagined inside her head that she yelled the next bit. *"Stop thinking and just listen to me! I'm near you, but you've got to communicate with me so I can find you!"*

Again, Veneta's side of the exchange was self-focused and frantic. Lane lifted her lashes to meet Jonas' gaze. In the dim glow from a streetlight farther up the street, his eyes looked the color of melted caramel.

"She just isn't hearing me," she told him.

"Okay." He drew her back into a walk. "Just keep trying. And really tune in to her thoughts. She may give you some kind of clue as to where she's being held. She has to be pretty sick by now. Maybe we're not close enough for you to get through to her." He dipped his head to plant a kiss on her crown. "I know it's draining for you, but just keep a steady flow of thoughts going out to her. Maybe you'll break through."

Lane did find it draining. But she kept trying. Veneta never once gave any sign that Lane was getting through to her. After an hour of listening to her sister's ramblings, Lane stopped walking and looked at the houses that lined each side of the block. She and Jonas stood beneath a gnarly old oak that grew in a grass median between the sidewalk and the street. Fallen leaves lay in pillowlike clumps all around their feet, as if someone had started to rake them into piles and had grown weary before finishing the job.

"She must be delirious," she told Jonas. "It's like listening to a broken record."

"All we need is an indication from her as to what house she may be in. Then we can call the cops and convince them to go in after her."

Lane stared up at him. "On what grounds could they legally do that? They won't take my word for it, Jonas. They'll just write me off as crazy for thinking I hear voices coming from a certain house."

His shoulders slumped. "Shit." Releasing his hold on her, he swung slowly in a circle to look at the houses. As he faced Lane again, he said, "I've got another idea. We keep walking, and you listen to see if her voice gets any louder in your head."

"It doesn't work that way. If Veneta grew up in southern Oregon as you've told me, I lived nearly the length of the state away from her, and her voice grew so loud inside my head sometimes that I couldn't think."

"But she's sick and weak now. Over at the motel, you couldn't pick up on anything she said, and we were in the same town."

Lane could understand Jonas' reasoning and struck off walking again. When he caught up with her, he said, "I didn't mean to piss you off."

She laughed softly, but there was no humor in the sound. "I'm not pissed off. I get what you're saying, and I think you may be right. It's just that"—she broke off to swallow and steady her voice—"I don't think she's going to last much longer. You know those films where people are racing against the clock? Maybe trying to disarm a bomb before it detonates and kills them all?"

"Yeah, I enjoy films like that."

"Well, it's not so entertaining in real life. That's how I'm feeling now—like every wasted second may make the difference of life or death for my sister. The clock is ticking, Jonas." She inclined her head at a house. "She could be in that dreary old place. I'm getting an unholy urge to just start breaking down doors to find her."

Jonas looped his arm around her shoulders again. "I get it. I've thought the same thing a few times. But we have to keep our heads. If we broke into the right house, by some incredible stroke of luck, that prick who isn't giving her food or water on a regular basis might get scared and kill her. Or us. When we determine for sure where she is, we have to call the cops and let them handle it. Jeff and I've talked about it."

"True. I'm just talking. This feeling I've got—that she's about to die—is freaking me out."

"We also have to remember that breaking and entering is against the law. If it comes right down to it, I'm willing to risk getting arrested, but only if you're sure Veneta is inside one particular building and I think we can get in without putting her in jeopardy. Fair enough?"

Lane nodded. "Fair enough," she agreed. "I'm just glad you're here to stop me from doing something stupid."

"I'm stuck to you like glue," he reminded her, and she was able to dredge up a smile.

Jonas took her hand. "Come on. We won't find her standing here."

Lane's frustration and sense of helplessness mounted as she and Jonas continued to wander aimlessly along one sidewalk after another. Without checking her phone for the time, she guessed that it was getting close to midnight. Occasionally, she heard Veneta's voice, but her sister's thought processes had become disjointed much of the time, offering Lane no hints or clues as to where Veneta was being held captive.

"Jonas." His name popped from her mouth without volition. She came to a sudden stop and made a fist on the side of his light jacket. "She doesn't know where she is."

He peered down at her through the moon-washed gloom. "What?"

Lane turned to press her palms against his chest. "Veneta doesn't know where she is," she repeated. "That's why her thoughts aren't providing me with any way to find her and probably never will, because she has no idea where she is."

Jonas seemed to ponder that for a moment. "Okay. That makes complete sense. If you kidnap someone, you don't want them to know much of anything, just in case the situation goes south and the abducted individual gets away or is freed by police intervention."

"A blindfold. Being careful about what is said within her hearing range. Boarding up the windows of her room so she can't see out. She has no idea where she is."

"Okay. I'm following. You're probably right."

They stood in front of a lovely older home with a dim porch light glowing on the spacious veranda. The lawn sloped in a graceful arc to the sidewalk and was bordered by a short rock wall. Jonas sat on the earth retainer and patted a spot beside him, inviting Lane to join him.

After she got settled, he said, "I'm no cop, but I've watched a lot of movies. When an abductee manages to call the police somehow—usually on a cell phone—and doesn't know where she is, they always ask her to listen for sounds that may tell them what area of town she may be in."

Lane went quiet and listened. She heard nothing that stood out. At this time of night, not even the residents of this neighborhood were driving the streets. She could hear a dog barking in the distance. Somewhere closer, the distinctive squeak and rattle of an old screen door echoed through the night. She also heard a clanking sound that might have been a metal lid being clamped back down on a garbage can.

"There's nothing distinctive here. No jets coming in for landings. No train whistles."

Jonas sighed. It was a defeated sound, indicating to Lane that he was losing hope. She didn't blame him for that, because she was feeling the same way.

"All we can do is our best." He turned to look at her. "Work that link with her as hard as you can work it. I can't bear the thought of her dying."

It occurred to Lane in that moment that maybe she

wasn't the only one linked to Veneta. Jonas also might be, but in a much more understandable way, by the strings of his heart. He'd never denied having loved Veneta once. Or at least thinking he did. And feelings like that didn't always just vanish. It was entirely possible and maybe even probable that he was still fond of Veneta, not in a romantic way, but as a friend.

Just then Lane heard a sound that made her heart leap. Church bells, ringing out the stroke of midnight. Lane forgot all about her personal issues and leaped to her feet. Wrapping her arms tightly around her waist, she squeezed her eyes closed and concentrated with everything she had to push into Veneta's mind.

"Veneta, can you hear the church bells?"

"Someone. Please. Help me."

"Veneta! Damn it, listen to me! Can—you—hear—the—bells? Can—you—hear—the—bells?"

A long silence followed, and then Veneta finally pushed back. *"What? Who is this?"*

Lane wanted to shout with excitement and joy. Wanted to turn and tell Jonas that Veneta had finally heard her. But instead she remained focused on the exchange. *"This is your sister, Lane. Your identical twin. I've been trying to find you, and I know I'm very close to where you're being held now. But I don't know what house you're in. Can you help me find you?"*

"How is this happening? God, he gave me something in that swallow of water. I'm hallucinating. Asshole, he's such an asshole."

"He didn't give you a drug, Veneta." Lane paused to lend that emphasis. *"I'm real. This is real. I can hear you, and you can hear me. But that's not important right now. Did you hear those bells?"*

"Yes. All the time—I hear them all the time."

"Stay with me. Okay? I'll be right back with you in a second." Lane turned to Jonas. "She's hearing me!"

He leaped to his feet. "How do you know?"

Lane smiled up at him through tears of pure joy. "She's talking to me. She hears the church bells all the time."

Jonas grasped Lane's arm, as if by doing so he'd have a hotline to Veneta himself. "Ask her if they sound close or distant."

Lane closed her eyes. *"Veneta, I'm back. I know this is all bewildering to you. I'll explain later. Okay? Just trust me. You're not losing your mind. You haven't been given a hallucinatory drug. I need you to focus and try to answer my questions. Can you do that?"*

"I'm dizzy. Very weak. I don't know. I'll try."

Lane nodded and then realized Veneta couldn't see her. *"When you hear the church bells, do they sound really close to you or distant, like maybe they're a few blocks away?"*

"Close," Veneta replied. *"Really close. No matter how sick I am, they wake me up. So loud! You can't believe how loud. The sound vibrates through the floor."*

Lane looked up at Jonas. "She says the bells are close. So loud they vibrate the floor when they go off."

Jonas gazed up and down the street. "We need to find that damned church."

He grabbed Lane's hand and set off up the sidewalk in a walk so fast-paced that she had trouble keeping up with him.

"Don't lose the connection with her," he warned. "Keep talking to her. I'll do the searching. You stay focused on your sister."

Lane stumbled along beside him and tried to do as

he said. Veneta seemed to be drifting in and out. Her thoughts were muddled. But Lane kept a dialogue going anyway. If Veneta lost consciousness, fell into a deep sleep, Lane wouldn't be able to connect with her again.

Lane didn't know how many blocks they covered or what was directing Jonas' footsteps. Dimly, she was aware that he was moving in circles. She guessed that he remembered where the sound of the church bells had seemed to come from, so he was covering the area by slowly narrowing their radius.

Half-running beside him, Lane grew a little breathless a few times, but being a regular jogger saved her from complete exhaustion. Finally, as they turned a corner, Jonas said, "Bingo. We've found it."

"We've found the church, Veneta! We must be very close to you."

The church, shrouded with shadows, sat halfway up the block from them, but even through the gloom, Lane could see a steeple rising from the apex of its sharply pitched roof. She supposed it housed the belfry. It was an old building, but it looked to be well-maintained.

"Get me out of here. Please. Call the police. This guy is crazy. If I don't die from lack of water first, he'll kill me."

Lane looked up at Jonas. "Now what? Do we assume she's in a house along this street?"

He shook his head. "We can't assume that. Sound travels in a radius around its source, so it stands to reason that while Veneta may be near the bells, the house where she's being held could be anywhere in a certain radius around this church." He gestured to indicate a block over from where they stood. "Maybe on this street, but possibly on others that are adjacent to it." He rubbed his jaw. "Ask her if she can tell if any lights are on inside the house where she's being held."

Lane asked the question, and Veneta replied. *"I can see a glow of light coming in under the door."*

"Yes," she told Jonas. "There's at least one light on in the house."

Jonas scanned both sides of the street that they were on. "We're on the wrong street, then. No lights on this block."

He grabbed Lane's hand and took off at another half run. Lane ran with him until they turned a corner on the sidewalk to the next adjacent street. When Jonas drew to a slower pace, she saw that seven homes along the thoroughfare had lights on. A couple of them had been renovated in grand fashion. Four more looked to be less fancy, but they'd been transformed, all the same. Only two were still ramshackle.

She spoke her thoughts aloud to Jonas. "She could be in one of those two places. They have lights on. No exterior work has been done on them, so I doubt they've been updated inside, either. The room I saw—well, I'm pretty sure it's in an old, dilapidated structure."

"We're close to her," Jonas murmured. "Just not close enough. We can't expect the police to invade either of those houses unless we're positive Veneta's inside."

Lane's heart sank, but her disappointment wasn't long-lived. "The window of the room is boarded up, both inside and out. We can creep around both of those houses to see if there are boards over one of the windows."

He nodded. "Good thinking. I would assume he'd

do that around back, though, so the boards couldn't be seen from the street."

Lane thought about that for a moment. Many of the homes in this older section of town had tall fences around the backyards. "We can probably climb over—or find a gate that's not locked."

"Let's go check it out."

Arm in arm, they walked along the wide ribbon of concrete to the first illuminated house. At the edge of the patchy front yard, Jonas drew Lane to a stop. "I'd rather do this without you," he said softly. "If I get caught, I can get back over that fence faster than you can."

Lane might have argued the point if she'd been wearing jeans and running shoes, but she wore a skirt and loose top with lace-up walking shoes. Her footwear was sensible, but her skirt wasn't good for fence climbing. "All right. But start a text to me and keep your screen active so the phone doesn't shut off. If you need me to call the police, just text me any letter. I'll get help."

He bent to kiss her cheek. "Stay right here. Unless, of course, he sees you or something. Then run like a scalded dog."

Lane watched him slowly vanish into the shadowy darkness along the side of the house. It seemed to her he was gone for a small eternity, but her cell phone told her he'd taken only four minutes.

"Anything?" she asked in a stage whisper as he returned to her.

"Nope. This isn't it."

By mutual and unspoken consent, they started down the block to the next house with lights on. Just as they got close, the front door of the home opened, and a tall, thin man emerged onto the porch. Jonas grabbed Lane's arm and pulled her behind a hedge that served as a barrier between one yard and the next.

Lane hunkered down beside Jonas. The smell of grass and boxwood leaves filled her nostrils. "That's *him*," she whispered. "Oh, God. That's him. Now what'll we do?"

Jonas placed a forefinger over his lips to silence her. Then he leaned sideways to look around the hedge again. "He's opening the garage door. I think he's leaving."

Lane heard a rattling, rolling sound and then a thump. Moments later, she heard a car door close, and then an engine started up. "A lucky break!" she said, excitement making her voice thin and high-pitched. "With him gone, it'll be clear sailing."

Jonas, eyes narrowed to see her in the darkness, slanted her a warning look. "He may have a partner who's staying at the house to look after her while he's gone."

Lane's elation turned to dismay. "Do you think? I saw no other man in any of my dreams."

Jonas drew out his phone.

"Who are you calling?" she asked.

"Jeff. To give him the address so he can get over here. I'll ask him to call the cops as well. More credibility with him being a deputy. They'll be more likely to take him seriously, even if he is out of his jurisdiction."

"Shouldn't we make sure this is where they're keeping her before we get the police involved?"

The sound of the car on the street faded away, and Jonas pushed to his feet. Giving Lane a hand up, he said, "Better to look stupid than be sorry. These people are killers, Lane. Even if they weren't, fear can push people into doing things they wouldn't normally. They've abducted a woman and held her against her will."

He pushed some numbers on his phone and held it to his ear. Lane heard the faint sound of Jeff's voice when he answered the call. In hushed and urgent tones, Jonas told his friend what was going down. He squinted to see the front of the house and recited the house number. "We need you here," he concluded. "We also need the cops and an ambulance. Veneta may be in a very bad way."

After finishing the call, Lane saw on Jonas' face that he intended to leave her behind the hedge while he went in alone. A faint glow from the porch light on the house shone over the hedge to illuminate his features. "No! No way. I'm going in. That's my sister in there. A sister I've never met, at least not that I remember. What if she's in such a bad way that she dies, despite emergency care? I'll never get to meet her, she'll never get to meet me. That isn't fair."

"Neither is taking a bullet between the eyes, but that could happen."

Lane stiffened her spine and lifted her chin. "I'm going in, Jonas. That's my sister, my identical twin. I'm—going—*in*! Nothing you say will stop me."

"Okay. But a few ground rules first." He reached under his jacket and drew out a handgun. As he jacked a casing into the chamber, he said, "You stay behind me at all times. If I tell you to hit the deck, I want you as flat against the floor as you can manage. That won't save you from taking a bullet, but at least you won't take one meant for me. It'll also make your vital organs harder targets to hit unless they aim for your head or get past me to stand over you."

Lane locked her knees. *Okay, I'm scared now*, she thought nonsensically. *Thanks for that*. Only she couldn't allow herself to hold on to the feeling. Jonas faced the same dangers, and he didn't seem afraid.

"Okay," she said. "I'd argue, but all I've got in my purse to use as a weapon is a fingernail file."

At any other time, Jonas would have made a joke about that, but tonight he just looked solemn. "Bring your phone in a pocket. Leave the purse here."

Lane already had her phone stashed in a skirt pocket. When he turned to go, she left her purse lying in the dark shadows cast by the hedge and followed him. He crouched low to the ground as he ran to the porch, Lane feeling like a waddling duck behind him. Once on the porch, he tried the door. It didn't open, so she presumed it was locked.

With a sweeping motion of his arm, Jonas moved her back several steps. Then, cocking one shoulder at an angle, he rammed the door with such force that the frame broke loose and crashed onto the entryway floor. The explosion of noise was almost deafening. He grabbed her hand to help her over the debris, pressed her against a wall after they cleared it, and whispered, "Behind me. Don't forget." Then, arms straightened, gun firmly gripped in both hands and pointed at the floor, he slid along the wall with his back pressed against it. Lane did exactly what he did, sans a weapon, deeply impressed by his courage.

It was an old house, the entry about the size of a large walk-in closet. The air was rank with the smell of cigarette smoke. An open door led into what looked like the dining room, only there was no furniture. Over Lane's right shoulder, she glimpsed a small, bare living room with a brick fireplace. Off to one side of the dining room was a closed door that Lane figured went to a bedroom. Jonas ignored it and moved beyond the dining area into a dated kitchen with windows overlooking what she presumed was a backyard. Off to the left was a pantry with a work counter that sported a half-used loaf of bread in a plastic wrapper and a jar of peanut butter, lid off, with a plastic table knife standing straight up in the thick spread.

After satisfying himself that there was no armed sentry in the house, Jonas relaxed and shoved the gun under the back of his belt again. He gave Lane a thumbs-up and returned to the dining area to try the only bedroom door.

"It's locked," he said. "Back up. I'm going in."

Lane skittered back several steps while Jonas broke the door down. After the splintered woodwork crashed into the bedroom beyond, she followed him into the room. Jonas reached past her, groping for the light switch. When the overhead fixture snapped on, Lane froze. Her sister lay on the floor on a thin and filthy cot mattress. Her skirt, which might have been pretty once, was now so dirty and caked with what appeared to be excrement that the stiff cloth was stuck to her legs in spots. The smell of urine that assailed Lane's nostrils almost turned her stomach.

Veneta had an expression of sheer terror on her face, but then she saw Jonas and began to sob. "Jonas!" Her voice was barely more than a gruff whisper, and she strained to free her hands, which were bound behind her back. "Jonas!!"

He knelt beside her and reached into his pants pocket, pulling out a small pocketknife. In short order, he cut through the ropes that encircled her wrists and ankles. Then he gathered Veneta into his arms.

"It's all right now, sweetheart. The cops are on their way. You're safe. It's all right now."

Barely able to move from weakness, Veneta managed to loop an arm limply around his neck. "You've saved me, Jonas. Thank God. You saved me. I'm sorry, so sorry. I never should have broken up with you. I love you. I do."

Jonas looked up at Lane and held her gaze for a long moment before redirecting his attention to Veneta. She was sobbing, but no tears slipped from her eyes. Lane stared at her, trying to come to grips with the fact that her sister was so dehydrated that she couldn't even cry.

It seemed to Lane that only seconds passed before she heard sirens in the distance. Jonas still held Veneta. "Should I go out on the porch to flag them down?" she asked.

He shook his head. "The porch light is on. They'll see the address and maybe even the broken door." He glanced down at the woman in his arms. "Plus, I'll worry less if you stay in here. We don't know what he left the house for, but if it was only for a pack of smokes, he may get back before the cops get here."

Lane hadn't thought of that possibility, and just then she heard a man's voice coming from the front of the house. Startled and suddenly afraid, she whirled to face the intruder. To her relief, Jeff appeared in the opening. With one look at Jonas and Veneta, he went into cop mode and hurried past Lane to lend his friend assistance. After going down on one knee at the opposite side of the filthy mattress, he pressed his fingertips against Veneta's throat and took her pulse. He looked alarmed by the count and shook his head slightly.

It hit Lane then that after all of their hard work and finally finding her sister, Veneta might still die.

Chapter Fifteen

Ever since learning that she had a twin sister, Lane had imagined their first meeting as an emotional and touching reunion. Instead, Lane had to stand with her back against the wall so she wasn't in the way of the medical responders and police. Jonas and Jeff joined her there, one on each side of her, making her feel like the filling in a sandwich. With amazing speed, the EMTs gave Veneta oxygen, got an IV in her arm, and radioed details of her physical condition to someone at the hospital, who in turn told them what medications should be administered to the patient during transport.

Before Lane knew it, her sister had been rushed from the dwelling, and the only personnel that remained were law enforcement officers, who gathered around Jeff, Lane, and Jonas to get more information. It seemed to Lane that everyone was talking at once. She was asked questions, but even as she gave responses, she wasn't sure what she said. Her thoughts were with her sister. Would she make it to the hospital alive? The EMTs had seemed to think her condition was very serious.

When the police gathered enough information to realize that Veneta's captor might return at any moment, they flew into action. Jonas, Jeff, and Lane were asked to vacate the house. A lower-rank officer was assigned to moving all the cars from in front of the structure while three other cops went to work propping the front door back into place.

"What are they doing?" Lane asked, feeling as if her brains had turned to pea soup.

"They're going to hide out front, maybe behind the hedge like we did, so they can try to catch the son of a bitch by surprise when he comes back," Jeff replied. "That means we need to vanish as quickly as possible ourselves."

Jonas swore under his breath. "I left my car clear over on Oak Street."

Jeff held up his keys. "I'll give you a lift over to get it. Then I need to pick up Carla from the motel." He rolled his eyes. "She's so pissed at me, it's not even funny, all because I wouldn't let her come with me. I had no idea what I might be walking into when I got here."

Three abreast, they hurried down the porch steps and cut across the neglected lawn. Lane darted around the hedge to grab her purse before she went to Jeff's car parked at the curb. She took the back seat so the guys could sit together up front. She doubted she could contribute intelligently to their conversation, anyway. She just wanted to get to the hospital. To be with her sister. To maybe get to hold her hand and let her know she wasn't alone anymore.

"You okay back there?" Jonas asked. "Lane?"

She jerked and focused. "I'm fine. Just worried. They seemed to think she was in immediate danger of dying."

"Severe dehydration puts a huge burden on the heart," Jeff said. "The blood grows thick, and it's harder for the heart to keep blood flowing. Dehydration also increases the sodium levels in the blood-stream, causing additional strain. Her pulse was weak and irregular when I took it. I didn't take that as a good sign. She may also have some kidney damage going on." He glanced back over his shoulder at Lane. "That doesn't mean she's going to die, though. It's bad. I won't lie and say it isn't, but she's in good hands, and they know exactly what to do. Right now, they're trying to get her hydrated, and they may be administering medications."

Just then Jonas' cell phone rang. Lane, intent on what Jeff was saying, jerked with a start.

"Hello, Jonas Sterling here. How can I help you?" A silence followed and then Jonas said, "Thank you, Officer. That's the best news I've heard all day. I just hope you can find out who the puppeteer is. I think this guy was acting on orders from above."

When Jonas ended the call, he gave Lane a thumbs-up. "They caught Veneta's kidnapper. Apprehended him before he ever reached the porch. They're taking him in to the station as we speak. There are already warrants out for his arrest, apparently. He's been dealing for a while. They just haven't been able to find him."

Lane's whole body went limp with relief. With that man still at large, Veneta would remain in danger. And so would Lane. "That's great news!"

"Yep. He's only a front man, though. The danger to you and Veneta isn't over yet. Hopefully, it will be soon. They have to find out who's in control of the operation."

Lane prayed that would happen soon. Veneta couldn't live in hiding for a prolonged period of time, and neither could Lane.

* * *

Once at the hospital, Lane and Jonas were directed to a sitting area where they could wait for word of Veneta's condition. Done in tones of green and blue, the area was comfortable, with magazine racks lining one wall and vending machines outside in the hall offering chilled sandwiches and salads, hot and cold drinks, candy bars, and individual-size bags of chips. Neither Lane nor Jonas was hungry, and neither of them felt like reading, either. They sat next to each other on a sofa with cushions that were a little too firm for comfort. Jonas kept an arm around Lane's shoulders, as if, even now that the danger was past, he still needed to protect her.

Finally, a nurse came out to speak with them. She was a plump, rosy-cheeked brunette in blue scrubs with a name tag that identified her as a registered nurse named Dani Tince. "We have an issue," she said, her voice filled with apology.

"What's that?" Jonas asked.

The woman put her hands on her hips. "I'll start with the worst part first. You aren't relatives of Ms. Monroe, and it's illegal for me to tell you anything at all about her condition."

Jonas removed his arm from around Lane and pushed forward to sit at the front edge of the sofa. "Not relatives?" he said, his tone ringing with incredulity. "Are you *serious*?" He gestured at Lane. "You can *see* that they're identical twins, just as Ms. Driscoll claims."

The nurse sighed and took a seat on a chair opposite them. "I know, but even though Ms. Driscoll is obviously related to our patient, she isn't legally a family member. From what I understand after reading the intake receptionist's notes, you were separated during an adoption process?" She leveled her gaze on Lane. "Is that the story?"

"Yes, essentially," Lane replied. "Can't you just ask Veneta for her authorization? We're the ones who rescued her. Surely she won't mind if you tell us how she's doing."

The nurse folded her hands in her lap. "Ms. Monroe is unable to talk at the moment." She sighed and bent her head to watch as she twiddled her thumbs. When she met Lane's gaze again, she smiled slightly. "I'm going to bend the rules a bit for you, Ms. Driscoll, by telling you that your sister is responding to treatment and resting peacefully. I'll speak with her at first opportunity. If she wants you to be informed of anything more or if she wishes to see you, we'll call you immediately. I'm sorry, but for the moment, I can say nothing more. We take the privacy of our patients very seriously here."

Lane couldn't quite believe this was happening, but she also understood the nurse's predicament. "Is she out of danger?" Lane asked.

"She's responding to treatment," the nurse said again. She looked at Jonas. "My advice is that you should both go home and get some rest. By morning, she may be awake and able to express her wishes. For now, there's nothing to be gained by you sitting up all night."

Lane asked, "If she takes a turn for the worse, will someone call me? They have my number at the front desk."

Dani shook her head. "I'm sorry. I can't really express just how sorry I am. This is an unprecedented situation. I can tell just by looking at you that you're a blood relative, but when I called HR, I was told that we still have to play this by the book. Legally, Ms. Monroe would have grounds to sue the hospital if we divulge any of her personal information to you."

Lane felt like screaming. What if Veneta died before the two of them ever even got to know each other?

"I'll tell you what, though," Nurse Dani went on. "If anything goes wrong—and I don't think, at this point, that it will—I'll call you. I won't divulge any information to you. I'll just say the cafeteria is open or something like that. At least, then, you can be in the building should she ask to see you." She stood and brushed the wrinkles from her scrub pants. "I'll also try to talk with her as soon as she's lucid."

"Thank you," Lane said.

As Jonas drove Lane back to the motel, he couldn't shake the feeling that something was off kilter between them. Going back over the events of the night, he tried to think of what he might have done to offend her. While trying to protect her, had he come off as overbearing? He supposed that was a possibility. While going into the house, he'd been pretty wound up and edgy, trying to anticipate danger before they encountered it. He might have spoken curtly to Lane a few times. He'd been extremely worried for her safety.

After he parked the car outside their room and cut the engine, he turned to look at her while the dome lights were still on. "Are you upset with me about something?"

She shook her head no. "Absolutely not, Jonas. You were amazing tonight. A loyal and caring friend. I don't know what I would have done without you."

A *friend*? Jonas searched her expression, hoping

against hope that she didn't mean that, because he wasn't just falling for Lane; he'd already taken the leap. "I want to be more than just a friend, Lane. Surely you realize that."

"Yes," she said softly. "I realize that, Jonas. I was hopeful for more, too. But now I think I was only wishing on rainbows." Just then, the dome lights blinked out, and Jonas strained to see her through the sudden gloom. "I saw how Veneta clung to you. She obviously still has feelings for you. She even said as much."

Jonas' heart sank. "Lane, you can't seriously believe that. She was the one who ended it between us, and she's never even been in touch with me since then."

"Yes, well. I can't ignore what I saw and heard. She clung to you as if she never wanted to let you go and said she still loves you. I'm not sure she was even aware of my presence in the room."

"I'm not responsible for Veneta's feelings, no matter what they may be. I can only speak for myself. I'm in love with *you*, Lane. Not with Veneta."

She opened the passenger door and swung out one leg. "I know that." Jonas saw a tear slip down her cheek. "And I love you back. Only where does that leave us?" When he started to speak, she held up a hand. "If Veneta still loves you, that puts me in an impossible position."

"She was just terrified, Lane. Half out of it as well. She's the one who broke it off between us. Why would she have done that if she still had feelings for me?"

"I only know that I couldn't live with myself if I stole the man my sister loves. Be honest, Jonas. How would you handle it if you fell in love with a woman and then found out your brother loved her?"

Jonas really didn't want to answer that question and

yet he knew there was no way around it. In order for him and Lane to be together and have a successful relationship, absolute honesty between them was a necessity. He swallowed hard before he spoke. "I love my brothers, so I'm not sure how I would handle it. But I do know I couldn't live with myself if I found happiness and broke my brother's heart in the process." He cleared his throat. "And I'd think of how painful it might be for him to see me with the woman he loved. So I totally get what you're feeling. I do. It's just that I don't think Veneta loves me. She was afraid for her life when I entered that room. She clearly saw me as her savior. She was also barely hanging on to consciousness. I don't think she meant it the way you interpreted it."

"Perhaps not," she said with hesitation. "But how can I move forward with you until I know that for sure?"

Jonas had no answers. "I truly have fallen in love with you." That was all he could think of to say.

She nodded, and in the dimness, her eyes sparkled with tears. He also saw her lips quiver as she said, "I know. And as I said, I feel the same way. You've become my best friend. You make me laugh. You build my self-esteem. You stand by me through thick and thin. I enjoy being with you. Talking with you never bores me. I feel as if I've been waiting for you all my life. But I can't be with you if Veneta is still in love with you, Jonas. For one, it would damage our relationship as sisters before we even get a chance to forge one. And I would feel guilty, as if I had betrayed her, for the rest of my life."

Jonas held her gaze. "As I said, I think it was only emotion and confused feelings at work when she said that."

"If that was the case, she'll reveal that to me sooner or later."

"And then?" he asked.

"Then I won't feel guilty about moving forward with you. But right now it's a big *if*, Jonas."

Jonas felt compelled to ask, "Where does this leave us, then?"

She shook her head. "I don't know." She reached over to touch his arm. "It'll be a wait-and-see thing, I guess. But please know that the waiting won't be easy for me, either. And if it turns out that she *does* still love you, it's going to be just as hard for me to end it between us as it will be for you to honor my decision."

Jonas tried to dredge up a smile, but he couldn't manage one. She got out of the car and stood by the door of their room because he had the keycard. He swore under his breath and exited the vehicle, wishing he could think of something to say that would ease her mind. But there was nothing. This was a complicated situation for Lane and for him as well. All he could do was hope that the issue would resolve itself.

When they got inside their room, Lane went directly to the closet after stashing her purse on the dresser. Moments later, she had erected their pillow barrier at the center of the bed. That act alone told Jonas that she'd decided against any more intimacy between them.

"Do you need to use the bathroom?" she asked. "I'd like to get cleaned up—unless you'd like to go first."

Jonas shook his head. "I'm fine for now. Go ahead and enjoy your shower. I'll grab one after you're finished."

Heavy of heart, Jonas threw on a T-shirt and sweatpants after she had collected her toiletries and vanished.

Then he stretched out on the bed, listening to Lane in the bathroom—the sound of the shower, the hollow thump when she dropped something, possibly a bar of soap—the metallic rasp of the grommets on the curtain rod. He remembered being with her under the warm spray, cherishing the feeling of having her in his arms with nothing between their naked bodies. It had been so—*beautiful* and had felt absolutely right. How had it all gone wrong so quickly? He felt dazed. Confused. Panicky. Deep down, he knew there was a good chance he might lose her over this, and he had no idea how to fix things between them. Certainly, nothing he said had done the trick.

He wanted to feel angry and resentful, but again, deep down where right and wrong didn't exist and only feelings dwelled, he understood where Lane was coming from. How would he feel if one of his brothers fell in love with Lane and took her away from him? Jonas felt fairly certain that he'd have bitter feelings toward his brother for the rest of his life. Even worse, Lane had a fledgling relationship with her sister that she needed to strengthen and protect. How could he blame her for taking a step back? He also realized that he had to accept her decision. If he resisted or pushed Lane to ignore her misgivings, he might only make matters worse.

When she emerged from the bathroom, she had her hair turbaned in a towel. In the oversize sleepwear, which had seen better days, she still managed to look adorable, with a ringlet of wet, strawberry blond hair dangling over her forehead to touch the bridge of her just-scrubbed and shiny nose. She grabbed her cell phone from the nightstand to check for messages or calls. Jonas could have told her that no one had been in touch, but the tension was so thick between them that he remained silent.

She finished towel-drying her hair and then fluffed it with her fingers, creating a swirl of curls around her head. "I left plenty of hot water," she told him.

Jonas sighed and swung off the bed. It had been a long night, and he was tired. Maybe a shower would relax him a bit and allow him to sleep.

Lane knew she needed to rest, but she was so wound up that she doubted she could relax. The entire night had been emotionally draining for her, and the adrenaline rush, brought on by excitement, fear for her life, and worry about Veneta, hadn't completely subsided yet. Her nerves felt raw. Her skin felt electrified. Her heart was still beating faster than normal. And none of that even touched how she felt about telling Jonas it might be over between them. There was an aching place within her chest that felt as large as a basketball. She wanted nothing more than to bury her face in a pillow and sob. How could she have ignored her misgivings and allowed herself to develop deep feelings for Jonas? She'd known he'd been in a romantic relationship with her sister. *Stupid, so stupid.*

Looking back on it, though, the two of them being together had seemed so perfect and right. Jonas was incredibly easy to love, bottom line. He had a fabulous personality, a great sense of humor, a loyal streak that was charming, and he was the quintessential nice guy, both strong and gentle, firm in his convictions and yet understanding of others. He'd become her friend— someone she trusted, someone who made her feel whole and special and normal. Because of her strangeness, Lane hadn't forged many close relationships, so meeting Jonas had been an amazing experience for her, and even now, she couldn't help but think of him as being the best friend that she'd ever had. In fact, when she thought about the bond that had grown between them, she treasured that even more than the incredible experience of making love with him. Over the last few days, he'd been a pillar of strength for her to lean on, a voice of reason, and a one-man cheering section, urging her to face her fears and overcome them.

How would she move forward now? The question lurked in her mind, making her doubt her decision to put their relationship on hold. Only then she remembered how Veneta had clung to him, and she knew it wasn't really a decision; it was a choice prompted by necessity. Lane would only ever have one sister, and she couldn't destroy that relationship because of her own selfish needs.

When Jonas emerged from the bathroom, his tawny hair darkened with dampness, he looked good enough to eat. The T-shirt clung to his moist skin and showcased his impressive physique. Watching him stow his soiled clothing in a laundry bag, she realized that she might never feel those strong arms around her again and felt bereft.

"Enjoy your shower?" she asked, trying to inject a note of cheerfulness into the query.

He closed his suitcase and turned to meet her gaze. "It was okay. Definitely not as spectacular as the last one I had."

Lane couldn't think what to say and groped for words. "I'm sorry, Jonas. For everything."

He shook his head. "It's not your fault or mine. And it's not Veneta's, either. We had a thing going for a while, it seemed great at the time, and then it all fell apart. I can't undo that, and neither can she. I wish I could." He gave his head another shake. "If I could go back in time, I wouldn't have a relationship with Veneta. I'd wait until I met you. Unfortunately, I didn't know you existed back then."

Lane felt the burn of tears in her eyes and was relieved when Jonas flipped off the light switches to plunge the room into blackness. The mattress shifted as he got into bed. Muscles stiff with tension, she lay on her back and stared at a ceiling she couldn't actually see. She wanted to offer him and herself a small measure of hope by saying, "Maybe it will all work out," but she knew she'd only be prolonging the inevitable. So instead she said, "You're the best friend I've ever had."

Long silence. Then he released a shaky breath. "If you're suggesting that we be only friends, I don't think it'll work. It wouldn't be enough for me, and I don't think it would be enough for you, either."

"No," she agreed. "We'd end up back in bed together." She no sooner spoke than she wanted to recall the words. "I mean—well, we're in bed together now, but—you know what I mean."

"Yeah. Oh, yeah."

His response made her smile even as tears leaked from the corners of her eyes.

Nurse Dani called Lane at a quarter after seven in the morning, startling both her and Jonas awake from a deep and much-needed sleep. The hospital employee had good news. Veneta was awake—not out of the woods yet, but conscious and coherent—and she'd asked to see her sister. Even as exhausted as she was,

Lane was delighted by the news, but she really hated to ask Jonas to get up and drive her to the hospital.

"I really don't mind," he insisted. "I'm awake now anyway." He met Lane's gaze. "I take it that Veneta didn't ask to see me, only you."

Lane nodded. "The nurse said nothing to me about it, if she did."

Jonas held up his hands, as if Lane were missing his whole point. "If she still has feelings for me, don't you think she would have asked to see me, too?"

Lane couldn't think how to answer him. "Maybe, maybe not. I have to feel my way through this, Jonas. Growing up as an only child, most kids yearn to have a sibling. I was no different, but my adoptive parents couldn't have more kids. Now—well, I won't say it's been a joyous experience—but I've discovered that I have a sister. I hope you understand how important it is to me to build a strong relationship with her."

He grabbed clean clothes from his luggage. "I completely understand. All I'm asking is that you keep your mind open to the possibility that Veneta didn't mean it the way you took it."

"That's me, open-minded. It's not as if I *want* it this way, Jonas."

While he was in the bathroom changing, Lane threw on a clean outfit herself. She was no sooner dressed than someone knocked at the door. She answered the summons to find Jeff standing outside. He grinned and winked.

"Good morning!" he said. "Since we've accomplished what we came to do, Carla and I are going to check out this morning and head back home. I just wanted to give you a heads-up."

Lane invited him in, sharing the news that Veneta

had woken up and was asking to see her. "The nurse was careful to make sure I understand that she's still not out of the woods, but I think it's good news that she's awake and thinking clearly."

"It's excellent news," Jeff agreed, rubbing his hands together. "And I've got even better news!"

"You do?"

Lane heard Jonas come out of the bathroom and felt him move to stand behind her. It was as if his body put off electrical signals that only she could feel. "What news is that?" he asked his old friend.

"I called the station this morning. Veneta's kidnapper started singing like a bird when they interrogated him. They now know the identity of the kingpin and several of the people who work under him. He even told the cops where they're holed up. The chief hopes to have all of them in custody before the end of the day. I think he's being a little too optimistic, but it's positive news. Once all those creeps are behind bars, Lane and Veneta should be safe."

A wave of relief washed over Lane, making her knees feel weak. She went to sit on the edge of the bed. "That's fabulous news. I'm surprised that guy gave up any information at all. I didn't have him pegged as a person who scares easily."

Jeff sat at the small table. "I'm sure he doesn't. But guys like him have been around the block a few times with the law. He knows he's in big trouble, and by cooperating with the police, he probably hopes to get a better deal when his case goes to court."

"I hope he never gets out of prison." Lane shuddered at the thought of that man being back on the streets. "Some people just have something missing inside of them. He's one of them."

"I agree." Jeff looked at Jonas. "It's been an amazing experience, buddy. Carla and I didn't really do all that much, but we're sure happy with the outcome and are glad we were on the winning team."

"So you're leaving for home?" Jonas sat in the chair opposite Jeff to pull on his shoes.

"Yeah. The fun's all over." Jeff chuckled. "Not that stakeouts at a grocery store were a laugh a minute. But now that everything's getting wrapped up, there's no reason for us to stay. We both made arrangements to be off for a week, so we're thinking about taking a few more days of downtime together. We may even take off down the coastline and do the tourist thing, an unexpected but welcome mini-vacation."

Lane's throat went tight. "I don't think I've adequately expressed how grateful I've been for your and Carla's support through all this. You've been good friends."

Just then Carla opened the door and stepped inside. "I could hear your voices, so I knew everybody was decent." She went to sit on Jeff's knee. "We're out of here—or soon will be."

Lane tried to tell Carla what she'd just told Jeff, but her new friend waved her off. "It was our pleasure. Now I know firsthand why Jeff whines so much about having to do stakeouts. It's kind of like sitting somewhere to watch paint dry. And we accomplished our mission! Well, not us, really, but we were involved and trying our best to help, so the outcome makes us feel good." She gave Lane a bright smile. "I hope you and I will see each other again, Lane. Maybe you can come to the coast with Jonas. We'll all do a weekend together, have some fun."

Lane glanced at Jonas and decided that, for the moment, the less said about their personal difficulties the better. "That would be great!" She tried to sound enthusiastic rather than sad. There was every chance that she might never see Carla again, and that seemed a shame. They'd hit if off right from the start. "I'll look forward to it."

The four of them hugged goodbye. Minutes later, Lane was in the car with Jonas as he drove her to the hospital. "Are you sure you don't want to stop somewhere for breakfast?" he asked.

"No, thank you," Lane told him again. She was upset about parting company with Jonas and nervous about having her first face-to-face with her sister. Food was the last thing on her mind. "If I get hungry, I can always go to the cafeteria."

"I'll stay out in the waiting room if that's all right. That way, you won't have to wait for me to come back when you need a ride to the motel."

Lane had no intention of staying another night with Jonas. She'd already texted her parents and made arrangements with them to stop by the motel later that afternoon to pick her up. It felt like an abrupt ending for her and this man who she'd come to care about so deeply, but in all practicality, it made no sense to drag their goodbye out, either. That would only prolong the pain of parting for both of them. She decided telling Jonas of her plans should wait until later, though. She'd surely be finished at the hospital early enough for Jonas to head back to Mystic Creek that afternoon, if he so wished. He'd be out the cost of lodging for another night, of course, but Lane truly did plan to reimburse him for everything, so she wouldn't let herself feel guilty about that.

He was uncharacteristically quiet as he escorted her

into the medical center and found them an elevator. At the front desk, they'd been told Veneta had been moved from ICU to a private room on the second floor.

As they stepped out of the car, Lane paused to look up at Jonas. "You'll be okay on your own?"

He nodded and forced a smile. She missed his real smiles. They'd always made her heart lift.

"Good luck," he said. "I know you're nervous about talking with her for the first time."

"I am," Lane confessed. "She's been inside my head for as long as I can remember, so this makes no sense, but she's still a stranger to me. I'm not sure I'll know what to say."

Jonas placed a hand on her shoulder. His touch set off emotions within her that made her want to weep. "Just be yourself. You're a wonderful person. She'll love you in two seconds flat."

Lane stuffed her hands into the generous pockets of her skirt and made tight fists as she left him to find Veneta's room. *I'm in love with him*, she thought. *I'm so deeply in love with him. I know I'm doing the right thing, but carrying through with it is going to be one of the hardest things I've ever done.*

Chapter Sixteen

With IVs in both arms and an oxygen cannula pressed to her nose, Veneta lay in a hospital bed, the head of it partially raised. Her eyes were closed, and Lane almost turned around to leave. But her sister must have heard her footsteps and lifted her lashes to reveal blue eyes exactly like Lane's own. Lane guessed that this moment was just as mind-boggling for Veneta as it was for her. They just stared at each other, trying to assimilate the fact that they each had a double.

"Wow," Veneta finally said. Her voice was hoarse, and she was still frightfully pale, but there was a spark of life in her this morning that had been all but nonexistent last night. "This is amazing." She slurred her words like a drunk. "Absolutely mind-blowing."

Lane pulled a visitor chair closer to the bed and sat down, removing the strap of her purse from her shoulder to set the bag on the floor at her feet. "It's difficult to wrap my mind around it, even now."

Veneta sighed and closed her eyes again.

"I can leave so you can rest," Lane offered. "You've been through a horrible ordeal."

Slitting open her eyes, Veneta said, "No way. I've been waiting for you to get here." She smiled slightly. "Do you remember me?"

Lane shook her head. "No. I think sometimes that I remember our mother. Just her face. Nothing about what she was like. I recall playing on the floor, but in my memory, I was playing alone. I also sort of remember her reading to me."

A surreal feeling enveloped Lane. She had imagined that this meeting would go so differently—both of them in tears, maybe, and even hugging each other. This was more like meeting a complete stranger.

Veneta nodded. "My memories are clearer than yours, but they only come to me in bits and pieces. She did read to us. Big storybooks with pictures. And sometimes as I fell asleep while growing up, I'd get flashes of memory about you. Not enough to make me suspect I had a sister, though. I thought maybe I'd seen myself in a mirror and was remembering images of myself."

"Nope. I'm real."

Veneta sighed. "The police were here earlier. They came to tell me my kidnapper is in jail and that they hope to apprehend the others by this evening." Her lip curled in a snarl. "As if. They have no idea who they're dealing with. Those guys are in up to their eyebrows and won't sit around waiting to be caught. By evening, they'll be on a beach somewhere, drinking margaritas."

The thought gave Lane the creeps. It also bothered her—although she was prepared to make exceptions because of Veneta's physical condition—that her twin wasn't solely focused on meeting her for the very first time. She regrouped and said, "Oh, but I hope they *are* caught. Neither of us will be truly safe until they are."

Eyes closed again, Veneta said, "From here on out, I'll be safe enough. They've been identified. Their mug shots are in the system already, I'm sure, so the cops have good physical descriptions. They're now wanted for two counts of murder and several counts of illegal drug distribution, not to mention kidnapping and a string of other charges. They won't be foolish enough to come back to Oregon to shut me up or get even. What I knew about them is out in the open now." She arched her brows but didn't lift her lashes. "I don't know how you ran afoul of them, but unless you know something the police haven't already been told by the creep they've got in custody, you shouldn't be worried."

Lane had never known anything much—except that her sister was in danger. She supposed Veneta's reasoning made sense. "Maybe not, but I'll still feel better when they're in custody."

"Don't hold your breath. They've got people in place to get them fake identifications, fake passports, and even makeup artists to alter their physical appearance so they won't be recognized in airports. They'll lie low for a while, and when they think it's safe, they'll set up shop again somewhere else. We'll be nothing but a bad memory."

"The two counts of murder . . ." Lane let her voice trail away, uncertain if she should continue. "I, um . . . I was told that you were good friends with the women who were killed."

Veneta finally opened her eyes. "I was." The blue depths of her irises went sparkly with tears. "I was both heartbroken and furious when they died. They'd gotten clean. They were picking up the pieces of their lives and starting over. They became targets because they knew the identity of the money person behind the drug ring. I couldn't let it go. I wanted the people who killed them to be held accountable. I know it was stupid of me to try to track those individuals down. Even stupider to pretend I was an addict and buy drugs from them to hopefully get information so I could turn them in. But at the time, I didn't feel I had a choice. My friends were wonderful women. Young and pretty and smart. How could I just let them be killed and do nothing to make the people who did it pay?"

Lane had no answers. "Is that what you did? You only *pretended* to be an addict? A bartender in Plover Bay said he had to make you leave his establishment because he saw you sniffing drugs while drinking at his bar."

Veneta wrinkled her nose. "Once upon a time, I was a pill popper, and when my doctor refused to prescribe for me any longer, I did buy pills on the street. Some were narcotics—and addictive. I used them as tranquilizers and sleeping aids. Another stupid thing that I did." She met Lane's curious gaze. "If you thought your newfound sister was a squared-away person who never makes mistakes, I'll be a big disappointment to you. I've made mistakes, and lots of them. But I quit the pills. Went for help. Dried out in a rehab center— they called it a retreat, trying to fancy it all up. That's how I met Dara McIntire, the first woman that was murdered. She was there to get clean, and we kind of did it together. You know? Jillian Foxglove was already clean, but she came to visit Dara at the center, and that's how she became my friend, too. No offense intended, but they were like sisters to me. I'll always miss them, I think." She sighed and let her eyes fall closed again. "The stuff I sniffed at the bar. It was fake cocaine, called inositol. It's actually a vitamin B powder, which gives users an energy boost. They substitute with it during the production of drug movies. They don't want their actors snorting the real thing."

"No, I don't suppose they would, and in most cases, the actors probably wouldn't be keen on the idea, either." Lane tried to imagine sniffing vitamin powder up her nostrils, thinking that it must burn. "So, can I ask you something?"

"I guess you can. Not like I can walk out of here yet. They say it'll be a week, if not longer."

Lane was just grateful that her sister would eventually leave this hospital under her own power. "You snorted what looked like cocaine in a quiet little coastal bar. Who were you putting the act on for?" Lane pushed at her hair, which had gone uncontrollably curly because she hadn't blown it dry last night. "I mean, well, it was to make them think you were an addict? Right?"

Veneta still had her eyes closed, which made Lane worry that she was growing exhausted. "Right. They weren't there, but the bartender was, and he's a snitch. I knew anything I said or did would go straight to the people I wanted to know about it."

Lane recalled the big bartender with the thinning blond hair. "He acted as if he was fond of you."

"Yeah." Eyes still closed, Veneta snarled her lip again. "I was like a daughter to him." Her lashes lifted slightly. "He got kickbacks for information and setting them up with customers. Do you think drug dealers actually stand on street corners to peddle their stuff anymore? Hell, no. Not these dealers, anyway. They're way more sophisticated than that. They enlist the aid of business people. Use them as go-betweens and reward them with monetary gifts. When it comes to the kind of bucks I'm talking about, there are a lot of people out there who would betray their own mothers to get a cut."

"So you essentially set yourself up?"

"Yep. Like I said—really dumb. My plan was to ar-range for a buy and get the cops in on it. I imagined a sting operation, basically, which probably means I watch too much TV. Obviously it didn't work. So that last night, I told Cliff—he's the bartender snitch—that some people had murdered my best friends and I meant to make them pay. Then I snorted the fake coke in front of him and said I was running low and needed to make a buy. I thought that would bring the big boss out of the woodwork, that he'd figure the easiest way to nab me would be to arrange for me to meet someone for the exchange. My plan was to call the cops, tell them when and where, and stand aside while the whole bunch of those bastards was arrested." She sniffed and swallowed. "Obviously it didn't go down that way. In-stead, I got a wool blanket thrown over my head and was tossed, none too gently, into the trunk of a car."

"Oh, God," Lane whispered.

"Yeah. Not fun." She finally made eye contact with Lane again. "They didn't tie me up in the trunk. I tried to keep my head. To remember stories I'd heard about how people alerted other drivers that they were trapped in the trunk and needed help. I drew back the carpeting and broke nearly all my fingernails ripping out the wir-ing to the taillights of the car, hoping they'd get pulled over by a cop. When that happened, I planned to kick, and bang, and scream my head off, and just pray to God the cop was faster to react than they were."

"But they didn't get pulled over?"

"Nope. I wished then that I'd tried to pull only one wire free to do an SOS signal, only I didn't know how to put the wiring back right, and I sure as fuck didn't know any SOS codes."

Lane couldn't help it; she laughed. That reminded her of Jonas, because she'd come to think of him as the person who'd taught her how. For a few minutes, she'd let go of the pain of losing him, the indecision, but now it slammed back into her again with a vengeance.

Veneta said, "It's not so funny when you're the one in the trunk of a car." Veneta turned her head slightly to look at Lane, really look at her. And then she said, "Jesus. Feeling like I do right now, seeing you is giving me one of those out-of-body experiences you read about."

Lane leaned over to collect her purse. "The nurse said I shouldn't stay too long. Right now, they mostly want you to rest. In order for you to recover, lots of sleep is just as important as the fluids and nourishment they're giving you through the IVs."

"Not so fast, Tinker Bell." Veneta flashed a smile that was all sarcasm and devoid of humor. "That was one of the stories Mama read to us, *Peter Pan*. I remembered bits of it, and I reread it as a teen, trying to remember more about her. I was desperate to remember—to see her face and know that at some point someone loved me. It sure as hell wasn't my adoptive parents. There were no more fairy tales once I went to live with them. More like a nightmare that never ended."

"I'm so sorry it was like that for you." Lane meant that from the bottom of her heart. She'd been adopted by wonderful people who'd loved her and read to her nightly. "It seems so unfair that I was adopted by fabulous parents and you weren't."

"Yeah. That's the breaks. My old man is a mean drunk, and my mom is a gutless wonder who decided when I was about seven that she'd rather take tranquilizers than endure reality. When I left at eighteen—I was close to graduating from high school—she was passed out on the couch with a bottle of pills and scotch."

Lane struggled to wrap her mind around how differently Veneta's adoption had gone. "That's terrible. Don't adoption agencies screen all the applicants?"

"There was no agency involved." Veneta squinted at her. "What's your name again?"

"Lane. Lane Driscoll."

"Well, Lane, welcome to the shady side of adoption. People who can't cut the mustard at regular agencies search for attorneys who handle private adoptions and sometimes, if the price is right, will dance around the law." She relaxed again and closed her eyes. "Those lawyers are only in it for the bucks. Not saying it's true of all private adoptions, but it happens. They offer a more expensive solution for couples who can't qualify to get a child the regular way. A pregnant girl who wants to carry her child to term and put it up for adoption. A greedy attorney. Couples who are desperate to get a kid and will agree to almost anything. The screening process may never occur. I was three, not a tiny baby, so not many applicants were interested in me. I never knew all these years that I was also part of a pair, which makes it even more understandable that I got overlooked. Adoptive parents usually want an infant, not three-year-old twins. Shit. Neither of us had a prayer of getting the cream of the crop when it came to parents. We were undesirables."

For the first time, Lane felt a burgeoning bond developing between her and her sister. *Undesirables.* She'd felt exactly that way for most of her life. As if she were a lesser being somehow. That her parents had been tricked into taking a lemon, only unlike a faulty car or appliance, they couldn't easily trade her back in for something better.

Veneta continued speaking. "You got inside my head last night. How did you do all that shit about the church bells? I'm glad you did. Don't get me wrong. But, *damn*, that was weird."

Lane gathered her composure. It didn't seem to be as hard for Veneta, but for her this was an unveiling that dug deep into her emotions. "I, um—was that the *first* time for you?" she asked. "The very first time you ever heard me?"

Veneta nodded.

Lane went limp on the chair. After searching for words, she said, "We're telepathically linked. You've been inside my head all my life, driving me half-crazy."

"I have?" Veneta sounded sincerely bewildered. "How'd I do that?"

Lane smoothed her skirt, wishing suddenly that Jonas were with them. *Jonas*. Oh, how she wished for his presence. "I can't explain it. You can burst through into my mind like an announcer with a megaphone." She went on to tell Veneta about awakening from a bad dream at four years of age with marks on her body and an arm that she cradled for weeks. About random events later that she particularly remembered. "I never knew when it would happen," she tried to explain. "It just did. I thought I was crazy. All these years, I truly believed I was emotionally unbalanced. My parents thought so, too."

Veneta said nothing for at least a full minute, leaving Lane to fidget on the chair. "Damn, that's totally psycho."

"Only it wasn't, not really," Lane pushed out. "For you and me, it's normal, Veneta. Jonas says your arm was broken by your father when you were little. He believes I somehow experienced that attack upon you when I was napping on the living room rug that afternoon."

Veneta lifted her lashes to stare at the ceiling. "So, let me get this straight. When you heard me in your head, it was never when I was happy and calm? Only times, like, when my dad was beating the hell out of me? Or something else bad happened?"

"I can't say that with absolute certainty," Lane replied. "But the way I remember it, it was mostly frantic or bad stuff." Lane thought back. "I was taking a math test once, and all of a sudden, I heard, 'Oh, God, I'm pregnant! He'll kill me if he finds out.' I got so weirded out that I flunked the final. There was all this craziness inside my head. That you had to get another pregnancy test. That it had to be a false reading. That somebody named Mark would dump you, for sure."

Veneta's lips went slack. "Wow." Her mouth tightened again and curved into a sad smile. "*Mark.* I'd forgotten all about him. The first love of my life. And I *was* pregnant; it wasn't a false positive. He did dump me over it. I was so scared. Kept it a secret until my father noticed the bulge. Then he took care of the problem."

Lane frowned. "He made you get an abortion?"

Veneta made one of those sarcastic faces again. "No. He beat the shit out of me, and I lost the baby."

Unpleasant memories flooded into Lane's mind. "Oh, God. I remember that. The beating. Blood in the toilet. Awful stomach pain."

"Oh, yeah. You tuned in for that mess?"

"I *never* tuned in," Lane corrected. "You *barged* in."

"Wow."

Lane wondered suddenly if any one person's life could have been as awful as she was suddenly imagining that her sister's had been. "Mostly, it was really bad stuff I saw and heard," she said. "I would have welcomed something good, I think."

"So you tune in only when my life has turned to shit."

Lane made fists on her knees. She'd entered this room thinking that Veneta might be the only person on earth, aside from Jonas, who could come close to understanding what she'd been through. "I don't deliberately tune in. It just happens. And it's screwed up my whole life."

Veneta took a deep breath and released it. "Well, excuse me for breathing. It wasn't my fault that I got the grab-bag parents who were monsters and consequently interfered with your cushy little life with a good mommy and daddy."

As frustrating as Veneta's reply was for Lane, she inhaled deeply herself and strove for calmness.

"I didn't get the luck of the draw," Veneta went on. "I haven't spoken to those screwed-up parents of mine for over eight years. When I turned eighteen, there weren't any candles on a cake for me. It was more, like, eighteen crushed beer cans scattered across the coffee table around my mom's jug of scotch. She was passed out on tranquilizers and booze. He was drunk as a lord. After school that day, I put everything I could in a pillowcase and left. I had nobody. I stayed at a girlfriend's house for a while to finish high school and get my diploma. That was important to me. I was dead set on doing something with my life."

"And did you?" Lane asked.

"Yeah. I was going to be an accountant, but after I

kicked Jonas to the curb"—she broke off and smiled slightly—"that was the worst mistake of my life, by the way, shoving him away. Anyway, after that, I decided I wanted to become a nurse instead. Now I'm an RN and, before all this crap happened, I was studying to become a nurse practitioner, specializing in family care."

Lane gulped. Her self-esteem took another nose-dive. "Oh. Wow. I'm impressed."

"Yeah, well, no need to be. I've got more schooling ahead of me, and I drink a little bit too much now. Maybe I'll settle for just being a drunk nurse, a chip off the old block, so to speak. Substance abuse runs in families, you know, and my folks are poster children for drug addiction and alcoholism."

"You aren't their biological daughter," Lane reminded her.

Veneta shot her a bleary-eyed look. "I was raised by the assholes, though. I think it just rubbed off on me."

Lane felt sick to her stomach. "I'm so sorry, Veneta."

"Yeah, well, I'm sorry that my fucked-up life has interfered with yours."

And then, as if someone had flipped a switch to turn off a robot, Veneta went to sleep. Lane sat there for several minutes, just staring at her sister.

Lane had just left Veneta's room and was trying to get her bearings to go find Jonas when he stepped out into the hallway and strode toward her. Hands in his pants pockets, the front panels of his lightweight jacket bunched over his wrists, he looked handsome, out-doorsy, and out of place in a clinical setting. Lane guessed that his casual, relaxed air probably disarmed his clients into trusting him enough to tell him almost anything.

"Hey," he said softly. "How'd it go?"

Lane parted her lips to speak and then realized that she couldn't think what to say. She settled for, "She tired quickly and went back to sleep. We chatted a little, though."

"And?"

"We didn't really accomplish much."

He grasped her elbow to guide her to the elevator. "What did you hope to accomplish?"

Lane shot him a sideways glance. "I hoped we might forge a friendship of sorts—that we'd at least feel kind of like sisters before I left. I guess that was unrealistic."

"Just a bit." His firm mouth tipped into a sad smile. "Twenty-three years of separation—that's a lot of catching up to do. With each visit, you'll learn more about each other. Just be patient and give it time."

Lane couldn't see that she had any choice. "Yeah, I guess." She watched him press the down button for the elevator. As the doors slid open, she said, "She cusses a lot."

Jonas chuckled as they entered the enclosure. "Ah, yes. That's Veneta. Mostly that happens when she's nervous or scared. She acts tough and street smart. It's a defensive mechanism, I think."

"It felt all"—Lane broke off and searched for the right word—"*wrong*. She looks like me. Her voice is similar to mine. But talking with her made me feel kind of like when I put a shoe on the wrong foot."

He leaned his hips against the handrail and folded his arms. Lane chose to stand with her back to another wall, keeping distance between them.

"Like I said, give it time, and try not to expect her to be exactly like you. Her life experiences have been totally different from yours."

"That may be the understatement of the decade," Lane volleyed back. "Her life experiences have been pretty awful. An abusive drunk for a father, a mom who took tranquilizers all the time and mixed them with scotch. Even with the voices and dreams to make me miserable, my life has been a walk in the park by comparison."

Jonas' eyes darkened with sadness. "That wasn't your doing."

Lane tucked in her chin to stare at her sandals. It would soon be too cold to wear them, and she'd have to retire them for the winter. She didn't know where that thought had come from. Her footwear had nothing to do with what she and Jonas were talking about. "I know that, but it still makes me feel guilty. How can one little girl be so lucky and the other one isn't lucky at all? I've always believed that adoption is a beautiful thing, bringing children and adoptive parents together to form a family. How could something that was so beautiful for me have been so horrible for my twin?"

The elevator gave that slight lurch that most elevators do when they hit bottom. Jonas straightened away from the wall and pressed his hand to the small of her back as they exited the enclosure. "Most adoptions *are* beautiful things, Lane. Sure, every once in a while the situation turns out bad. But just think of all the kids who find wonderful parents who love them and offer them a happy home. We shouldn't get soured on the adoption process because of one instance of failure."

Lane thought of her parents—how devoted they'd always been to her—and a smile curved her lips. "You're right. For me, it truly was beautiful. I'm just feeling bad for Veneta, is all. She deserved a happy life just as much as I did, and she didn't get one. She says our adoption was handled by a greedy attorney who didn't bother with screening the parents. A private arrangement. I'm not sure if she knows that because her parents told her or if she's just guessing."

"The next time you visit with her, maybe you should ask her. Or, better yet, ask your own parents."

They went single file through revolving doors to reach the covered ambulance lane just outside the hospital. An elderly man in a wheelchair had apparently just been released, and a nurse was trying to help him get into a waiting car.

Jonas stopped. "Do you need a helping hand?"

The nurse flashed a grateful smile. "Please. Mr. Everett is still a bit weak."

Jonas leaned around to introduce himself to the man. "Hi, Mr. Everett. My name's Jonas Sterling. Do you mind if I give you a hand up?"

Watching Jonas, Lane felt her mouth quiver at the corners. He was such a kind person and had a way of putting perfect strangers at ease. The elderly man chuckled and said he definitely needed a hand. "My old legs turned to jelly from lying in bed for so many days."

Jonas helped the old fellow into the car, striking up a conversation with Mrs. Everett, who sat behind the steering wheel. White-haired and frail, she looked to be about the same age as her husband, and Lane guessed that they'd probably been married for at least sixty years. What would it be like, she wondered, to be with a man she loved for over half a century? Wonderful, she decided. And there was no denying, not even to herself, that she wished that man could be Jonas. As a girl, she'd never dreamed of the perfect man, but if she had, she felt certain that she would have imagined someone exactly like him.

And now she had to walk away.

Once back in their room, Jonas half expected Lane to tell him she'd called her parents and arranged for them to pick her up at the motel, but it still hurt when she actually said the words. He tried to keep his expression blank, not wanting to make this any harder for her than it had to be. He'd had time to think about everything, and he understood the predicament she was in. And, for at least right now, trying to build a relationship with her sister had to be her first priority. Jonas could only hope that Lane would eventually come to realize that Veneta no longer had deep feelings for him. What he felt for Lane was real and true. It would be such a shame if they could never be together.

As she packed her things into her suitcase, Jonas sat on the bed watching her. When she latched the carryall, she turned to face him, her eyes so big and blue that they dominated her delicately carved features. She clasped her hands, then pulled them apart to let her arms hang straight at her sides.

"I, um, don't know how to say this." Her voice quivered. "But when I go back to Mystic Creek, it'll only be to get my things and my car. My dad will probably come with me to help me load everything into a trailer. We may stay over a night and make the drive back here to Maple Leaf the next day."

Jonas felt sick inside, and he wanted so badly to take one more stab at convincing her to stay with him. Only doing that would go against all of his conceptions of what a solid and loving relationship was supposed to be about. Being with him had to be Lane's choice. He had to let her come to him without any misgivings, or not at all. He couldn't, in good conscience, pressure her. A memory of an embroidered wall hanging of his mom's came into his mind. A beautiful saying that read, IF YOU LOVE SOMEONE, SET THEM FREE. IF THEY COME BACK, THEY'RE YOURS; IF THEY DON'T, THEY NEVER WERE. Jonas believed that. Love shouldn't be a form of emotional bondage.

"So you won't be working with Ma? You've given up on the possibility of becoming part owner of the shop."

She sighed and raked a hand through her hair. "I just don't think I can live there now."

Because I'll be there, he thought, and that was another knife in his heart. "I hope you'll keep in touch," was all he said, even though he wanted to say so much more.

"Do you think that's really a good idea?"

Jonas met her gaze. "We were friends before we made love, Lane. And really special friends are hard to find."

"Obviously," she said with a little laugh that lacked humor. "You're the best friend I've ever had, barring none."

Jonas rubbed his jaw. "Well, then, it seems silly to me to toss a friendship like ours away just because it's complicated. Communicating long distance is harmless."

"Yes, but it may keep these crazy feelings we have for each other alive. Sometimes, it's best to make a clean break."

It took all of Jonas' self-control not to shout, *Our feelings for each other aren't crazy!* Instead, he said, "Then do what you think is best for you. But I'll hope to hear from you. Regardless of everything, I care about you as a friend. I'll be curious about how your relationship with Veneta is progressing and will want to know how you're doing as well. Just ordinary, every-day stuff, not sappy letters."

She gave him a tremulous smile. "I'll try. That's all I can promise."

Jonas heard a car pull up out front, and his guts clenched. He could only wonder how in the hell this had happened. He'd fallen head-over-heels in love with this woman, and watching her walk out of his life was going to rip his heart out. How had he fallen in love so quickly? Why had he let himself go there when he'd once been involved with her identical twin? From the start, this whole situation had been a perfect recipe for heartbreak.

A heavy knock came at the door. Lane jumped and flattened a hand over her heart. "My dad."

Jonas stepped over to open the door. A tall, dark-haired, brown-eyed man who looked nothing like Lane stood outside. *But, of course, they look nothing alike*, Jonas thought. *They aren't blood relatives.* He proffered his right hand.

"Mr. Driscoll, I'm Jonas Sterling. It's a pleasure to finally meet you."

"Brent," he replied. "My wife tells me that I owe you a big thank-you for watching after our daughter."

Jonas shot Lane a look and then smiled at her dad. "I think it was a toss-up, with her watching out for me as much as I watched out for her." Uncertain of exactly how much Brent knew, Jonas chose to let it go at that and went to get Lane's luggage. "Are you sure you got everything?"

"I think so."

She looked up at him with tears swimming in her eyes. Jonas felt his own misting up and blinked. "Take care, Lane. Keep me updated if you can."

She nodded, brushed moisture from her cheek, and hurried out the open door. Brent Driscoll followed his daughter with his gaze and then gave Jonas a questioning look. "Are you certain it's safe for her to be in Maple Leaf? My wife says the guy who attacked her on the sidewalk is behind bars, but if he's involved with a drug ring, how can I be sure someone else won't come after her?"

Jonas realized that Lane had shared very little of what had happened with her mom, and he was glad he'd kept his lips zipped. Lane would tell them the whole story when she saw fit, and until then, he didn't want to drop any word bombs. "I'm fairly confident that the danger to Lane is over," he said. "I'm sure she'll give you and your wife all the details later, but, yes, I think she's safe now."

Brent's shoulders slumped with relief, which told Jonas that the man truly did love his daughter no matter what kind of shenanigans he might have pulled in order to adopt her twenty-three years ago. Desperate people sometimes resorted to desperate measures.

He walked outside with the man. Lane stood by the car. Jonas carried her suitcase out, opened the rear passenger door, and deposited it on the seat. Then he turned toward Lane. "You take care of yourself," he said. Lowering his voice, he added, "Work with Veneta to control her thoughts, if you can. Maybe over time she can learn not to transmit them to you."

She nodded. Tears streamed down her pale cheeks. In a choked voice, she said, "Goodbye, Jonas. I'll never forget you. Really, I never, ever will. Please, be happy."

Jonas wasn't about to promise that he'd be happy. He had a very bad feeling that he'd never forget her, either. "Same back at you. And if it works for you, please do keep in touch. Texts, emails, even a call now and again would be awesome."

She nodded and climbed into her father's car. Brent, who'd walked around to the driver's door, waved farewell over the cab of the vehicle. "It was good to meet you," he said. "And thank you again for everything."

Jonas stood outside the motel room to watch the car go out of sight. Then he went in to pack his shit and head home. There was nothing to keep him here now. Just like that, and she was gone.

Chapter Seventeen

Once back in Mystic Creek, Jonas faced the challenge of moving forward with his life without Lane in it, and within a week, he realized how difficult that was going to be. Prior to meeting her, he'd hoped to find the woman of his dreams and create a future with her, which had motivated him to focus on building his business while he was still single. He'd wanted to be successful when he finally met Miss Right, to be a *good catch*, so to speak. But now, having found that woman and then losing her, he wasn't sure what life was supposed to be about. If he couldn't be with Lane, if he couldn't build a life and raise a family with her, what was his incentive to work and save and try to get ahead? He'd resumed seeing people for counseling, but his heart was no longer in it. They had problems, but he had bigger ones, and nobody seemed interested in trying to fix his.

His family tried to be supportive. His dad kept him busy by calling him out to the farm to help with first one chore and then another. His mom invited him to dinner and fussed over him while he was there. His sisters baked him cookies and delivered them to his apartment. His brothers appeared at his door with six packs of cold beer, ready to talk and listen and advise.

Only Jonas didn't really feel like talking, and all the good advice in the world wouldn't fix his problem. He hadn't heard anything from Lane, and he was starting to fear that he never would.

Tired after back-to-back counseling sessions all morning and mucking out stalls at the farm that afternoon, Jonas took an order of enchiladas upstairs to his apartment for his Wednesday night dinner. He wasn't really hungry or interested in eating, but he knew his body needed nourishment. Weird, that. He'd always loved food—all kinds, he wasn't picky—and now he didn't really care if he ate. He sat at his desk, determined to go over his chart notes, pay a couple of bills, and check his mail before he poured himself a glass of wine and crashed in his recliner to stare stupidly at the television until he could sleep.

After taking a bite of enchilada, Jonas set the plate near his elbow, thinking that the blob of goo in his mouth was as tasteless as sawdust. *It's just me*, he reminded himself, *not the food. José is a great cook.* Only lecturing himself didn't make the enchilada any more flavorful. As he booted up his computer, he managed to swallow, but it took effort. He got back up and went to the kitchen, deciding he'd enjoy a glass of vino *before* he got in the recliner. Something wet to make the enchiladas go down easier.

After plucking a bottle of merlot from the counter-top rack, Jonas peeled away the neck foil and then froze, staring at the cork. *Memories. Lane, coming to the rescue with a fingernail file to open our wine. Me, pushing too hard on the cork, splashing my shirt, drenching the table.* He wished he could turn back the clock and relive those moments with her. Wished he'd paid more attention to detail and appreciated each second more. Now, looking back, he promised himself that he'd never take special moments for granted again.

He opened the wine, sloshed some into a tumbler, and went back to his desk. His computer had been busy loading, and the Windows page was up. He opened Outlook to check his emails. His gaze snagged on one sender, *LDriscoll*. He stared at the ID for a long moment, part of him bursting with joy, another part of him afraid to open it. *Lane*. She'd finally gotten in touch. Only why? Maybe she'd written to say she never wanted to see him again. Right at that moment, Jonas felt pretty certain a letter like that would push him over the edge. *Nonsense*, he scolded himself. *She already pretty much said that, and you lived through it.*

As he moved his cursor over the message, he felt like a kid about to open his Christmas packages, hoping to get his most-wanted present but afraid he'd be disappointed. *Click.* The letter popped up. He stared at the blur of words, not really making them out for what felt like a full minute. Then he focused. *"Dear Jonas,"* it read. *That's positive*, he assured himself. *Ah, but don't forget that Veneta broke up with you in a letter, and she started it with the same salutation.*

He forced himself to read on.

I've wanted to write to you a dozen times, but every time I tried, it felt all weird and I hit the delete button. I miss you so much! I can't believe just how much. I keep telling myself that these feelings will pass, but so far, the ache in my chest only seems to get worse, not better. It's so bad that sometimes I think I've made a terrible mistake and almost call you to say I've changed my mind. But fortunately, sanity always prevails, and I'm right back where I started, knowing deep down that I can't be happy with a man that my sister loves, and as yet, she has said nothing to disabuse me of that belief.

That said, it surely can't do any harm for us to write to each other. Maybe it will help both of us move on with our separate lives. I'm happy to report that the drug boss and his cohorts have been arrested, and the evidence against them is so strong that it's unlikely their high-end lawyers will be able to get them off the hook. They'll be doing time in prison for what they've done, and I hope they're never on the streets again. Wish we were back at the motel together so we could celebrate!

Veneta is recovering nicely, but the doctors want to keep her in the hospital for a day or two more. After she's released, she plans to stay with a friend over on the coast until she can find a job. She's as excited as I am about trying to find our birth mother. I told her about discovering a little town named Veneta in Lane County, and she, too, believes our real mom was trying to leave us clues so we might find her or each other someday. Neta will be giving me all her contact information before she leaves Maple Leaf, and we've promised each other that we'll never lose touch again.

It has been a difficult and yet wonderful experience getting to know my sister. We're so alike that it's eerie. We both like the same foods, the same style of clothing, and even wear our hair alike.

But, then, in other ways, we're also different. Only in small ways, though.

Jonas drew his brows together into a scowl of bewilderment. In his opinion, Lane and Veneta were very different in so many ways that he couldn't count them.

As time wears on, we hope to forge a strong and wonderful bond to make up for all the years we've been apart. Oh, and another interesting thing. Remember me telling you that I got better for almost two years? No voices, no horrible dreams. And then, bang, she was back in my head? Well, we've talked about all of that, and it appears that I get signals from Veneta only when she's in trouble of some kind. Her life settled down for nearly two years. She went into rehab and got off the pills. She had two good friends to support her. She was doing well with her university coursework and became a registered nurse. Then her friends were murdered, and her life went off course again. And, like always, my life was derailed right along with hers.

Jonas smiled slightly. Lane wrote great letters. It was almost like having a conversation with her, only one-sided.

The situation with my folks was extremely difficult at first. (I'm still staying with them.) At first they denied everything, but after a couple of days they finally confessed the truth to me. My adoption wasn't handled by a certified adoption agency. My father was married once before, and when the relationship began to fall apart, his first wife grew vindictive and told the police terrible lies about him, which his little girl verified with her testimony in closed chambers. He was arrested and convicted. He did time for two years and then got parole. When he married my mom, they both wanted a family, but my mom couldn't conceive. Adopting a child was their only option. With a felonious conviction of child abuse on his record, Dad could never adopt through a regular, state-affiliated adoption agency, so their only recourse was an independent adoption, a private arrangement. When my birth mother put out feelers to find suitable parents for me and Veneta, she couldn't find a couple willing to take two kids. For health reasons—I'm not sure what kind of health issues she had—she was frantic to see her little girls settled into wonderful homes, so she finally agreed to separate us. Veneta had already been adopted by the time my mom and dad came along, and they were never told that I had a twin.

So my parents didn't know of Veneta's existence. The reason my dad acted so weird on the phone when I asked them if I had a twin was, as I suspected, borne of a guilty conscience and a feeling of shame, I suppose, but it was because he didn't want to tell me that they essentially bypassed the law by coughing up enough money to adopt me. It's hard for me to forgive them, Jonas. I'll be honest. It bothers me that they essentially purchased a child. But things you said to me about how childless couples can feel desperate has really helped me sort it out. I will never approve of their methods, but I'm glad they're my parents. I was so much luckier than Veneta, after all. My mom and dad have done their very best.

Jonas shifted to get more comfortable and stuck his elbow into the enchiladas. He swore under his breath and stood to strip off the soiled shirt. After throwing it in the laundry basket, he returned to the computer.

Neta and I are really excited about trying to find our birth mother. My mom—my adoptive mom—gave me my birth mother's name. That's the only information she has about my real mother, but I'm hoping it'll help us find out what happened to her and if she's even still alive. Her name is Dallas Chastain. Pretty surname. It's strange to think I might have grown up being called Lane Chastain. (Kind of glad that didn't work out. It sounds like a brand of handbags.) We hope to learn what forced our mother to give us up, and, on a more practical note, a little about our family medical history.

Jonas wished he could go with Lane to the town of Veneta, that he could help track down her birth mother. But he knew he was dreaming. She'd made it clear that it was over between them romantically unless Veneta changed her tune about loving him, and he'd made it equally clear that being only friends would never be enough for him.

Being adopted sucks when it comes to knowing if you're at risk for certain diseases. Does breast cancer run in our family? How about diabetes and heart disease? In that regard, we don't know anything about either of our parents. It would be nice to at least find our birth mother's medical records.

Jonas hadn't ever considered the family history aspect of adoption. What Lane said was true. Adopted children normally grew up with no health information about their biological parents.

Well, Jonas, I've got to sign off. I'm cooking dinner tonight to give Mom a break. Eating a little late because Dad's working longer than usual. I'm making lasagna with a side salad. No dessert. They're both watching their weight. After hanging out with you, I miss having something sweet at the end of a meal. I'll probably just have some fruit.

Please know that I think of you about a dozen times a minute, and I wonder if you're feeling as miserable as I am. I'm a terrible person, I guess, because I hope you are. Misery enjoys company, I suppose.

Until next time,
Love, Lane

Jonas sat back and stared at the screen. He wanted to write her back, but he was terrible at letters. They always sounded like technical reports, not chatty and natural like Lane's. His stomach growled, but he felt no hunger pangs. A glance at the plate of cold enchiladas with an elbow print in the middle did nothing to improve his appetite. Maybe he'd just have a bowl of cereal later. Or not.

He got up to get another measure of wine. *You can't drown your sorrow, man. Drinking every night isn't good.* But he poured himself a second round anyway. *Why worry about your health? Like you want to live to be a hundred without her?* Jonas returned to his desk and started a reply to Lane's email. Everything he wrote sounded corny, and he ended up deleting the whole attempt. *Tomorrow, I'll write to her tomorrow.* Only Jonas didn't know if he would be able to even then. What he wanted was to pour his heart out to her, to tell her that he couldn't live without her. Chitchat wasn't his forte.

He adjourned to his recliner and turned on the television. After three generous glasses of wine, he fell asleep with his chin resting on his chest.

For the last week, Lane had been driving her parents' spare car, an old PT Cruiser that her dad had bought for a song and fixed up. After parking in the visitor section of the hospital, she grabbed her purse, locked the vehicle, and ran toward the entrance, eager to see her sister. They'd developed a habit of going down to the cafeteria each morning for a very late breakfast, because Veneta couldn't tolerate the meals that were brought to her room. Lane wasn't sure the cafeteria fare was that much different, but it brightened Veneta's day to do one meal downstairs. Lane had lent her sister a lounging kimono that fell to her ankles and covered her hospital gown, which opened at the back. At least the kimono allowed Veneta to walk the hallways without feeling exposed.

When she entered Veneta's room, she found her twin sitting on the adjustable bed with a plastic bag on the mattress beside her. She was wearing the black kimono with gold flowers cascading down the front. "I'm out of here," Veneta announced. "The doc just signed my release forms."

Lane had been bracing herself for this moment, but now that it had arrived, she wasn't ready for Veneta to leave town. They still had so very much to learn about each other. "Oh."

Veneta smiled. "That doesn't sound enthusiastic. Aren't you glad for me? I'm so sick of this bed that I'm about to go nuts."

Lane set her purse on the visitor chair. "I'm happy for you. Really, I am. It's just sad to think of you leaving."

With a sigh, Veneta said, "Yeah, well, all good things must end. I won't be that far away. I'm assuming that my car was impounded in Plover Bay. As soon as I can afford to pay the fees to bail it out of jail and get a new driver's license issued to me, we can start meeting halfway. It won't be the same as seeing each other daily, but just think how fun it'll be when we do get together."

Lane sat next to her on the bed. "I just wish—oh, I don't know what I wish. It seems a shame that we can't live in the same town for a while."

Veneta fiddled with the bag beside her. "I know. But truthfully speaking, I've got to start digging myself out of this mess. My apartment in Plover Bay has been rented out to someone else, and God only knows what they did with all my shit. My clothes, my makeup, my dishes and pots and pans. You name it. When you get kidnapped, they don't let you pack for the trip."

"Oh, Veneta. I didn't stop to think!" Lane patted her sister's knee. "All your things are gone."

"Yeah. I'm hoping my landlord put them in storage. That would be a stroke of luck. But I have a bad feeling he sat it out at the curb and let passersby help themselves."

"I don't think that's legal. It was *your* stuff. Not his to do with as he wished. There are laws in Oregon that protect tenants. I think he's required to keep your things for a period of time."

"I don't know what the usual procedure is when a tenant disappears, but in my case, he wasted no time in renting my place out to somebody else. I guess people figured I was dead." She shrugged. "What the hell? Right? I had no family members to go in and save my things for me." She rolled her eyes. "I don't even have my purse. I believe I dropped it when they threw the blanket over me, and I'm guessing they grabbed it, afraid that something inside might implicate them. My phone was in it, too. All my credit cards, gone. All my IDs, gone. It's going to be sort of like coming back from the dead. I'll have to start over from scratch." She lifted one foot, encased in a blue, disposable slipper. "My one and only pair of shoes. For some reason, it didn't occur to me until now that I have absolutely nothing to wear." She patted the bag. "Only what I had on when they brought me in, and all of it stinks so bad, I don't know why they saved it."

"In other words, you're in a heck of a fix." Lane felt guilty for not having anticipated this. "But I've got a solution. You can come home with me, at least for tonight. I didn't take all my clothes to Mystic Creek. Initially, I planned to be there for only a short while. We can sort through what I've got in boxes at my parents' place. We're the same size. I've got lots of shoes, dresses, and skirts in styles I think you'll like. And tomorrow, I can take you to your bank. You can get your credit card problems sorted out. Withdraw some funds.

And we'll go shopping. And given that I haven't gone back to work yet, I can use my parents' spare car to drive you to Plover Bay. We'll get your vehicle out of jail. Get you settled in at your friend's place. By the time I leave, you'll have your life sort of glued back together."

Veneta shook her head. "I dunno about staying the night at your place. Your parents will be there. Meeting them might be kind of uncomfortable—for them and for me."

"Why will it be uncomfortable? They know about you now. In fact, they told me that they would have adopted you if they'd had all the information early enough. My dad says he would have come up with the money somehow. He never would have allowed us to be separated."

Emitting another sigh, Veneta said, "I wish to hell they had. I might be a totally different person if I'd been raised by them. All squared away. More like you."

"Squared away?" Lane laughed. "That is *so* not me." She grabbed her sister's hand. "Come on. Just say yes. It'll be fun!"

Puffing air into her cheeks, Veneta said, "Only if you run it by your parents first. Make sure I'm welcome there."

Lane hopped off the bed to grab her purse. Drawing out her cell phone, she speed-dialed her mother. Ann answered on the fourth ring, and Lane put her on speaker. "Mom, how would you feel about having Veneta stay with us for a couple of days? She's being released from the hospital in a few minutes, and she has nothing to wear but my old kimono and a pair of disposable slippers. I'd like to help her get lined out to reenter the world."

"Oh, the poor *dear.*" Ann clucked her tongue. "She has nothing to wear?"

"She was kidnapped, Mom. She put it best, I think. When you get kidnapped, they don't let you pack for the trip. She doesn't even know what happened to her purse."

"Your father and I would love to have her. If she's your size, we can probably go through your things and find her a few outfits that she can wear until she can do some shopping."

When Lane ended the call, she winked at her twin. "You're more than welcome there. You heard her."

Veneta nodded. "She sounds like a really nice person."

"She is. I'm sure you'll like her."

Having Veneta to worry about was the perfect distraction for Lane, allowing her to go at least ten minutes at a stretch without thinking of Jonas. The ache of loss that had centered in her chest as they said goodbye was still there, a constant throb that she was almost getting used to. Lane wished she could just ask her sister if she still loved Jonas, but then she reasoned her way past the urge. Veneta was in no position at the moment to analyze how she felt about an old flame. Her whole world was up in the air, and Lane didn't feel right about pressing her to sort through her feelings just yet.

Veneta was quiet as Lane wove her parents' car through Maple Leaf's lunch-hour traffic to reach the other side of town. Lane was about to ask her twin if everything was all right when Veneta suddenly said, "Oh, look! A liquor store. Can we stop?"

Lane drove around the block to find a parking place. After cutting the engine of the PT Cruiser, she turned to ask, "Are you going in like that?"

Veneta looked down at herself. "Well, fuck. I totally forgot I'm wearing a lounging robe." Then her frown deepened. "Shit. I can't even buy myself a bottle. No *dinero*."

"I can buy it for you," Lane told her. "What do you want?"

"Vodka. Whatever's cheapest, but get a half-gallon. I don't mess around with pints."

Lane ran inside the liquor store to make the purchase. When she returned to the car, Veneta snatched the bag from her hand, took the cap off the bottle, and took a swig of vodka. Lane nearly gagged. She occasionally enjoyed a mixed drink, but she would never forget how awful the nearly straight vodka had tasted in Plover Bay.

Veneta sighed and leaned her head back against the rest. "Thanks. I needed that."

Lane pulled the car back out into traffic. "We all need a drink sometimes."

"Yeah. Me more than most."

Lane glanced at the digital clock on the dash and saw that it was only one o'clock. In her estimation, it was a little early for cocktails, but it wasn't her place to point that out to her sister. "I didn't know what you like as a mixer."

"Nothing. Vodka on ice is my go-to. Without ice is fine when I'm desperate, and right now I'm desperate." She drank from the bottle again. "Whew. How I missed this feeling. All my problems melting away. All my muscles starting to relax."

By the time Lane pulled into her parents' driveway and parked at the outer edge of the concrete apron in front of the attached garage, she was fairly certain that her sister was well on her way to getting drunk. Somehow, she didn't think the doctor who had been overseeing her care would approve. During the first part of Veneta's hospitalization, there had been a lot of concern about her kidneys, and straight vodka probably wasn't a wise choice for her. But, there again, it wasn't Lane's place to tell her sister what she should or shouldn't do.

As always, Ann was a gracious and welcoming hostess. She gave Veneta an enthusiastic greeting and then served them lunch at the dining room table. Nothing fancy, just turkey sandwiches and vegetable soup, but Lane deeply appreciated her mother's attempt to make Veneta feel at home.

"Love your house," Veneta said as she poured more vodka into her glass. Ice cubes chinked as she took a drink. "Classy. Now I know where Lane gets it."

Ann watched Veneta guzzle more booze and shot Lane a look of alarm. "That's a very nice compliment. Thank you."

"Only the fucking truth. Like mother, like daughter. Two very classy chicks. I feel completely out of my element."

Lane's cheeks grew warm. She sent her mom an apologetic glance. The *F* word was frowned upon in the Driscoll household.

By the time Lane's father got home, Veneta was laughing over nothing, slurring her words, and was laterally challenged when she tried to walk.

"So you're the good daddy Lane's told me so much about." Veneta flashed him a wide smile. "Too bad you came around too late to adopt me. I'd've been a lot better off."

Brent Driscoll shook her hand. "Welcome to our home." He studied Lane's face and looked Veneta over again. "It's amazing. I'd be hard put to tell you apart if you wore the same clothing."

"That's why we're called iden-ti-cal twins," Veneta told him. "Cuz we're exack-ly alike."

Before dinner was served, Lane had to put her exack-ly alike twin to bed in the guest room. Veneta's head had barely touched the pillow before she was asleep. Well, Lane guessed it would be more correct to say that she passed out, but even thinking along those lines was rather alarming. Before rejoining her parents in the kitchen, she drew the curtains, turned out the lights, and pulled the door closed so Veneta could sleep.

"Will she be all right?" Ann asked. "I don't think I've ever seen anyone drink that much alcohol straight."

Lane had never witnessed such a thing, either, and it bothered her more than she could say. "I'm sorry she got so smashed. Jonas mentioned that she didn't have a stop button with wine. I guess I should have expected it."

Brent got a cold can of beer from the fridge. "I'm sure glad I don't have a problem like that," he said with a grin as he popped the tab.

Lane couldn't help but laugh. Her dad rarely drank more than two beers, normally only one to relax when his workday was over. "Thank you, guys. You're good sports. She's been through a pretty horrible ordeal. I don't suppose I can blame her for having a little too much."

"A little?" Ann raised her eyebrows. "I think she had a whole lot too much. It worries me. Do you think she has a problem?"

Lane lifted her hands. "I don't know. If so, she hasn't—oh, wait, she did mention it once. Said she was drinking too much. I think it may have interfered with her college studies. She became a registered nurse and wants to continue her schooling to become a nurse practitioner."

"Being a nurse practitioner is a great profession," Brent said. "I read just the other day that it's currently rated as being *the* best job in the country. Great pay. Lots of demand. A nurse practitioner doesn't make as much as a doctor, of course, but they do really well, and if they have their own clinic, they don't usually get emergency calls like a full-fledged physician does. Better quality of life, all around."

Ann had prepared a beef roast with potatoes and carrots for dinner. Lane set a place for Veneta just in case she woke up, but her sister never made an appearance. As Ann set out sugar-free pudding parfaits for dessert, she mused aloud, "I expected the two of you to be more alike, but I already see differences."

"Yes," Lane agreed. "We're the same on the outside, and in many ways, we're alike in our tastes, but we're definitely different in many ways."

Lane cleaned up the kitchen as her contribution to the evening meal and then watched a little television with her parents. She was pleasantly tired by the time she retired to her childhood bedroom, which her mom had cleaned up after the burglary and restored to its former appearance, minus a few mementos of Lane's from high school that had been destroyed. After showering and putting on pajamas, Lane crept down the hall to check on her sister. Veneta appeared to be sound asleep, so she returned to her own room.

Since writing Jonas, Lane had started checking her emails each night before she went to sleep. After opening her laptop, she was delighted to see a letter from him. She opened the missive.

Hi, Lane. I tried to write you something similar to what you wrote to me, mostly about what's happening in my life now that I'm back in Mystic Creek without you. I'm sorry to say that didn't work out for me. The truth is, my life sucks right now, and the little things that happen are just that, little. I know that pressuring you to come back to Mystic Creek is the wrong tactic to take, but that's undoubtedly exactly what I'll do. I'm a guy who says what's on my mind. Always have been, probably always will be. I love you, and I honestly don't know how to move forward without you.

Lane had to stop reading for a moment and close her eyes. *Jonas.* She pictured him—the tawny shock of hair that always lay over his forehead, the expressive shimmer of his hazel eyes, the way his smile creased his lean cheeks and transformed his face. She didn't know how to move forward without him, either. Lovemaking with him had been incredible, but that wasn't why she yearned to be with him again. It was because he made her feel whole, as if by being together they created a perfect balance.

She forced herself to stop being sappy and started reading again.

You said in your letter that you and Veneta are very alike. I can only hope that, over time, you begin to realize how wrong you are about that. In my professional opinion, it's unhealthy for you to believe you're exactly like her, or for her to believe she's exactly like you. On the surface, yes. But your looks only go skin deep. Really focus on the differences between you. You talk differently. You walk differently. You think differently. You laugh differently. You believe in different things. Don't lose your individuality. It's important for you to know who you are and to remember who you are. Don't allow the differences between you and Veneta to change you.

I'm not knocking Veneta. She's got a lot of issues, but she's a good person. Being different from you doesn't make her bad. That said, being in a relationship with her can be an emotional roller coaster ride, and as sisters, you're beginning a very important relationship. Don't get lost in the maze. You're a very special person, loyal, brave, honest, and caring. Remain true to yourself, no matter what.

I'd like to end this letter with a list of reasons why you shouldn't end things between us, but I'm going to employ all my self-control and not do that. I wish you luck in locating your biological mother or at least unearthing her medical records. It's important to know if we may be inclined to get cancer or heart disease. Important to know if diabetes may run in our family. With some warning, we can take preventative measures to protect ourselves. Please keep me posted on the search for your biological mom and on how everything else is going.

Things in Mystic Creek are pretty much the same. I think that's probably one reason I love it here.

There's a rhythm to daily life that never seems to change all that much. Ma Thomas is still hoping you may come back. I know you've told her otherwise, but she's not ready to accept that yet. Ben asked me to extend his apologies for questioning the validity of your story and not readily accepting that you weren't Veneta. He's pretty embarrassed about that. I told him he deserves to feel embarrassed.

That made Lane smile, because she could almost hear Jonas saying exactly that. He was a man who spoke his mind and didn't play games.

I'll end by saying that I truly do love you and I miss you more than words can say. I can't open a bottle of wine without remembering the night we didn't have a corkscrew. I'd happily strain wine through my teeth for the rest of my life in order to be with you.

Be safe, be happy, and please, don't forget me.
Love, Jonas

Lane started to close the laptop, but she glimpsed more writing down below. Had he decided not to use some parts of what he'd originally written, moved it downward, and then forgotten to delete the evidence? She had done that herself a couple of times.

Feeling like a sneak, she scrolled down, and then burst out laughing.

Okay, I have ZERO self-control when it comes to my feelings for you. So if you see this and read it, please don't hate me. If you don't see it, no harm done.

I have this weird theory inside my head about how people fall in love. My mom's always told me that we all have one special person waiting for us out there and that we'll know it when we meet them. I've also had lots of men tell me that they knew the instant they clapped eyes on their wives that "she was the one." I know it sounds corny, and I didn't really think there was anything to it before I met you. But now I'm believer.

I now think that my mom has it right; there is one special person out there for each of us, and when we meet them, we just know. It's instinctive, I think. And, as we both discovered, you can't fight it when it happens. You had no intention of falling in love with me. In fact, you were dead set against even feeling attracted to me from the very start, because I'd once been in a relationship with your identical twin. You made that pretty clear to me, so, like you, I guarded against wanting you or developing feelings for you. Where did that get us? Looking back on it, it was as if we were drawn to each other by a force greater than our mutual determination to remain apart.

Thus my crazy theory. I think I was searching for that one special woman that God had set aside for me, and when I met Veneta, something within me recognized her. I just had this sense of rightness, of familiarity. But once I got into the relationship with her, that initial feeling started to fade. She wasn't right for me. Even my friends saw that. My parents and siblings also saw it. Veneta did as well. I was the only one who kept blinders on. Why? Why did I remain in that relationship until Veneta gave me no choice but to end it?

You may think I'm nuts, but here's what I think happened. I met the wrong twin, but even when the relationship started to fall apart, I was determined to hang on. I'd gotten that feeling when I met her, that sense of just knowing, like my mother describes, only it wasn't Veneta who was my special person; it was you. Veneta even said as much to me once, that I'd fallen in love with the wrong part of her. It made no sense to me at the time, and she was drunk, so I laid what she said off on the booze and muddled thinking. But now I'm convinced that she was absolutely right.

Remember telling me that night as we walked the sidewalks (it was when Veneta had gone silent) that you felt as if a part of you was gone? Like you'd lost an important part of yourself? Well, I haven't been able to get that off my mind. I think Veneta always sensed you as well—as a part of herself—and that night when she told me I'd fallen in love with the wrong part of her was an attempt on her part to explain to me what she didn't really understand herself. And how could she? The link between you and her defies all logic.

You don't feel free to move forward with me because you believe Veneta still loves me. I honestly don't think she does, so I'm hoping and praying that she eases your mind on that score soon. I've gotten that feeling my mom told me about twice now, once with a woman who was wrong for me and the second time with a woman who is absolutely perfect for me. It doesn't seem quite fair. You were always the one I was searching for. I just met the wrong twin before I met the right one. Think about that and get the straight scoop from Veneta as soon as you feel she's recovered enough.

Love,
Jonas

Chapter Eighteen

Lane stared at the screen for several seconds before she closed the laptop. Then she grabbed a robe, drew it on, and went out to the kitchen. Jonas' letter had upset her in ways she couldn't really get straight in her head, so she wanted to snitch a bottle of her parents' wine and take it to her room. Tomorrow would be a long day, and she needed to sleep. The way she felt right now, she'd toss and turn all night and not get a wink.

She froze under the archway that led into the kitchen and dining room, because her parents sat at the table talking as they sipped glasses of wine. "Great minds must think alike," Lane called out.

Ann and Brent both jerked with a start and looked momentarily flustered before they collected their composure, which made Lane wonder if they'd been talking about her.

"Please, join us!" Ann said. "Grab a glass on the way. We were just debating about opening another bottle. Now we've got a good excuse!"

Lane drew a goblet from the cupboard and sat with her parents at the table. It felt like old times, because her father sat at the head and her mom sat to his right. Lane had grown up eating most of her meals sitting in the chair to his left. Brent grabbed her glass and filled it while Ann went to the kitchen for a second bottle. After pulling the cork, she resumed her seat and set the wine in front of her husband.

"Cheers!" Brent said.

Lane forced a smile and took a sip of merlot. "Mmm. The stuff I buy is never quite as good as this."

"Your mother is an expert and always chooses nice wine that's within our budget."

Lane smiled again. Her lips felt stiff. "Maybe that's it, then. Your budget and mine aren't exactly the same. I watch for the six-ninety-nine specials."

Her parents laughed, and then her dad reached over to rub her mom's arm. It occurred to Lane while watching them that their love for each other had never faded. Realistically, she knew they had experienced rough patches in their marriage. Couples who yearned for children and couldn't have them often ended up divorced. There was the stress involved with trying to get pregnant and then dealing with all the disappointments. And the blame factor normally came into play as well, the man saying it was the woman's fault and vice versa. In her parents' case, there had also been their yearning to adopt a child and Lane's father being deemed unsuitable to be a parent by all the agencies. How had their marriage withstood all of that?

"You guys amaze me," Lane blurted. "Look at you, still in love after all these years. What's your secret?"

"We found the real deal," her dad popped back.

Ann said, "Nuh-uh. *I* found the real deal. I had to track you down and ask *you* to dance. You took one look at me, our eyes met, and then you ran."

Brent winked at Lane. "I'll let her go with it and take the credit, but the truth is, I saw her, knew in a heartbeat that she was the one, and I avoided her because I was scared." He shrugged his broad shoulders. "I had only been out of prison for about three months. Even though it was an unmerited charge, a conviction of child molestation has a way of turning women off. And I knew I didn't have it in me to keep that from a woman in order to have a relationship with her." His shrug deepened, bringing his shoulders up almost even with his ears. "So, yeah, I ran. Well, I just mingled with other people at the other end of the hall, but your mother likes to say I ran."

Ann giggled. She'd clearly had enough wine to do her for the night, which made Lane wonder why her parents had both been thinking about opening another bottle. They weren't normally heavy drinkers.

"He ran," Ann insisted. "Trust me." She leaned forward to give Lane a conspiratorial look. "We women know when a man is running. Right, sweetie?"

Lane felt some of the pain in her chest start to ease away. She loved these people so much. They'd taken a confused, troubled, and traumatized little girl into their hearts and had never once withdrawn their affection or abandoned her, no matter how costly she was or how much worry she caused them. They had stuck with her through thick and thin.

"I don't know," Lane replied in all honesty. "I've never had one run from me."

"Well, your dad did." Ann held up her hand with a forefinger raised. "But I went and found him. So much for getting rid of me that easily." She dimpled her cheek at Lane. "I wasn't about to let him ignore me. It was like—I can't explain it—our gazes met, and it felt to me as if everyone else in the hall faded away. There was only him, looking straight at me! And this feeling. I can't explain that, either. I just knew if I let him walk away and I never saw him again that I'd always kick myself."

"Did you hear what your mother just said?" Brent asked. "She said she couldn't let me *walk* away. So there you go. I walked; I didn't run."

As upset as she was after reading Jonas' letter, Lane couldn't help but giggle. She wondered why her parents had never told her this story, but in the next instant, she knew exactly why. They'd been hiding things from her all her life. Her father's criminal record, for one. His former marriage, for another. The shady arrangements they'd made in order to adopt her.

"So what happened when you ran him down?" Lane asked her mom.

"I asked him to dance, and he was so besotted with me that he couldn't say no. So he led me out onto the dance floor. The first song was fast." Ann pursed her lips and briefly narrowed her eyes. "He looked like an ape having an epileptic attack." She took another sip of wine and then lifted her eyebrows at Lane. "You've seen your father try to dance without a partner. He's great in a waltz or two-step, a disaster when the arms and legs are left to flop around all on their own."

Lane laughed again. "I take it that you weren't so put off by his lack of grace that you made a U-turn."

Ann reached over and clasped her husband's hand. "Nope. I was afraid if I walked off the floor that I'd miss the real dance—the most important one, the one that lasts for the rest of your life. So I stuck it out, and the next song was slow." She sighed dreamily and then snapped erect. "The first thing he said to me was, 'I just got out of prison. I was convicted of sexually molesting my daughter.' I have to admit, that gave me pause." Ann rolled her eyes. "But the fact that he told me, right off the bat—well, I couldn't help but think there was a lot more to the story."

"And she stayed to hear it," her dad interjected. "Even more incredible to me was that she believed it. That I was innocent, I mean."

Ann nodded. "I did believe him. I absolutely believed him. And now, looking back, I'm so glad I did." She smiled at Lane. "You know your dad. And he's paid in the most painful of ways for that woman's vindictive lies. He was never allowed to see his little girl again, and when we tried to contact Alyssa after she became an adult, she refused to meet with us. She grew up believing what her mother told her, we guess. She was so very little when it all happened. Three or four years old?"

Brent nodded. "Three." His expression grew solemn. "Just a tiny, innocent little girl. It was her testimony in private chamber with the judge that got me convicted, but I'll go to my grave never blaming her for a single word she said. I was her father. I took care of her." His took a sip of wine. "My wife back then was a couch potato, which was one of the reasons our marriage fell apart. She didn't take proper care of Alyssa. I'd come home from work, and my baby girl's hair wasn't combed. She hadn't been helped to brush her teeth. Half the time she was still wearing pajamas. During the day, her mother gave her sugar-coated cereal, maybe a peanut butter sandwich if she felt ambitious, so I always cooked a nice dinner. I figured that at least then Alyssa would get one balanced meal a day. And then I cleaned up the kitchen, which was always a total disaster, and then tried to make time to play with her. After play, it was bath time and story time."

Lane well-remembered her dad reading to her. She couldn't count the times that she'd fallen asleep to the melodious intonations of his deep voice. But never once in her memory had Brent Driscoll bathed her and gotten her dressed for bed. Her mom had always done that part. "You never gave me a bath." The words popped out without Lane weighing them, but even as she said them, she knew why. "Oh, dear God, Dad. You went to prison for bathing your little girl?"

He shrugged again. "Someone had to keep her clean, and Marion didn't." He held up both hands. "I swear to you, I never touched my baby girl inappropriately, but I did have to wash her until she was able to do it properly herself. So when she was asked, 'Did your daddy ever touch you here?' she said yes." He did the shrug thing again. "She was only telling the truth. I don't even blame the judge. In fact, I'm glad we have judges out there who make rulings to protect the kids. There are men out there who *are* sick, men who violate their own children."

Lane knew that was true, but she also knew, deep in her heart, that this man had never been one of them. "Oh, Daddy. I'm so sorry."

"I only did two years. It wasn't so bad. I was a grown man. I understood what had happened and why. I won't say it was easy. I'll never say I was glad to serve the sentence for something I hadn't done. But what haunted me was that my ex-wife lied and my little girl ended up without a real parent. I was judged to be an animal who was never allowed near her again."

"And," Ann interjected, "she is now doing time for drug possession."

"I have a sister in prison?"

"Not your sister, biologically," Brent pointed out. "You don't need to worry that you have a criminal mind."

Lane might have laughed if her father's story

weren't so sad. "You had a little girl that you lost in the worst possible way and yet you still found it in your heart to love me?"

He stared at Lane for what seemed a long while. "Of course I loved you, sweetheart. From the moment we brought you home, you were also my very own little girl. I'm sorry I never gave you a bath, but given what had happened, it never struck me as being a wise idea."

Lane burst out laughing. It wasn't really funny, but her parents joined in, and pretty soon, they all had tears of mirth streaming down their cheeks.

"Oh, dear," Ann finally said, sighing as if the laughter had drained her of energy. "I don't know why we're laughing. What Marion did to your father and her daughter was monstrous, and now Alyssa is paying the price. She lost the only parent who truly loved her, who truly cared what became of her. Growing up without love or parental supervision pretty much dooms a child most of the time."

Lane wiped under her eyes, and so did her dad. What had seemed so funny only a moment ago now only seemed indescribably sad. Lane wondered how her father had lived through it and retained his sanity. Or how her mom had fallen in love so deeply that nothing could shake her faith in her husband. Lane only knew she was very glad it had happened that way, because these people had raised her and loved her and stood behind her, no matter how much she may have bewildered them over the years.

"I love you both so much," she said. "Seeing you together, seeing how happy you are. It makes me wish I could find that with someone, but now I'm afraid I never will."

"You're only twenty-six," Ann said. "What on earth makes you believe that?"

Lane hadn't intended to tell her parents about her feelings for Jonas, but suddenly the words were there, and she blurted them out. "I've fallen in love with someone, and it isn't working out."

Her father straightened at that announcement. "Who's the man?"

Lane wished she hadn't said anything, but she had, and there was no undoing it now. "Jonas."

"Jonas Sterling, the guy I met?" Brent asked. "The one who once dated Veneta and helped you find her? He seemed like a really decent young man."

Lane nodded. "Yes, that's Jonas."

Her father considered that news for a moment. Then he glanced at Ann and directed another question to Lane. "What's the problem, then? He doesn't love you back?"

"No, he loves me back. Or at least that's what he tells me."

Brent frowned and glanced at his wife again. "Okay. So why isn't it working out?"

Lane felt her face twist, and the pressure of tears pushed against the backs of her eyes, leaking out no matter how hard she tried to stop them. In a voice she despised because it was squeaky and whiny, she said, "Because Veneta may still be in love with him. They dated in college. Then she broke it off. But when we found her in that house, she clung to Jonas as if he were her lifeline and said she still loved him."

"Oh, boy, that's not good," Ann inserted. She glanced toward the hallway that led to the bedrooms. "Has she said anything about it since then?"

"Once in the hospital," Lane replied. "I think it was the morning after she was rescued. Nothing since then."

"Does she talk about him?" Ann asked.

Lane shook her head. "No. Maybe she senses that I have feelings for him, too, and is avoiding the topic. Or she's still standing on such shaky ground emotionally after all that's happened that she doesn't feel ready to examine her own feelings."

"What does Jonas have to say?" Brent asked.

"He doesn't believe Veneta loves him. She was the one that ended their relationship, and she never once got in touch with him afterward."

Brent lowered his glass to the table. "That seems odd. That she doesn't mention him, I mean. Normally, when we love people, we talk about them a lot."

Ann ran her fingertip around the rim of her goblet. "If she senses that you care for him, too, she might not feel comfortable doing that, though. If it were me, I think I'd just ask her. It would be a shame for you to end things with Jonas over a misunderstanding." Directing a questioning glance at her husband, Ann asked, "What do you think, darling?"

Brent's brow knitted in a thoughtful frown. "As soon as you think Veneta's ready for a heart-to-heart talk, I agree with your mother that you should ask her about her feelings for Jonas. And hopefully that will be soon. A man can't be left dangling forever."

"It's only been a little over a week," Ann reminded him.

Brent shrugged. "When we love someone and we aren't sure we can ever be with that person, a week can seem like forever."

* * *

Lane still felt heavy of heart the next morning when she emerged from her room, ready to face the day. She found Veneta in the kitchen with Ann. Fully expecting her sister to have the mother of all hangovers, she was surprised to find her laughing, talking, and apparently feeling fine.

After a quick breakfast, the three women adjourned to Lane's bedroom and began going through the boxes of Lane's clothing in the closet. Veneta found several ensembles that she liked and then narrowed her choices down to three, saying that she didn't want to cut Lane short.

"I'll be back to work soon," she said. "All I need are enough outfits to get me by until I get paid and can go shopping."

Once they had unearthed enough clothing for Veneta to wear, Lane drove her sister into town to shop for other necessities, like underwear, cosmetics, and hair tools. After two hours of walking through stores, Veneta's energy flagged.

"I'm still not back to normal," she said. "What do you say we go to that little cheese and wine place for a break?"

Lane was getting hungry. "They offer some nice lunch options. My treat."

Veneta laughed. "That goes without saying. I really need to visit the bank and make a withdrawal. I don't have all that much in there, but I'll have enough to pay you back for all of this." She held up a shopping bag. "And hopefully enough to get my car out of jail after I get to Plover Bay."

Lane didn't mind paying for their lunch, and she

had no intention of allowing Veneta to reimburse her for what she'd already purchased. Her sister was in an unprecedented situation, possibly stripped of nearly everything she'd owned, and the months ahead would be tough for her as she struggled to get back on her feet.

They found a corner table at Andy's Cheese and Wine. They decided to share a Reuben sandwich, because they both loved them. Lane ordered a diet soft drink to go with her meal. Veneta ordered wine.

"It's only half past noon," Lane pointed out.

Veneta shrugged her shoulders. "Sorry. I know I drink too much, but it's not really a problem unless I want to quit. Right?"

Lane saw holes in her sister's reasoning and didn't think her attempt at humor was funny. "Overindulgence can be bad for your health. That's especially true for you, given what your body's been through."

"I'll be fine. If you're worried about the cost, I'll pay you back. Truly, I will."

Lane wasn't worried about the money; she was worried about her sister.

After finishing lunch—during which Veneta consumed two glasses of wine—they drove to a branch of Veneta's bank, where she got temporary checks, applied for a new credit card, and withdrew all but five dollars from her savings account. As she stuffed the money into the inexpensive purse that Lane had gotten for her earlier, she said, "We'll tally up all the receipts tonight, and I'll settle up with you then. Okay?"

"I really don't want you to pay me back just yet," Lane told her. "Why don't you wait until you're settled in over on the coast?"

"You are so sweet. I suppose waiting would be

smarter. I have no idea what expenses I'll be faced with over there. I do know it costs money to get an impounded car back, and I'll definitely need transportation to hold down a job. You know how it is over there, most of the businesses strung out along the beach. I'll definitely need wheels."

Once they were back in the car, Lane asked, "Have we forgotten anything?"

"I think this is as good as it's going to get until I go back to work. You gave me shoes. I've got clothes and undies. Tomorrow morning, I can even put on some makeup and do my hair."

"Let's head back to the house, then. See what we can do to help my mom with dinner."

"I take it she doesn't work."

"Oh, yes. She used to be a full-time teacher. Now she just substitutes. Mostly she gets called in to work only a couple of times a week. Now that she's older and she and Dad are pretty much financially set, she enjoys having time off. She has hobbies, friends, loves to read. It's the perfect situation for her."

"And your dad just goes along with it?"

Lane raised a questioning brow as she stopped at a red light. "Of course. Why wouldn't he?"

Veneta snorted with laughter. "Because he's a man? They're all into career women now, and they expect their wives to pull in half the money. Even better if she makes double what he does. Then he can afford more toys."

Lane signaled for a turn and kept her eyes on the road as she rounded the corner. "My dad isn't like that. Mom basically worked two jobs once I was old enough for school. She taught all day and ran our household at night. Dinner on the table. Dishes afterward. Laundry n the evenings. Touch-up vacuuming. Deep cleaning on the weekend. On top of that, she had lesson plans. Dad says it's time for her to be able to slow down, that she's worked hard for the privilege."

"Wow. When I get married—if I ever do, anyway—I hope I'm lucky enough to get a husband like that. I'll probably end up with someone who lazes around in his recliner, drinking beer and farting."

Lane had been hoping for an opportunity to talk with Veneta about her feelings for Jonas, and she decided this might be her only chance. "Maybe you should have kept Jonas on the hook. I can't picture him doing that. He'll be a wonderful husband to some lucky woman."

The interior of the car went suddenly silent. A heavy, uncomfortable silence. Then Veneta broke it by saying, "Apparently you're very fond of Jonas. Are you hung up on him or something?"

Lane glanced over at her sister. "If I am, are you going to hate me for it?"

Veneta smiled. "I can see that my answer is extremely important to you, so let me set the record straight on Jonas. Okay? I have deep feelings for Jonas as a friend, but I never really loved him. I'm not sure I'm even capable of loving a man. My father pretty much turned me sour on members of the opposite sex. I did *care* about Jonas, though, and I probably always will. For a while, I even toyed with the idea of marrying him, not for romantic reasons but for practical ones. He was close to getting his degree. I knew he'd be a great psychologist and probably make good money." She narrowed her eyes at Lane. "Don't look at me like that. I'm not the only woman who's ever considered marrying a guy for his potential earning power. In the end, I didn't, though, and it wasn't because I suddenly got noble. Jonas bored me. That's the truth of it. He's a rule follower. It's against the law to drink and drive, so he'd either pace himself or not drink at all if he had to be behind the wheel. One night a bunch of us rented a motel room, and the pool closed at ten. I wanted to go for a swim anyway, but Jonas refused to go in with me. I'm the kind of gal who'll strip off to her underwear and climb over the hurricane fence. You know? Some other people did go in, but Jonas wouldn't. I felt like I had hooked up with an old man."

Lane found it difficult to understand how anyone could think Jonas was boring. He had a wonderful sense of humor. He was a fabulous lover. And what was so wrong with abiding by rules? "Did you get caught?" she couldn't resist asking.

"Of *course* we got caught. Knowing we might was what made it so fun."

"Did you get in trouble?"

"The manager yelled at us, made us get out of the damned pool. What was he going to do, have us arrested?"

Lane took a deep breath and released it. "So you honestly don't love Jonas."

"No, I don't. And just in case you're wondering, I don't think he ever really loved me. For a while, he loved what he imagined me to be, but toward the end, he was pissed off at me most of the time because I couldn't keep pretending to be someone I wasn't. By cutting him loose, I did him a big favor. I think he realizes that now. It never would have worked for us long-term, and Jonas is a forever kind of guy."

Up ahead, Lane saw the old maple tree that marked the corner of the street her parents lived on. It was nostly bare of leaves now, with only a few splashes of orange and gold clinging to its branches. She reduced her speed and flipped on the turn signal.

"I'm curious," Veneta said. "Why has it taken you so long to tell me that you have feelings for Jonas?"

"I wanted to, but I couldn't think how to broach the subject. And you've been through such a horrific ordeal that I didn't feel right about bringing it up until I thought you were ready for a serious and possibly upsetting conversation."

"Do you love him?" she asked. "I mean, having feelings for someone and really loving him can be two different things."

"I really love him."

"But you're not with him. Please tell me I'm not the reason for that."

Lane pulled the car into her parents' driveway and parked on the swath of gravel next to the concrete apron. "You are, in a way. That night when we found you in the house, you said you never should have broken up with him and that you still loved him."

"I *do* love him, but only as a friend. And in that moment, I meant it when I said I should never have broken up with him. He's so solid and steady. Nothing that happened to me ever would have happened if I'd stayed with him."

Lane turned off the car engine. "So you honestly don't love him except as a friend?"

"That's about as deep as it goes for me," Veneta replied. She studied Lane for a seemingly endless moment. "God, I'm so sorry about this, Lane. People tend to throw the *L* word around. I'm certainly guilty of it. I never intended to make you think I was still into him in that way."

Lane sighed and closed her eyes for a second.

"What are you going to do?" Veneta asked.

"I don't know. I told him I couldn't move forward with him if you still loved him. I came home, and he left for Mystic Creek. I need to fix it between us. If I can."

"If he loves you, he's hoping and praying for you to come back to him. I doubt it will be a difficult situation for you to fix."

"True enough." Lane slid her palms along the curve of the steering wheel. "Well, at least now I know that it won't matter to you if we end up together."

"Nope, not one whit. The only thing that will piss me off is if the two of you get married and you don't ask me to be your maid of honor."

Lane couldn't help but laugh. Veneta chuckled and opened the passenger door. "Come on, sister dear. We can't help your mom cook dinner while we're sitting out here."

If Ann was surprised when they joined her in the kitchen, she didn't let on. Instead she assigned Lane the task of making a salad and Veneta was stationed at the sink to peel potatoes. Ann was making au jus to go with the steaks, which she planned to grill out on the patio. The meat would be cooked last, because it was always Ann's aim to put a freshly prepared meal on the table shortly after her husband got home.

Somehow the conversation turned to Ann's hobbies, one of which was sewing, which seemed to pique Veneta's interest. "So, do you have a sewing machine?"

"Oh, yes," Ann assured her. "One with all the bells and whistles. Brent bought it for me for Mother's Day one year, and I absolutely love it."

"After dinner, would you mind if I use it?" Veneta asked.

"Not at all. Does something Lane gave you need mending?"

Veneta hunched her shoulders. "Um, no. It's more that I'd like to revamp the stuff she gave me. When it comes to clothes, I prefer my outfits to be a little flashier and a bit more revealing."

Ann sent Lane a slightly bewildered look, but after dinner was over and Brent was settled in his recliner to watch a little news, she led the way to a small bedroom that she'd transformed into her craft area. Before Lane knew it, a skirt and blouse that she'd given her sister was being transformed, a lower, more revealing neckline on the blouse and to-the-thigh slits in both sides of the skirt. Veneta donned the outfit, and it became Lane's job to pin and tuck until her sister was satisfied with the effect when she turned back and forth in front of the full-length bathroom mirror.

"Awesome!" Veneta pronounced as she grabbed Ann's scissors and started deepening the neckline of a blouse. She glanced up once. "I hope you're not offended, Lane. You look beautiful, the way you dress. But it just isn't *me*. You know?"

Lane wasn't offended at all. When she examined her feelings, she decided she was more fascinated than anything else. Veneta was turning her former clothing into something Lane would never feel comfortable with. *Sexy*, Lane decided, but way too bold for her taste.

By eleven, when the women decided it was time to turn in, all three of Veneta's ensembles were finished. "Thank you both so much for all the help. Tomorrow I'll feel more like *me*."

Lane remembered the advice Jonas had given her in his letter, and she made herself focus on the fact that her and Veneta's taste in clothing, while similar, was also noticeably different. Lane was happy with a simple Boho look; Veneta wanted to make a man's eyes pop out of his head.

Once in bed, Lane had every intention of going straight to sleep. Over the course of the evening, Veneta had talked about returning to the coast as soon as possible. Her plan was to work as a waitress for a few months to get back on her feet, and then she hoped to relocate and resume her nursing career while furthering her education to become a nurse practitioner. For all Lane knew, she might be driving her sister to Plover Bay bright and early tomorrow morning.

A part of her wanted to contact Jonas to tell him that Veneta's feelings toward him were only about friendship. Only it seemed all wrong to tell him in a letter or over the phone. She wanted to see his reaction when she told him. Besides, she needed to get some rest, which she wouldn't if she wrote a long email.

Her plan to fall fast asleep was foiled by a light knock on her door. Lane guessed it was Veneta, because her mother had gone to bed. She called out for her to come in as she sat up and flipped on the light.

"Sorry. I know you're tired." Veneta sat on the edge of the mattress, ice clinking in a twenty-ounce tumbler of clear liquid. Lane hoped it was water and not vodka. "I just wonder when you think you'll have time to take me back to the coast."

Lane pushed a shank of hair from her eyes. "I haven't gone back to work yet. We can go any time you like."

Veneta took a large swig from her glass. "Okay." She

shrugged and wrinkled her nose. "I need to get my life put back together, and you need to get yours sorted out as well. I heard your dad worrying aloud to your mom about the things you left behind in Mystic Creek, your car and some household items that he'll have to trailer back here. You've also left Jonas hanging, and that's not good. I don't like the thought that you're putting things off because I'm here and you feel obligated to help me."

Lane shook her head. "I don't feel *obligated*. You're my sister. We've only just found each other. And there's no real hurry to get my car and the other stuff. My rent's paid through the end of November, and I signed a six-month lease. As for Jonas . . ." Lane sighed. "I almost emailed him to say I'm coming back. But it just feels off to tell him in a letter. I'd rather do it in person."

"You're nervous," Veneta observed.

"As you said, I've left him hanging. What if he's fed up with the uncertainty and tells me to get lost?"

Veneta chuckled. "If he really loves you, that won't happen. But having said that, I can almost feel the butterflies flopping around in your stomach. I'd be a little nervous, too."

"Correction. I'm a *lot* nervous."

Veneta took another gulp of vodka. Lane could now detect the faint smell of the alcohol. "Well, no matter how we slice it, we've both got shit to take care of. I need to get my life back in order. You need to get your relationship with Jonas back on track. The sooner we both do that, the sooner we can meet in the Eugene area to see what we can find out about our birth mother. I'm looking forward to doing that. Are you?"

Lane nodded. "I can't help but wonder if she's still alive."

"Wouldn't that be awesome? I'd love to meet her. My memories of her are sketchy, but judging by what I can recall, I think she loved us very much."

They chatted for a few more minutes. After Veneta left, Lane went to the kitchen for a glass of water. When she entered the room, the lights were on, and she saw her father standing in front of the open refrigerator.

"Dad! What are you still doing up?"

He glanced back over his shoulder. "I couldn't sleep, and I don't want to disturb your mother with my tossing and turning."

Lane grabbed a glass from the cupboard and stepped over to the sink to fill it from the tap. "Are you upset about something at work?"

"Things are fine at work." He closed the fridge and rested his shoulder against the door. "It's you I'm worried about."

"Me?"

Brent inclined his head toward the dining area. "Sit with me for a minute? I'd like to talk with you."

As Lane trailed behind her dad to the other room, she wondered what this was about. Veneta, possibly? Her sister had a talent for using curse words as if they were sentence enhancers, and she tended to be a loud person at times. Maybe her dad worried that those undesirable habits might rub off on Lane. Or maybe having Veneta in the house was wearing on his nerves.

She set her water on a place mat and took a seat. Brent sat at the head of the table. For the first time, Lane noticed that he was going slightly gray at the temples.

"I'll be taking Veneta back to Plover Bay tomorrow, if that's what you're worried about."

Brent shook his head. "She's a sweet girl. Your mom and I don't mind having her here. It's you I'm concerned about."

"Why? I'm fine."

"You're sad," he countered. "You're putting up a good front, but I see right through all the forced smiles and laughter." He fiddled for a moment with his wedding band. "Do you have any idea how many people live their entire lives without ever finding true love?"

Lane was momentarily bewildered by the question, but then she realized her father meant to lecture her about Jonas. "I haven't given it much thought."

"You heard the story of how your mother and I met. Do you know how many times over the years I've thanked God she followed me that night? What if she hadn't? I think about that sometimes. My first marriage was such a mess, and after doing time, I had low self-esteem. I didn't think any woman worth having would ever be interested in me. She was one in a million, Lane. I've always believed that each of us has one special person in the world that we're meant to be with. For me, it was my Annie. What if she'd chickened out at the last second and hadn't asked me to dance? I might never have found anyone else, and I would have missed out on so many things that make a person's life worth living. The joy of building a life with someone I love. The miracle of bringing home a beautiful little girl that we could love and raise together. When I contemplate how easily I could have missed out on that, it frightens me."

"I have a feeling you want to talk with me about Jonas. Am I right?"

"I just don't think you should leave him wondering very much longer. Have you spoken with Veneta yet?"

"As a matter of fact, I asked her today, and she doesn't have romantic feelings toward him."

"Fabulous. Then the way is clear for you."

Lane nodded. "Yep, and I'm scared half to death. What if Jonas has decided he dodged a bullet?"

"Then he didn't really love you, honey, and you dodged one, too."

Brent didn't wait for Lane to reply. He pushed to his feet and left the room. Lane sat there in the shadows, alone with only her thoughts and a glass of cold water.

Chapter Nineteen

Jonas walked aimlessly along East Main, stopping occasionally to stare at Thanksgiving window displays without really seeing them. It had been Halloween only a week ago, and he didn't really understand why people were in such a hurry to decorate for the next holiday. He knew from experience that immediately after Turkey Day, if not before, the Christmas theme would make an appearance. Normally, he enjoyed the cheerful brightness of the holiday season, but this year, it all seemed superficial and meaningless. Thinking that way made him feel like a scrooge, but he couldn't muster up any enthusiasm, no matter how hard he tried.

He stepped off the curb into the town center, which was essentially a brick traffic circle that surrounded a fountain where people threw coins to make wishes. Jonas had never been a believer, but he couldn't help but smile slightly when he saw a little girl in a red hat, coat, and winter boots standing by the water feature with her eyes squinted closed and her lips drawn in over her teeth as she thrust her hand out over the pool to drop in a coin. Jonas guessed she was concentrating on making her wish. He hoped it came true for her. Then, maybe, at least someone would be happy. He definitely wasn't.

Lane still hadn't returned to Mystic Creek, not even to get her car. Each evening, he drove out to her cottage to see if her Hyundai was gone. It was always still parked right where she'd left it the night they'd driven to Maple Leaf. After writing that last letter to her, Jonas hadn't heard a word back. No text, no email. He knew he needed to accept that he probably would never hear from her again. When she came back with her father to collect her car and belongings, she might not even stop by his apartment to tell him goodbye. They were finished. The way she undoubtedly saw it, they'd already said their goodbyes. It was just incredibly difficult for him to wrap his mind around the finality of it. How could it happen that he'd fallen so deeply in love with someone only to face living the rest of his life without her?

Jonas slowed his steps at the fountain and pulled a quarter from his pocket. He stared for a long moment into the clear blue water where a carpet of coins flashed like a copper and silver mosaic under glass.

"You just make a wish and fro it in," the little girl told him.

Startled, Jonas saw that she'd come to stand beside him. He looked down into her upturned, chubby-cheeked face. When she smiled at him, he saw that she was missing her two front teeth, which explained her slight lisp. "I'm not very good at making wishes," he said. "Mine never come true."

"Oh." She pushed her tiny hands into her coat pockets, which reminded Jonas that winter temperatures had definitely arrived in Mystic Creek. "You prob'ly just aren't doing it right. You need to have your wish all figured out and practice saying it inside your head. And then you gotta b'lieve it'll come true. You gotta b'lieve it wif your whole heart."

"Ah, okay. I've been doing it wrong, then. Since none of my wishes have ever come true, I don't believe the next one will."

She sighed and wrinkled her nose. "It won't come true, then. You gotta b'lieve wif all your heart."

Jonas couldn't resist asking, "Do your wishes come true?"

"Yup. Every time. Like when my daddy left, I wished for him to come back, and he did."

"Wow. You're really good at wishing." Jonas held out his quarter. "Maybe you can make a wish for me, and it'll come true."

The child took the quarter and nodded. "What do you want me to wish for?"

"There's a lady I love a whole lot, like you love your daddy, and I really miss her. I'd love it if she'd come back to me."

"What's her name?"

"Lane."

The child squinted her eyes closed again and held her arm out over the pool. The coin made a plopping sound when it landed on the water. Then it flipped slowly, end over end, as it sank to the bottom of the fountain.

"There," the little girl said, dusting off her hands. "The lady should come back now. Well, I dunno if wishing stuff for someone else really works, but I did believe wif my whole heart when I wished it, so maybe it will."

Jonas placed a hand atop her bright red hat. "Thank you. I really appreciate it."

"You're welcome. I gotta go now. My mom is at the grocery store, and I promised I'd make my wish and go right back."

Jonas followed her with his gaze as she crossed East Main to gain the opposite sidewalk. Then he couldn't stop himself from yelling, "What did you wish for yourself?"

She stopped by the pedestrian light pole and turned to call back, "A puppy for Christmas! Don't tell anybody, though, cuz then my wish won't come true!"

Jonas smiled, feeling somewhat humbled by the little girl's simple faith in what seemed to him an impossibility. When wishes came true, it was only a coincidence. He sure did hope she got that puppy, though. He'd grown up with dogs and believed that every child needed the responsibility and companionship of a pet. Caring for the family dogs had taught him to be conscious of other's needs instead of only his own.

Following the child's example, Jonas shoved his hands into his jacket pockets and walked along West Main. *If only wishes could come true*, he thought.

And it was then that he saw her—a diminutive strawberry blonde enveloped in a puffy blue parka. She stood in front of the Straw Hat, looking lost and uncertain of what to do next. Jonas' heart leaped with pure happiness. *Lane*. He was so excited that he almost broke into a run. *But, no. She may have stopped by only to say goodbye. Don't be an idiot and make her feel uncomfortable with romantic theatrics.*

When she saw him striding toward her, her face lit up and her blue eyes sparkled. "Jonas! I've been looking everywhere for you!"

He allowed himself to smile, but the gesture was guarded. The emotional pain he'd endured over the last few weeks had made him wary, he guessed. He wasn't sure what had prompted her to stop by, and he didn't want to open himself up to even more heartbreak. "Hello, Lane." His voice shook slightly, but he thought, over all, that he'd pulled off the greeting without revealing his inner turmoil. "It's so good to see you. What brings you by?"

Her smile faded, and she just stood there, hugging her jacket against the cold. The jagged hem of what looked like a gray wool skirt hung below the coat bottom, V-shaped panels cascading to hit her mid-shin. She wore a pair of matching gray shoes with a short heel, footwear that definitely wouldn't do in Mystic Creek once snow fell. Here, even women who enjoyed making a fashion statement wore boots in the winter with good grips on the soles. The slipping danger was too great with slick-bottomed heels. Not that Lane would be around for any white stuff. He sternly reminded himself not to be stupid and get his hopes up.

"I, um . . ." She broke off, and he saw her larynx bob in her slender neck as she swallowed nervously. Then she closed her eyes for a moment. "I feel ridiculous," she told him. "I know I stayed away too long. That I should've written or texted or called. But I just didn't know how to say it without being face-to-face."

Jonas searched her gaze. She looked like she was about to cry, and he knew how she hated it when she did. "Well, we're face-to-face." He braced himself for a blow. "So just say it."

Her eyes went bright with tears. "I love you. I'm in love with you. I'll always be in love with you."

That wasn't what he'd expected her to say, and the only thing he could think of as a reply was, "Oh."

She stared up at him. Tears spilled over her lower

lashes onto her cheeks. Then she spun on her heel to walk away. Jonas gazed after her for a moment and then broke into a run to catch up with her. He caught her by the arm and whirled her around. "If you love me, where are you going?"

"To my car." She was really crying now, the facial muscles in her delicately carved countenance twisting in spasms, her mouth trembling. "You obviously aren't glad to see me!"

Jonas caught her by the shoulders, and all his guardedness disintegrated. "I've never been so glad to see anyone in my life." He cupped her face in his hands and began thumbing away the wetness on her cheeks. "I love you, too. And I always will. That's just not what I thought you'd come here to say."

Bewilderment shone in her beautiful eyes. "What *else* would I come here to say?"

"I don't know. Maybe to finish things between us. To tell me you can never be with me. Something more final than last time. The situation between us was kind of left up in the air, and it's been a whole month. I thought you'd decided it just can't work between us."

"Is that how you feel? That it just can't work?"

"No!" Jonas decided then and there that sometimes he did his best talking with his actions, so he drew her into his arms and embraced her as tightly as he could without hurting her. "I think it can work. I always believed it could."

She went up on her tiptoes to hug his neck. "I love you. I'm sorry it took me so long to talk with my sister. And I'm sorry I ran into such a mess, trying to get her settled. I wanted to call you or email you to tell you I was coming back, but every time I tried, I chickened out."

Jonas couldn't help but get tears in his own eyes. "You're here now. That's all that matters."

"I'm scared," she said shakily. "I won't lie to you about that. It's a risk when you love someone. There are no guarantees. You just have to take your chances."

Jonas swayed with her in his arms. He didn't care who might see them. Nothing mattered to him but holding this woman and finally knowing that there was now no obstacle to keep them apart. She loved him as much as he loved her. He didn't know how long they stood there, locked in an embrace. She whispered things to him; he whispered things to her. He wasn't sure what he said or what she said, but that didn't matter, either. They were together again.

"Let's walk," he said as his senses began to clear.

Holding hands, they set off toward the town center, where plenty of sidewalk stretched before them. Jonas led her to the natural bridge, a place that held center stage in much of his family lore. It had been along the banks of Mystic Creek where his parents had first met and fallen madly in love.

"Have I ever told you the legend of Mystic Creek?"

Her face still tear-streaked, she shook her head.

"It's just a silly superstition, I suppose, but a lot of people believe it, including both my parents. Supposedly any man and woman who stand together by Mystic Creek are destined—or some say, doomed—to fall in love."

"Really?" She looked ahead at the bridge. "Since we're already in love, I guess we're safe enough."

Jonas laughed. "Or maybe it'll work its magic on us, too, and make us fall even more deeply in love."

They gravitated toward a park bench just north of the bridge and sat down, his arm around her shoulders, their legs pressed together over their winter clothing like two pieces of bread over sandwich filling. Then they both started to talk at once, which made them laugh.

"You first," he said. "You started to say something about Veneta?"

She nodded. "Nothing that you haven't already said, only that the more I was around her, the more I finally started to realize, despite all the similarities, how different we actually are." She flashed him a slight smile. "And even if it makes no sense to others, I think, by getting to know each other, that both of us are finally better able to understand ourselves." She held up a slender forefinger. "For instance, I've had this thing all my life about looking distinctly different from everyone else. I never knew *why* that was so important to me, only that I was almost phobic about it. But now I totally get it. When we were little, I think our birth mother may have dressed us exactly alike, and I believe I felt sort of erased and that Veneta did as well. Identical twins in identical outfits. We couldn't define ourselves as separate individuals."

Jonas pushed a lock of reddish-gold hair from her eyes. "That's deep," he said, knowing even as he spoke that he'd just pulled a professional response out of his hat. Lane wasn't a client. She didn't need to be psychoanalyzed. But she *did* need to sort through her feelings and begin to understand them, and talking it out was the best way he knew for her to reach her own conclusions. "And fascinating."

"For as far back as I can remember, I felt compelled to have my own look. I didn't know why, but I refused to follow fashion trends because, in my mind, that would have made me just like everyone else. I didn't know I had a twin. I only knew there was a fierce need within me to stand out, to look different, to be *me*. The irony of it is that Veneta has the same quirk, and unbeknownst to us at the time, we both chose bohemian-style clothing to make a statement. So when we finally got together as adults, we were still wearing twin outfits. Or almost, anyway."

"Uh-oh. Does this mean you're about to throw out your whole wardrobe and buy a new one?"

She laughed softly. "Probably. Only I'll need to confer with Veneta to make sure she isn't going with the same style."

Jonas couldn't help but chuckle. "The mental link is definitely problematic."

She nodded. "A problem and yet a gift. It's fun to have a sister, and over time, we'll iron out the wrinkles."

Grasping her hand, Jonas began toying with her slender fingers. "I hope none of those wrinkles involve me."

She rested her head on his shoulder. "Absolutely not. Veneta does still love you, but only as a friend. She called it using the *L* word loosely. And that night when we found her, she says she absolutely meant what she said about regretting that she broke up with you, not because she loved you in a romantic sense, but because she never would have landed in the mess she was in if she'd still been with you." She lifted her gaze to his. "Because you're steady and solid and think before you act."

With a nod, Jonas acknowledged the possible truth in that. "How's she doing with the substance thing?"

"No more pills. She kicked that habit in rehab. Unfortunately, she basically just switched substances and is now hooked on vodka. Straight vodka, sometimes cut with a little water."

"Vodka? That's so *not* Veneta. She was always a wine lover."

"She says it doesn't give her the same punch, whatever that means." Her forehead furrowed in a thoughtful frown. "I think she seeks oblivion. Her life hasn't been easy, you know. Lots of horrible memories that haunt her, which explains her past dependency on sleeping pills. They knocked her out. She could slip away into blackness and no longer think."

"Have you suggested that she seek help?"

"I have, and I hope she listened. But at this point, there's really not a whole lot more I can do. It's up to her, and all I can do is be available when she wants to talk."

"When people are troubled, that's all any of us can do." Afraid Lane might be getting cold, he tightened his arm around her shoulders and drew her snugly against his side. "It's basically what I do as a counselor. You listen. Try to guide the person into self-examination. After an hour of that, they leave."

"Isn't that frustrating?"

"No, actually, it's rewarding. And someday, hopefully sooner than later, when Veneta decides to deal with her drinking problem, you'll understand just how rewarding it is. You planted the seed in her mind. When she acts on it, you'll know that seed put down roots."

She nuzzled her cheek against his jacket and released a deep breath. "Enough about Veneta. I'd rather talk about us. I was a nervous wreck driving over here. I imagined you telling me to get lost. That you'd be angry. I wanted to call or text or email you, but things got so crazy over on the coast that it wasn't a case of just dropping Veneta off at her friend's place and leaving. Her car had been impounded. That was a thousand dollars, plus towing fees, and she didn't have that much cash. On top of that, everything in her apartment had been thrown into boxes, helter-skelter, and dumped in a storage unit. What a nightmare that was. Just for an example, I finally found her underwear with the pots and pans."

Jonas laughed. "Poor Veneta."

"Yes, and poor me. All she wanted was to find the necessities. Her clothing. Her shoes. Her toiletries and makeup. She can't afford to buy replacements. And we were faced with what seemed like a hundred boxes, and with nowhere to unpack them to sort through the contents, it was as if the original hundred boxes gave birth to babies. It took two solid days just to find all the essentials, and even then she was still missing a lot of stuff. My dad came to the rescue, bless his heart." She glanced up. "He and Mom are fond of Veneta, so they're sort of adopting her. When Dad heard she couldn't afford to rent a place where she could unpack and get her life sorted out, he coughed up the money for her to get an apartment. Finding her a place took the better part of a week, and then, because she wasn't yet working, no landlord wanted to take a gamble on her. My folks saved the day by guaranteeing that her rent will be paid for the first six months."

"That was really good of them."

"Dad says he and Mom are the lucky ones. They're getting a second daughter out of the deal."

"I hope Veneta doesn't disappoint them," Jonas said.

"They know she has issues. After raising me, they're experts at rolling with the punches. They want to help her, and she definitely needs it. But more than that, I think she'll benefit from knowing she has people she can count on for the first time in her life. As difficult as it is for me to wrap my mind around it, she's never had anyone. How awful it must be to feel that alone."

Jonas ran his hand up and down her jacket sleeve, acutely aware of how slender her arm was beneath all the fluff. "Do you realize what an amazing person you are?"

She gave him a bewildered look. "It's my parents who are offering her the helping hand, not me."

"But some people might resent that. They're *your* parents, not hers. If they take her under their wing and start to think of her as a second daughter, you'll no longer be the only child."

"I never wanted to be. All my life, I wished for at least one sibling. Now maybe I'll have one." She waved her hand. "Well, obviously, I *do* have one now, but it'll be even better if she's welcomed into my family as a daughter."

"Amazing," he said again.

"I thought you'd be angry with me for leaving you hanging for so long."

Jonas shook his head. "Not angry. Maybe frustrated and a lot sad, but never angry. You're the love of my life, and I was afraid I'd lost you. But there was also a part of me that not only approved of your decision but also admired you for making it. You couldn't bring yourself to seek your own happiness when you thought it might cause your sister pain. I understood that. I've had a lot of time to think about it and try to put myself in your place. If in the same situation, I don't think I could live with hurting one of my brothers. So I couldn't blame you for doing what I might have done myself." He shrugged. "And, honestly, all it did was make me love you all the more."

"Thank you for granting me the time," she said softly. "As much as I wanted to be with you, it was good for me—and possibly even necessary—to really get to know my sister. It allowed me to realize that even though we have marked similarities, we're also extremely different in other ways."

Still not quite able to believe that Lane had come back to him, Jonas rested his cheek against her curly hair and smiled. "Veneta's childhood was completely different from yours," he pointed out. "You can take two cake mixes that are exactly alike, whip them up using the same directions, and have two markedly different outcomes if you bake one in a Bundt pan and the other in a sheet cake pan."

"I think I'm probably more like a sheet cake without icing, the plain one."

Jonas tightened his arm around her. "You're beautiful and sweet just as you are, and I wouldn't change one thing. All I care about is that you're here. I was really starting to think you might never come back to me."

She released a shrill little sigh. "It was a scary decision to make, staying on to help Veneta get settled on the coast. Remember when I compared my feelings during our search for her to a ticking bomb? Every second I was over there, that feeling was there again. I knew I'd left you hanging, and instead of racing back here to settle things between us like I should have, I was looking at apartments and then helping my sister unpack and get her life back in order. I started to call you at least twenty times, but how do you say all this over the phone? And, to be honest, I was chicken, afraid you'd tell me to never call again or something. As crazy as it may sound, I hoped it'd be harder for you to do that if we were standing face-to-face. I never realized until I fell for you that loving someone is a gamble. We can promise each other forever, but we can't look into the future. We have no idea what may happen next."

"True," he conceded. "But now, Lane, we'll face it together, and as long as we love each other, we'll overcome it or die trying."

She drew back to look up at him with her heart shining in her blue eyes. "I actually believe that now. I just needed to see you again to feel certain of it."

"I won't pretend the waiting hasn't been pure hell, but I'm glad you helped Veneta get things sorted out. She's a good person with a big heart even though she's sometimes abrasive and difficult to understand. And she needs to be loved, not merely by friends who may or may not truly care about her, but by family—people who love her no matter what."

"She has some qualities that I wish I had. She's braver than me, for one. Just look at how she went after the kingpin who murdered her friends. That took incredible courage."

"Yep." He pressed a kiss to the tip of her nose. "That level of courage almost got her killed, though. When courage isn't accompanied by common sense, it can be dangerous."

"Are you saying my sister has no common sense?"

Jonas chuckled. "Don't get your back up. I'm only saying that one woman who decides to go after a drug ord might land herself in more trouble than she can handle, and Veneta apparently didn't think of all the ways her plan might backfire."

"In the end, she accomplished her goal, though. He's in jail, and unless the judicial system fails us, he'll never be on the streets again."

"True."

She lay her hand on his knee and pressed in hard with her fingertips, a telltale sign to Jonas that she felt tense again. "May I ask you a very personal and inappropriate question?"

"No question you ask me will ever be too personal or inappropriate."

She licked her lips and drew them in over her teeth, looking adorable as she wrestled with whatever it was worrying her. "I remember you saying that you and Veneta could only be together intimately when her roommate or yours weren't at home. But things she said led me to think"—she broke off and took a bracing breath—"that maybe the two of you never actually went all the way."

Jonas was taken aback by the question for a moment, and he knew it was never wise to divulge details about a past relationship to a current lover. In his short professional career, he'd already counseled several men and women who had nearly destroyed their marriages by being too open about past sexual exploits. But this was Lane, one of the most caring and understanding women he'd ever met.

"Kind of, sort of," he began. "We'd start, but at the last second, she always called things to a halt. I tried to talk with her about it, but she'd just hold up her hands and say I wouldn't understand. So, even though we necked and petted and got close a few times, she always asked me to stop before we actually—well, you know—connected, I guess, is a polite way to put it."

"I *knew* it," she said. "The last night I spent with her at the apartment, she said she'd never be with a man that way again, and I got the impression that something really horrible happened to her. Since I couldn't believe, even for a second, that you could have been responsible, it made me wonder. You know?"

"You called that right. It definitely wasn't me." He bent his head to stare at the grass. "I'm sorry for misleading you. We did seek time alone for romantic interludes, and each time I thought she truly intended to go through with it, but she could never get past a certain point, and afterward she'd huddle in a corner and refuse to even talk about it. As I told you, she was mercurial. Up one minute, down the next."

"I think it may stem from her childhood. She didn't offer any details." She gave his knee a hard squeeze and smiled up at him. "And you needn't apologize for glossing over those details. It's really none of my business, and if she weren't my sister, I wouldn't have asked. I've tried tuning in to her thoughts, not only about that, but also her feelings for you, but she has to be thinking about something for me to pick up on it, and all I got was regular stuff. I'm just hoping to learn all I can so I'll understand her a little better."

Jonas gazed across the park, dotted with picnic tables, fire pits, and playground equipment. In his mind's eye, he pictured himself and Lane bringing their kids here to play, but before the image gained clarity, it occurred to him that nothing between them had really been finalized yet. Did Lane plan to return to Mystic Creek? Or was she hoping Jonas might move to Maple Leaf? Was she contemplating marriage, or was she toying with the idea of just living together for a while so they could try each other on for size?

"So where do we go from here?" The moment Jonas asked the question, he wondered if he was pushing for too much, too soon. "I mean—well, you're here, but I don't really know what your plans are."

She snuggled closer to the wall of his chest. "I haven't made any decisions yet. If we're going to be together, we need to make decisions together that meet both our needs. I've been in touch with Ma. She says I can have my job back. In fact, she seems to be delighted at the prospect. But I couldn't accept the offer until I talked with you. The lease on my cottage is for six months, so whether I live there or not, I'll still have to pay the rent. It seems a shame to let it sit there empty, but I don't know how you'd feel about living there. In short, I can't fly solo anymore."

"And neither can I." And as Jonas said that, he realized he didn't want to. From this moment forward, he wanted to shape his world around this woman. "Lane, I know this won't be every ladies' dream proposal, but I think we need a clear idea of where we're going before we figure out how to get there." He swallowed hard and hoped she didn't hear the nervous plunk in his throat. "Will you marry me?"

She turned her face up to his. "I was starting to think you might never ask. That's why I'm here. I can't imagine spending the rest of my life without you in it."

"Is that a yes?"

"Yes, yes, *yes*!" She giggled and threw her arms around his neck.

Jonas pushed to his feet, drawing her up with him. Embracing her around the waist, with her parka billowing over his arms, he buried his face in her hair and breathed in the scent of her, a pleasing mixture of feminine smells that intoxicated him. Recalling the little girl he'd met earlier at the fountain, he realized that he'd been wrong about wishes never coming true.

Sometimes they did.

Epilogue

It was a beautiful and sunny afternoon in Mystic Creek, an ideal, late spring day for a wedding. Clinging to her father's arm, Lane wore a handkerchief dress of eyelet that draped from the fitted bodice in a graceful froth of white. She'd almost chosen a more traditional gown, but Jonas had discouraged that, saying that she should wear what she loved and not focus on the expectations of others. Now, he stood with the pastor atop the natural bridge, waiting to make her his wife. The processional music had already been played by the string quartet her dad had hired, so everyone in the wedding party stood behind Jonas and the officiant. His three older brothers had formed a rank off to one side of him, leaving room for Lane's maid of honor, none other than her twin, Veneta, and his two sisters, whom Lane had asked to be her bridesmaids. It was a nearly perfect picture of what Lane had imagined it would be. She'd wanted a small, simple wedding, with limitless room for all the many guests, which was why she'd decided on an outdoor ceremony. Off to the right of the bridge, picnic tables, laden with food, elegantly wrapped gifts, and a three-tier wedding cake, had been positioned for an on-site reception, which would occur right after the nuptials.

"Nervous, sweetheart?" her dad asked.

"I just keep thinking that nothing can go this smoothly. Something is bound to go wrong."

"I can tell you're nervous. You're hugging my arm so hard, it's going to sleep." He grinned down at her. "Life itself rarely goes as planned, so why should a wedding? You're a beautiful bride. All the people you love are here. If the sky cracks open and it starts to rain, it won't be the end of the world. We'll have a good laugh, get soaking wet, and eat soggy wedding cake."

Lane knew he'd meant to make her laugh, but picturing the wreckage that a deluge of rain would cause made her heart leap into her throat. "I should have rented those tents." She squinted up at the aqua-blue sky. "Oh, *no*! There's a cloud!"

"Thank you for not getting tents. You saved me two thousand bucks." Brent laughed. "And you're worrying over nothing. That is *not* a storm cloud."

Just then the quartet started to play "Here Comes the Bride," and Lane stepped forward with her father, following the flower girl, Ben and Sissy's three-year-old daughter, Katie Lynn, who looked adorable in a frilly little dress the same shade of rose pink that the bridesmaids wore. As the child first started off, she forgot to throw any flower petals, and then, when she remembered, she began to walk too fast.

"Do you vote for a footrace? Or shall we just hang back?" Brent asked.

Lane had just met Jonas' gaze, and the expression on his face made her heart soar with gladness. He loved her, and he didn't try to hide it. Nothing could spoil this day for her, not even if it rained. Her father was right; everyone she loved and who loved her was here. Because Lane had chosen not to divide the seating for relatives and friends of the bride and groom, her mom, Ann, sat with Jonas' parents, Kate and Jeremiah. When she glanced their way, she saw that they were all beaming with gladness for her and her groom.

"Take it slowly, as we rehearsed," Lane said. "I want to remember these moments for the rest of my life."

Brent kept the same pace, allowing Katie Lynn to get way ahead of them. The guests chuckled. Lane heard Ma Thomas' familiar voice say, "Oh, isn't she darling?" And Lane knew that the flower girl was stealing the show. It didn't matter a whit to Lane. As she walked along beside her dad, she knew she wasn't here to have all the attention focused on her. In only minutes, Katie Lynn Sterling would be her niece, and Jonas' family would be her family, just as hers would become his. On this beautiful day, they were officially beginning their life together, even though in reality, they'd already started carving out their future. They'd recently purchased the cottage from her landlord, and they'd already hired an architect to draw up plans to enlarge the house. Jonas had been living there with Lane since her return to Mystic Creek, so his apartment now served as only office space for him and a newly hired receptionist who would hopefully keep Jonas organized and busy with clients. Lane, now working full-time at Simply Sensational, would become part owner of the business as soon as she'd saved back enough money to buy in. Everything was falling into place.

As Lane's father led her up the steep slope of the arched bridge, she saw that Veneta had tears streaming down her cheeks, but her smile was joyous. Over the last many months, they'd become the most wondrous of things, true sisters. With a lot of encouragement from Lane, Veneta had gone back into rehab to get a handle on her drinking problem. Since then, both of them had been busy, Lane with work and wedding plans, Veneta with moving inland to Mystic Creek, where she now had a full-time job as a registered nurse at the emergency clinic and pursued her education online and at the college in Crystal Falls to become a nurse practitioner. As a result, they hadn't had time to search for their birth mother yet, but that was something they both looked forward to doing together over the summer. Maybe they would find Dallas Chastain, if she was still alive, but if nothing else, both of them hoped to unearth some of their mother's medical history, and if they got lucky, maybe even learn their real father's name so they might track him down.

That all remained to be seen and didn't truly matter to Lane. The man who stood at the apex of the bridge had become her everything, and she didn't need or want anything more than to be with him, today, tomorrow, and always.

As her father placed her hand in Jonas', Lane felt tears gathering in her eyes and hoped her short veil would hide them. Jonas gave her hand an encouraging squeeze as he turned with her to face the pastor. The nuptials passed in a blur for Lane. She heard Jonas say, "I do," in a firm and steady voice, and moments later, when she was prompted to say the same, she hoped her own voice rang out with the same strength and clarity.

When the minister finally pronounced them man and wife, Jonas lifted her veil and bent to kiss her. In that moment when their lips met, Lane felt almost dizzy with happiness. This was the kiss that marked the beginning of their lives together. It would be an adventure, with twists and turns, successes and failures, joys and heartbreaks. But whatever came their way, they'd face it together.

Don't miss

HUCKLEBERRY LAKE

by Catherine Anderson, available now!

Erin De Laney's hands were already shaking when her old Honda decided to get a bad case of mechanical indigestion. Just as she maneuvered the car around a sharp curve, it belched like a locomotive suddenly out of steam, lurched three times, and stopped on the gravel road with a shudder. The ensuing silence was punctuated by popping sounds from the cooling engine. She released a pent-up breath and let her shoulders go limp against the back of the driver's seat. A local mechanic had warned her the Honda's fuel pump was about to cock up its toes, but she'd taken a gamble that it would keep working until payday. Since Lady Luck had never been her friend, she was tempted to thump herself on the head. Now, here she sat, miles from home, in a vehicle that wouldn't move until a tow truck transported it into town.

Erin gazed out the dusty windshield dappled with afternoon sunlight that slanted through the needle-laden boughs of countless ponderosa pines. At least she would have a pleasing view while she waited for help. She loved her new hometown of Mystic Creek, Oregon, and the beautiful, mountainous terrain that surrounded the small valley where it rested. No matter where she was, she could find something lovely to admire. Unfortunately, that was the only plus in her otherwise dead-end life. Maybe Mary Poppins or Pollyanna would look on the bright side, but Erin's inner sunshine had blinked out.

Normally she didn't embrace gloomy thoughts, but having just attended her uncle Slade's wedding and witnessing so much love and hard-won happiness, she felt depression riding her shoulders like an oxbow. *True love, a reason for being.* She was glad that her uncle had finally found that. In fact, she was pleased for everyone involved that all had come right for Slade and his new wife, Vickie, in the end. But seeing so many faces aglow with joy had filled her with yearning for a taste of the same, and it was such an unlikely scenario that it made her feel empty and alone. She hated her job as a county deputy. Her social life consisted mostly of chatting with old ladies about their cats. She couldn't get a guy to give her a second look. She wasn't even sure anyone gave her a *first* look. And now her only form of transportation had petered out on her. Where in all of that was a silver lining?

She drew her cell phone from the pocket of her floral-pattern skirt to call for a tow truck, but before she dialed, it struck her that she should probably at least get out and lift the hood of her car. Otherwise she'd look like a helpless female, and that wasn't and never would be her MO. Other wedding guests would be traveling this road soon as they drove back to town. It was one thing for Erin to know she was pathetic; it was quite another to allow herself to *look* pathetic.

After releasing her seat belt and gathering the folds of her skirt, she pushed open the driver's door and stepped onto the gravel road. Sharp-edged rocks rolled under the soles of her pink heels, reminding her of how sore her feet were from wearing impractical footwear on a lumpy lawn all afternoon. Given her druthers, she chose to wear boots, county-issue riding boots when she was on duty and black commando boots when she wasn't. They never pinched her toes, and she didn't wobble like a tightrope walker when she wore them.

Tottering and wincing, she circled the front bumper of her car and popped up the hood. One thing her father had never insisted that she learn was how to do mechanic work. She peered into the greasy abyss and acknowledged that she recognized three things: the battery, the oil cap, and the windshield-cleaner reservoir. The unpleasant smell of gasoline wafted to her nose, verifying that the fuel pump had indeed malfunctioned. She deserved a gold star just for figuring out that much. Automobiles mystified her. Half the time, she wasn't sure what a warning light meant.

She wanted a life partner, not just someone to cheer her on when her confidence flagged, but a companion to watch movies with, dine out with her, and believe in her. She was lonely, damn it. Oh, sure, she had her best friend, Julie Price, to keep her company, but that was different. And, of course, she had Uncle Slade, who loved her dearly and was always there if she needed him. With his marriage to his lifelong sweetheart today, Erin had accumulated a heap of new relatives as well: her first cousin, Brody; his wife, Marissa; and their three sons, plus a gaggle of cousins and second cousins by marriage. Raised as an only child by parents who didn't socialize much with relatives, Erin appreciated having extended family for the first time in her memory. But having friends and relations wasn't the same as having one special person she could call her own.

Just then, she heard the rumble of a diesel engine. She quickly got a little grease on her hands so it would appear that she'd been tinkering with the engine. Then she straightened and peered around the uplifted hood. When she saw a late-model, silver Dodge pickup, she almost groaned. *Not Wyatt Fitzgerald. Please, God, not now.* Only it was Wyatt, of course. After being the recipient of his disdain all afternoon, she wanted to grind her teeth.

The driver's door opened. His dog, Domino, leaped out and raced toward Erin. A beautiful border collie mix, he had long, silky black fur splashed with white.

"Hello, sweet boy." Erin didn't want to pet him with greasy hands, but Domino reared up, planted his paws on her chest, and bathed her chin with doggy kisses, which gave her no choice. "Yes, I'm glad to see you, too."

She wished she could say the same for his owner, who strode toward her with a well-oiled shift of his narrow hips. She had just seen Wyatt a few minutes ago at the reception, and there was no reason for her to drink in every detail of his appearance again, but he'd changed out of a Western-cut suit into work clothes, and he looked as sexy as a guy could get. Tall, well-muscled, and lean, he had the broad shoulders and deep chest of a man who pitted his strength against the elements every day. Beneath his tan Stetson, hair the color of an August wheat field fell as straight as a bullet to the yoke of his red shirt. His eyes, as blue as laser beams, struck a startling contrast to his sun-burnished face.

She forced her attention back to the dog before Wyatt could chastise him for jumping up and said, "It's been at least twenty minutes since we saw each other, which is seven times longer for a dog than it is for people, so I understand his excitement. Please don't scold him."

The last person Wyatt Fitzgerald wanted to see was Erin De Laney. For a man like him, she meant nothing but trouble. For starters, she was pretty, with her wealth of dark hair, dainty features, and expressive blue eyes. And she obviously felt as attracted to him as he was to her. *Not happening.* He'd sworn off women six years ago, and that was one promise to himself that he meant to keep. He'd be especially cautious with Erin, a county deputy. If he messed up with her, she wouldn't have to call the law on him; she *was* the law.

"Most people try to coast over to the side of the road when their cars break down," he called out. "When I came around that curve, I had to lock up the brakes to keep from turning that car into a Honda pancake."

She continued to pet his ill-mannered dog. "You're assuming that all cars continue to roll after the engine dies. My Honda did a three-count burp and stopped dead in its tracks."

"You should have recognized trouble with the first burp and steered toward the ditch on burps two and three. A stalled car in the middle of a curvy road is a hazard."

She gave him a syrupy-sweet smile that didn't reach her beautiful blue eyes. "How remiss of me. I'm sure you would have kept a much clearer head if you'd been behind the wheel. Unfortunately, not all of us are superior beings."

Wyatt knew he was being a jerk, but he had no experience with women who had romantic notions about him. He didn't know how to discourage Erin and be nice to her at the same time. So he was being a jackass. That worked. She didn't flirt with him when she was pissed off.

He shifted his attention to his dog, who was not aiding his cause. For reasons beyond him, Domino had fallen in love with Erin at first sight last September and remained besotted ever since. "Domino, *off*!" Wyatt ordered, disregarding Erin's plea for leniency. It wasn't her dog, and Wyatt didn't want Domino to develop bad manners. "Off, I said!"

Erin dimpled a cheek and said, "He's fine, Wyatt." Then she resumed ruffling the animal's fur. "Yes, you're wonderful," she told the dog. "It's good to know that at least somebody likes me."

Reading her lips to determine each word she uttered, Wyatt found himself wishing he could hear the intonations of her voice. Why, he didn't know, because he felt sure every syllable dripped with sarcasm. During the wedding reception, she'd attempted to chat with him, and he'd shut her down. So now she was all butt-hurt about it. A part of him felt bad about that, but he couldn't afford concern over her. For him, holding her at arm's length was a matter of self-preservation. Today, he found her even more tempting than usual. The silky blouse and flowery skirt displayed her body in a way that a shirt and trousers didn't, making him acutely aware of her physically. Not a good thing. Because of this woman, he'd recently awakened in the middle of the night from the first wet dream he'd had in at least fifteen years. Talk about embarrassing. He'd been surrounded by other men in the bunkhouse, and when he woke up, every other guy in the room had been sitting straight up in bed. Now, whenever Wyatt thought about that night, his stomach felt as if it shriveled up like a rotten walnut. *Dear God.* In his dream, he'd been making love to Erin, no holds barred. And although he hadn't asked, he knew all the other men had guessed what was going on. *Just our foreman, getting his rocks off. Poor, deaf bastard.*

"What?" Erin demanded. "You're glaring at me like I just popped your last birthday balloon."

He hadn't meant to scowl at her. Trying to smooth the wrinkles from his brow, he curved his lips in what he hoped resembled a smile. It wasn't that he disliked Erin. Far from it. She just resurrected yearnings and feelings that he couldn't allow himself to have. He wished he knew how to distance himself from her without making her feel rejected. Only how could a guy do that? He guessed he could explain, but in order to do that, he'd have to tell her things about himself she had no need to know. His checkered past was his business and only his business.

Deciding to ignore her comment, he said, "What seems to be the issue with the car?"

She gave Domino a final pat and gently pushed him down. "The fuel pump bit the dust." She held up greasy hands. "There's nothing for it but to get a new pump. That means my car will be at the repair shop for a few days."

Wyatt dragged his gaze from her full lips to the exposed engine. He'd never met a woman with so many talents. He wasn't really surprised to learn that they included shade-tree mechanics. She could make a guy feel inadequate without half trying. "Any way to jerry-rig it so you can make it into town?"

She shook her head. "Nope. Replacing the pump is my only option. I was about to call for a tow truck."

Wyatt's boss, Slade Wilder, was Erin's uncle, so Wyatt knew she didn't make much money as a junior deputy. Towing services didn't come cheap, and the expense would put a dent in her budget. "No coverage for roadside services, I take it."

"I canceled it last month. Doesn't that figure? I paid the premiums for fifteen years and never needed to use it. Then, right after I drop the coverage, bang. Call it bad karma, I guess."

Wyatt preferred to think of it as plain old bad luck, at least for him. She needed help, and he was elected. His pickup was capable of towing her car into town, and he couldn't in good conscience allow her to call for assistance she couldn't afford when he was already on-site.

"I can tow it in for you."

She shook her head. "I appreciate the offer, but I don't want to bother you."

She bothered him more than she could possibly know. "I carry everything I ever need in my toolbox, including a heavy tow chain. Unfortunately, I don't have a tow bar, but that only means you'll have to steer the vehicle and tap the brake when necessary so you don't rear-end me. Think you can do that?"

She folded her arms at her waist. And a very slender waist it was. When she wore a uniform, which was most of the time, her attractive figure was buried under loose-fitting clothing, and her waistline was bulked up by a belt loaded with cop paraphernalia. Today, dressed in feminine attire suitable for a backyard wedding and reception, she looked good enough to make a man's mouth go dry. And that was his whole problem with her. He couldn't be around her without wanting to taste that kissable mouth of hers—and other parts c her as well.

"I can do that, yes. But, like I just said, I don't want to be a bother." She rested a slender hand on Domino's head, her fingertips absently stroking his silken fur.

"No bother. I'm making a grocery run for the bunk-house, so I'm going into town anyway. I'll drop your car off at the Timing Light and then give you a lift home."

"It's Sunday," she said. "Buck won't be there."

"He has a drop box for car keys. You can just lock up the Honda, drop your keys through the slot, and then give him a call in the morning to get an estimate."

"An estimate won't be necessary. That's the only auto repair shop in town. Taking the car into Crystal Falls for competitive bids would cost so much that any money I saved would be wiped out by towing fees."

Wyatt couldn't argue the point. He placed a hand on the side of the truck box and vaulted into the bed, landing on his feet. Without glancing back at Erin, he opened the lid of his diamond-plate toolbox, grabbed the tow chain, which lay at the top because he used it often on the ranch, and then leaped back onto the roadway. "I'll pull around and get in front," he told her.

"I really don't need a tow. I've got this."

Wyatt was reminded of the first time he met Erin. She'd been just as stubborn about accepting his help then as she was now, and he responded with almost the same answer. "The boss won't be happy if I leave you stranded out here."

Her chin came up a notch. "It's not exactly remote here. Dozens of cars will be returning to town on this road in a matter of minutes."

"Exactly. And every single driver will see that I drove right past you."

"I'll tell them you offered to help and I declined."

"Why not just accept the tow?" he pressed. "It's a favor between friends."

"We aren't friends. You make no secret of the fact that you don't like me. Now that I've made friends with Doreen at dispatch and get time off, I can finally visit the ranch more often, and whenever I do, you vanish as if I have a contagious disease."

Wyatt knew he was guilty as charged. But he didn't steer clear of her because he disliked her. The truth was that he liked her too much. "Whenever you visit, I'm on the clock. On any given day, I have a list of stuff to get done that's as long as my arm. I don't deliberately avoid you. I'm just busy."

Her expression told him she wasn't buying that. "Look," he went on. "Whether I like you or whether you like me isn't the point. Your uncle is my employer, and he'll be pissed at me if I don't lend you a hand. I need to keep my job, if it's all the same to you."

A subtle slump of her shoulders told him he'd won this round. "Oh, all right," she said with a flap of her wrist. "I'll let you tow the car into town, but only because I don't want to cause any trouble between you and Uncle Slade."

Wyatt didn't care what her reasons were, only that she'd finally accepted his help.